epic!

Written by
Matthew Cody

Illustrated by
Yehudi Mercado

Andrews McMeel
PUBLISHING®

For Meika Hashimoto, editor extraordinaire,
and Cat Ninja's unsung superhero
—MC

For Asher Warfield
—YM

Andrews McMeel Publishing
a division of Andrews McMeel Universal
1130 Walnut Street, Kansas City, Missouri 64106

www.andrewsmcmeel.com

Epic! Creations, Inc.
702 Marshall Street, Suite 280, Redwood City, California 94063

www.getepic.com

21 22 23 24 25 RR2 10 9 8 7 6 5 4 3 2

Paperback ISBN: 978-1-5248-6094-3
Hardback ISBN: 978-1-5248-6138-4

Library of Congress Control Number: 2020933940

Design by Dan Nordskog
Additional art assistance: Sophia Hoodis, Dave Wheeler,
Mary Bellamy, and John Padon

Made by:
LSC Communications US, LLC
Address and location of manufacturer:
1009 Sloan Street
Crawfordsville, IN 47933
2nd Printing – 1/15/21

ATTENTION: SCHOOLS AND BUSINESSES
Andrews McMeel books are available at quantity discounts with
bulk purchase for educational, business, or sales promotional use.
For information, please e-mail the Andrews McMeel Publishing
Special Sales Department: specialsales@amuniversal.com.

Chapter 1:
The Great Hamster Heist

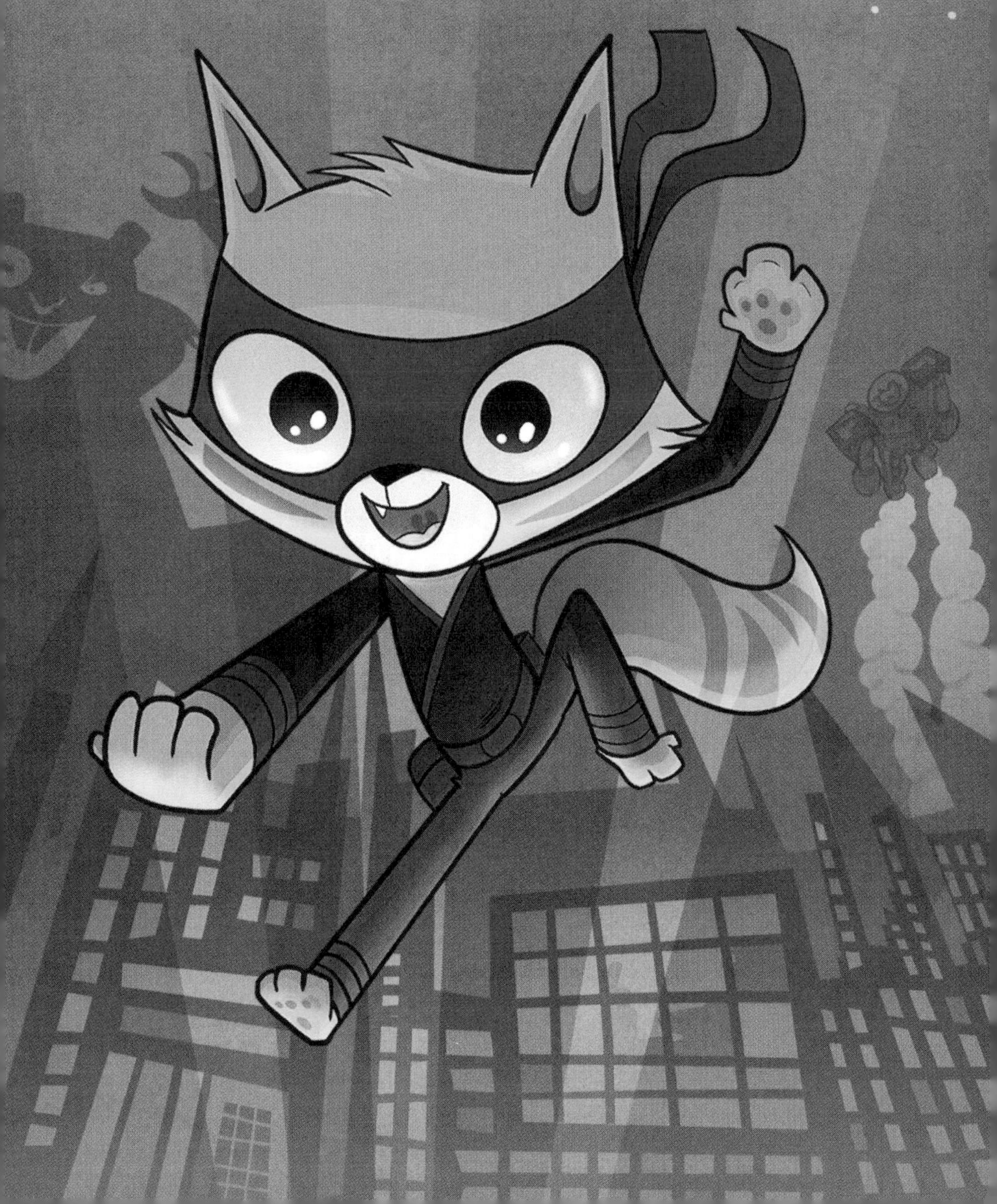

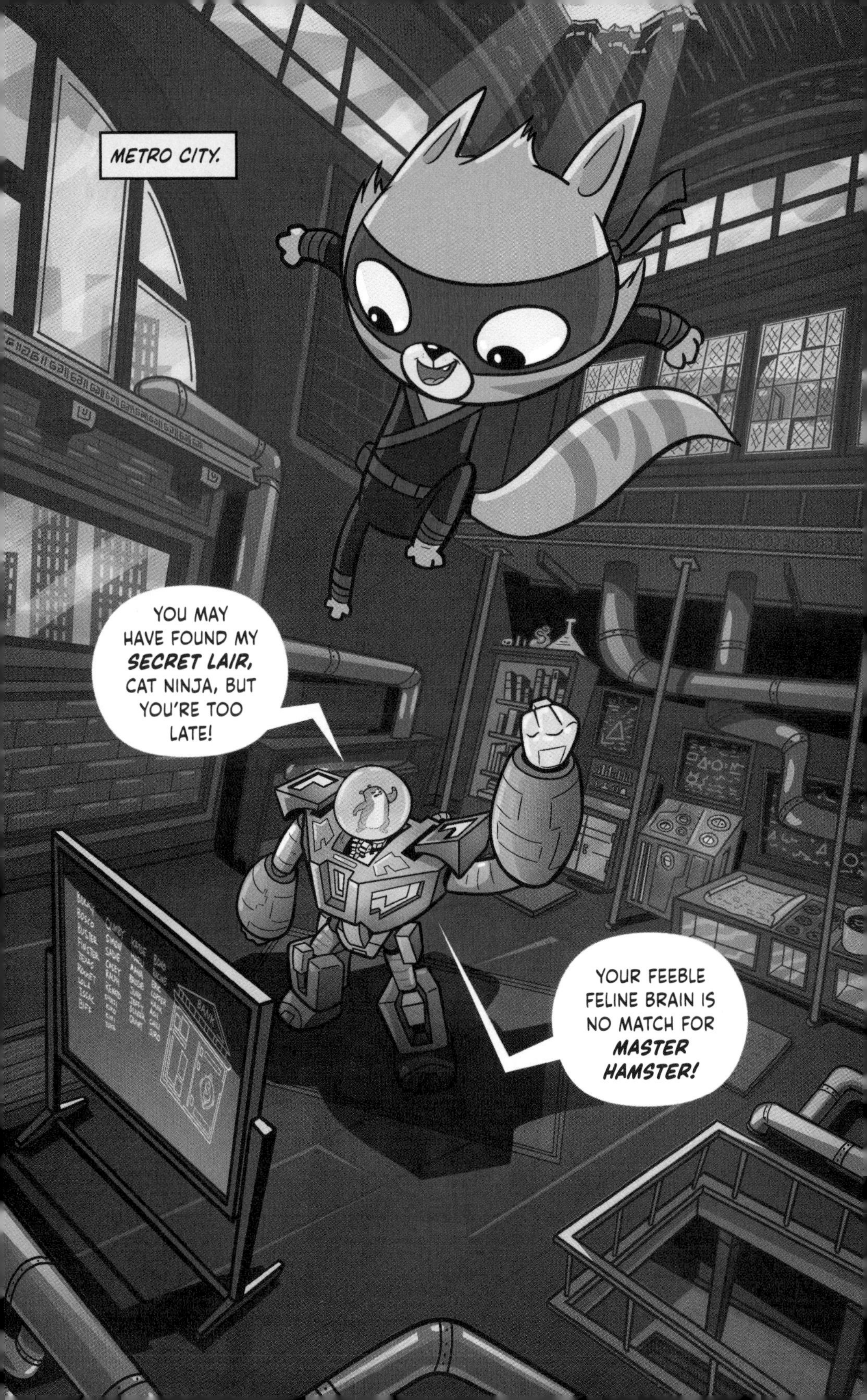
METRO CITY.
YOU MAY HAVE FOUND MY SECRET LAIR, CAT NINJA, BUT YOU'RE TOO LATE!
YOUR FEEBLE FELINE BRAIN IS NO MATCH FOR MASTER HAMSTER!

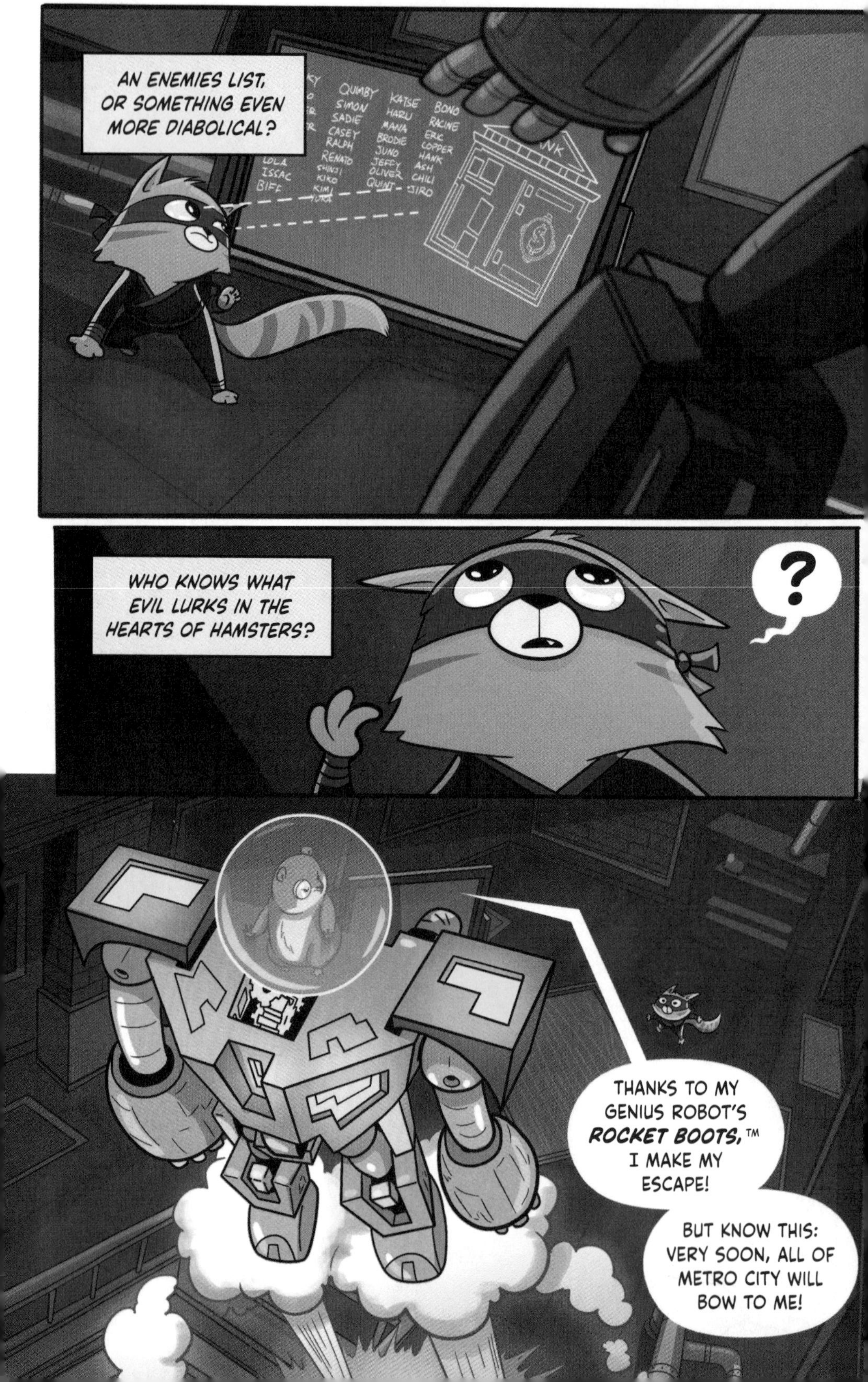
AN ENEMIES LIST, OR SOMETHING EVEN MORE DIABOLICAL?
WHO KNOWS WHAT EVIL LURKS IN THE HEARTS OF HAMSTERS?
?
THANKS TO MY GENIUS ROBOT'S ***ROCKET BOOTS,***™ I MAKE MY ESCAPE!
BUT KNOW THIS: VERY SOON, ALL OF METRO CITY WILL BOW TO ME!

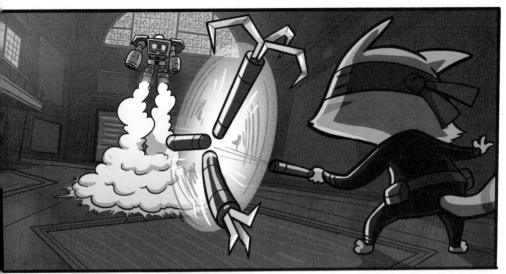

GET OFF ME,
YOU FIENDISH FURBALL!
YOU'LL CRASH
US BOTH!

KA-CHUNK

3

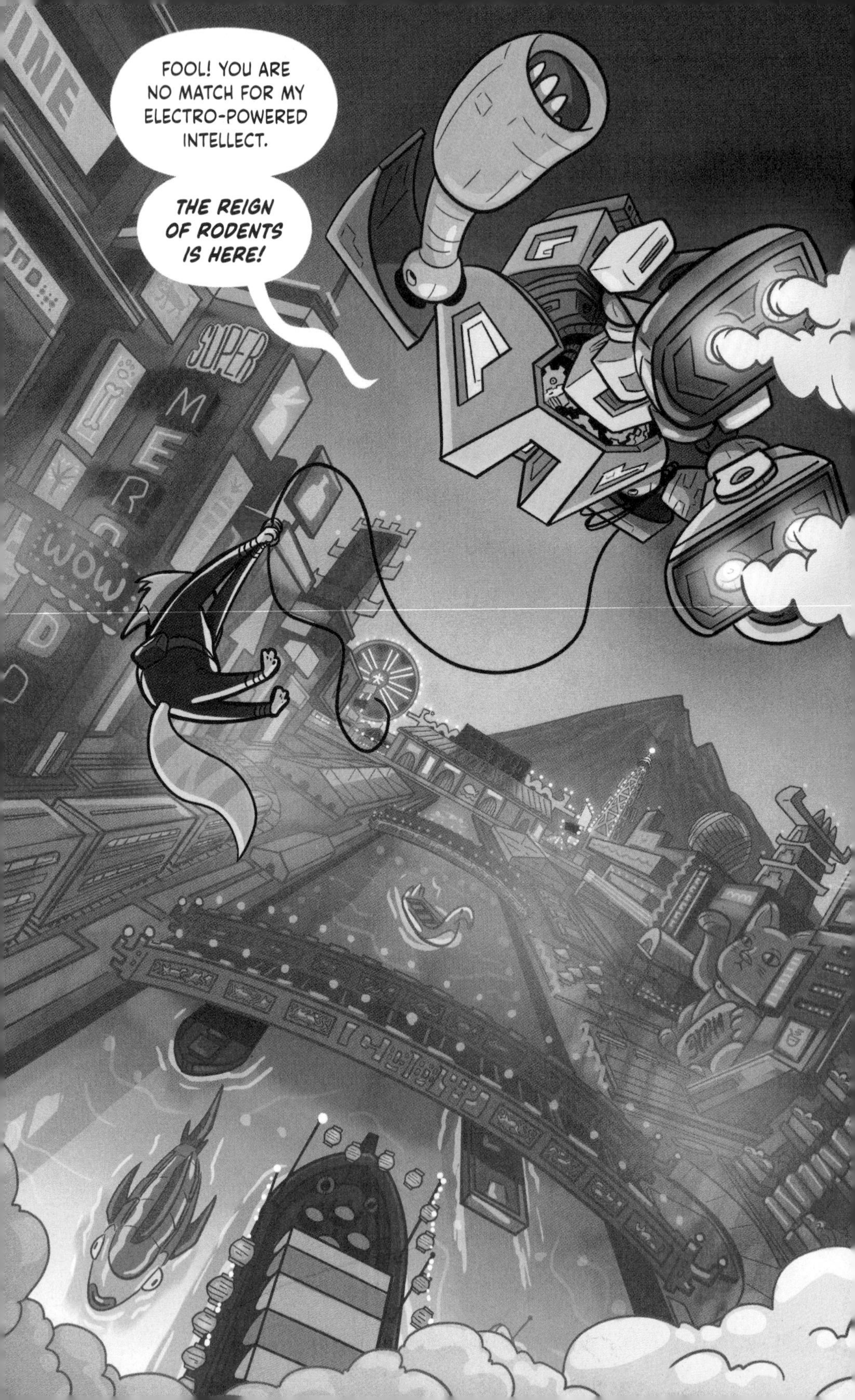
FOOL! YOU ARE NO MATCH FOR MY ELECTRO-POWERED INTELLECT.
THE REIGN OF RODENTS IS HERE!
SUPER
WOW

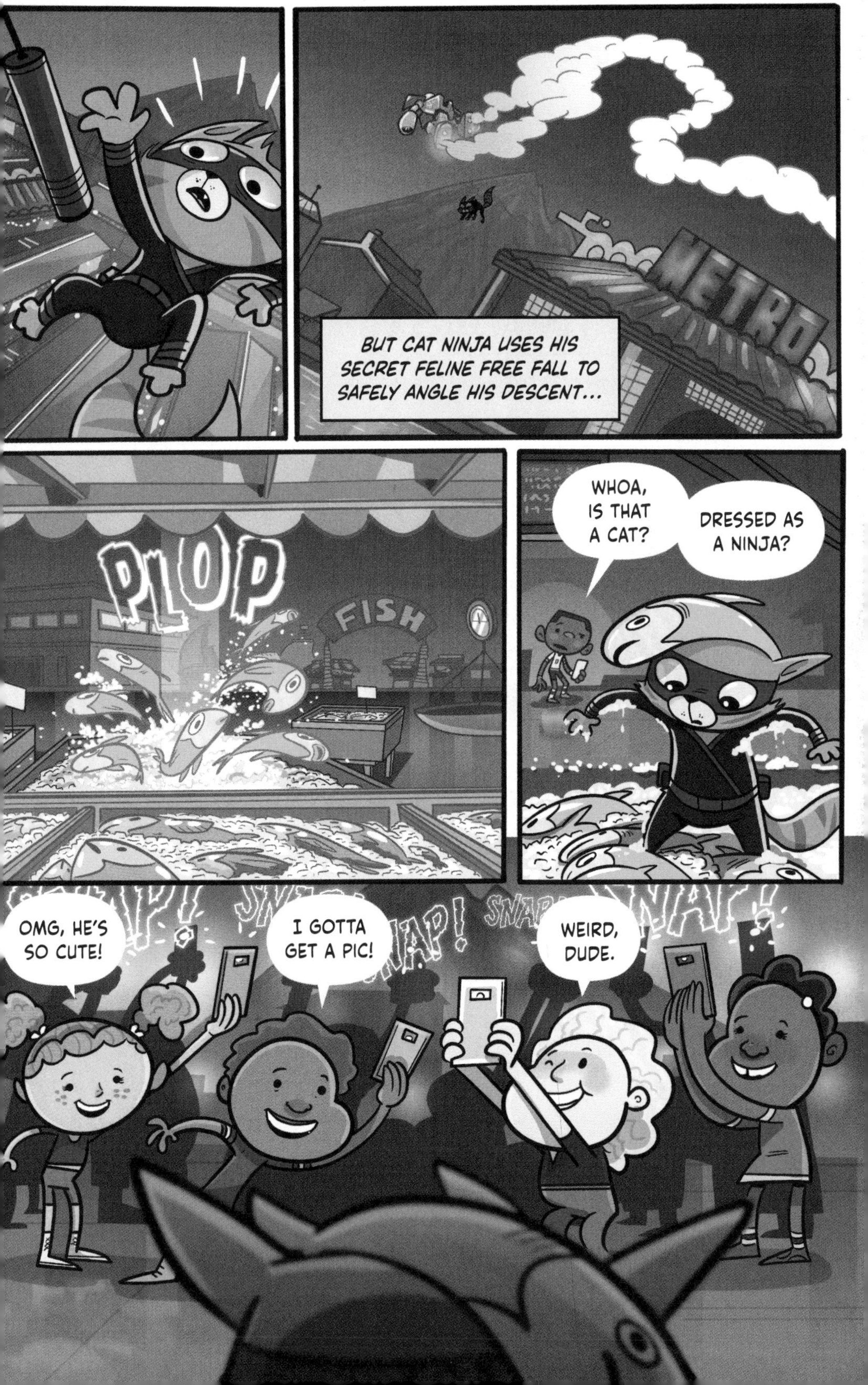
METRO
BUT CAT NINJA USES HIS SECRET FELINE FREE FALL TO SAFELY ANGLE HIS DESCENT...
PLOP
FISH
WHOA, IS THAT A CAT?
DRESSED AS A NINJA?
OMG, HE'S SO CUTE!
I GOTTA GET A PIC!
WEIRD, DUDE.

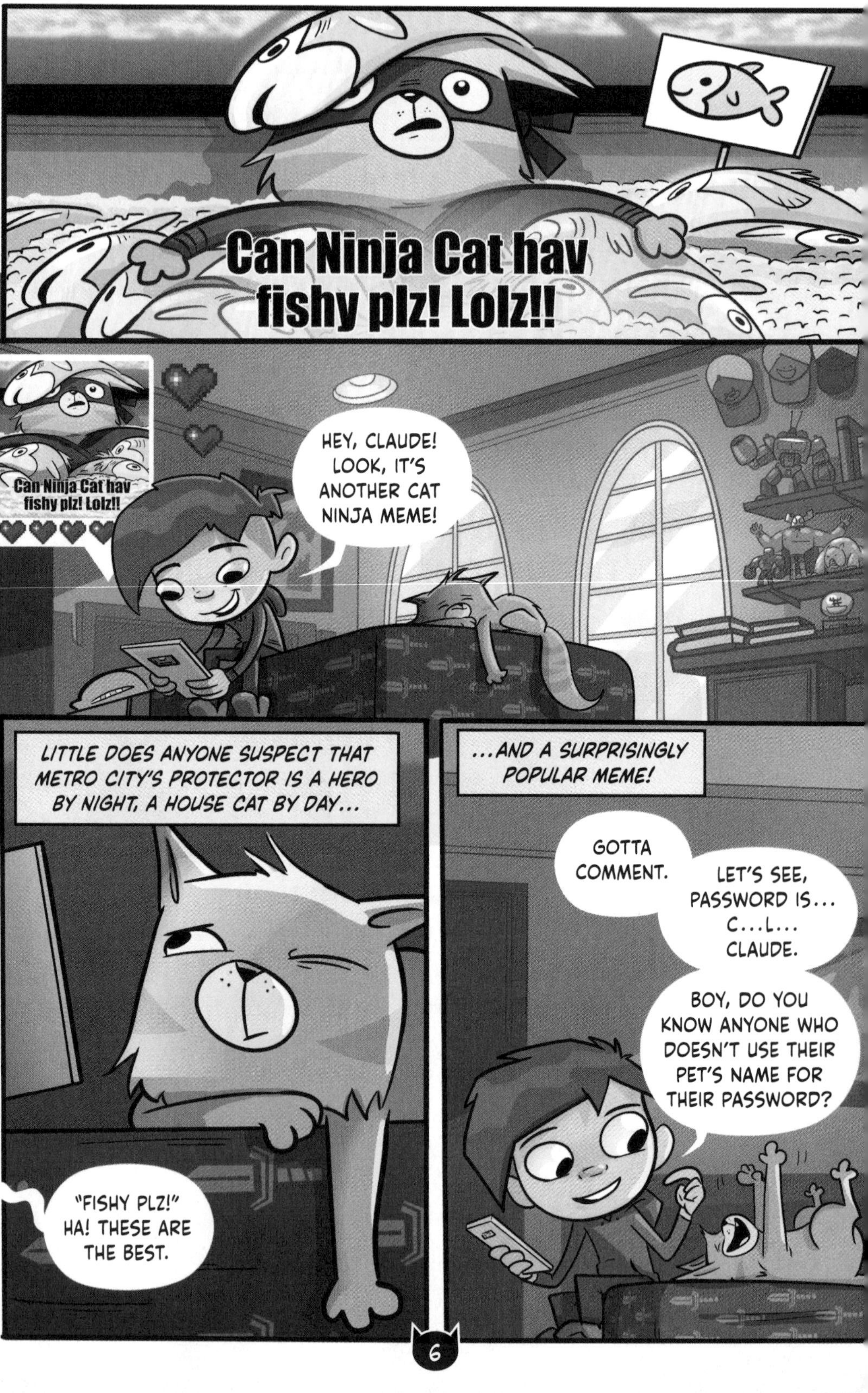
Can Ninja Cat hav fishy plz! Lolz!!
Can Ninja Cat hav fishy plz! Lolz!!
HEY, CLAUDE! LOOK, IT'S ANOTHER CAT NINJA MEME!
LITTLE DOES ANYONE SUSPECT THAT METRO CITY'S PROTECTOR IS A HERO BY NIGHT, A HOUSE CAT BY DAY...
"FISHY PLZ!" HA! THESE ARE THE BEST.
...AND A SURPRISINGLY POPULAR MEME!
GOTTA COMMENT.
LET'S SEE, PASSWORD IS... C...L... CLAUDE.
BOY, DO YOU KNOW ANYONE WHO DOESN'T USE THEIR PET'S NAME FOR THEIR PASSWORD?

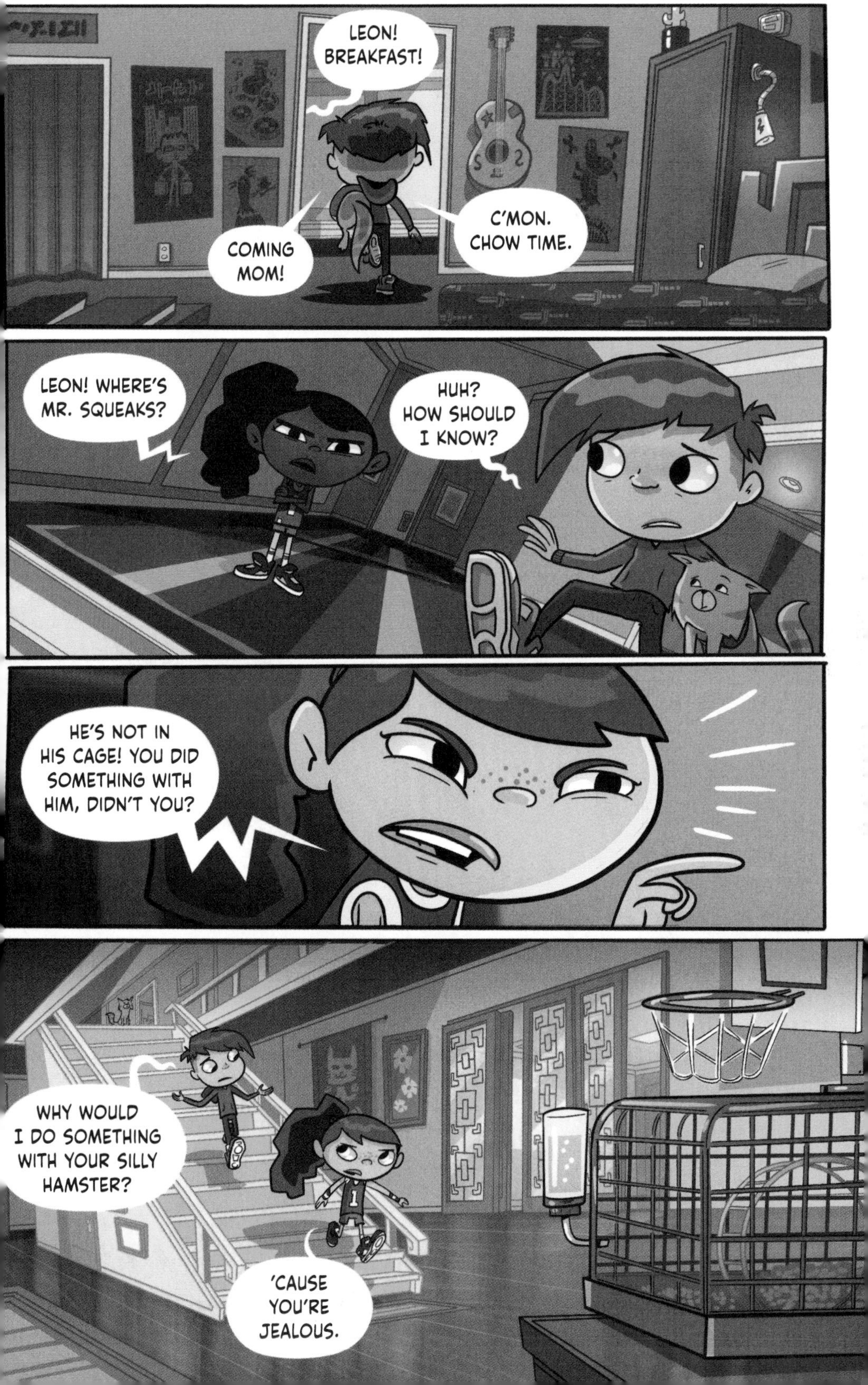
LEON! BREAKFAST!
COMING MOM!
C'MON. CHOW TIME.
LEON! WHERE'S MR. SQUEAKS?
HUH? HOW SHOULD I KNOW?
HE'S NOT IN HIS CAGE! YOU DID SOMETHING WITH HIM, DIDN'T YOU?
WHY WOULD I DO SOMETHING WITH YOUR SILLY HAMSTER?
'CAUSE YOU'RE JEALOUS.

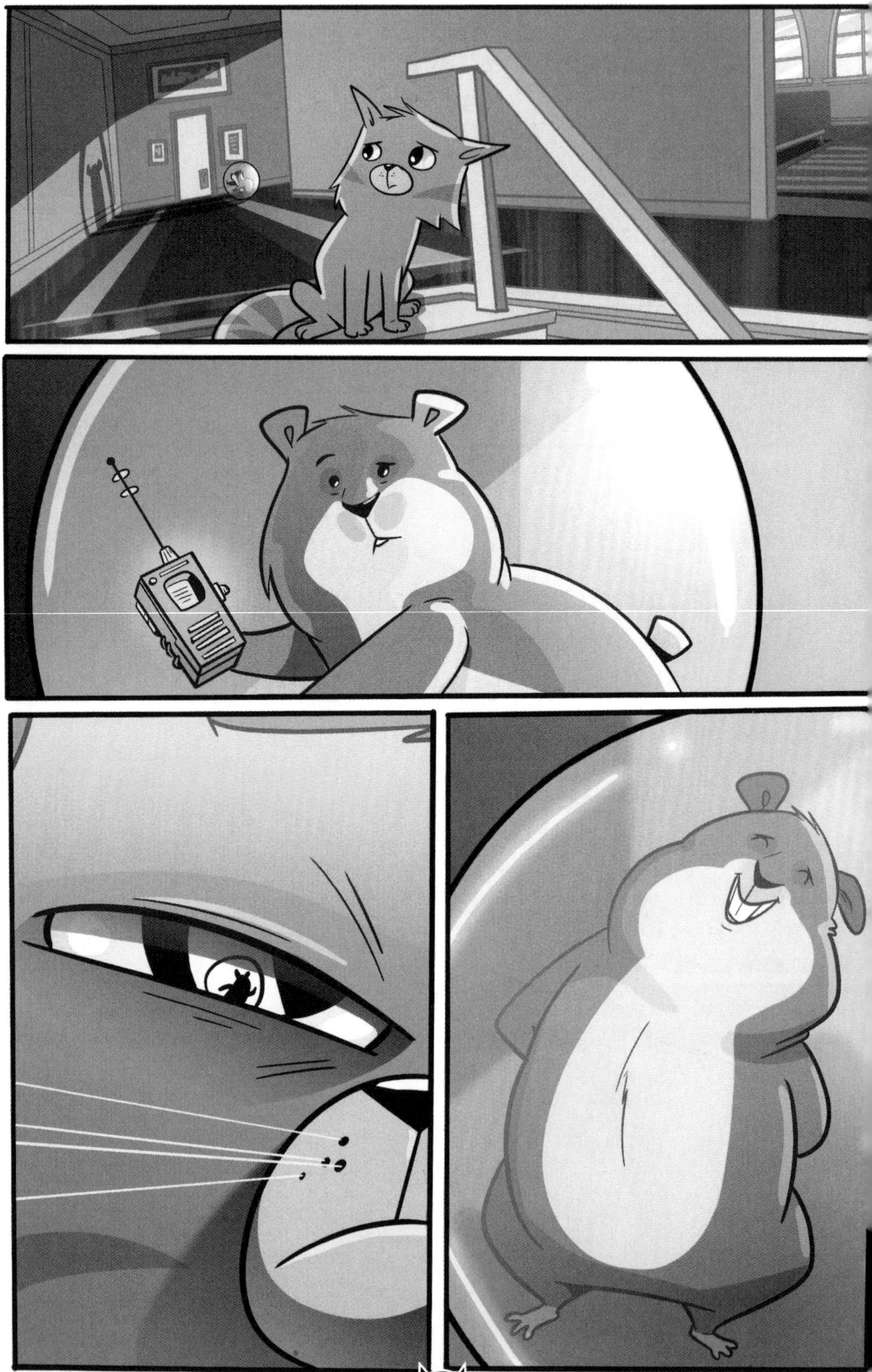

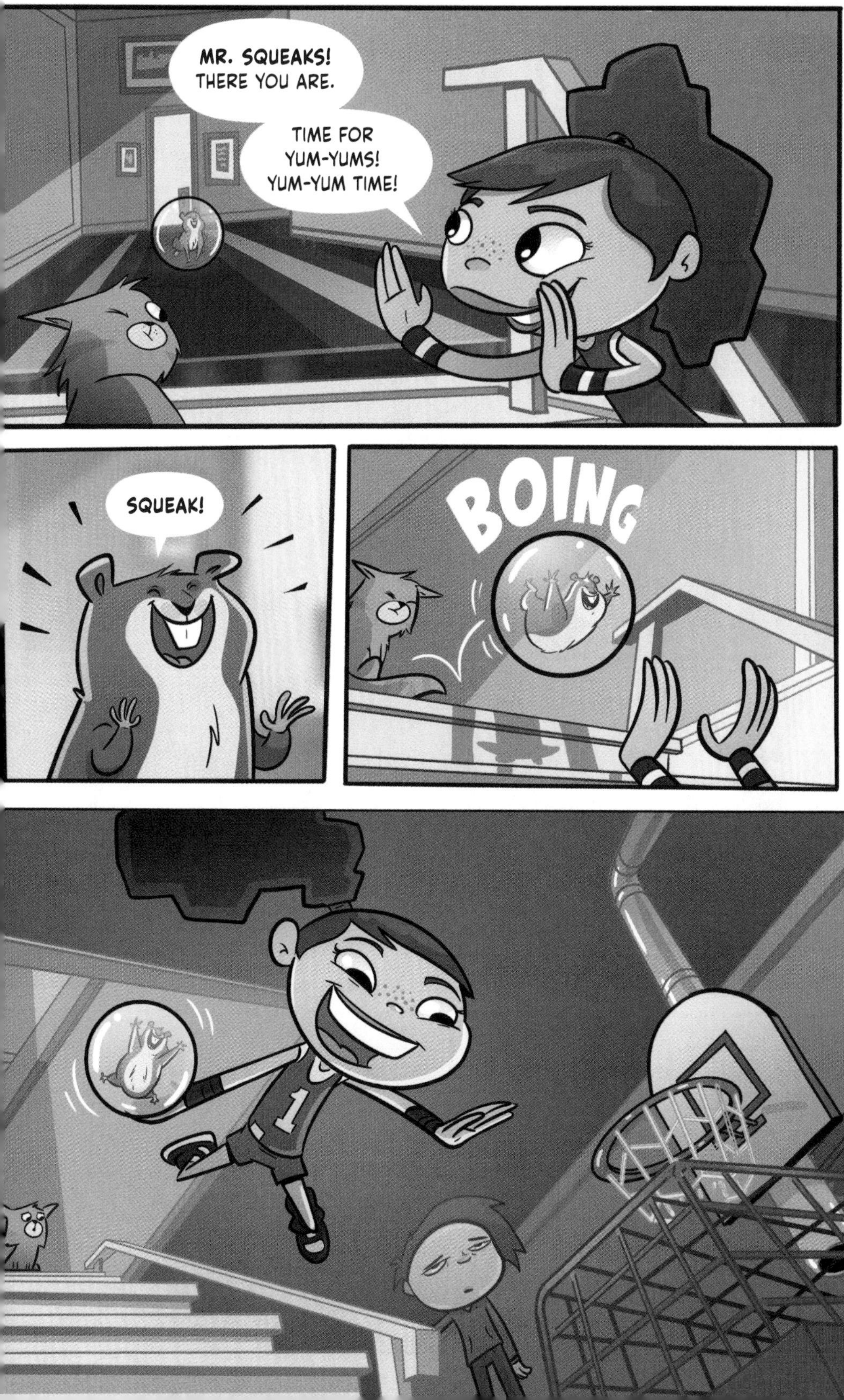
MR. SQUEAKS!
THERE YOU ARE.
TIME FOR
YUM-YUMS!
YUM-YUM TIME!
SQUEAK!
BOING
1

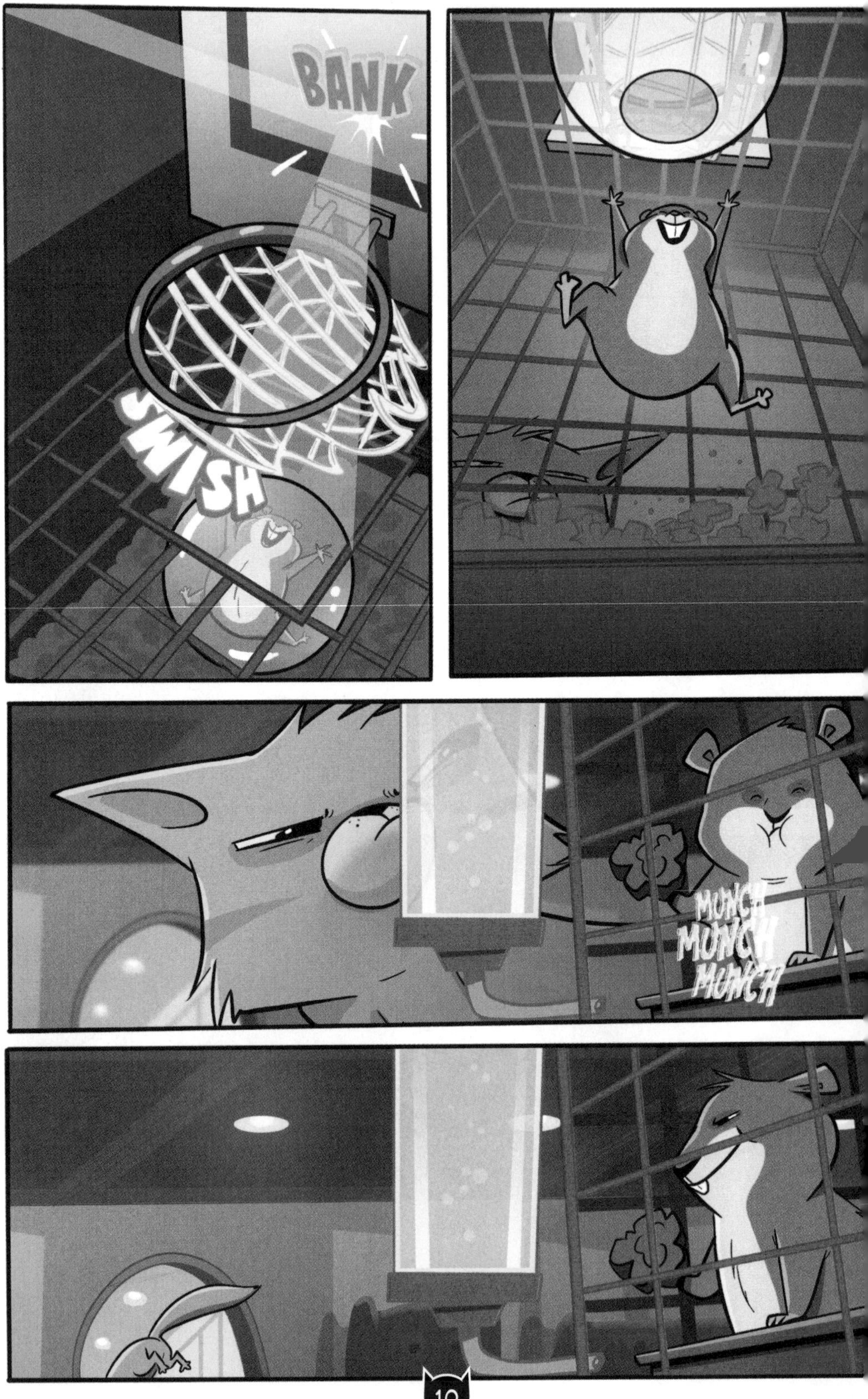
BANK
SWISH
MUNCH
MUNCH
MUNCH

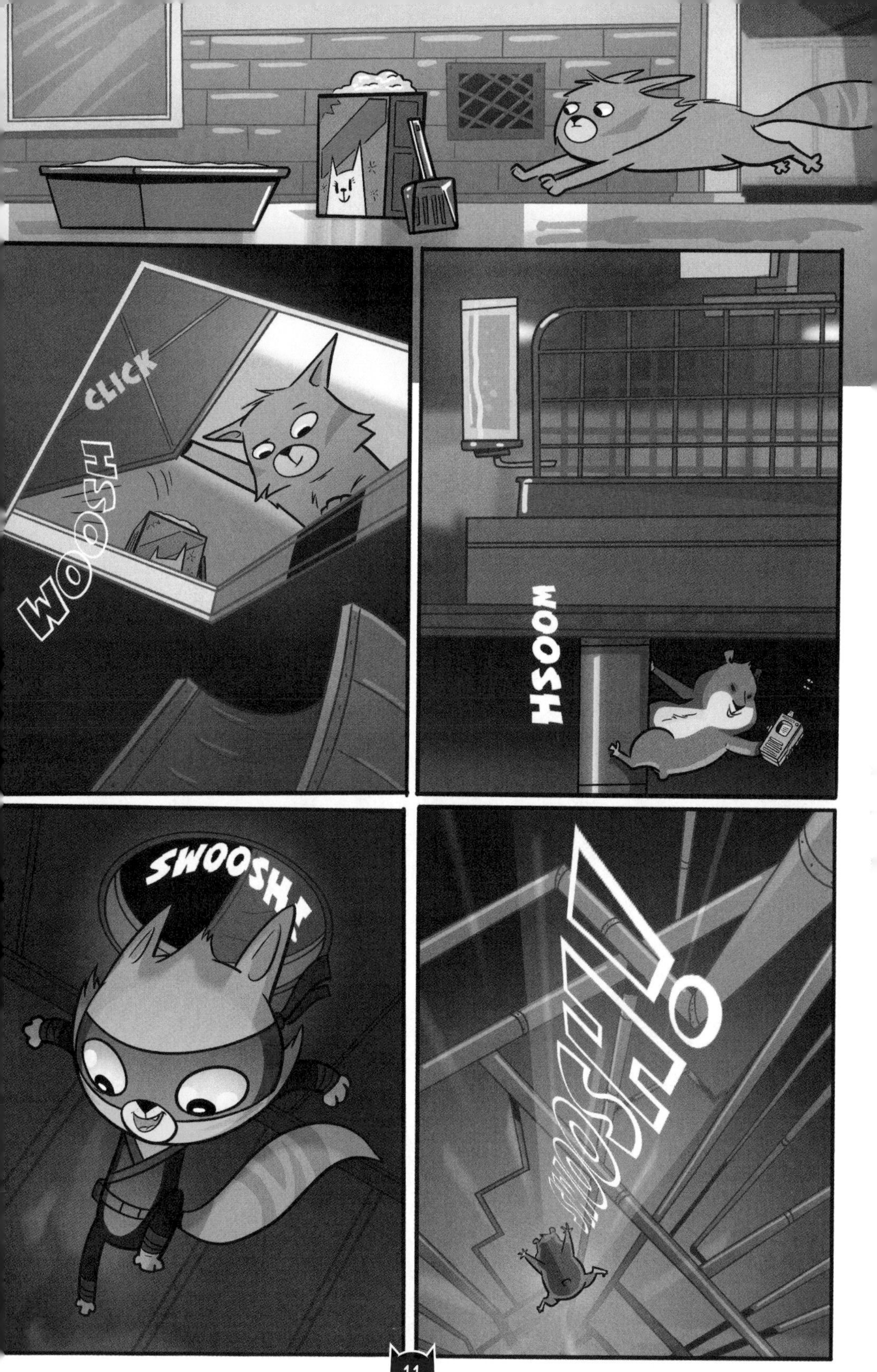
CLICK
WOOOSH
WOOSH
SWOOSH!
SWOOSH

Interlude: Origin Stories starring Cat Ninja and Master Hamster!

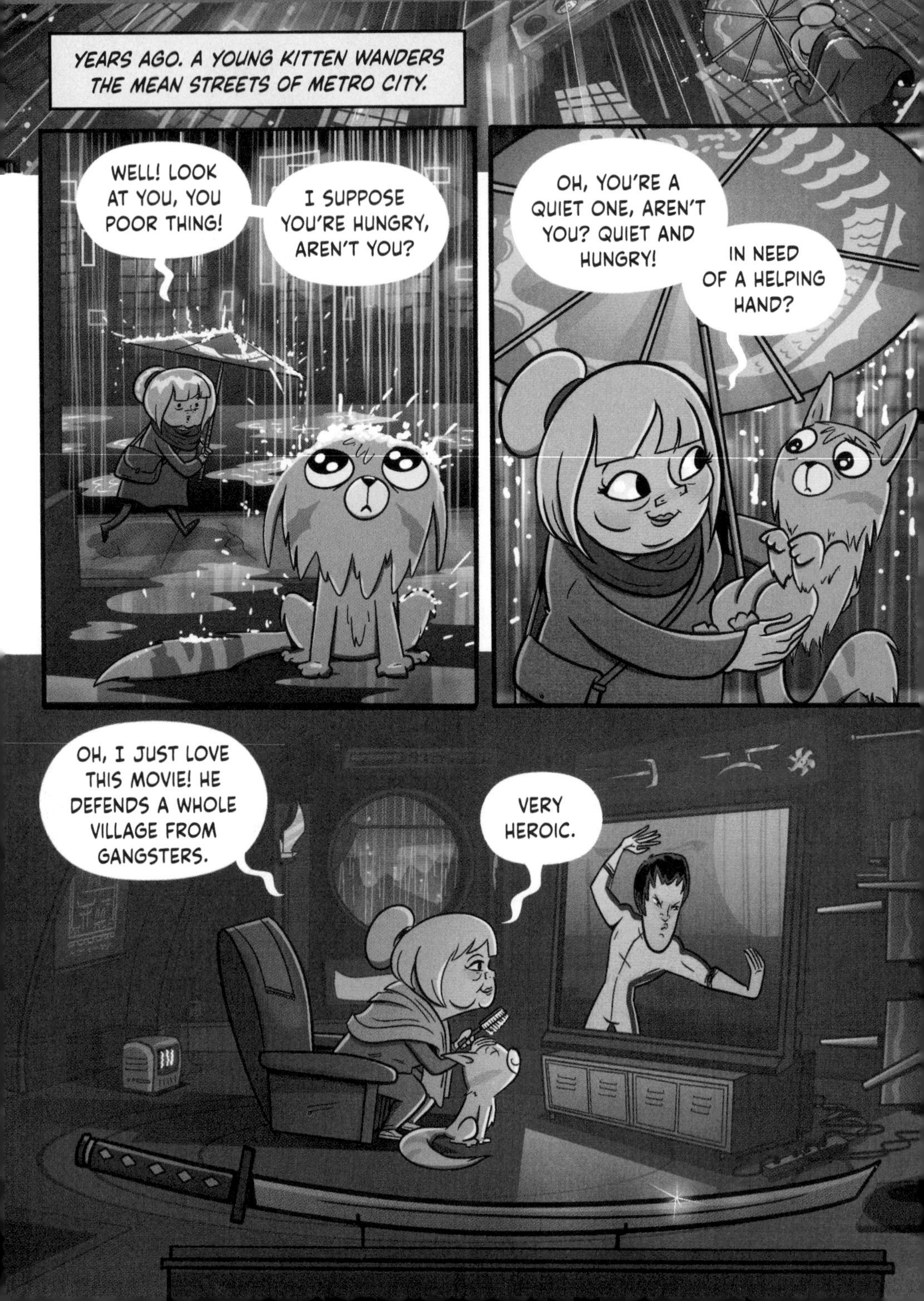
YEARS AGO. A YOUNG KITTEN WANDERS THE MEAN STREETS OF METRO CITY.
WELL! LOOK AT YOU, YOU POOR THING!
I SUPPOSE YOU'RE HUNGRY, AREN'T YOU?
OH, YOU'RE A QUIET ONE, AREN'T YOU? QUIET AND HUNGRY!
IN NEED OF A HELPING HAND?
OH, I JUST LOVE THIS MOVIE! HE DEFENDS A WHOLE VILLAGE FROM GANGSTERS.
VERY HEROIC.

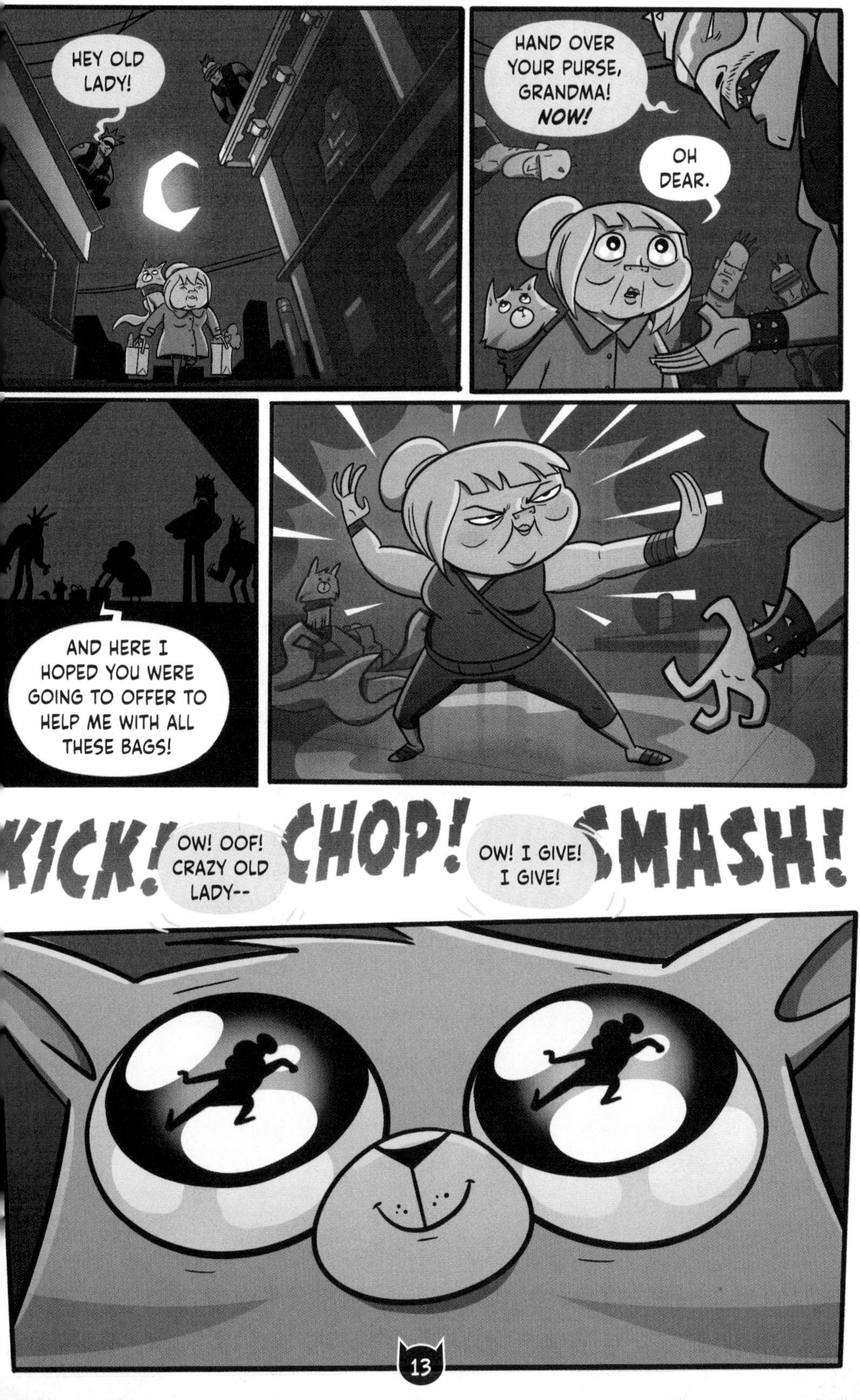
HEY OLD LADY!
HAND OVER YOUR PURSE, GRANDMA! *NOW!*
OH DEAR.
AND HERE I HOPED YOU WERE GOING TO OFFER TO HELP ME WITH ALL THESE BAGS!
KICK!
OW! OOF! CRAZY OLD LADY--
CHOP!
OW! I GIVE! I GIVE!
SMASH!

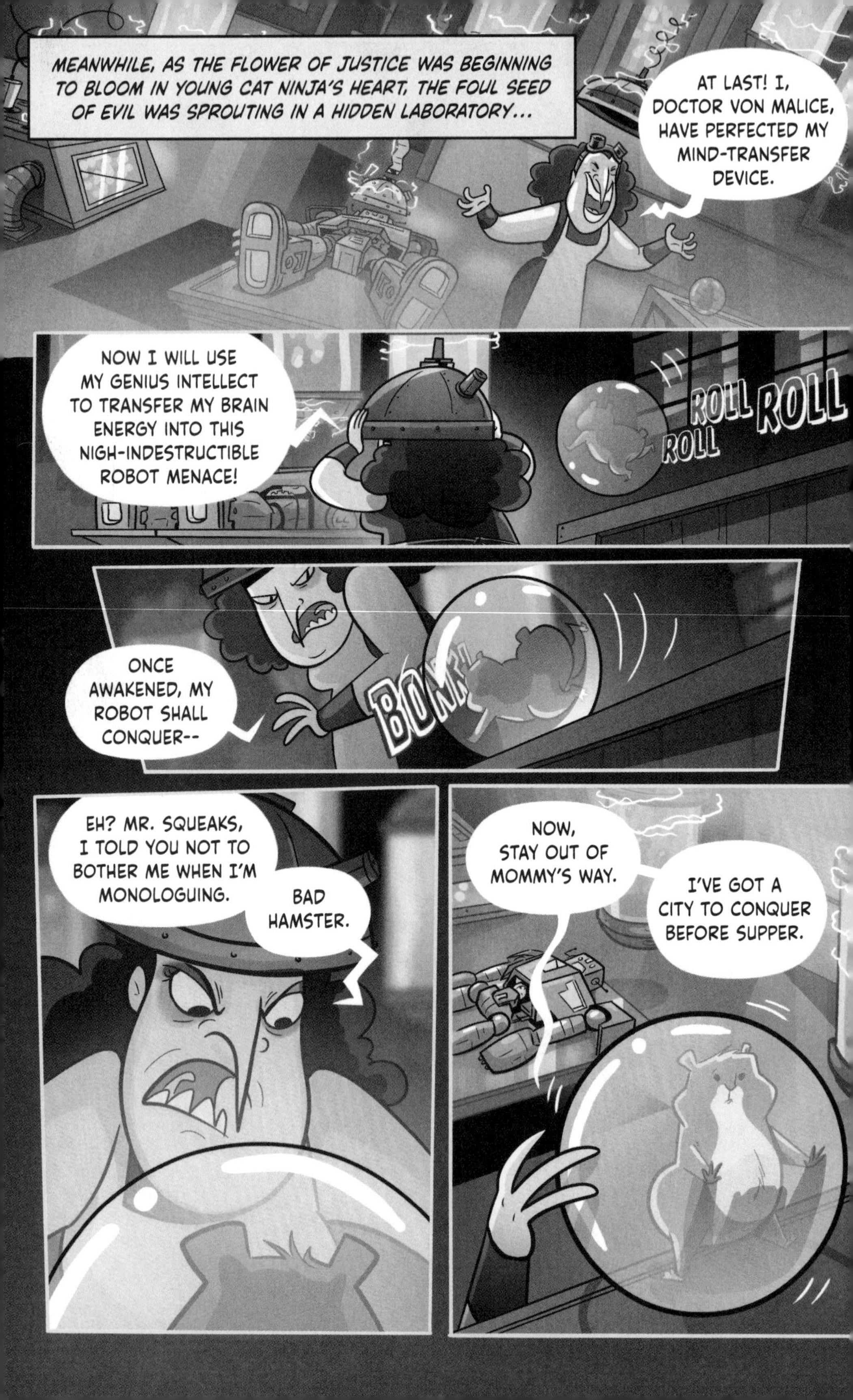
MEANWHILE, AS THE FLOWER OF JUSTICE WAS BEGINNING TO BLOOM IN YOUNG CAT NINJA'S HEART, THE FOUL SEED OF EVIL WAS SPROUTING IN A HIDDEN LABORATORY...
AT LAST! I, DOCTOR VON MALICE, HAVE PERFECTED MY MIND-TRANSFER DEVICE.
NOW I WILL USE MY GENIUS INTELLECT TO TRANSFER MY BRAIN ENERGY INTO THIS NIGH-INDESTRUCTIBLE ROBOT MENACE!
ROLL ROLL ROLL
ONCE AWAKENED, MY ROBOT SHALL CONQUER--
BONK!
EH? MR. SQUEAKS, I TOLD YOU NOT TO BOTHER ME WHEN I'M MONOLOGUING.
BAD HAMSTER.
NOW, STAY OUT OF MOMMY'S WAY.
I'VE GOT A CITY TO CONQUER BEFORE SUPPER.

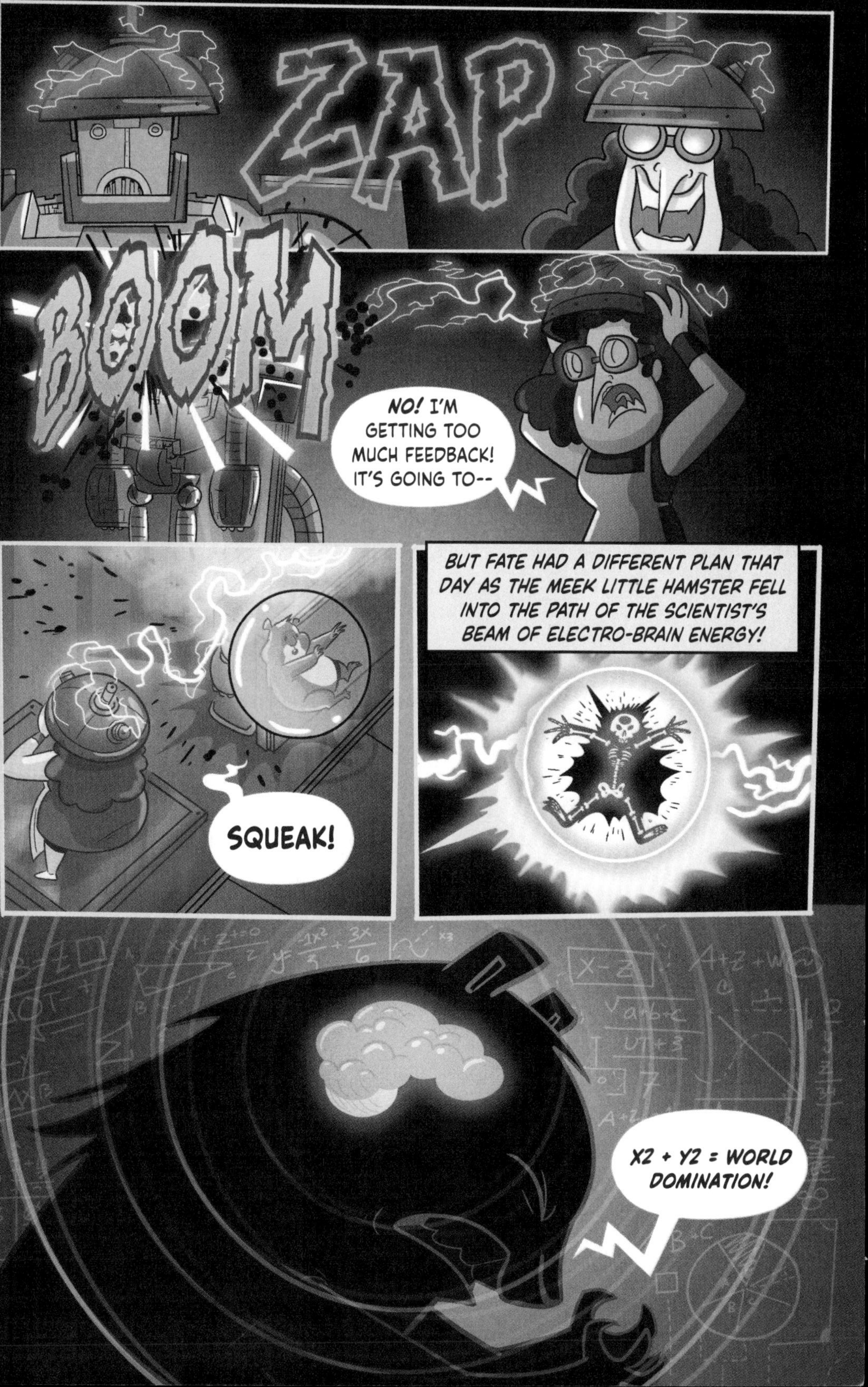
ZAP
BOOM
NO! I'M GETTING TOO MUCH FEEDBACK! IT'S GOING TO--
BUT FATE HAD A DIFFERENT PLAN THAT DAY AS THE MEEK LITTLE HAMSTER FELL INTO THE PATH OF THE SCIENTIST'S BEAM OF ELECTRO-BRAIN ENERGY!
SQUEAK!
X2 + Y2 = WORLD DOMINATION!

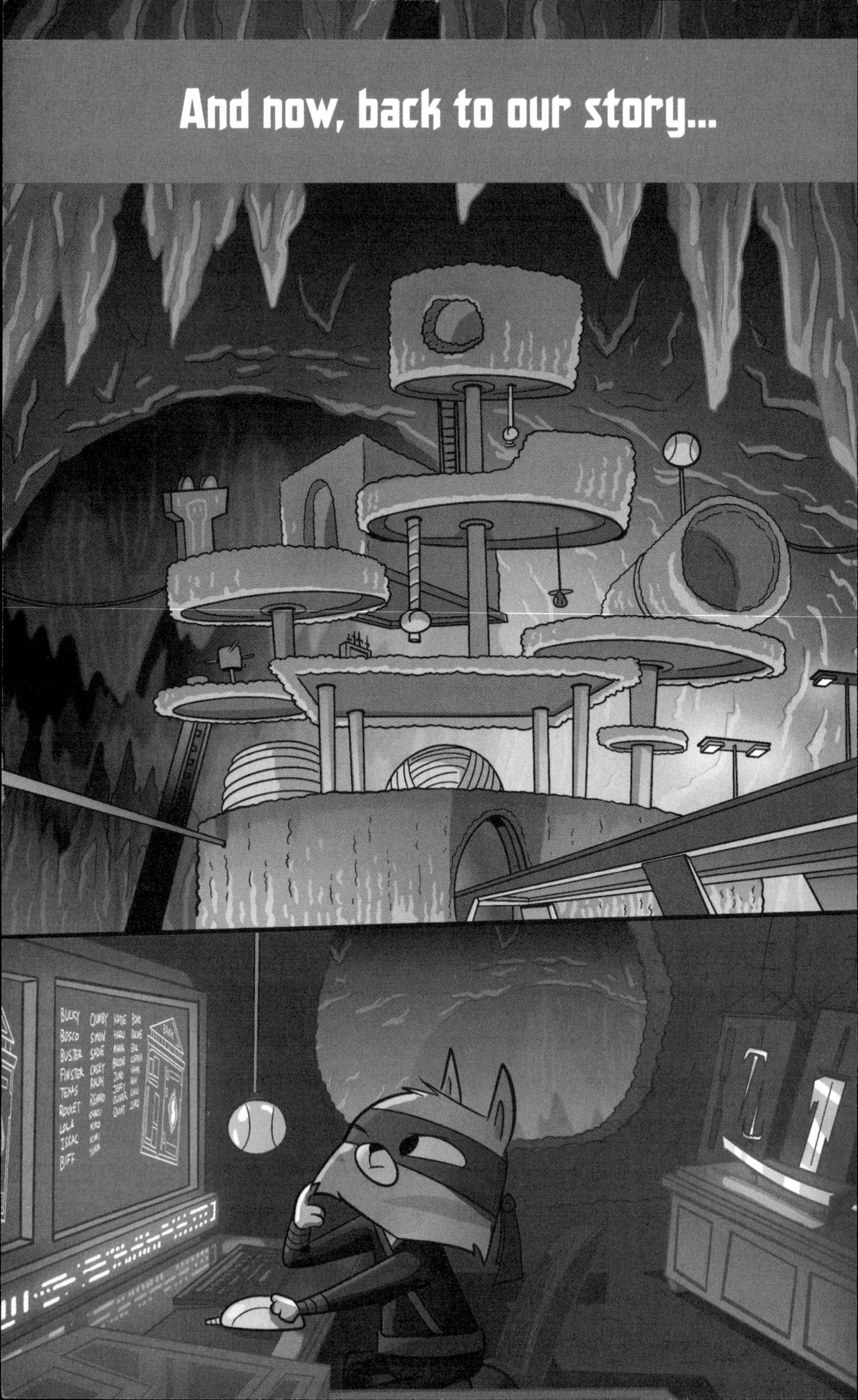
And now, back to our story...
BUCKY
BOSCO
BUSTER
FINSTER
TEXAS
ROCKET
LOLA
ISSAC
BIFF
QUIMBY
SIMON
SADIE
CASEY
RALPH
RENARD
KIKO
BANK

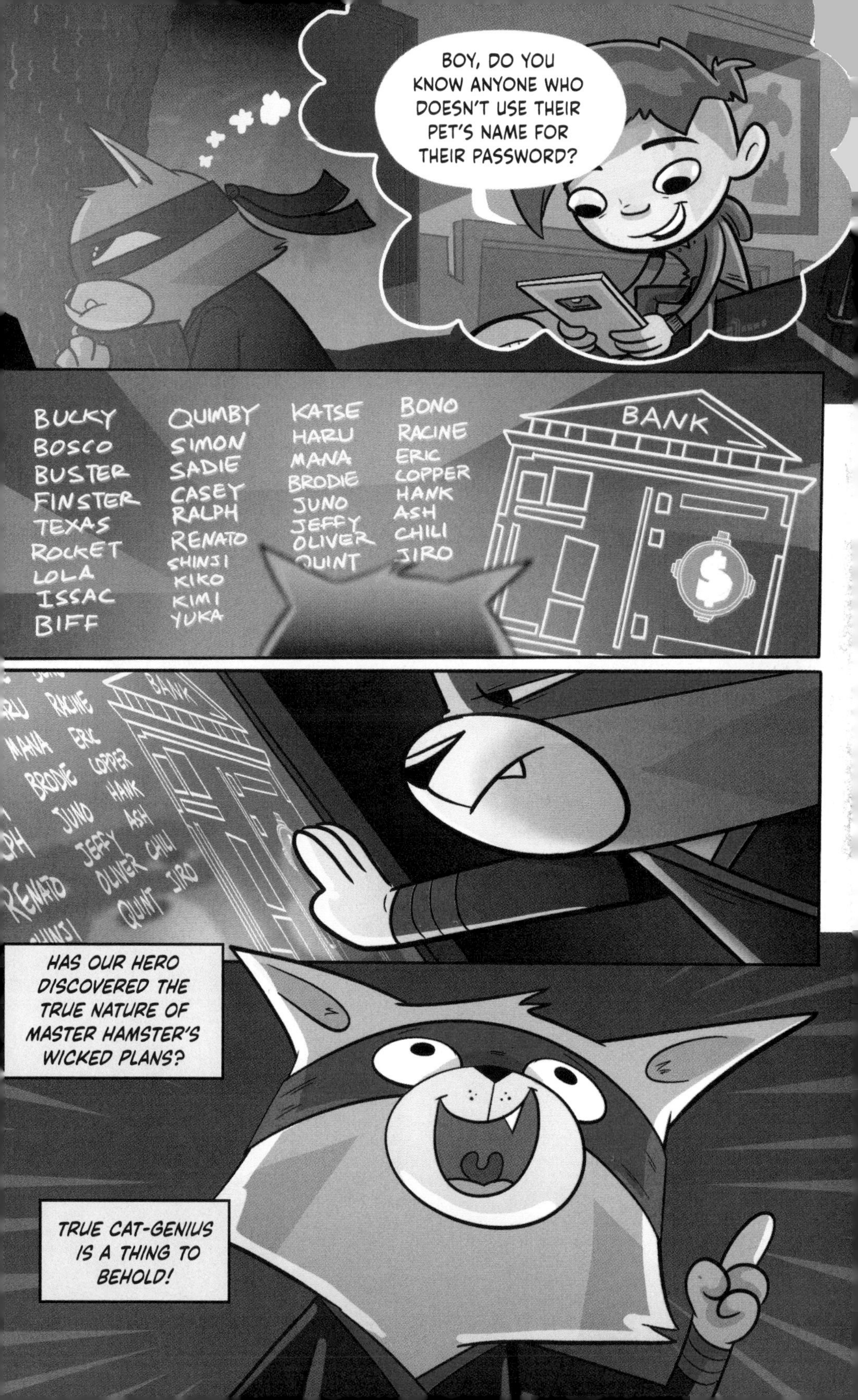
BOY, DO YOU KNOW ANYONE WHO DOESN'T USE THEIR PET'S NAME FOR THEIR PASSWORD?
BUCKY
BOSCO
BUSTER
FINSTER
TEXAS
ROCKET
LOLA
ISSAC
BIFF
QUIMBY
SIMON
SADIE
CASEY
RALPH
RENATO
SHINJI
KIKO
KIMI
YUKA
KATSE
HARU
MANA
BRODIE
JUNO
JEFFY
OLIVER
QUINT
BONO
RACINE
ERIC
COPPER
HANK
ASH
CHILI
JIRO
BANK
HAS OUR HERO DISCOVERED THE TRUE NATURE OF MASTER HAMSTER'S WICKED PLANS?
TRUE CAT-GENIUS IS A THING TO BEHOLD!

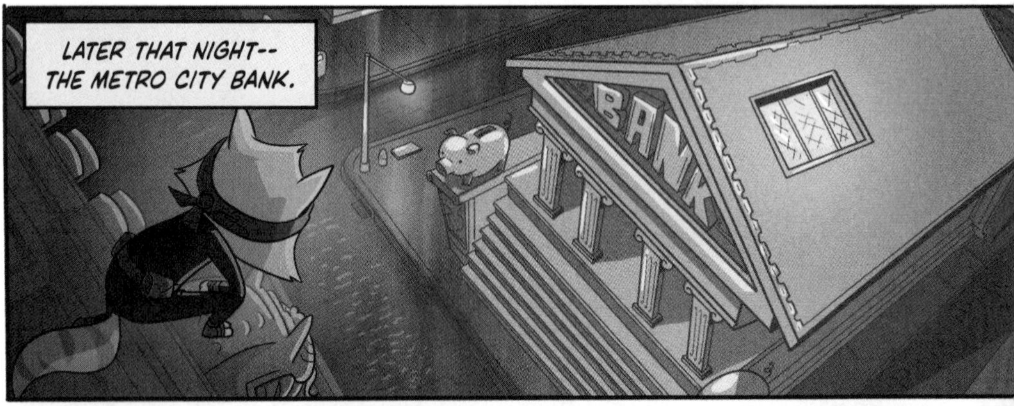
LATER THAT NIGHT--
THE METRO CITY BANK.
BANK

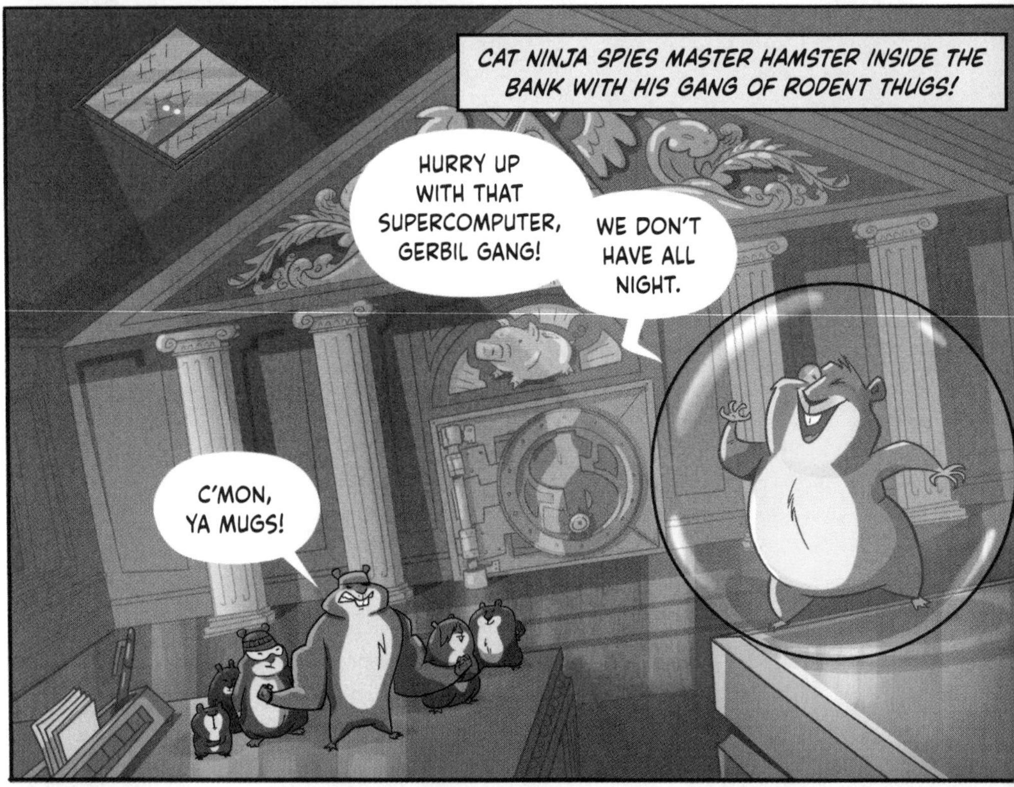
CAT NINJA SPIES MASTER HAMSTER INSIDE THE BANK WITH HIS GANG OF RODENT THUGS!
HURRY UP WITH THAT SUPERCOMPUTER, GERBIL GANG!
WE DON'T HAVE ALL NIGHT.
C'MON, YA MUGS!

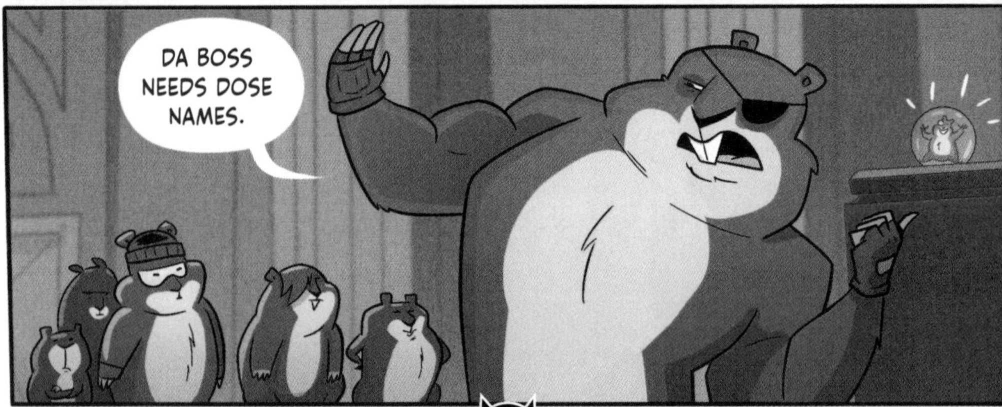
DA BOSS NEEDS DOSE NAMES.

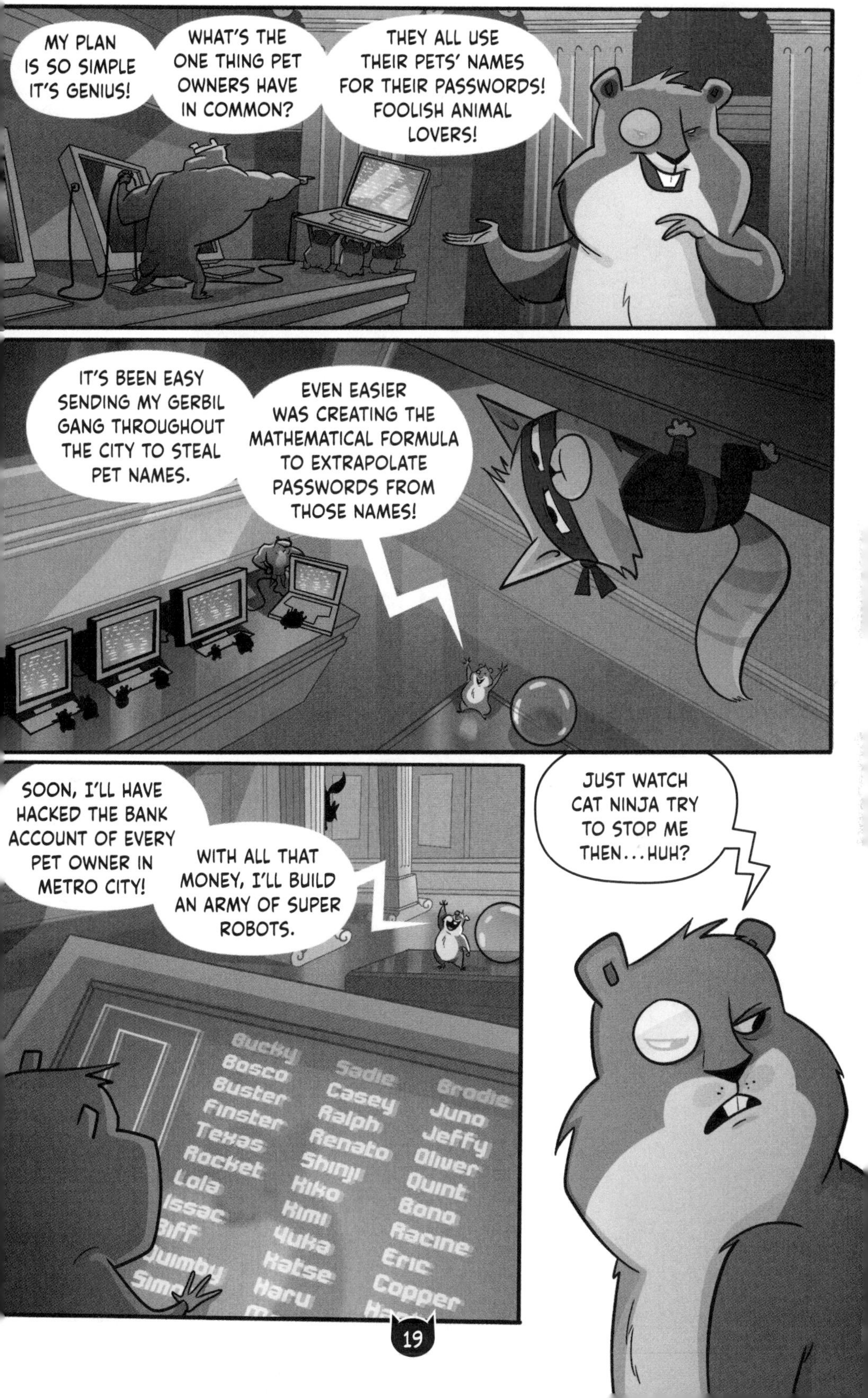
MY PLAN IS SO SIMPLE IT'S GENIUS!
WHAT'S THE ONE THING PET OWNERS HAVE IN COMMON?
THEY ALL USE THEIR PETS' NAMES FOR THEIR PASSWORDS! FOOLISH ANIMAL LOVERS!
IT'S BEEN EASY SENDING MY GERBIL GANG THROUGHOUT THE CITY TO STEAL PET NAMES.
EVEN EASIER WAS CREATING THE MATHEMATICAL FORMULA TO EXTRAPOLATE PASSWORDS FROM THOSE NAMES!
SOON, I'LL HAVE HACKED THE BANK ACCOUNT OF EVERY PET OWNER IN METRO CITY!
WITH ALL THAT MONEY, I'LL BUILD AN ARMY OF SUPER ROBOTS.
Bucky Bosco Buster Finster Texas Rocket Lola Issac Biff Quimby
Sadie Casey Ralph Renato Shinji Kiko Kimi Yuka Katse Haru
Brodie Juno Jeffy Oliver Quint Bono Racine Eric Copper
JUST WATCH CAT NINJA TRY TO STOP ME THEN... HUH?

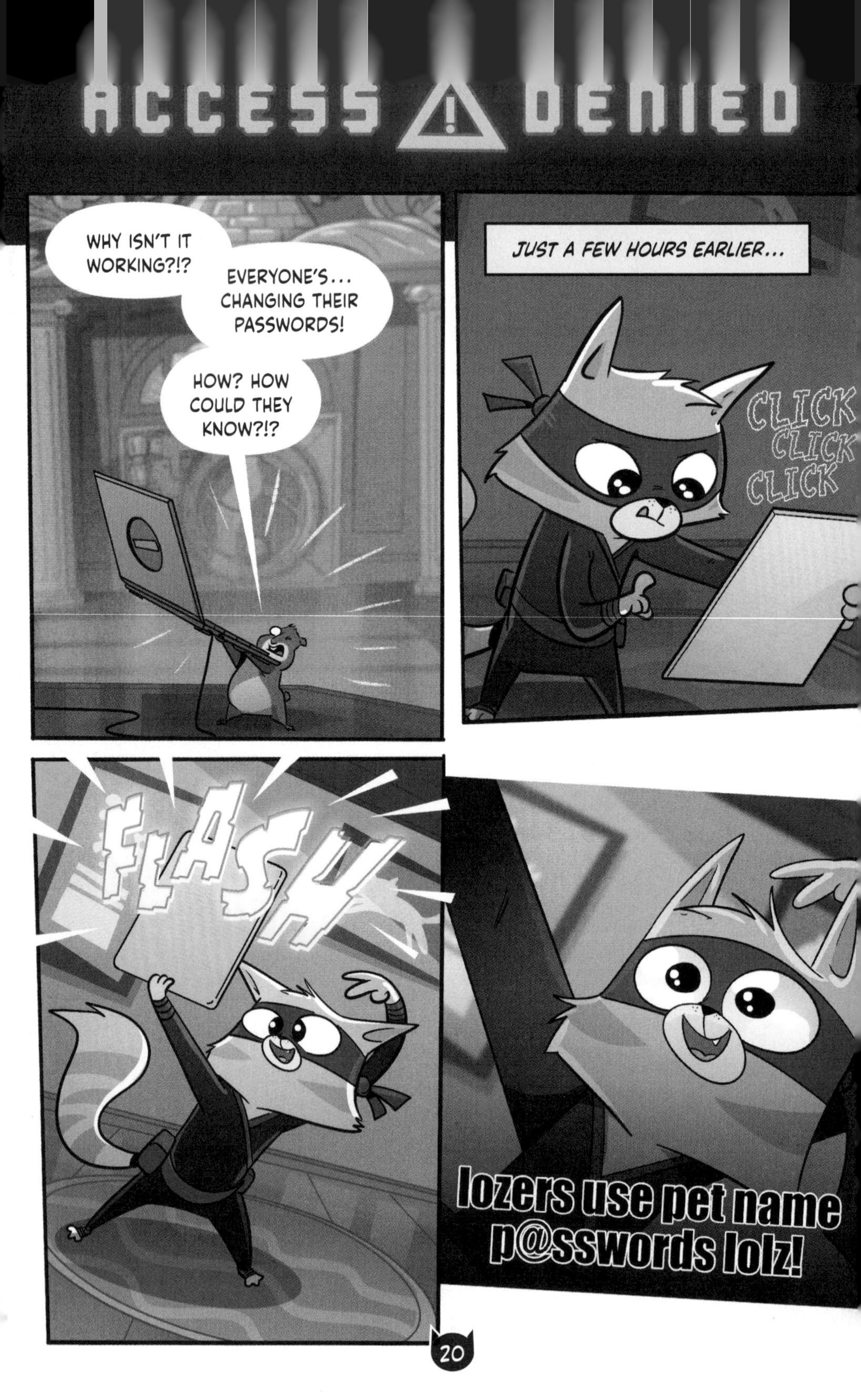
ACCESS DENIED
WHY ISN'T IT WORKING?!?
EVERYONE'S... CHANGING THEIR PASSWORDS!
HOW? HOW COULD THEY KNOW?!?
JUST A FEW HOURS EARLIER...
CLICK CLICK CLICK
FLASH
lozers use pet name p@sswords lolz!

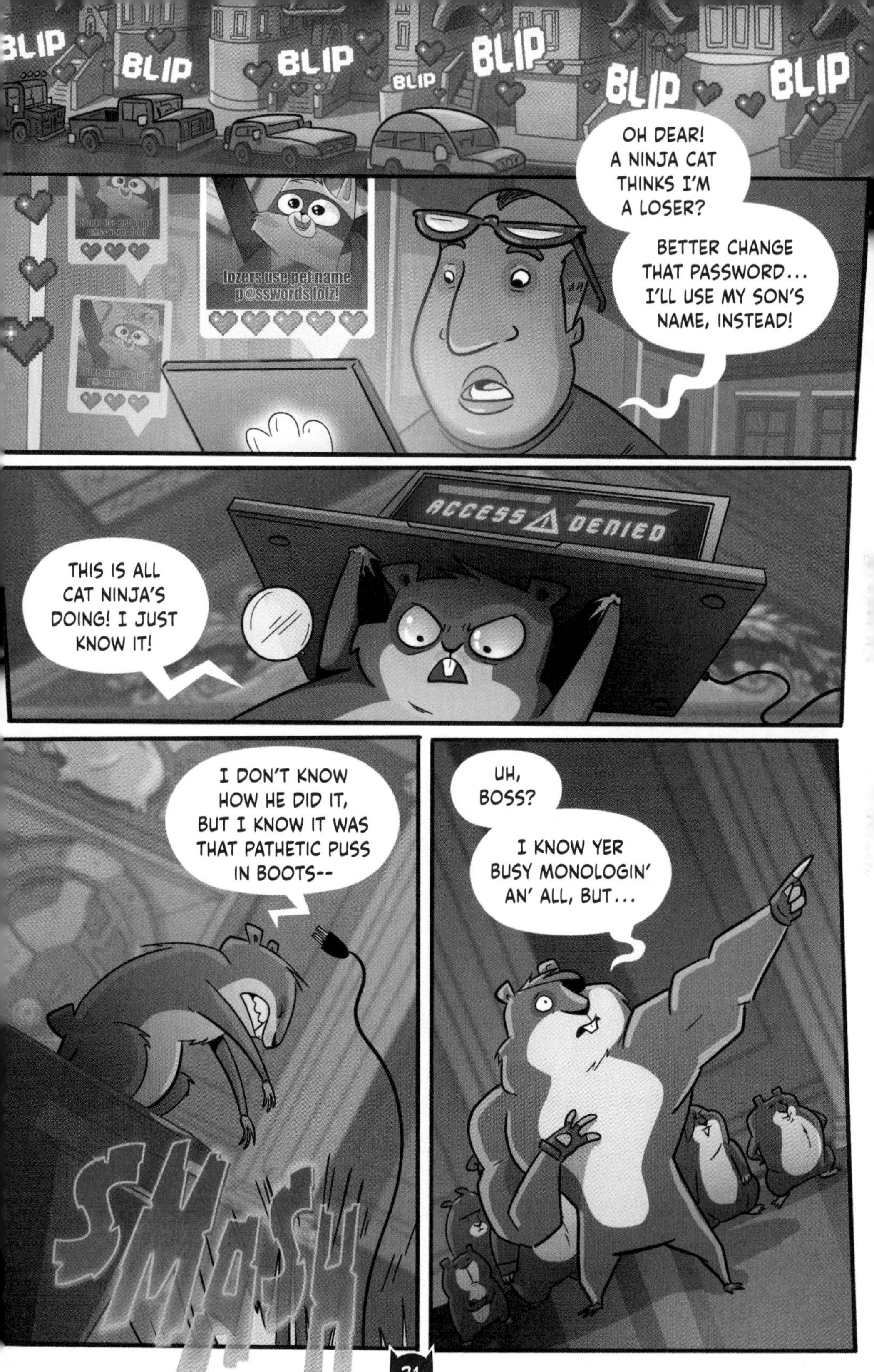
BLIP
BLIP
BLIP
BLIP
BLIP
BLIP
BLIP
OH DEAR! A NINJA CAT THINKS I'M A LOSER?
BETTER CHANGE THAT PASSWORD... I'LL USE MY SON'S NAME, INSTEAD!
lozers use pet name p@sswords lolz!
ACCESS DENIED
THIS IS ALL CAT NINJA'S DOING! I JUST KNOW IT!
I DON'T KNOW HOW HE DID IT, BUT I KNOW IT WAS THAT PATHETIC PUSS IN BOOTS--
SMASH
UH, BOSS?
I KNOW YER BUSY MONOLOGIN' AN' ALL, BUT...

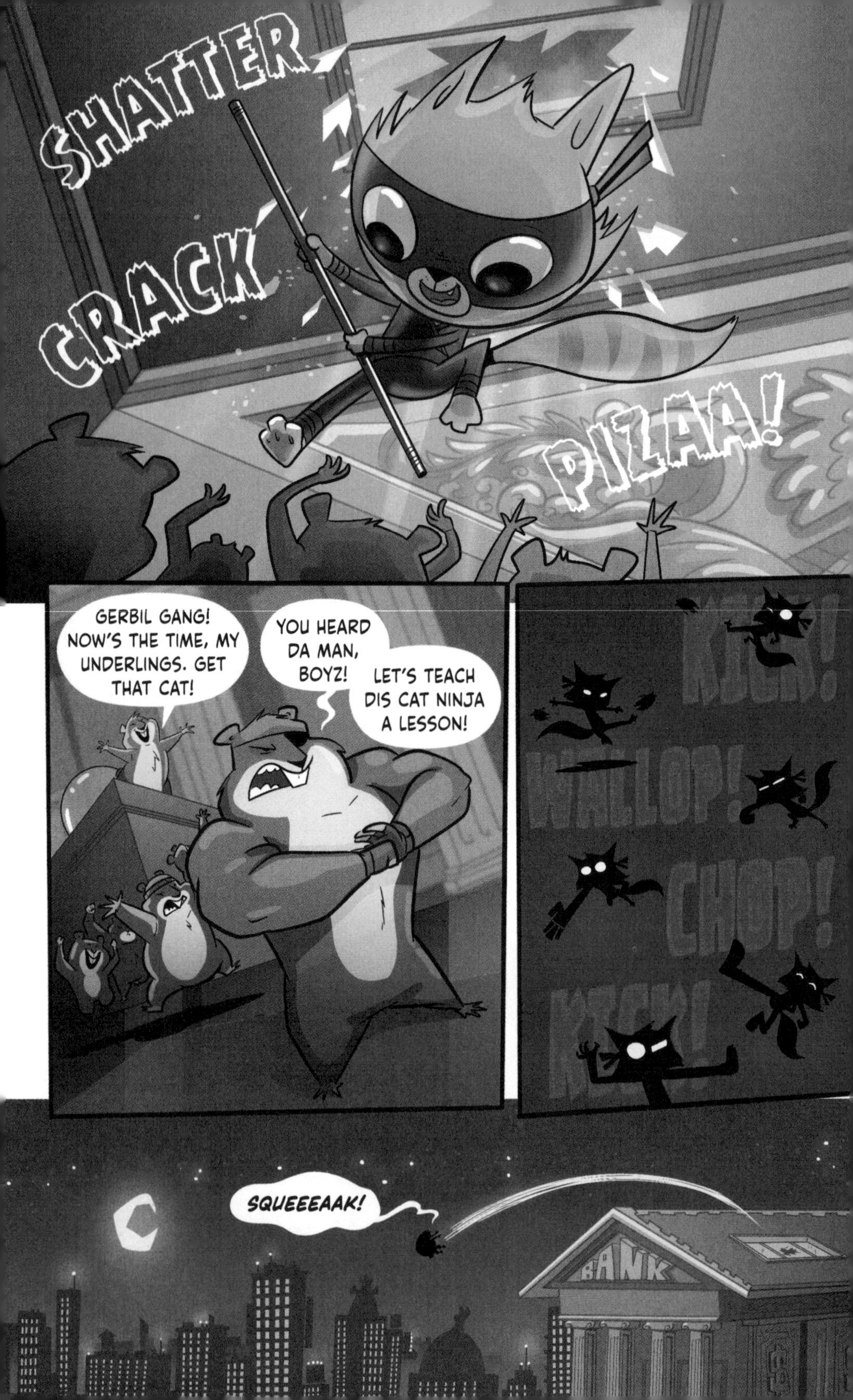
SHATTER
CRACK
PIZAA!
GERBIL GANG! NOW'S THE TIME, MY UNDERLINGS. GET THAT CAT!
YOU HEARD DA MAN, BOYZ!
LET'S TEACH DIS CAT NINJA A LESSON!
KICK!
WALLOP!
CHOP!
SQUEEEAAK!
BANK

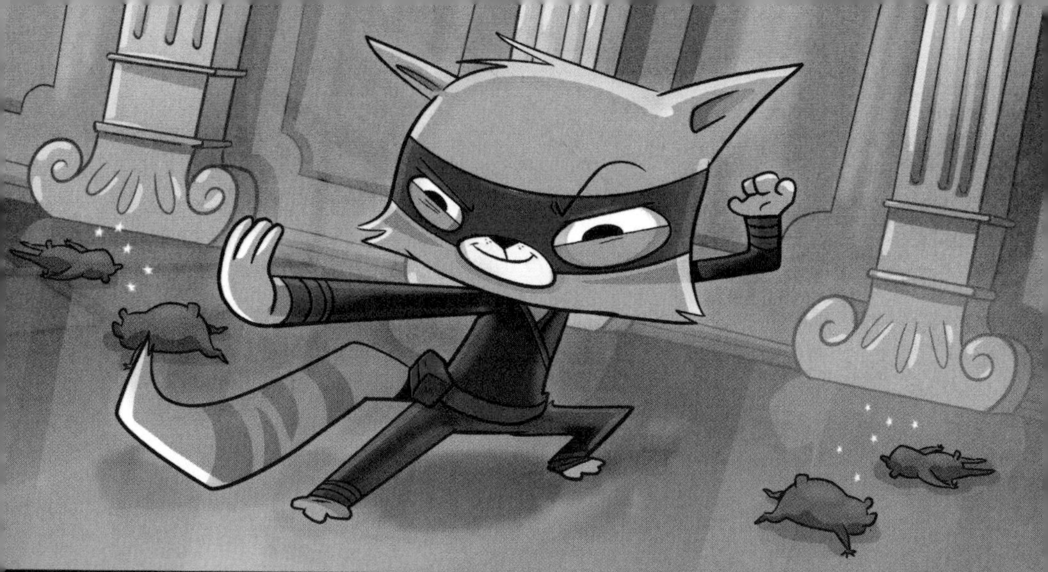

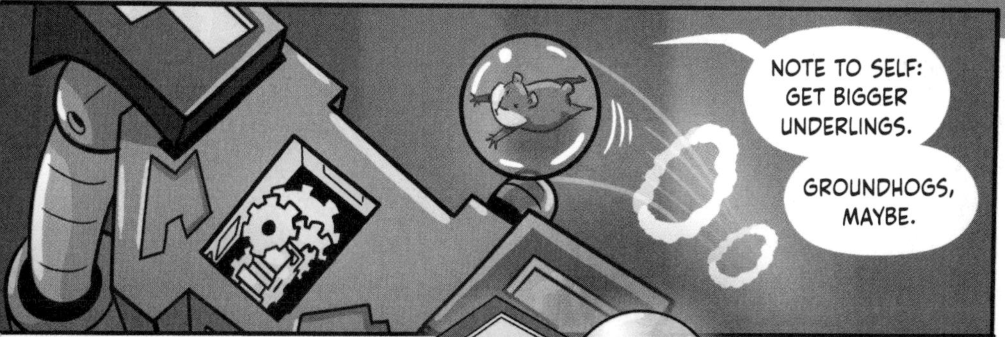
NOTE TO SELF: GET BIGGER UNDERLINGS.
GROUNDHOGS, MAYBE.

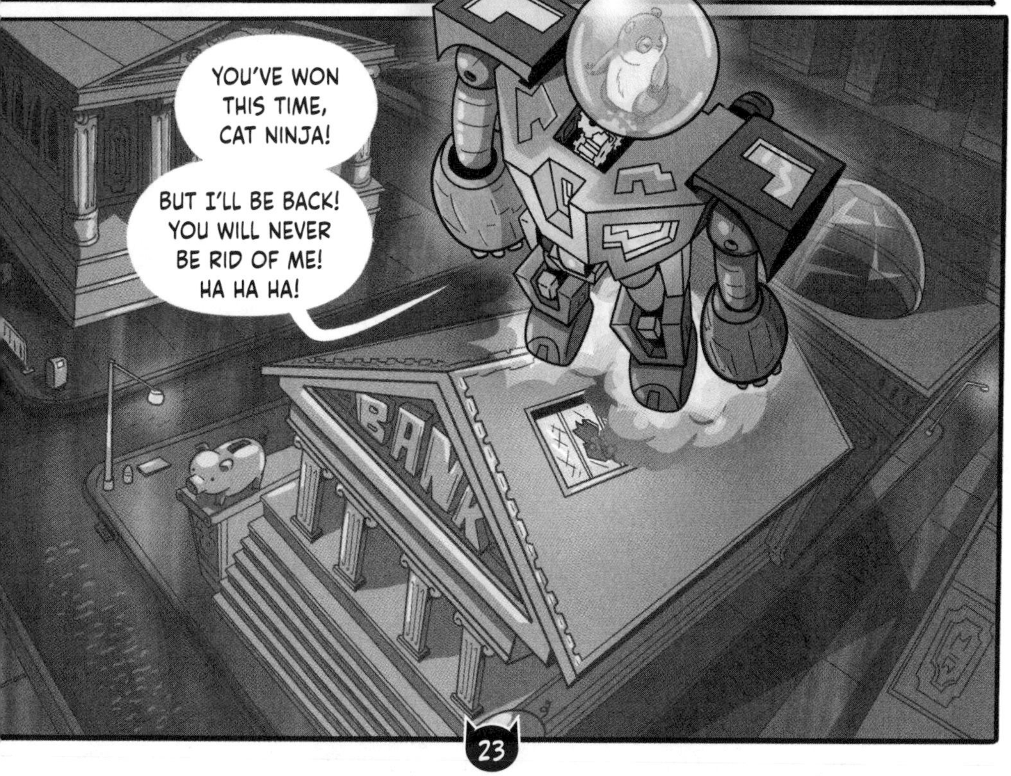
YOU'VE WON THIS TIME, CAT NINJA!
BUT I'LL BE BACK! YOU WILL NEVER BE RID OF ME! HA HA HA!
BANK

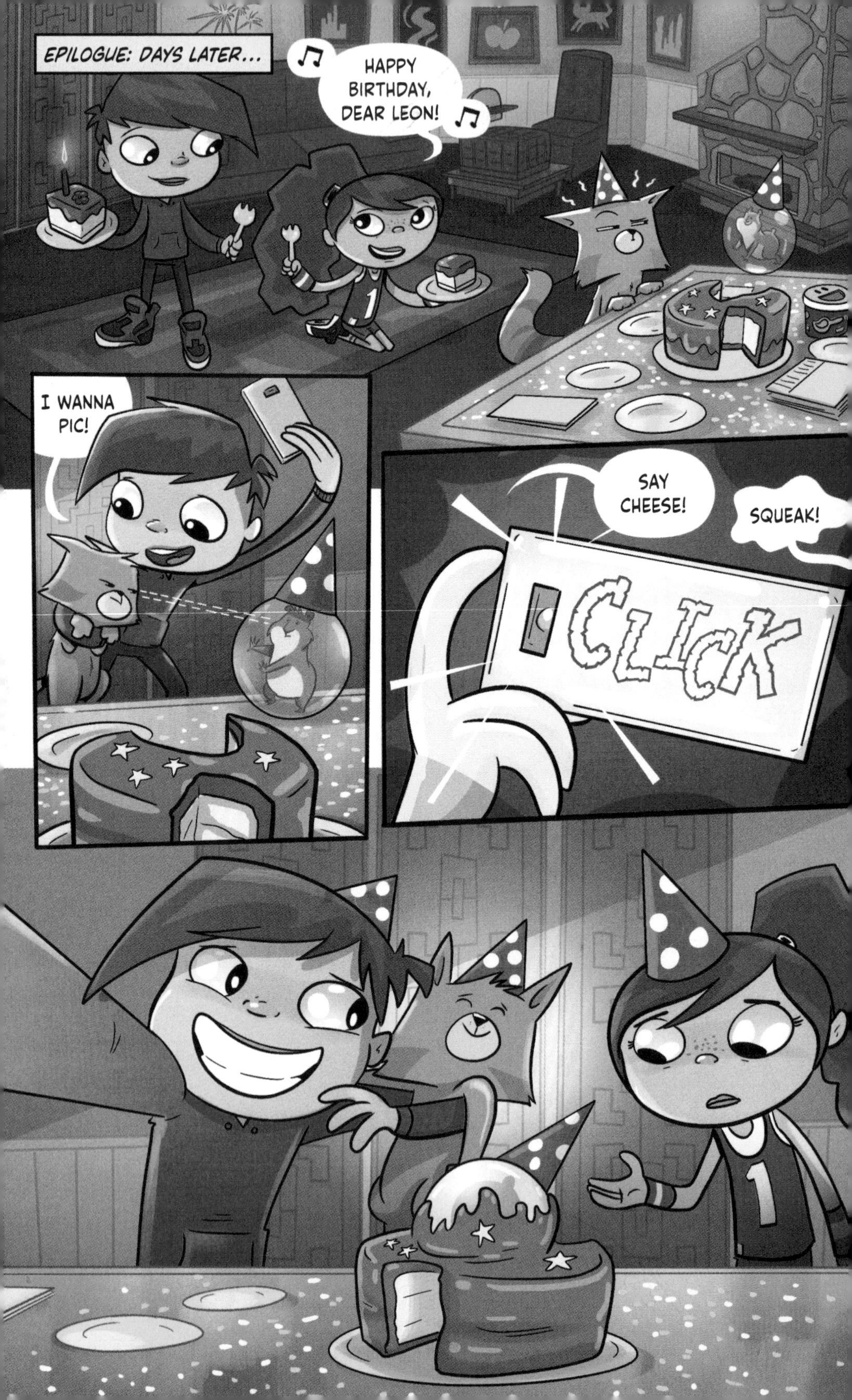

EPILOGUE: DAYS LATER...
HAPPY BIRTHDAY, DEAR LEON!
I WANNA PIC!
SAY CHEESE!
SQUEAK!
CLICK

Chapter 2:
Le Chat Noir!

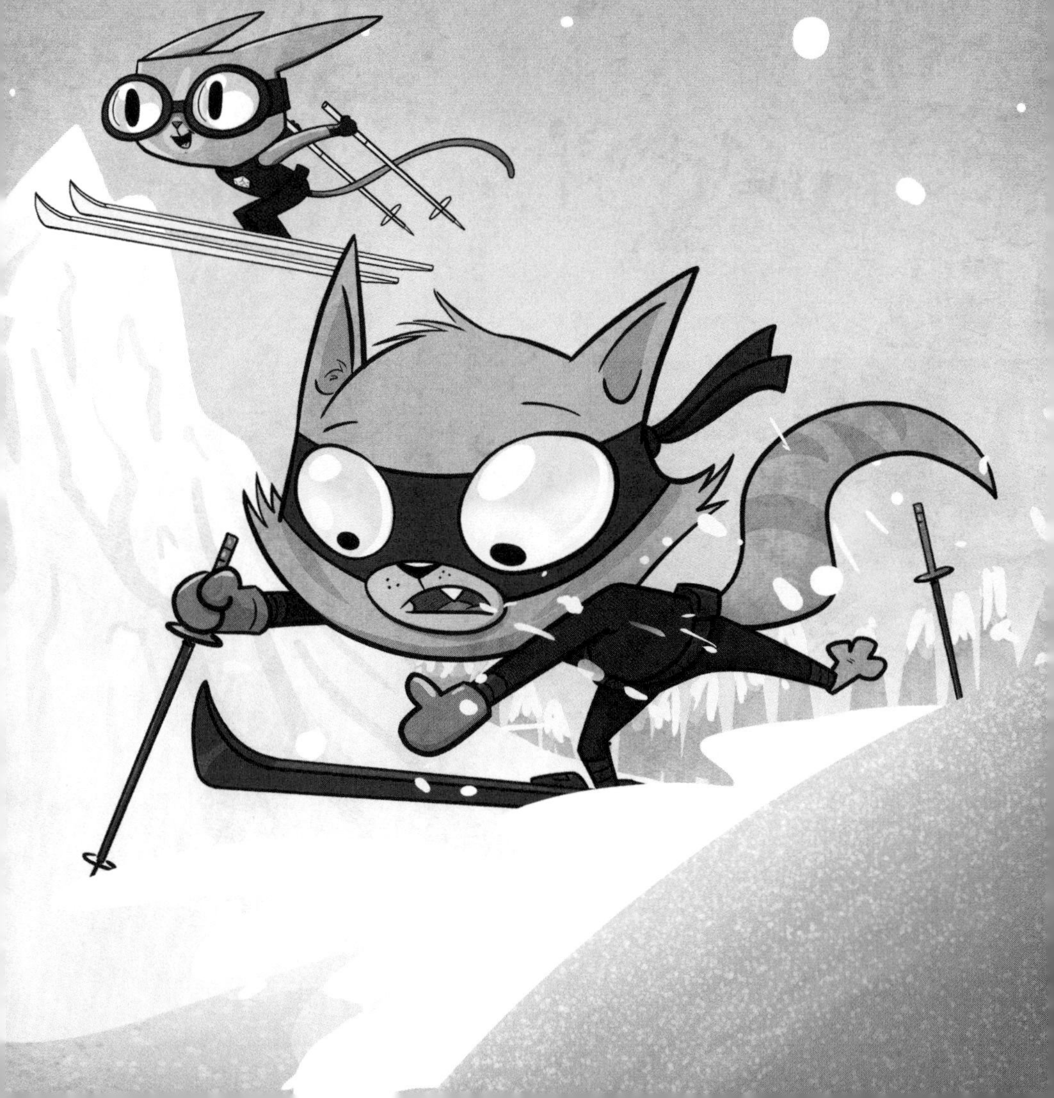

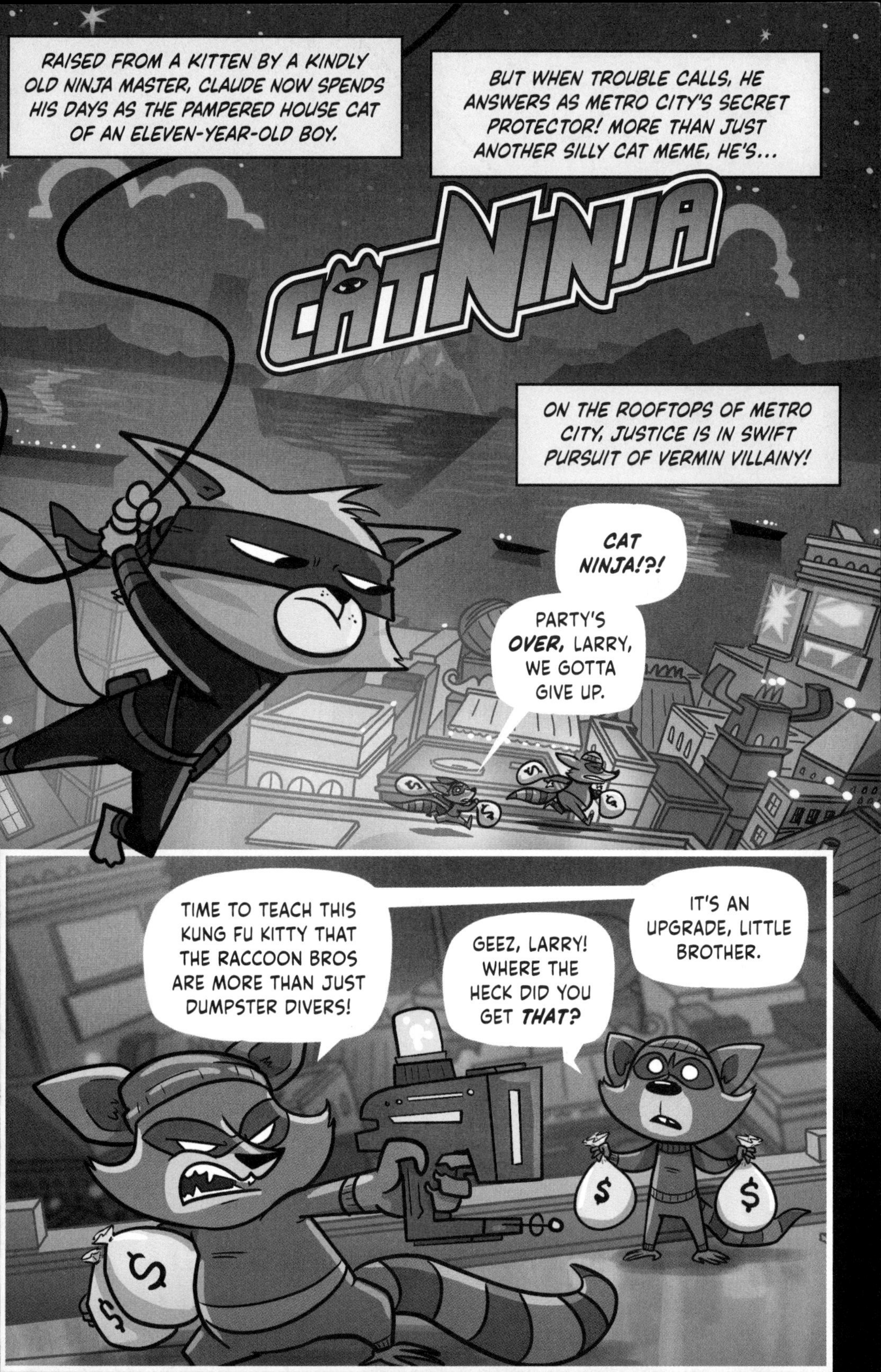
RAISED FROM A KITTEN BY A KINDLY OLD NINJA MASTER, CLAUDE NOW SPENDS HIS DAYS AS THE PAMPERED HOUSE CAT OF AN ELEVEN-YEAR-OLD BOY.
BUT WHEN TROUBLE CALLS, HE ANSWERS AS METRO CITY'S SECRET PROTECTOR! MORE THAN JUST ANOTHER SILLY CAT MEME, HE'S...
CAT NINJA
ON THE ROOFTOPS OF METRO CITY, JUSTICE IS IN SWIFT PURSUIT OF VERMIN VILLAINY!
CAT NINJA!?!
PARTY'S OVER, LARRY, WE GOTTA GIVE UP.
TIME TO TEACH THIS KUNG FU KITTY THAT THE RACCOON BROS ARE MORE THAN JUST DUMPSTER DIVERS!
GEEZ, LARRY! WHERE THE HECK DID YOU GET THAT?
IT'S AN UPGRADE, LITTLE BROTHER.

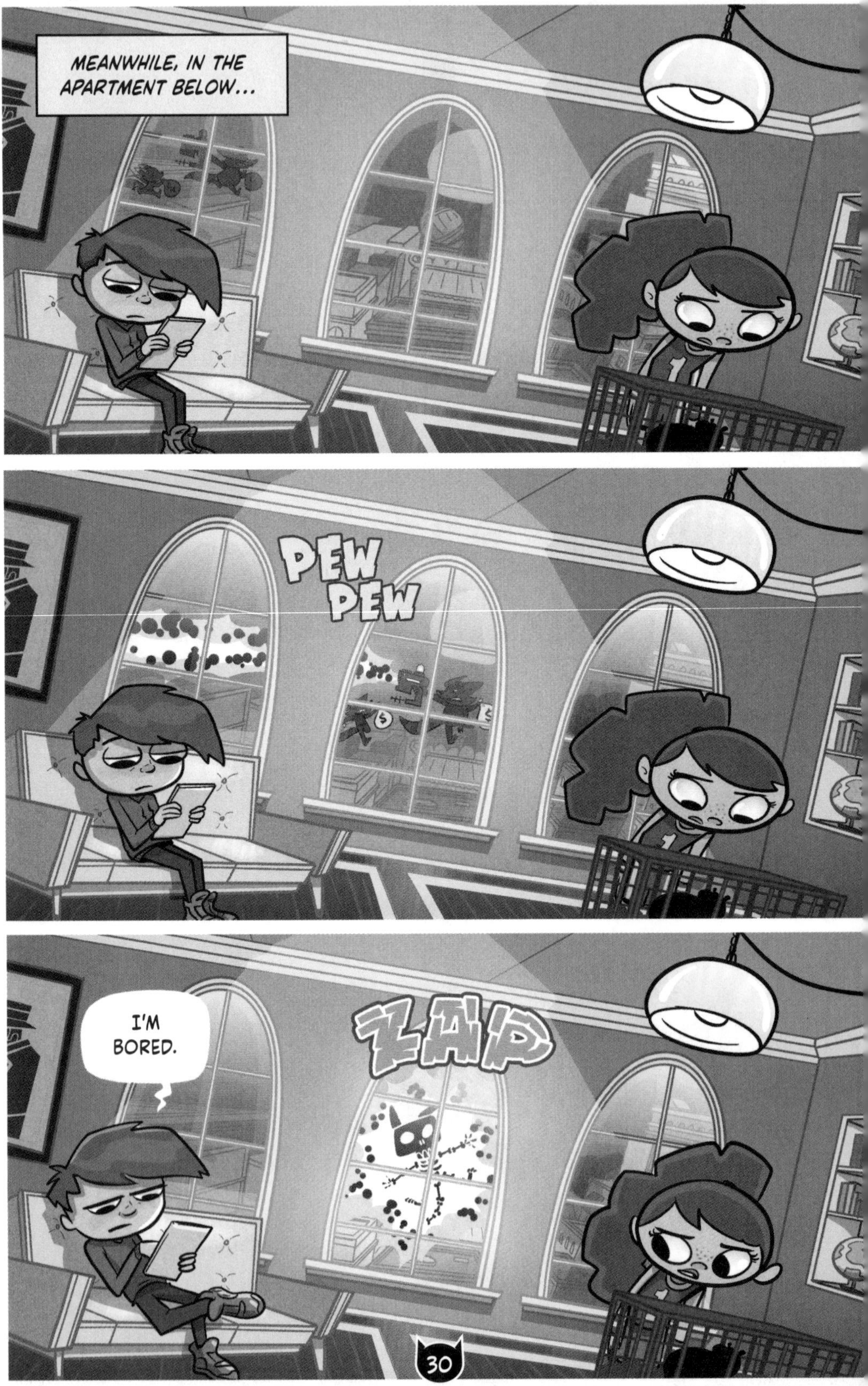
MEANWHILE, IN THE APARTMENT BELOW...
PEW PEW
ZAP
I'M BORED.

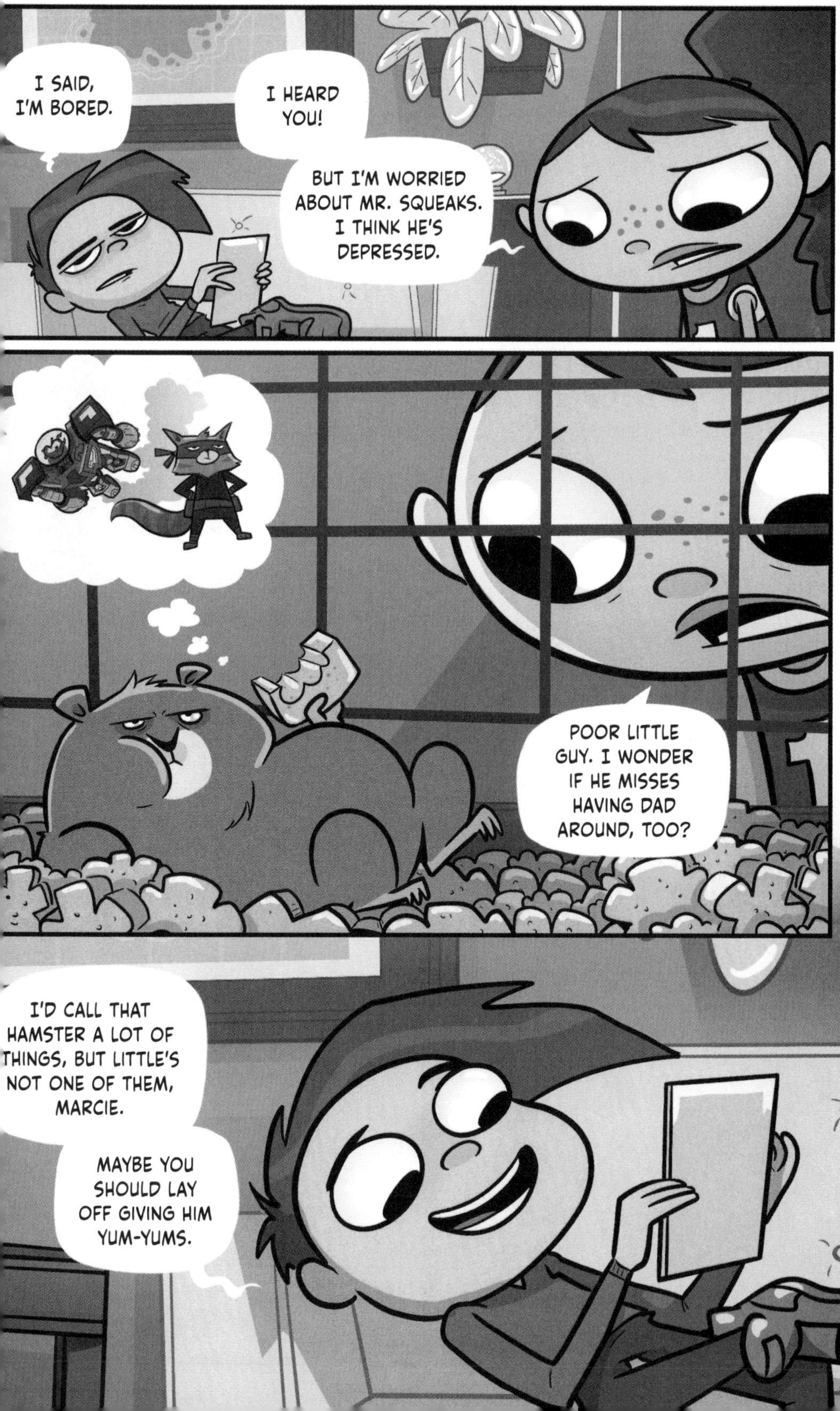
I SAID, I'M BORED.
I HEARD YOU!
BUT I'M WORRIED ABOUT MR. SQUEAKS. I THINK HE'S DEPRESSED.
POOR LITTLE GUY. I WONDER IF HE MISSES HAVING DAD AROUND, TOO?
I'D CALL THAT HAMSTER A LOT OF THINGS, BUT LITTLE'S NOT ONE OF THEM, MARCIE.
MAYBE YOU SHOULD LAY OFF GIVING HIM YUM-YUMS.

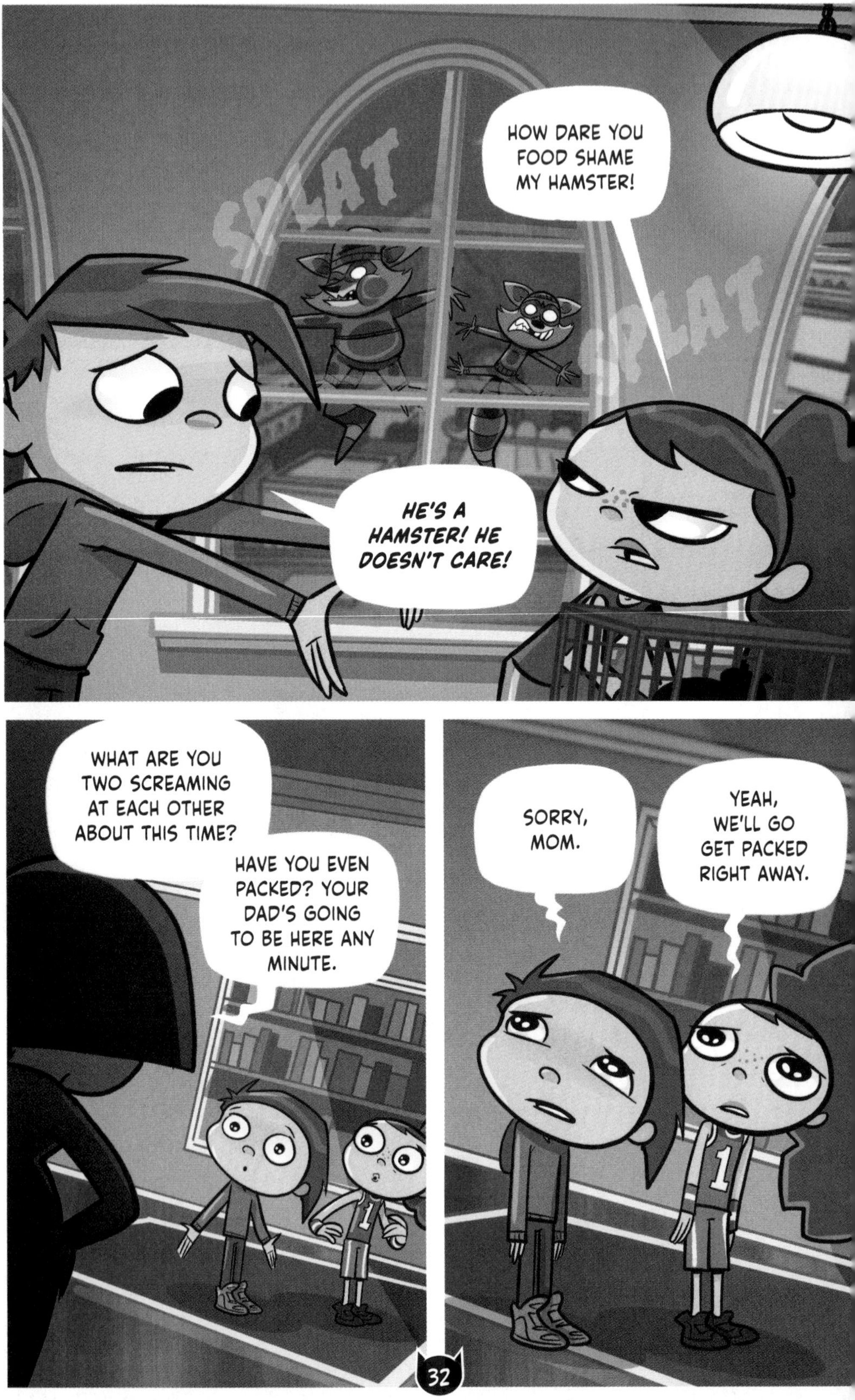
HOW DARE YOU FOOD SHAME MY HAMSTER!
SPLAT
SPLAT
HE'S A HAMSTER! HE DOESN'T CARE!
WHAT ARE YOU TWO SCREAMING AT EACH OTHER ABOUT THIS TIME?
HAVE YOU EVEN PACKED? YOUR DAD'S GOING TO BE HERE ANY MINUTE.
SORRY, MOM.
YEAH, WE'LL GO GET PACKED RIGHT AWAY.

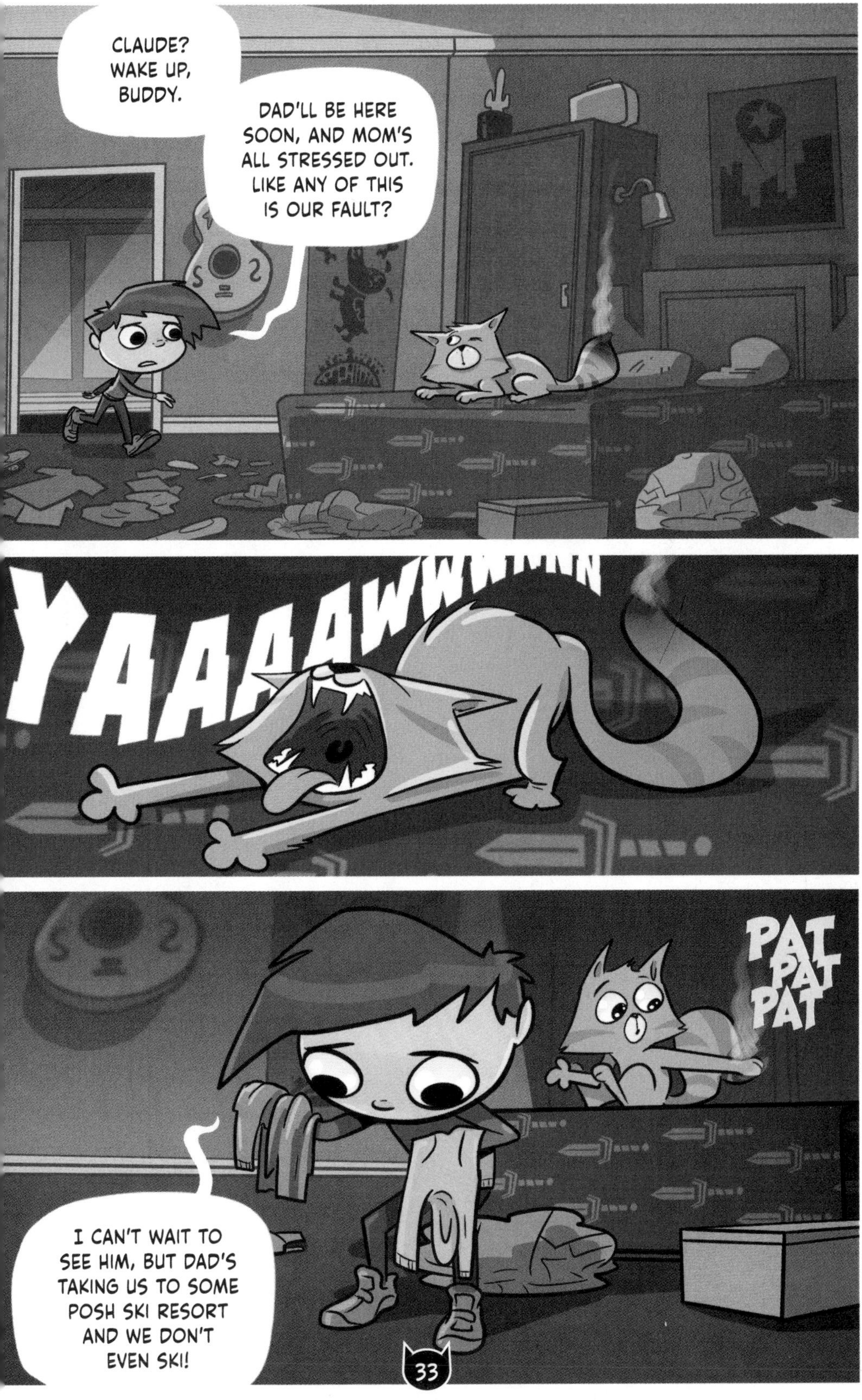
CLAUDE? WAKE UP, BUDDY.
DAD'LL BE HERE SOON, AND MOM'S ALL STRESSED OUT. LIKE ANY OF THIS IS OUR FAULT?
YAAAAWWWNNN
PAT PAT PAT
I CAN'T WAIT TO SEE HIM, BUT DAD'S TAKING US TO SOME POSH SKI RESORT AND WE DON'T EVEN SKI!

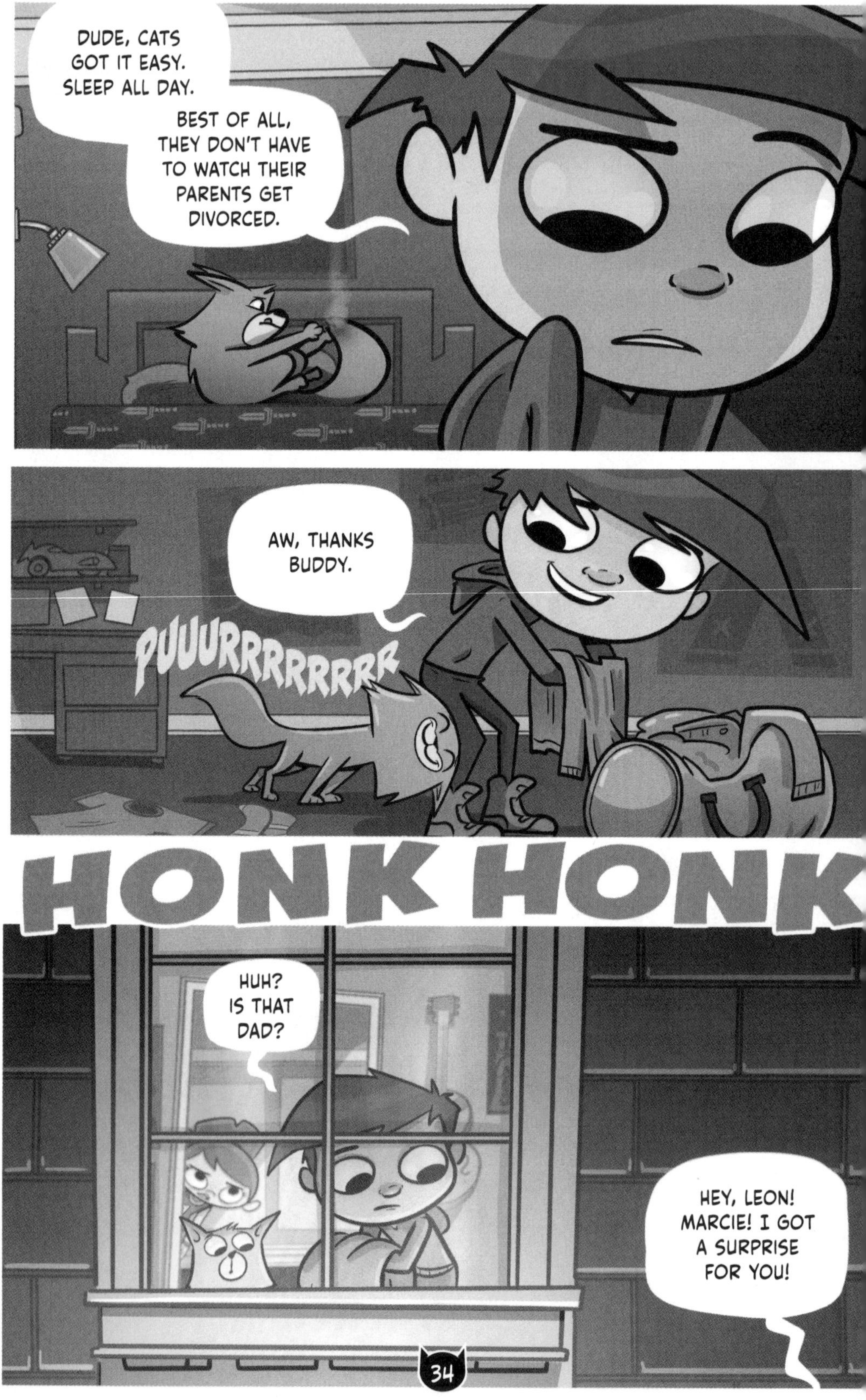
DUDE, CATS GOT IT EASY. SLEEP ALL DAY.
BEST OF ALL, THEY DON'T HAVE TO WATCH THEIR PARENTS GET DIVORCED.
AW, THANKS BUDDY.
PUUURRRRRRRR
HONK HONK
HUH? IS THAT DAD?
HEY, LEON! MARCIE! I GOT A SURPRISE FOR YOU!

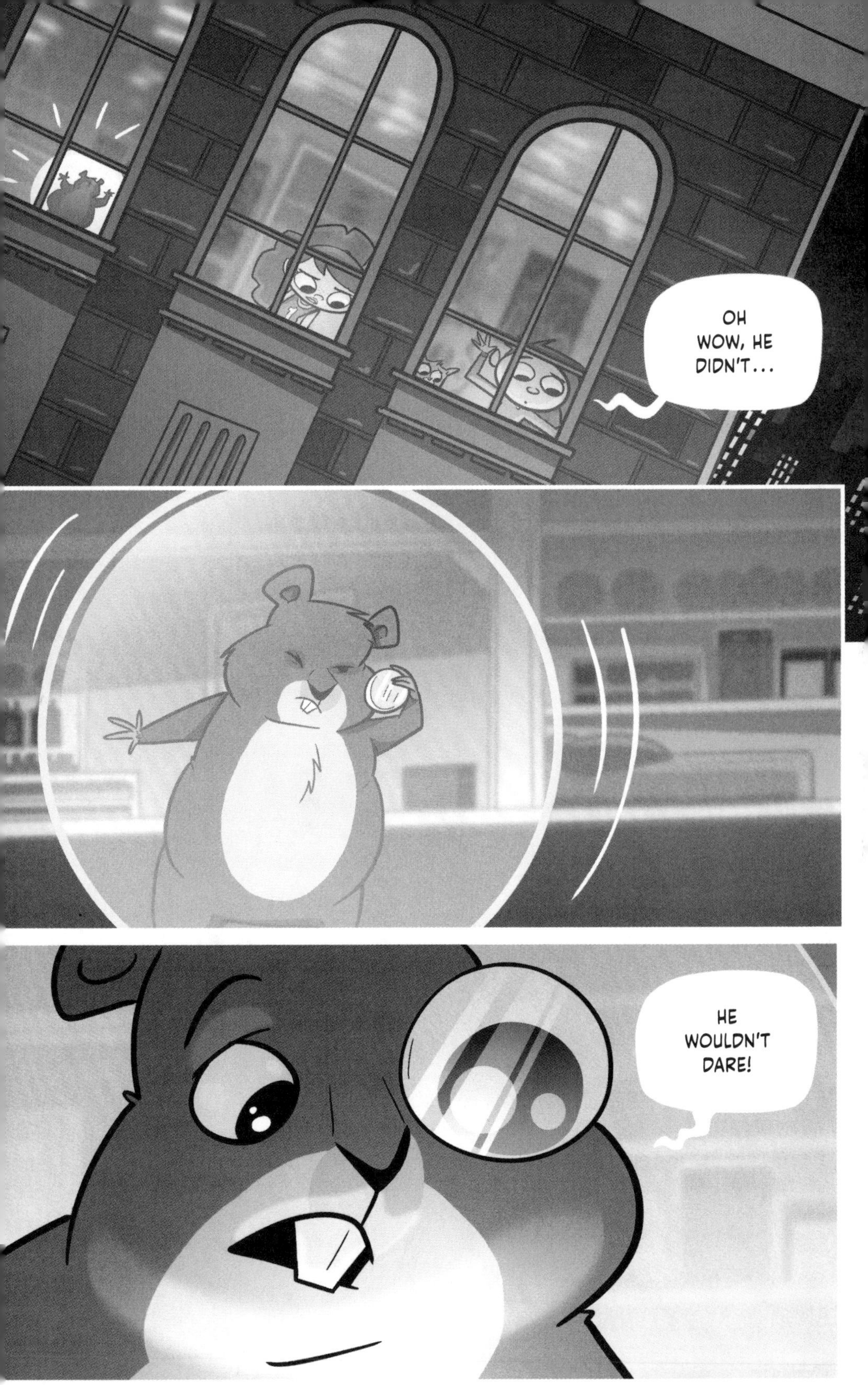
OH WOW, HE DIDN'T...
HE WOULDN'T DARE!

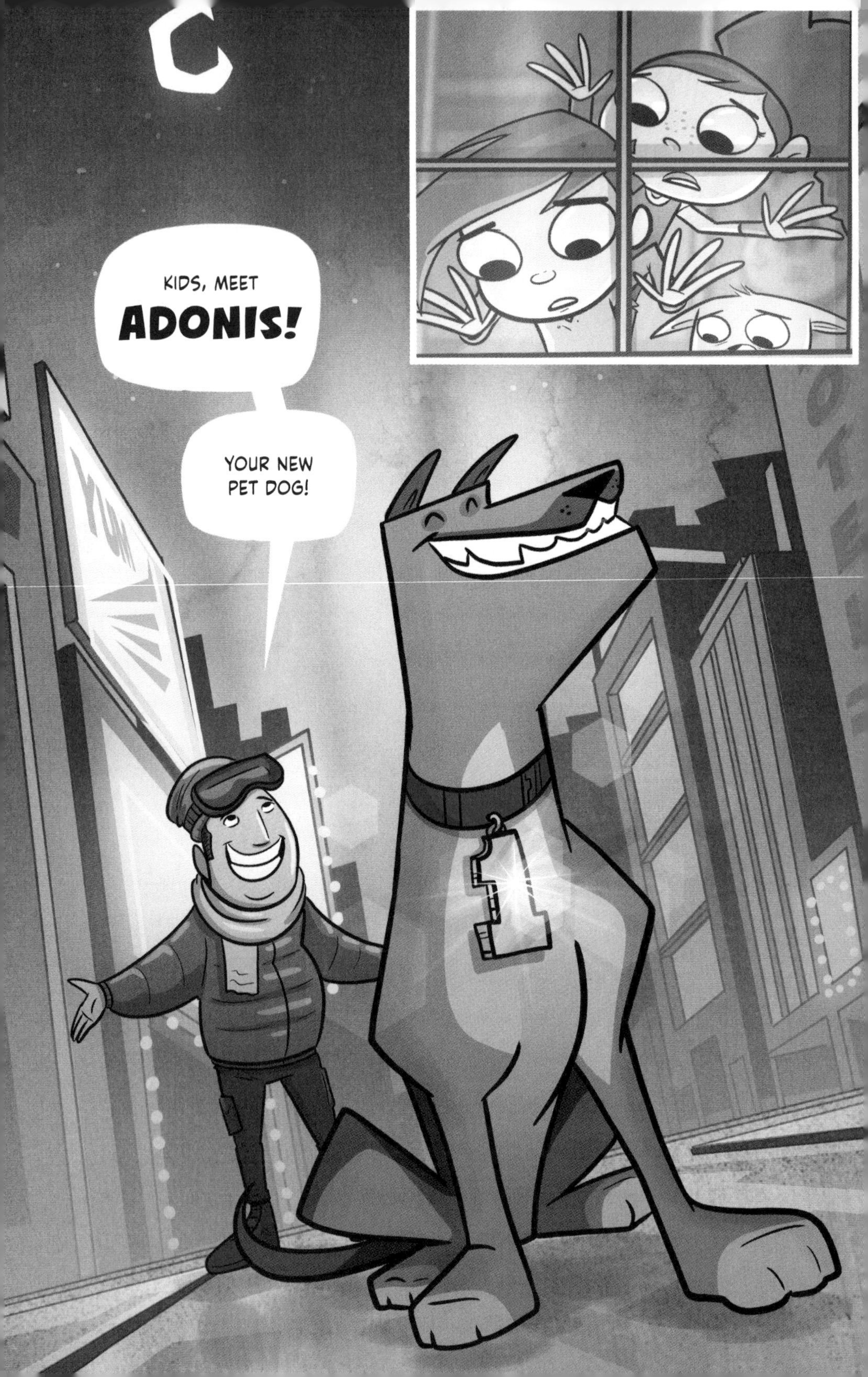
KIDS, MEET
ADONIS!
YOUR NEW
PET DOG!

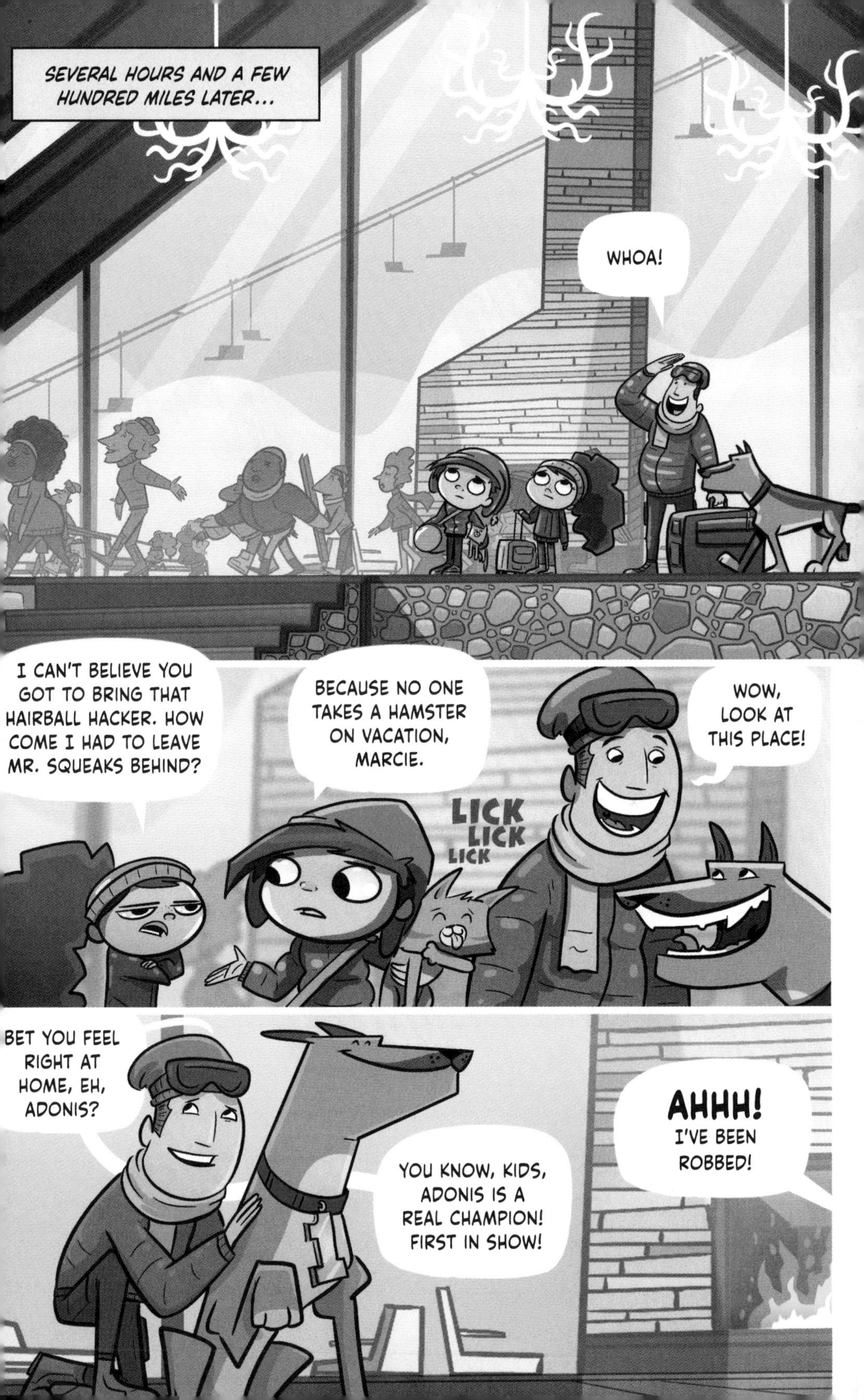

SEVERAL HOURS AND A FEW HUNDRED MILES LATER...
WHOA!
I CAN'T BELIEVE YOU GOT TO BRING THAT HAIRBALL HACKER. HOW COME I HAD TO LEAVE MR. SQUEAKS BEHIND?
BECAUSE NO ONE TAKES A HAMSTER ON VACATION, MARCIE.
LICK LICK LICK
WOW, LOOK AT THIS PLACE!
BET YOU FEEL RIGHT AT HOME, EH, ADONIS?
YOU KNOW, KIDS, ADONIS IS A REAL CHAMPION! FIRST IN SHOW!
AHHH! I'VE BEEN ROBBED!

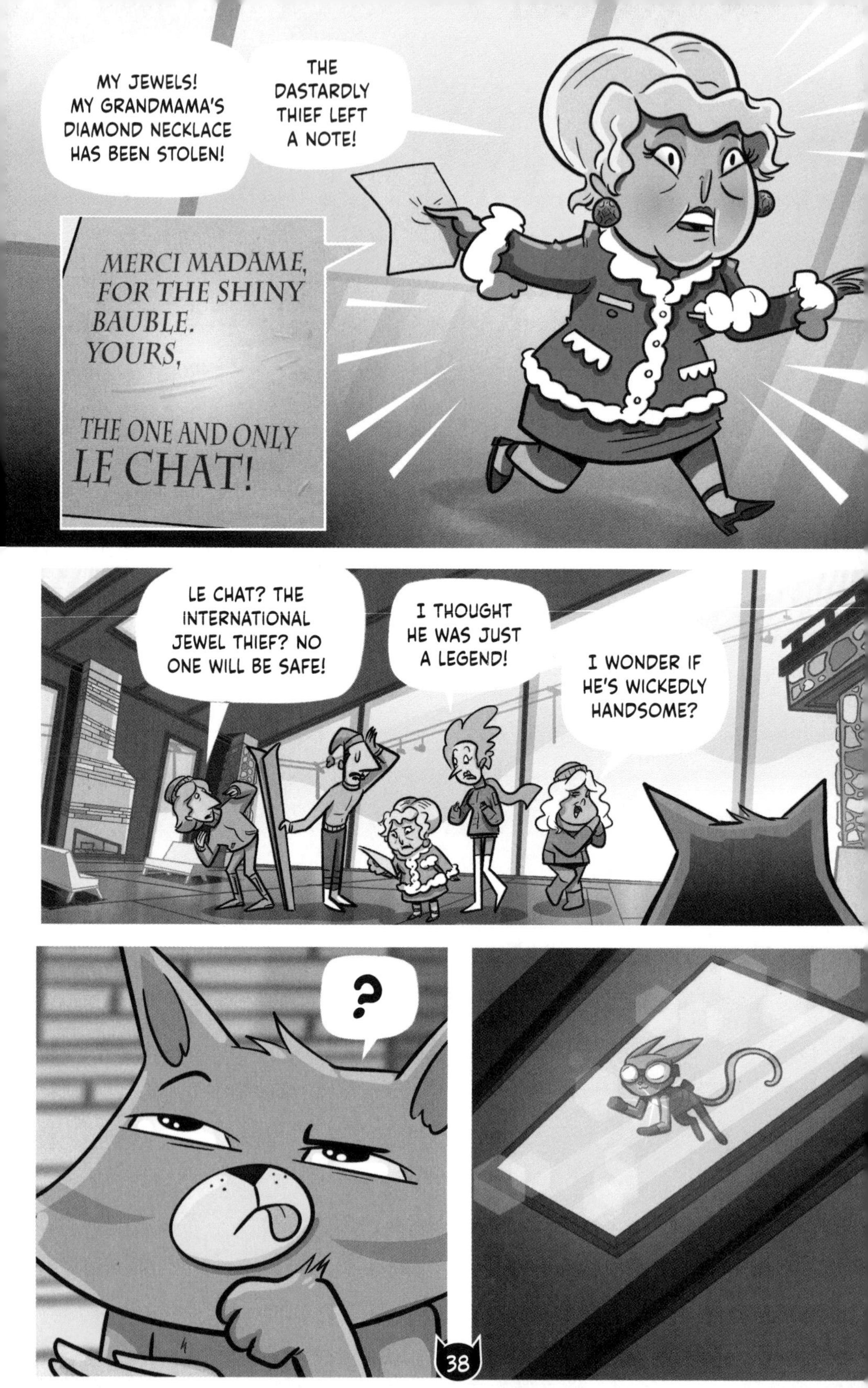

MY JEWELS! MY GRANDMAMA'S DIAMOND NECKLACE HAS BEEN STOLEN!
THE DASTARDLY THIEF LEFT A NOTE!
MERCI MADAME, FOR THE SHINY BAUBLE. YOURS,
THE ONE AND ONLY LE CHAT!
LE CHAT? THE INTERNATIONAL JEWEL THIEF? NO ONE WILL BE SAFE!
I THOUGHT HE WAS JUST A LEGEND!
I WONDER IF HE'S WICKEDLY HANDSOME?
?

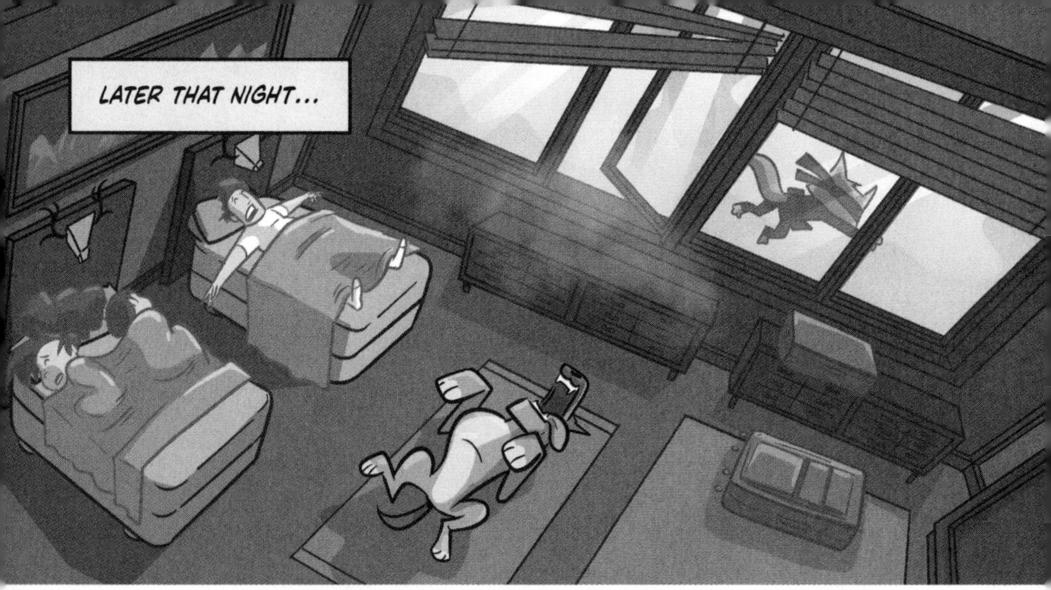
LATER THAT NIGHT...

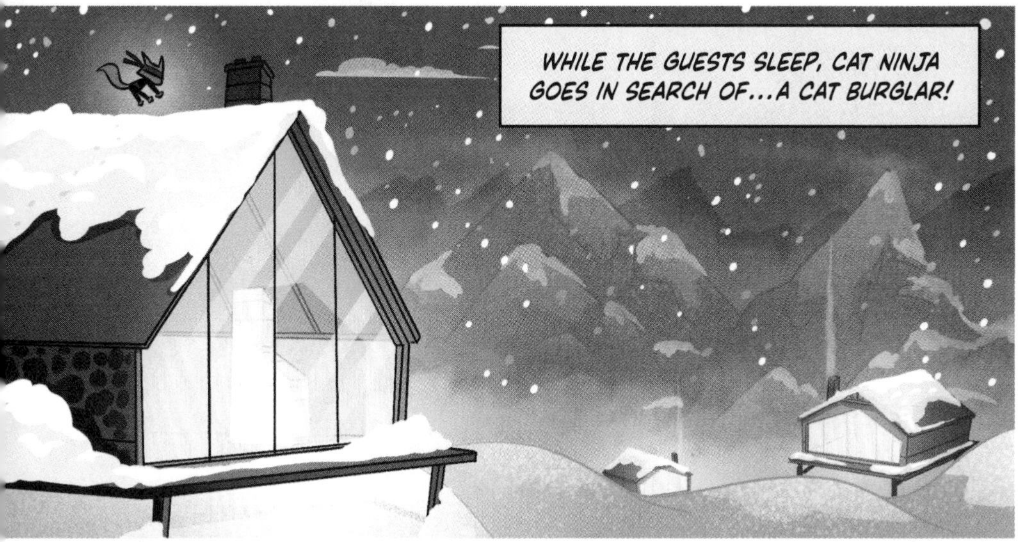
WHILE THE GUESTS SLEEP, CAT NINJA GOES IN SEARCH OF...A CAT BURGLAR!

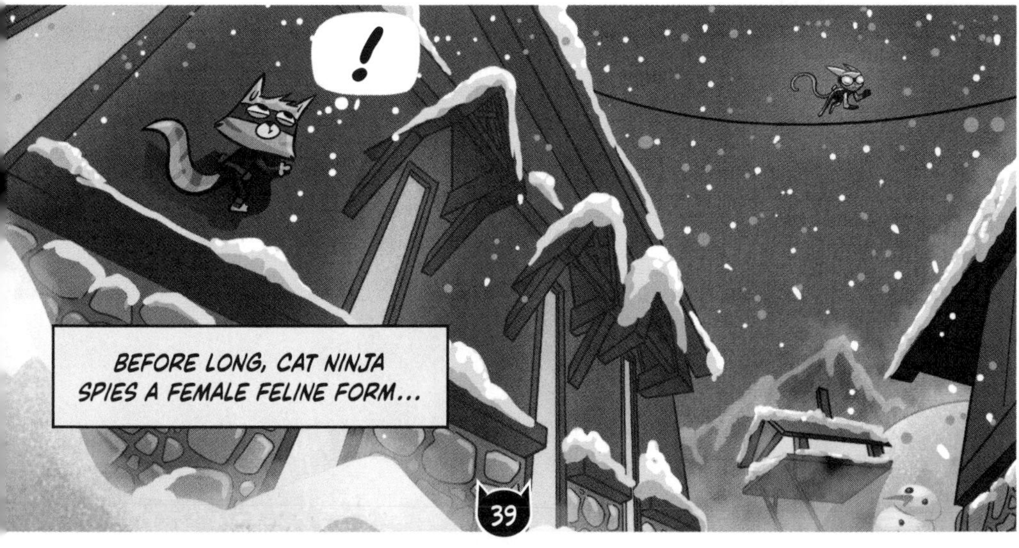
!
BEFORE LONG, CAT NINJA SPIES A FEMALE FELINE FORM...

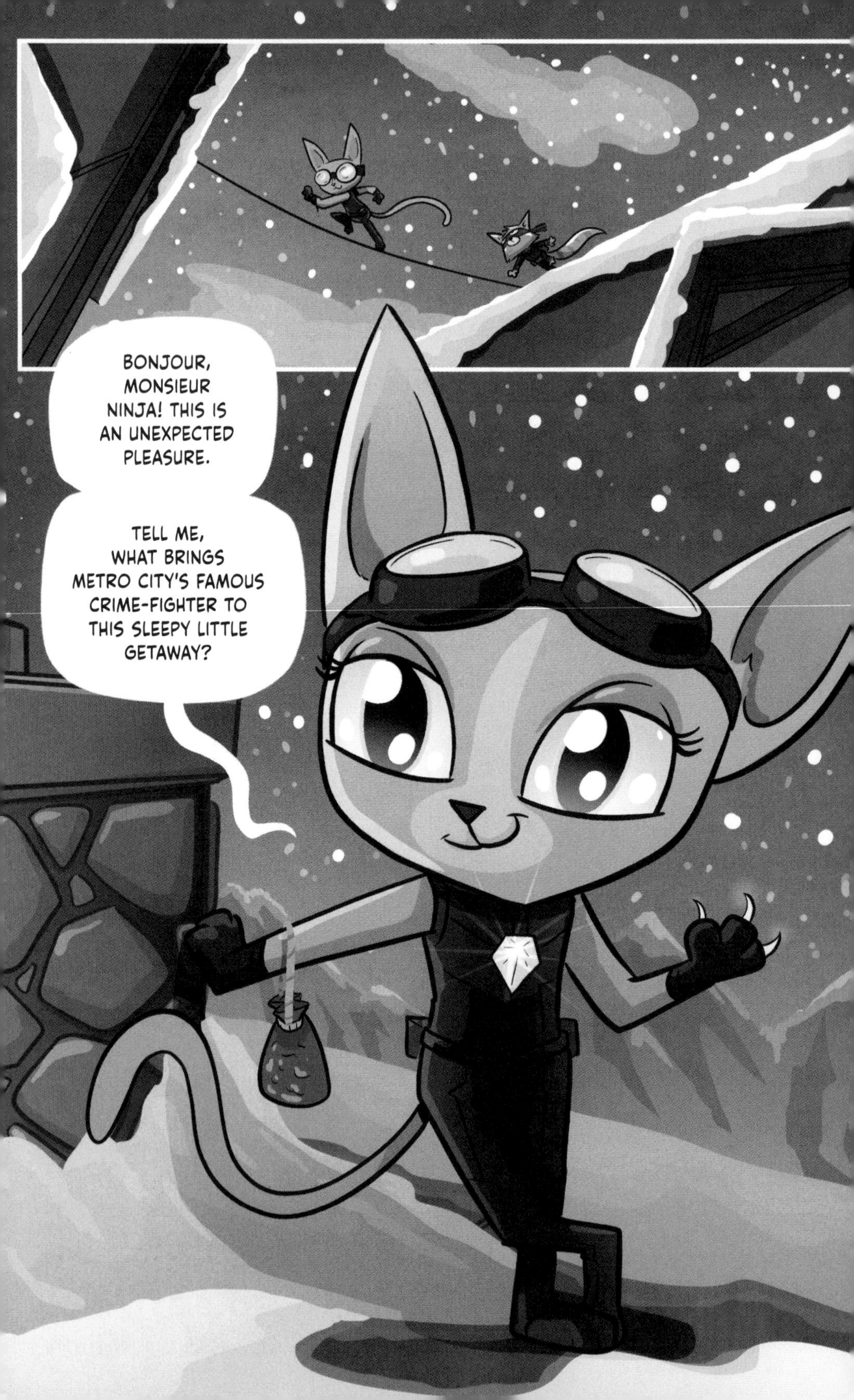
BONJOUR, MONSIEUR NINJA! THIS IS AN UNEXPECTED PLEASURE.
TELL ME, WHAT BRINGS METRO CITY'S FAMOUS CRIME-FIGHTER TO THIS SLEEPY LITTLE GETAWAY?

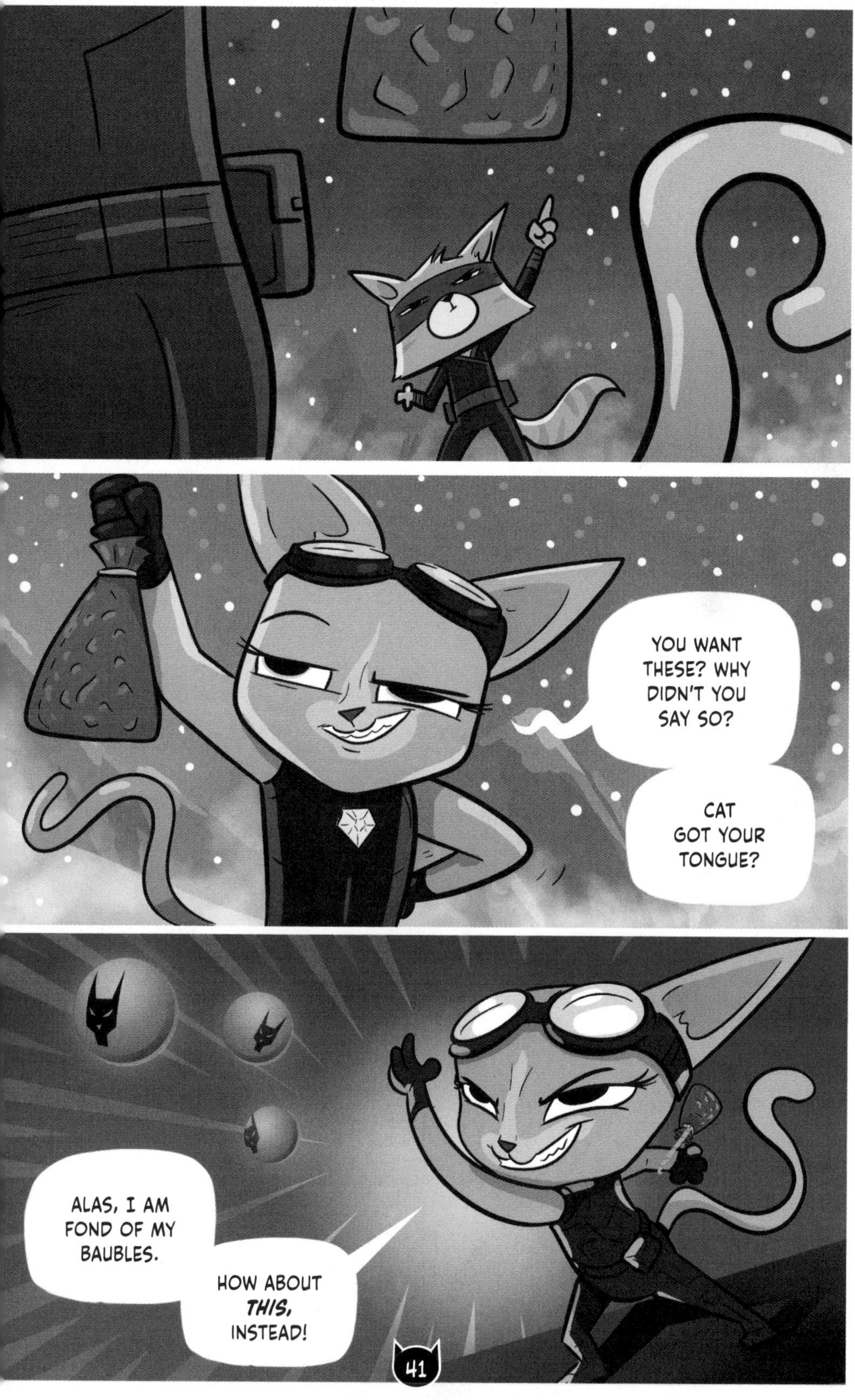
YOU WANT THESE? WHY DIDN'T YOU SAY SO?
CAT GOT YOUR TONGUE?
ALAS, I AM FOND OF MY BAUBLES.
HOW ABOUT *THIS,* INSTEAD!

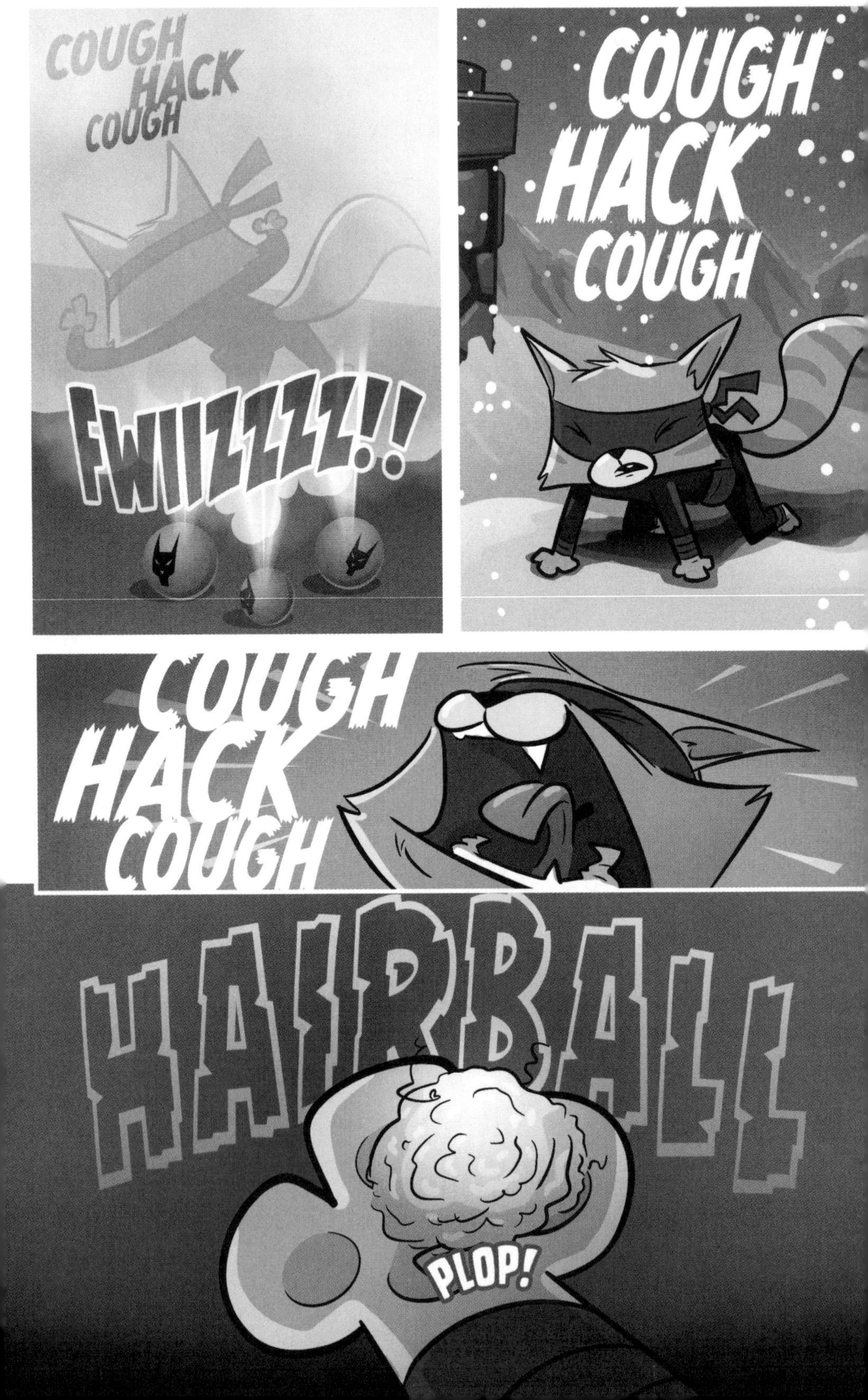
COUGH
HACK
COUGH
FWIIZZZZ!!
COUGH
HACK
COUGH
COUGH
HACK
COUGH
HAIRBALL
PLOP!

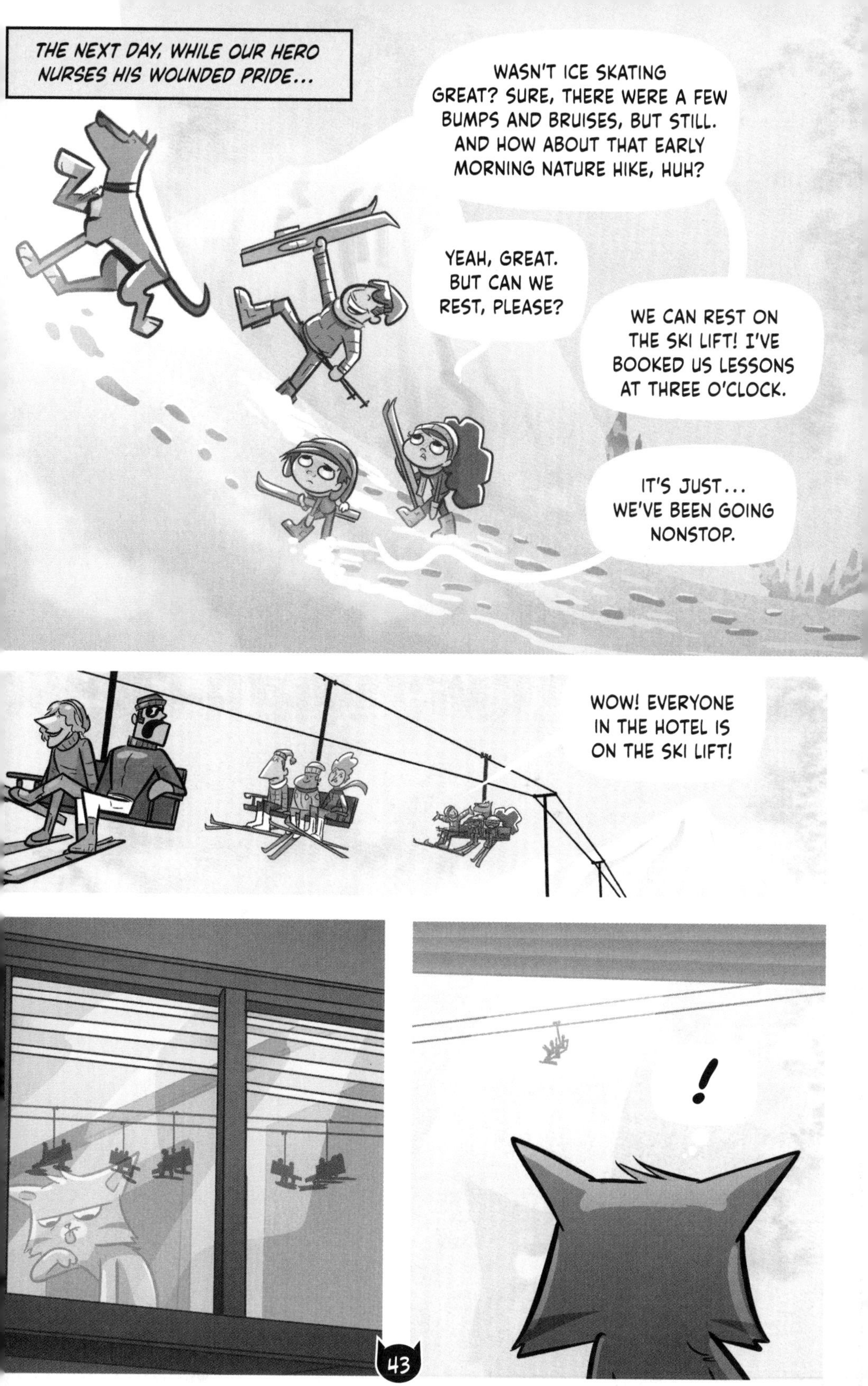
THE NEXT DAY, WHILE OUR HERO NURSES HIS WOUNDED PRIDE...
WASN'T ICE SKATING GREAT? SURE, THERE WERE A FEW BUMPS AND BRUISES, BUT STILL. AND HOW ABOUT THAT EARLY MORNING NATURE HIKE, HUH?
YEAH, GREAT. BUT CAN WE REST, PLEASE?
WE CAN REST ON THE SKI LIFT! I'VE BOOKED US LESSONS AT THREE O'CLOCK.
IT'S JUST... WE'VE BEEN GOING NONSTOP.
WOW! EVERYONE IN THE HOTEL IS ON THE SKI LIFT!
!

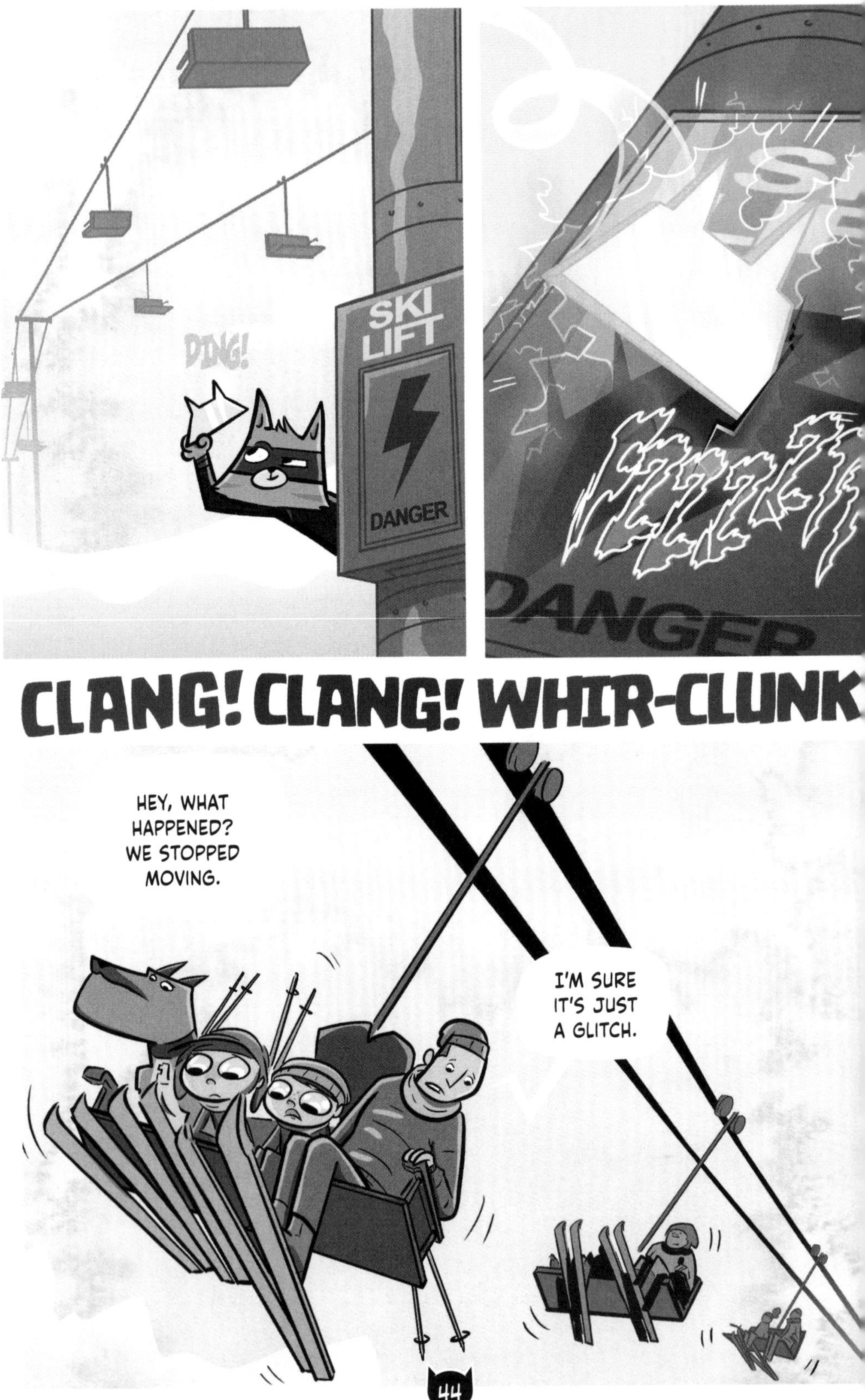
DING!
SKI LIFT
DANGER
DANGER
CLANG! CLANG! WHIR-CLUNK
HEY, WHAT HAPPENED? WE STOPPED MOVING.
I'M SURE IT'S JUST A GLITCH.

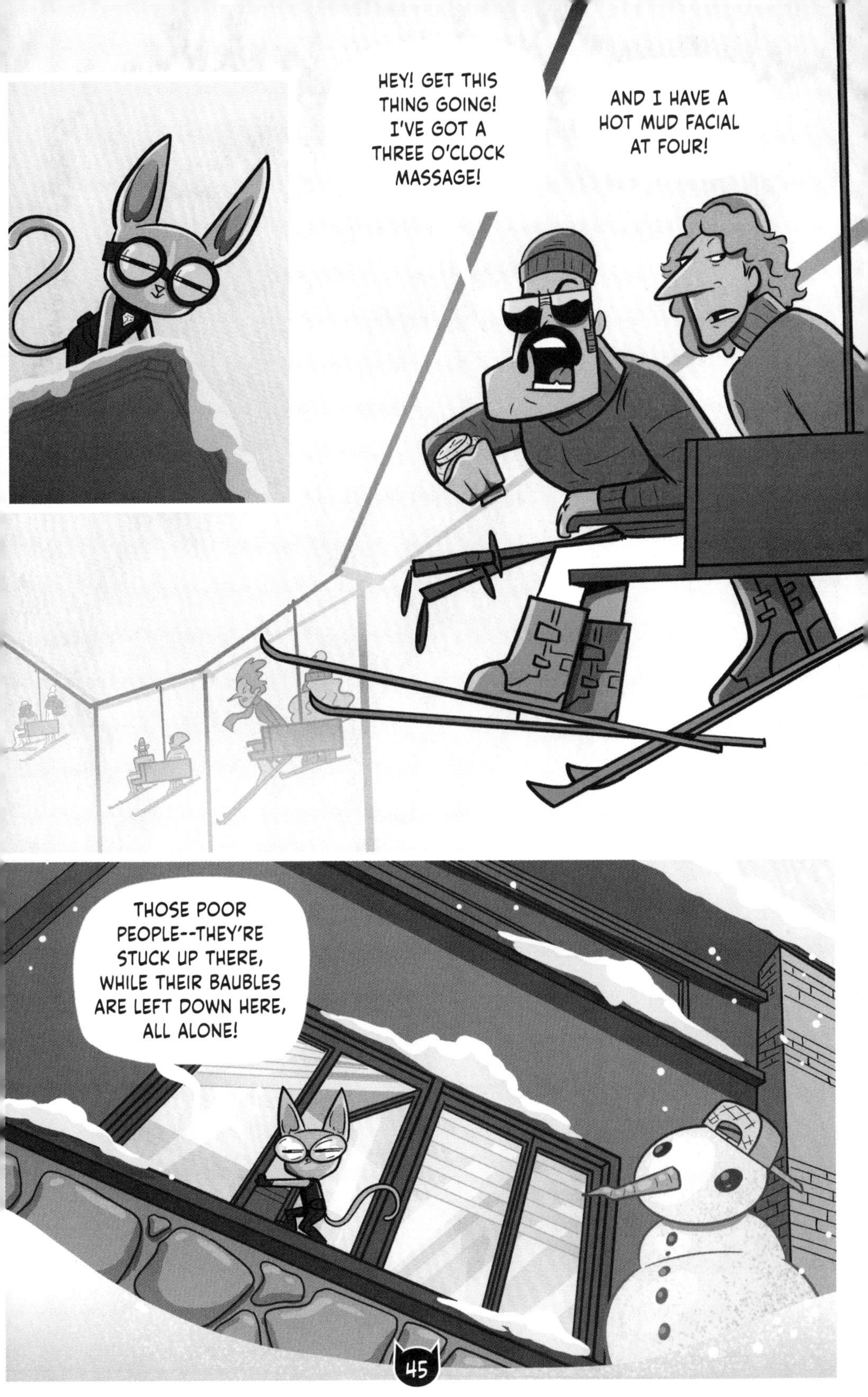
HEY! GET THIS THING GOING! I'VE GOT A THREE O'CLOCK MASSAGE!
AND I HAVE A HOT MUD FACIAL AT FOUR!
THOSE POOR PEOPLE--THEY'RE STUCK UP THERE, WHILE THEIR BAUBLES ARE LEFT DOWN HERE, ALL ALONE!

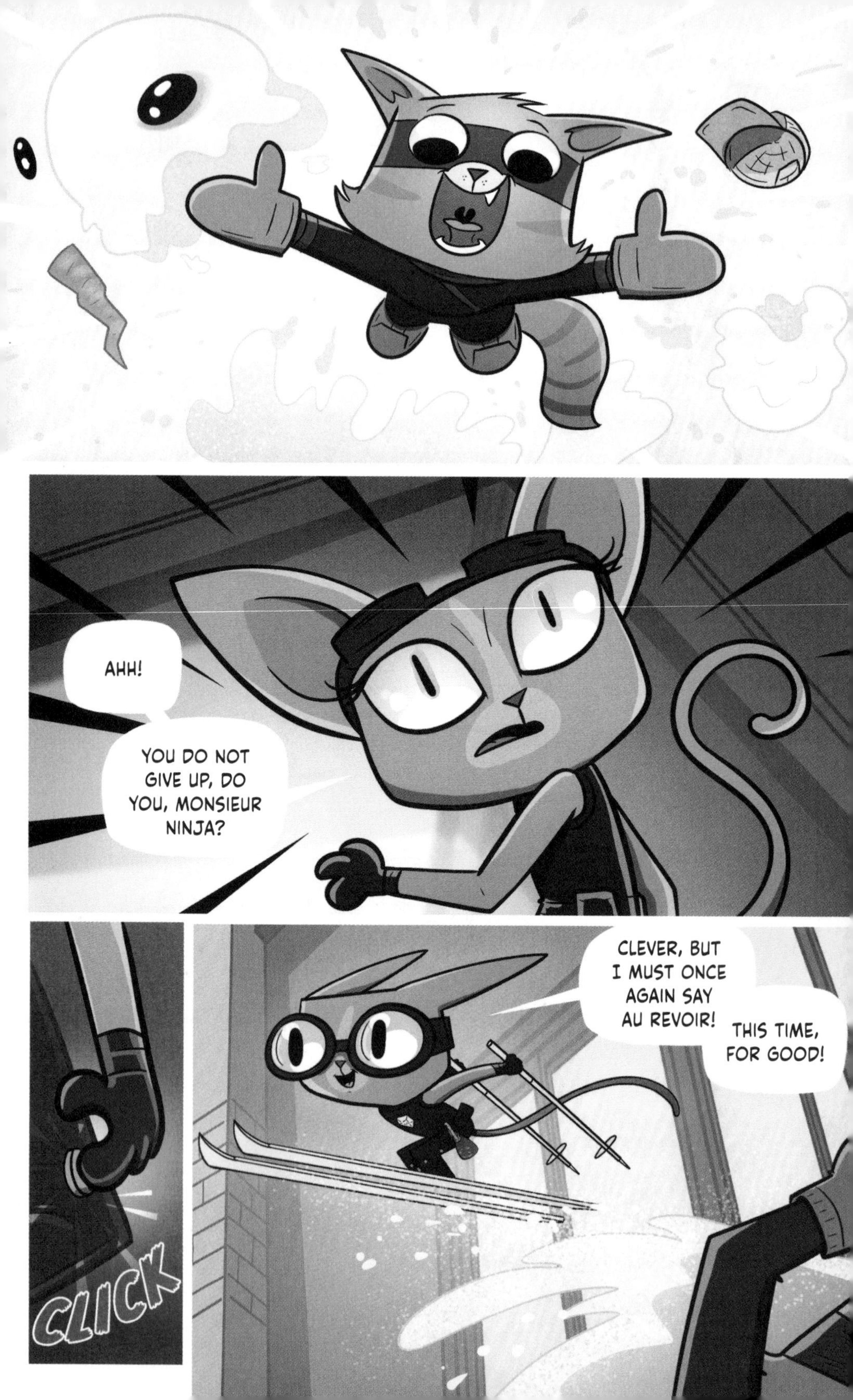
AHH!
YOU DO NOT GIVE UP, DO YOU, MONSIEUR NINJA?
CLICK
CLEVER, BUT I MUST ONCE AGAIN SAY AU REVOIR!
THIS TIME, FOR GOOD!

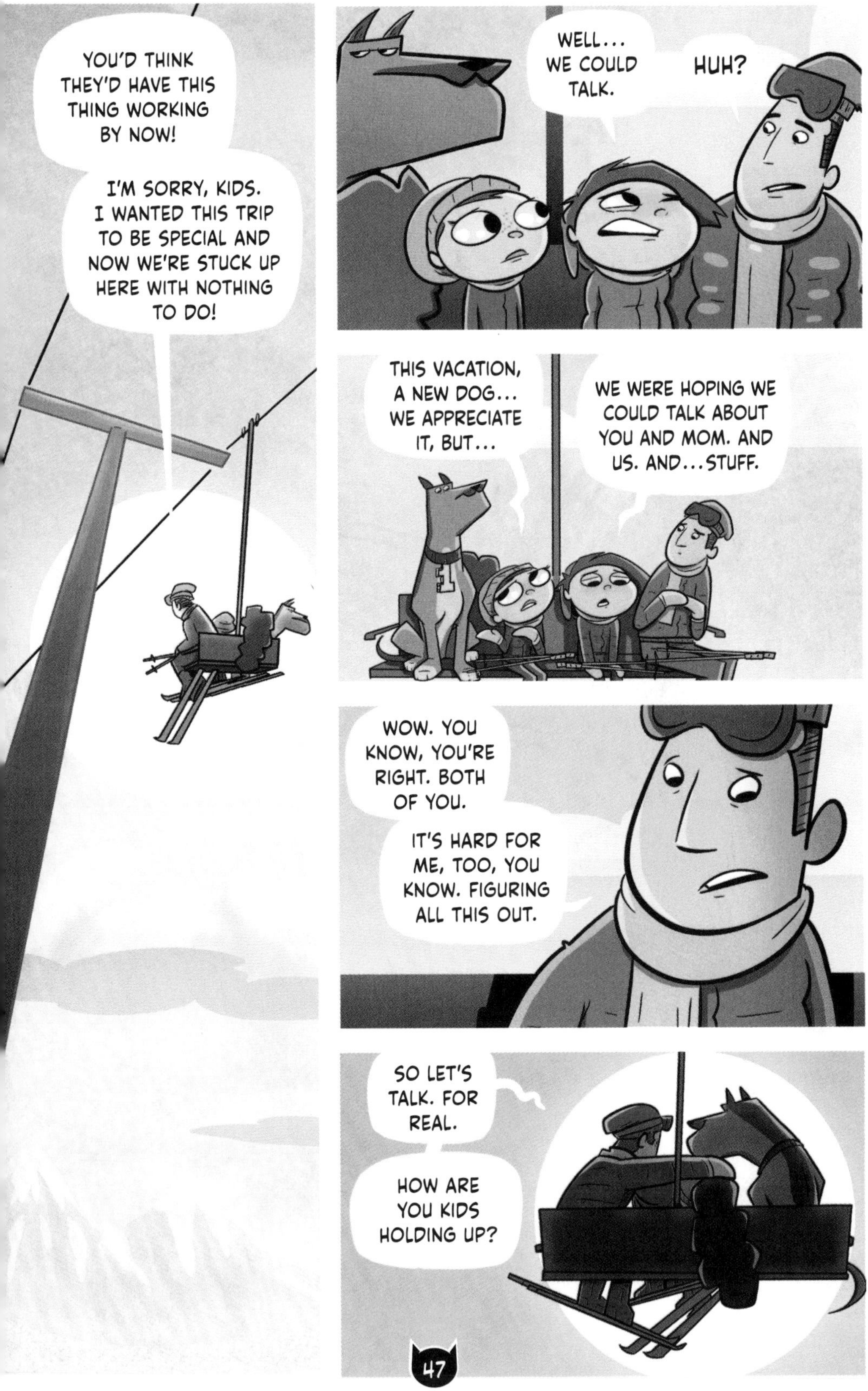
YOU'D THINK THEY'D HAVE THIS THING WORKING BY NOW!
I'M SORRY, KIDS. I WANTED THIS TRIP TO BE SPECIAL AND NOW WE'RE STUCK UP HERE WITH NOTHING TO DO!
WELL... WE COULD TALK.
HUH?
THIS VACATION, A NEW DOG... WE APPRECIATE IT, BUT...
WE WERE HOPING WE COULD TALK ABOUT YOU AND MOM. AND US. AND...STUFF.
WOW. YOU KNOW, YOU'RE RIGHT. BOTH OF YOU.
IT'S HARD FOR ME, TOO, YOU KNOW. FIGURING ALL THIS OUT.
SO LET'S TALK. FOR REAL.
HOW ARE YOU KIDS HOLDING UP?

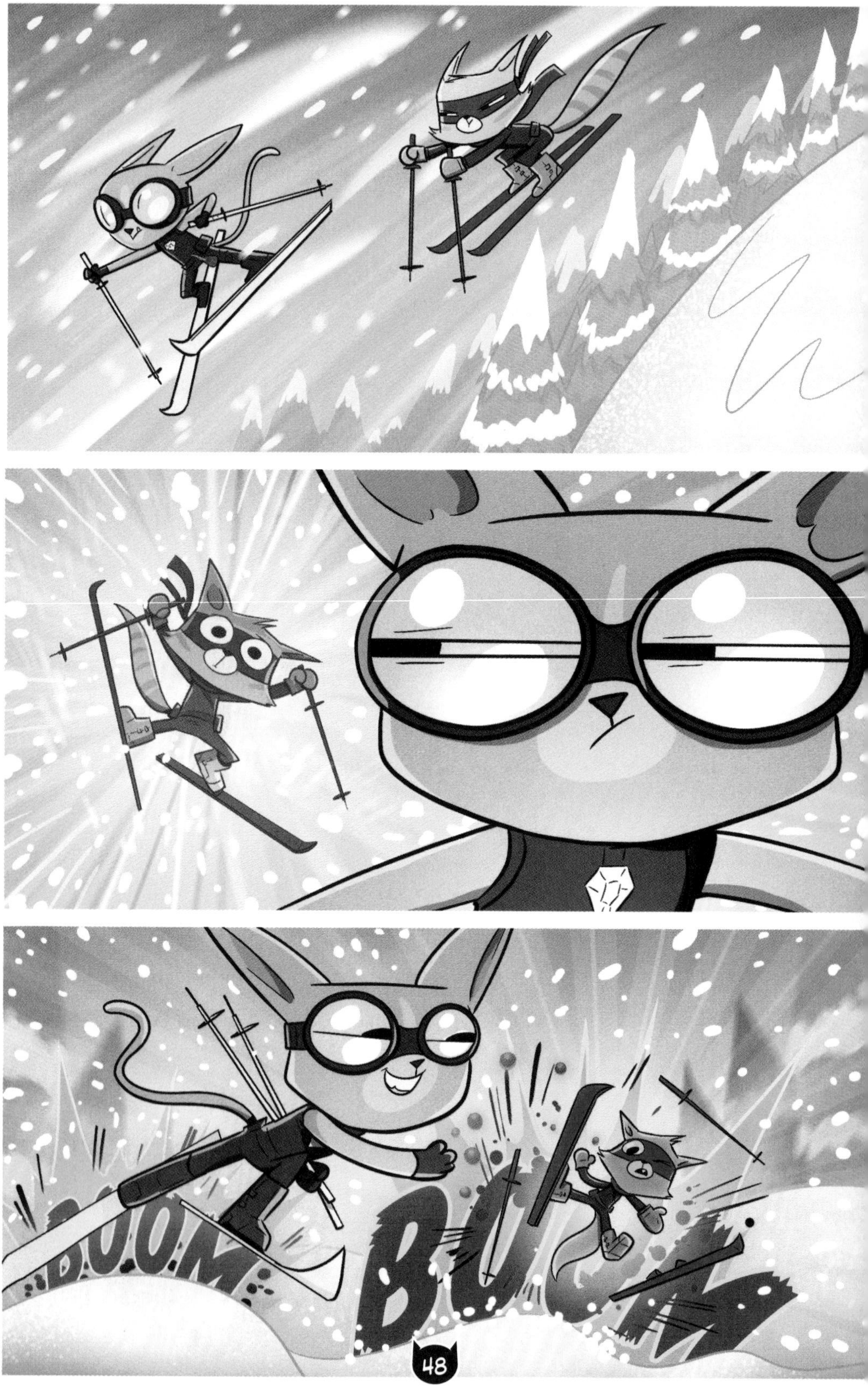
BOOM

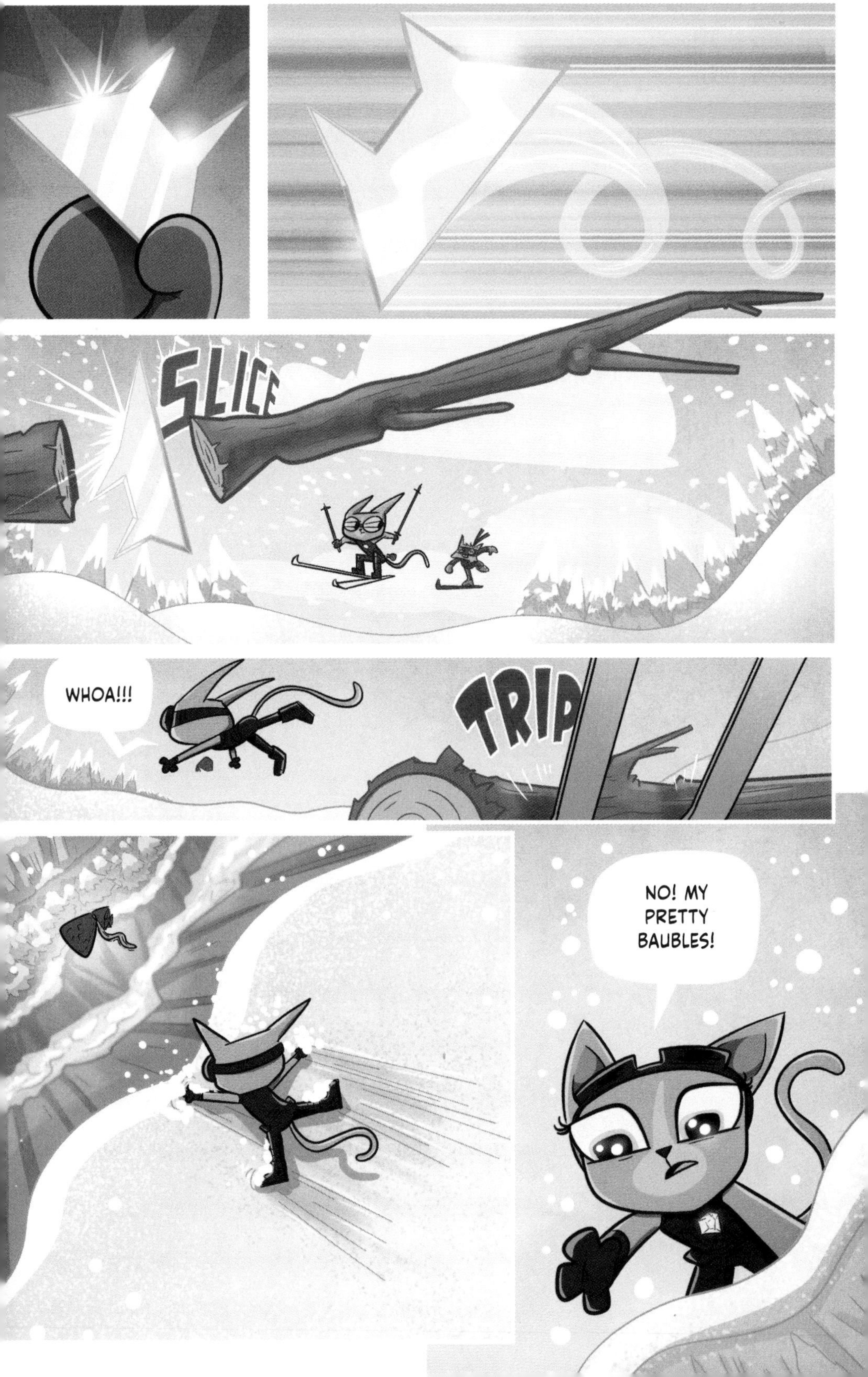
SLICE
WHOA!!!
TRIP
NO! MY PRETTY BAUBLES!

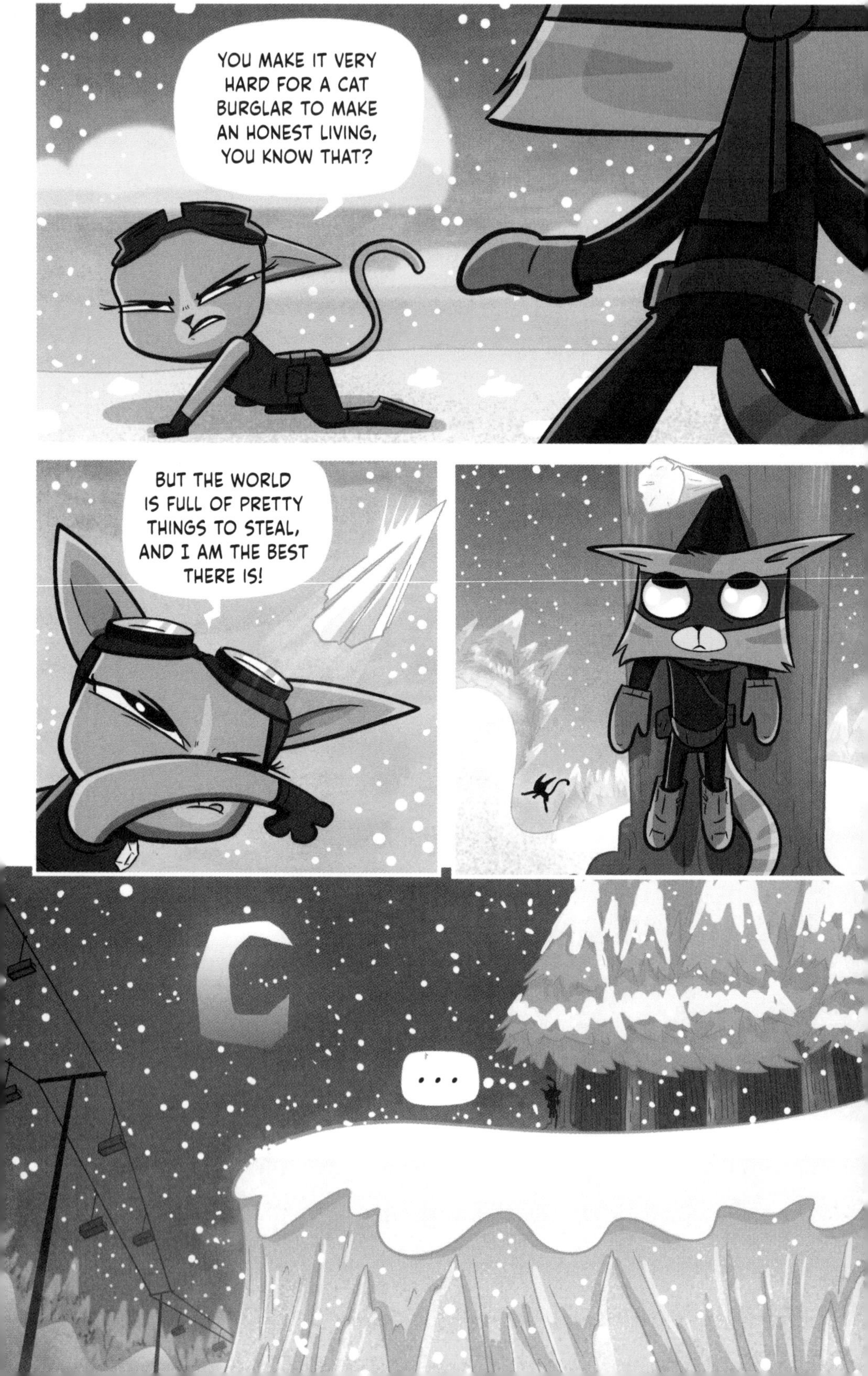
YOU MAKE IT VERY HARD FOR A CAT BURGLAR TO MAKE AN HONEST LIVING, YOU KNOW THAT?
BUT THE WORLD IS FULL OF PRETTY THINGS TO STEAL, AND I AM THE BEST THERE IS!
...

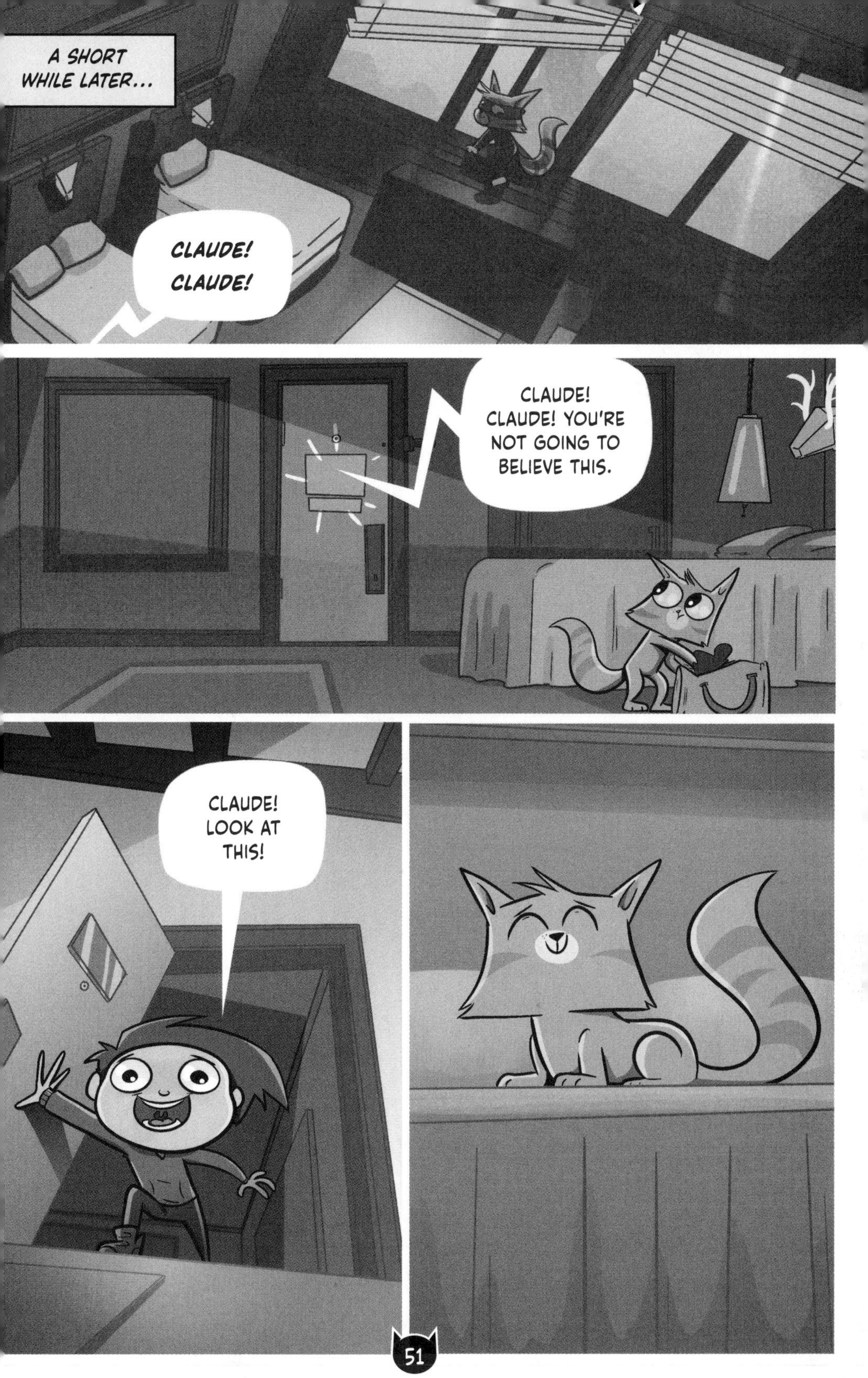
A SHORT WHILE LATER...
CLAUDE! CLAUDE!
CLAUDE! CLAUDE! YOU'RE NOT GOING TO BELIEVE THIS.
CLAUDE! LOOK AT THIS!

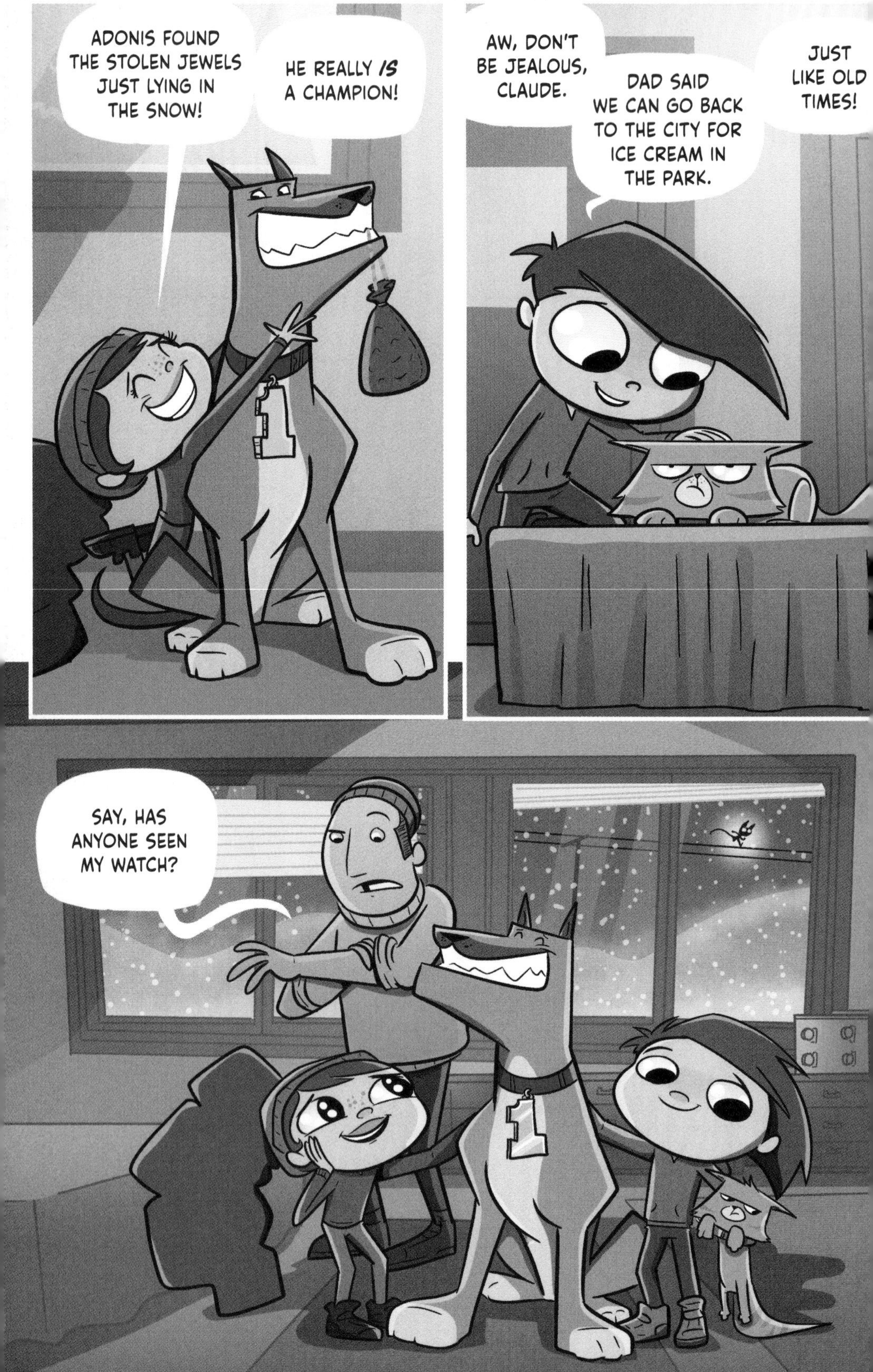
ADONIS FOUND THE STOLEN JEWELS JUST LYING IN THE SNOW!
HE REALLY *IS* A CHAMPION!
AW, DON'T BE JEALOUS, CLAUDE.
DAD SAID WE CAN GO BACK TO THE CITY FOR ICE CREAM IN THE PARK.
JUST LIKE OLD TIMES!
SAY, HAS ANYONE SEEN MY WATCH?

Chapter 3:
You Only Live 9 Times

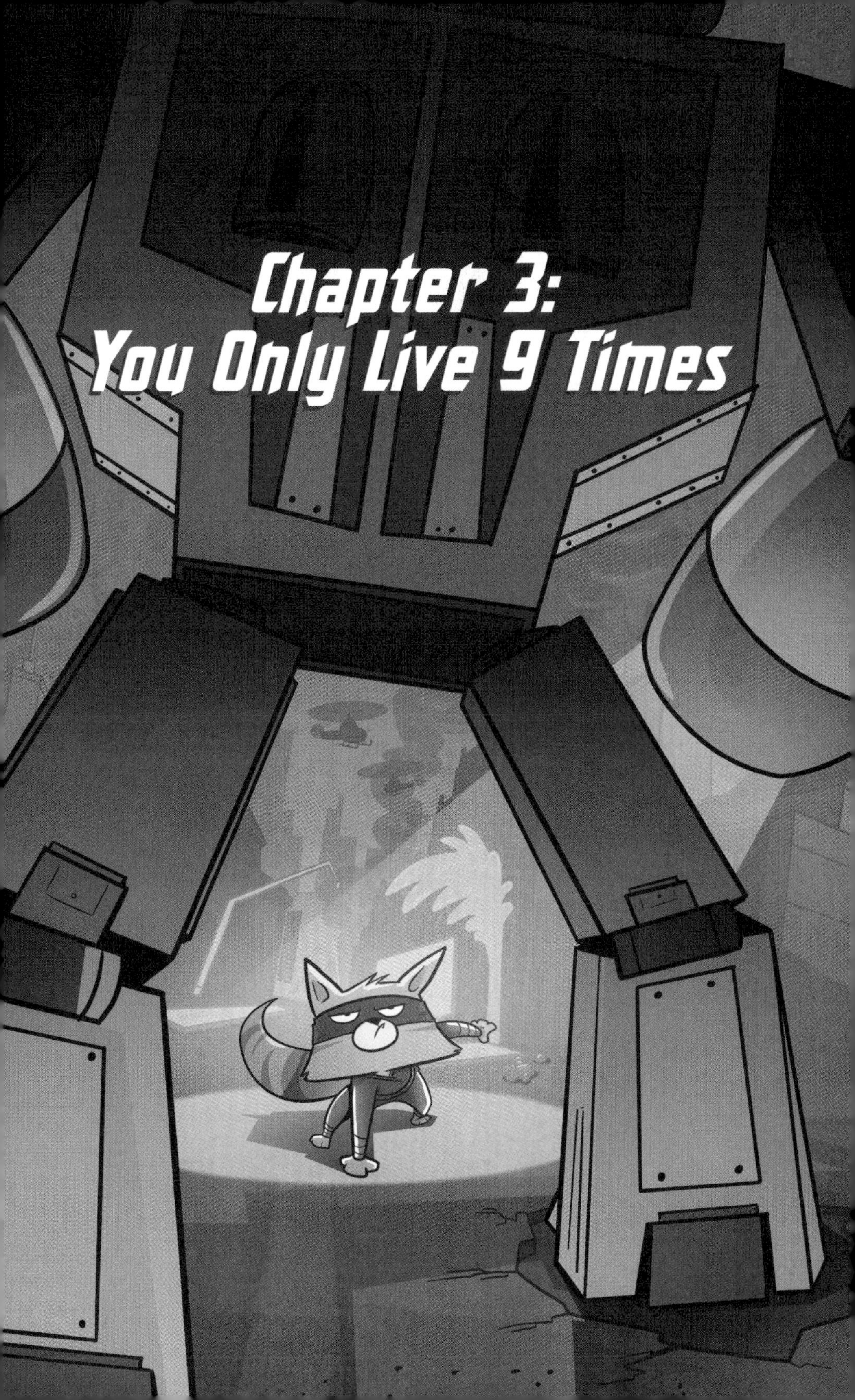

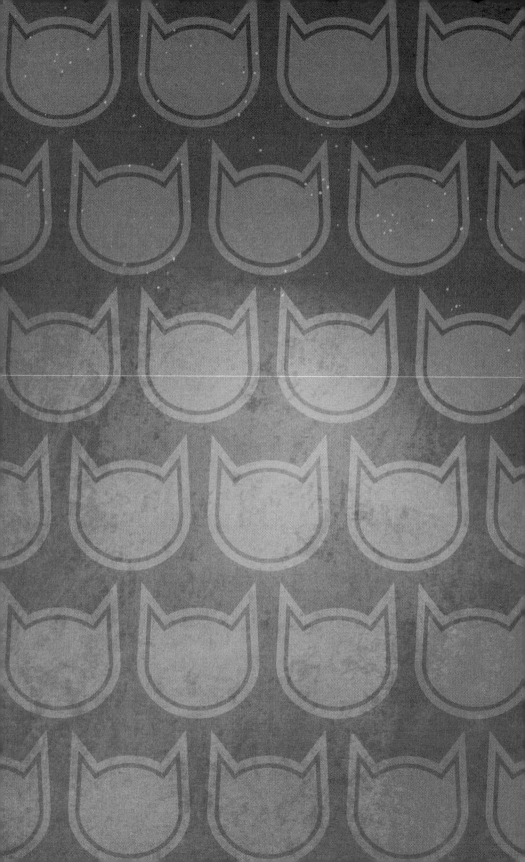

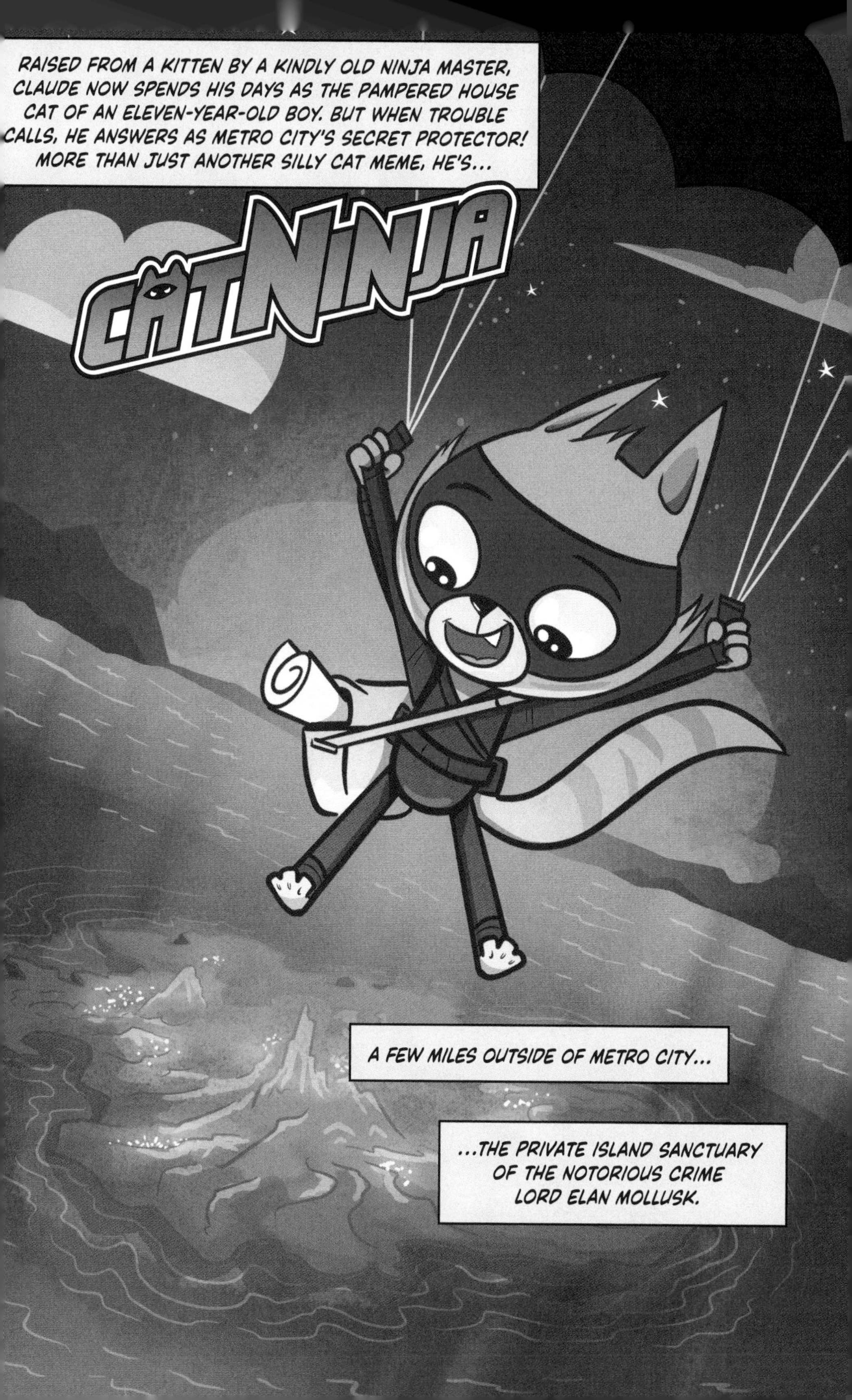
RAISED FROM A KITTEN BY A KINDLY OLD NINJA MASTER, CLAUDE NOW SPENDS HIS DAYS AS THE PAMPERED HOUSE CAT OF AN ELEVEN-YEAR-OLD BOY. BUT WHEN TROUBLE CALLS, HE ANSWERS AS METRO CITY'S SECRET PROTECTOR! MORE THAN JUST ANOTHER SILLY CAT MEME, HE'S...
CATNINJA
A FEW MILES OUTSIDE OF METRO CITY...
...THE PRIVATE ISLAND SANCTUARY OF THE NOTORIOUS CRIME LORD ELAN MOLLUSK.

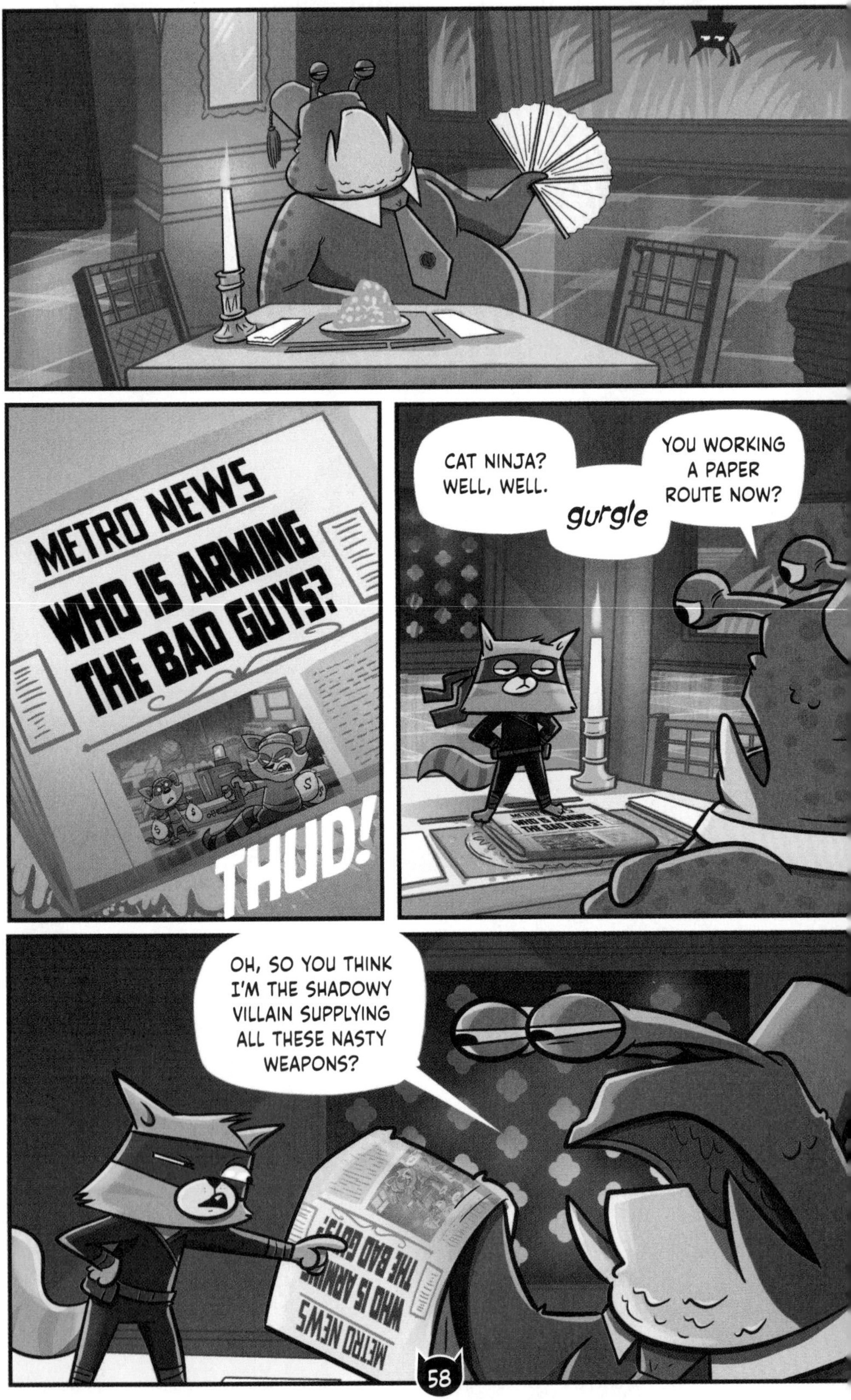
METRO NEWS
WHO IS ARMING THE BAD GUYS?
THUD!
CAT NINJA? WELL, WELL.
gurgle
YOU WORKING A PAPER ROUTE NOW?
OH, SO YOU THINK I'M THE SHADOWY VILLAIN SUPPLYING ALL THESE NASTY WEAPONS?

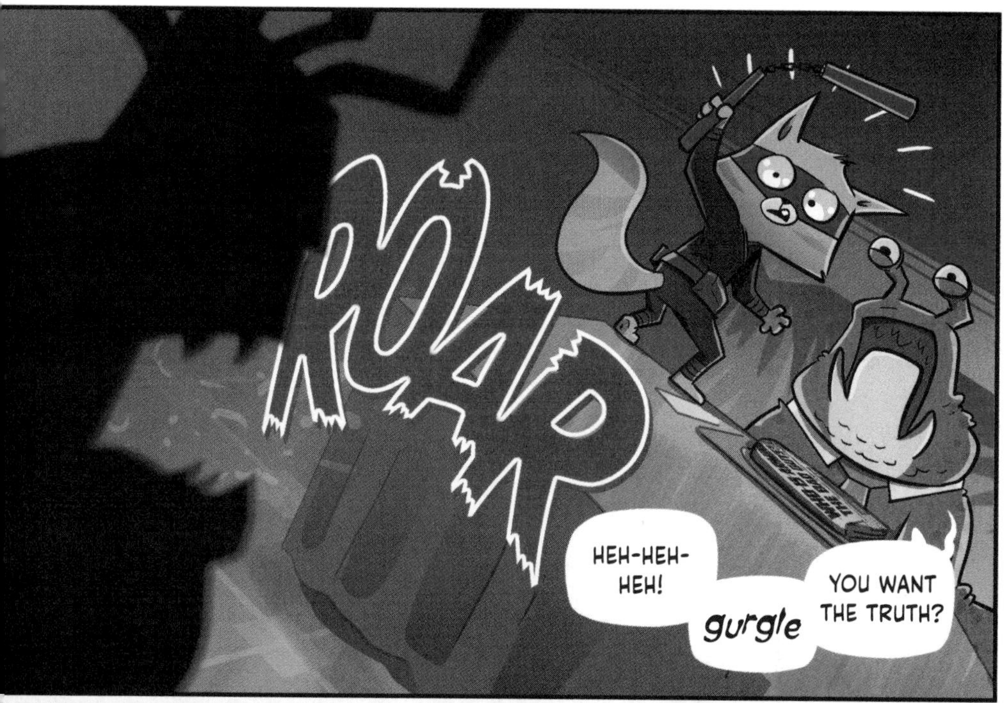
ROAR
HEH-HEH-HEH!
gurgle
YOU WANT THE TRUTH?

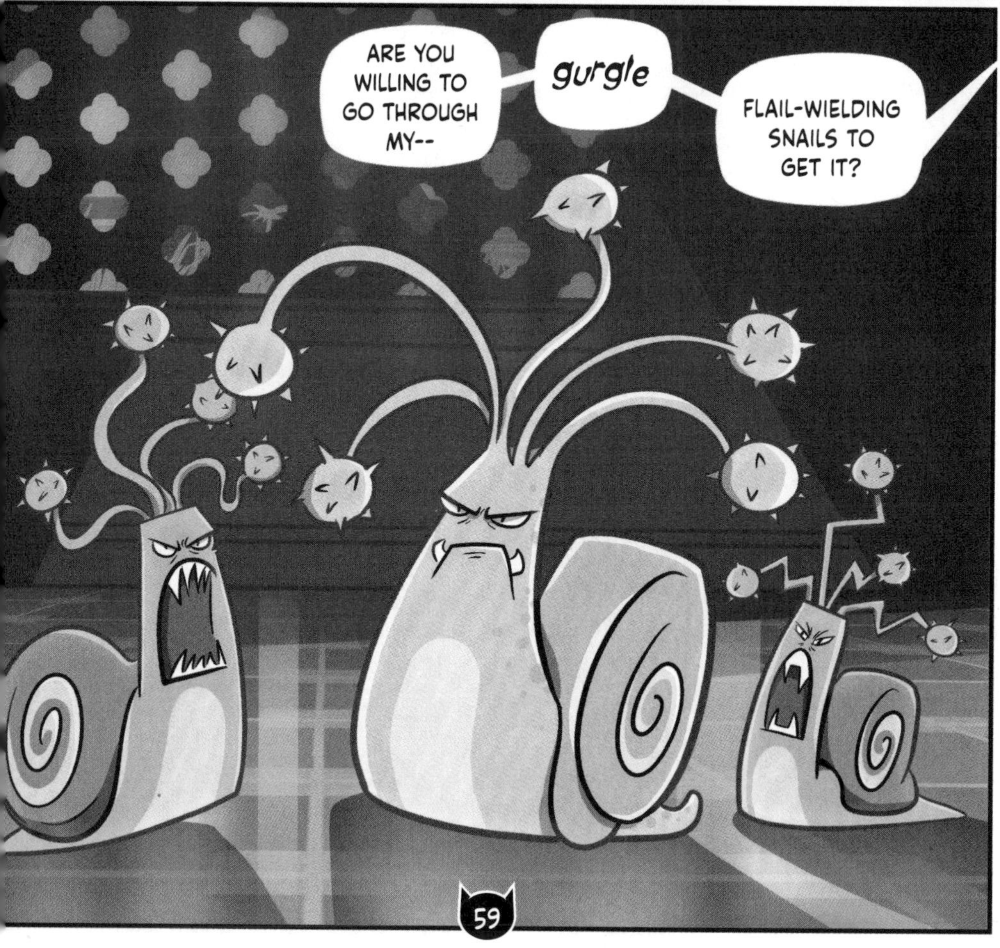
ARE YOU WILLING TO GO THROUGH MY--
gurgle
FLAIL-WIELDING SNAILS TO GET IT?

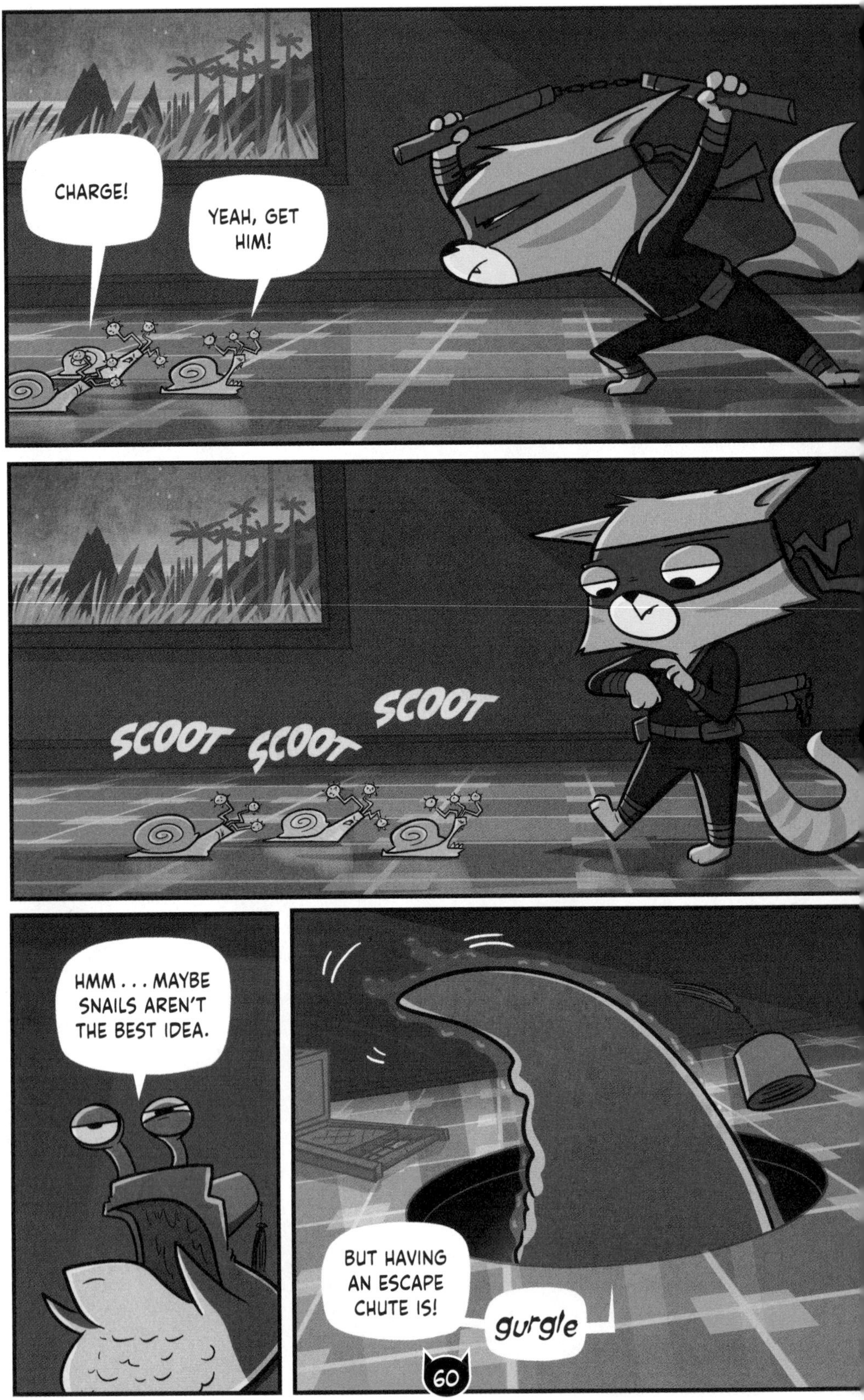
CHARGE!
YEAH, GET HIM!
SCOOT SCOOT SCOOT
HMM . . . MAYBE SNAILS AREN'T THE BEST IDEA.
BUT HAVING AN ESCAPE CHUTE IS!
gurgle

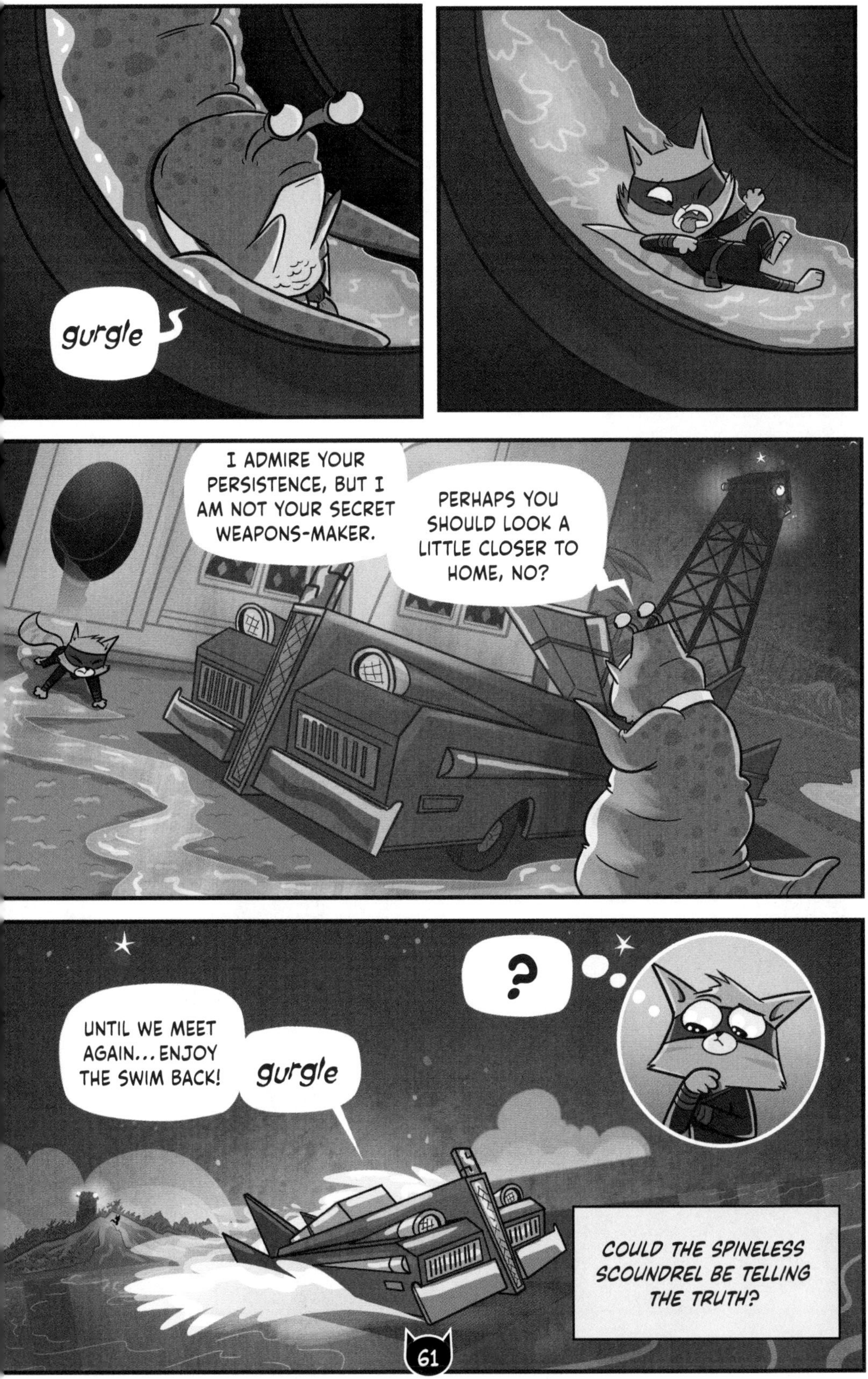
gurgle
I ADMIRE YOUR PERSISTENCE, BUT I AM NOT YOUR SECRET WEAPONS-MAKER.
PERHAPS YOU SHOULD LOOK A LITTLE CLOSER TO HOME, NO?
?
UNTIL WE MEET AGAIN... ENJOY THE SWIM BACK!
gurgle
COULD THE SPINELESS SCOUNDREL BE TELLING THE TRUTH?

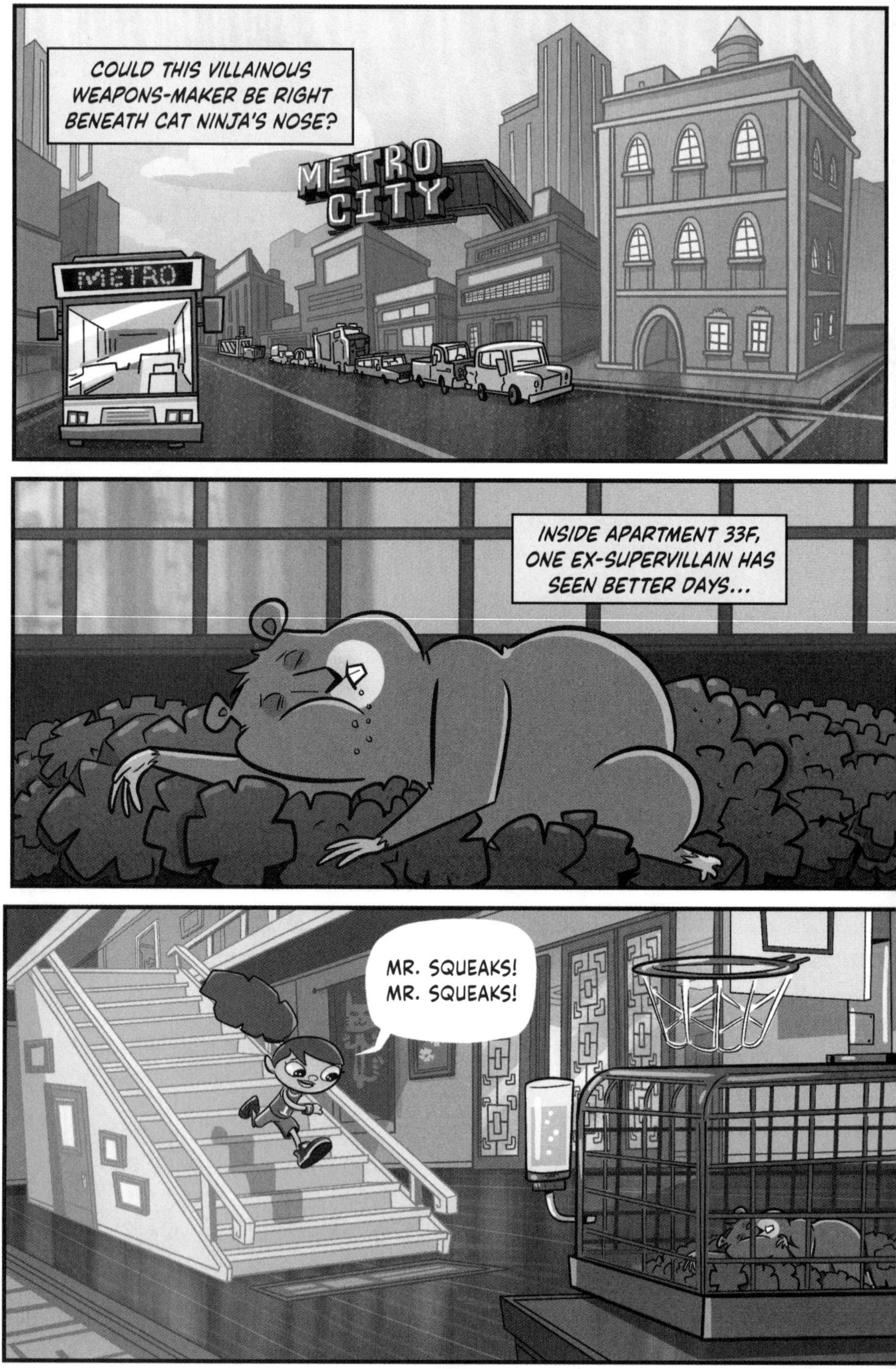
COULD THIS VILLAINOUS WEAPONS-MAKER BE RIGHT BENEATH CAT NINJA'S NOSE?
METRO CITY
METRO
INSIDE APARTMENT 33F, ONE EX-SUPERVILLAIN HAS SEEN BETTER DAYS...
MR. SQUEAKS! MR. SQUEAKS!

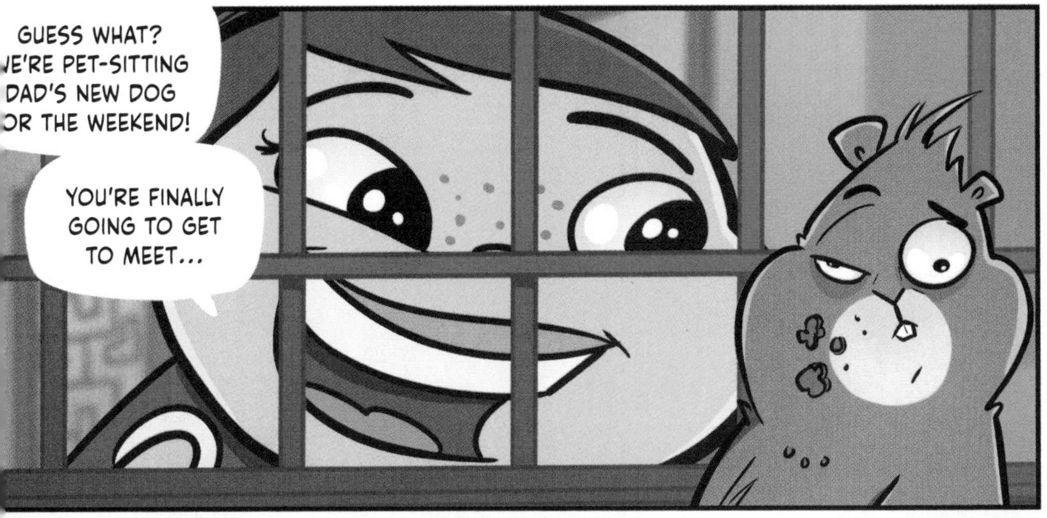
GUESS WHAT? E'RE PET-SITTING DAD'S NEW DOG OR THE WEEKEND!
YOU'RE FINALLY GOING TO GET TO MEET...

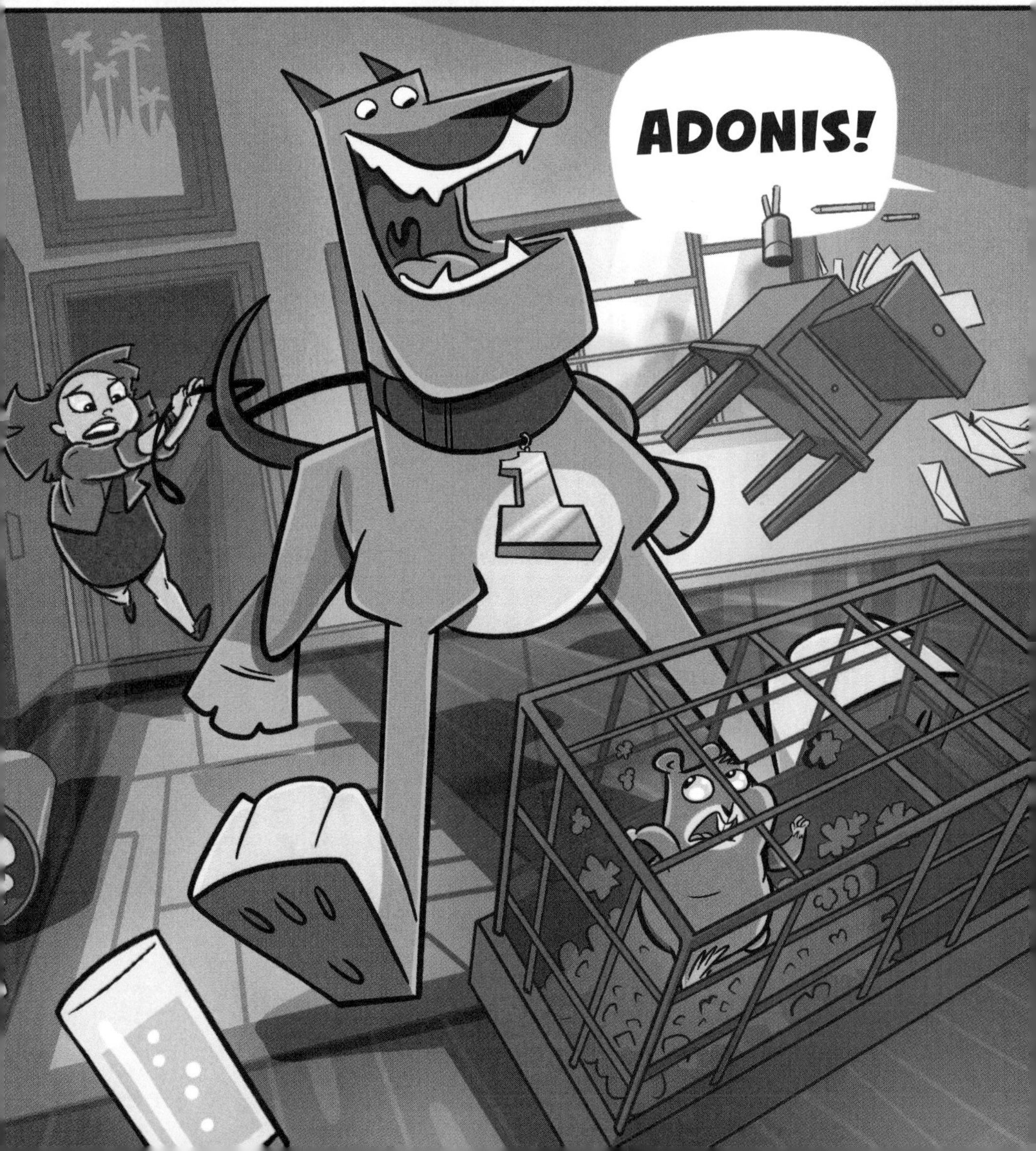
ADONIS!

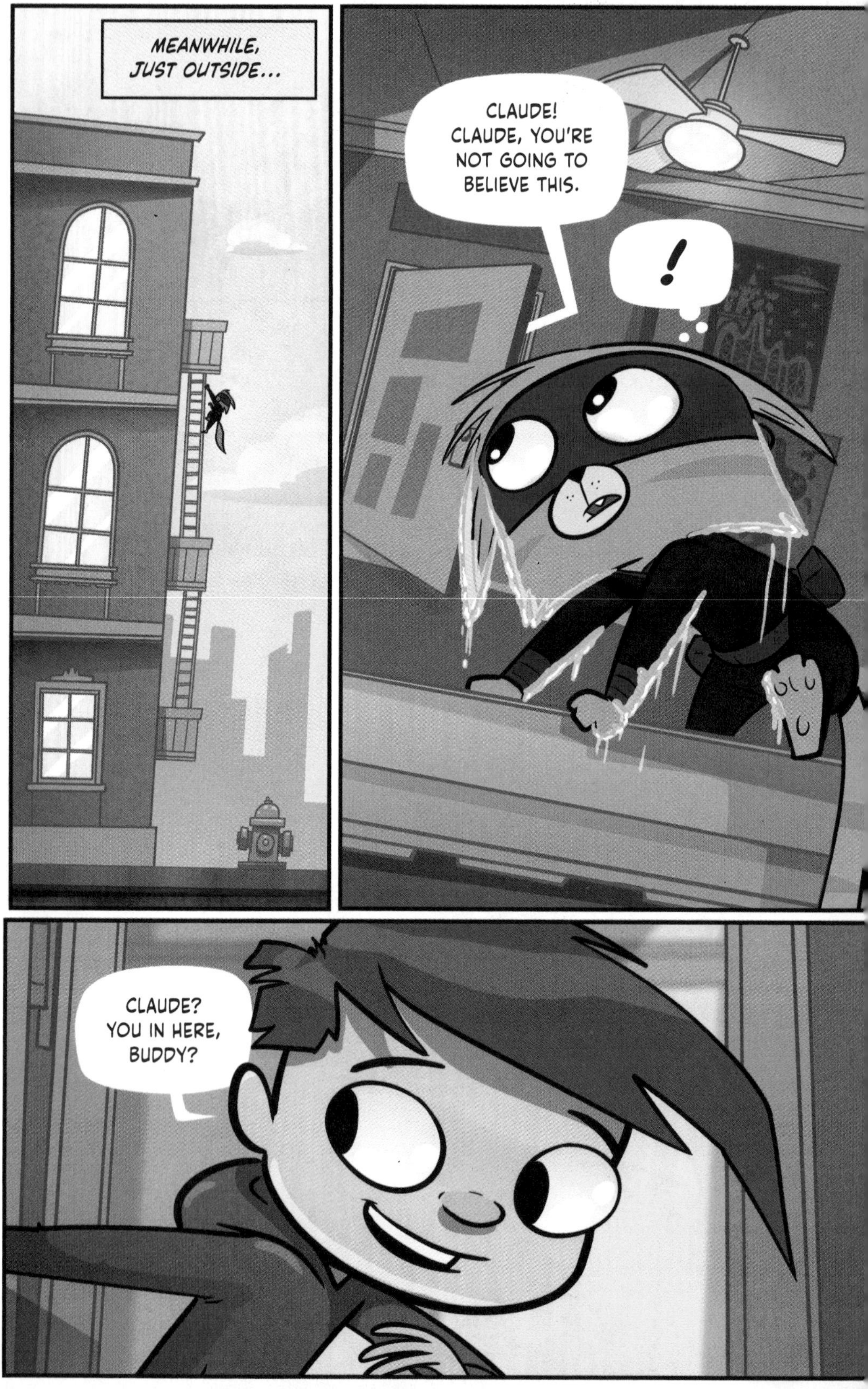
MEANWHILE, JUST OUTSIDE...
CLAUDE! CLAUDE, YOU'RE NOT GOING TO BELIEVE THIS.
!
CLAUDE? YOU IN HERE, BUDDY?

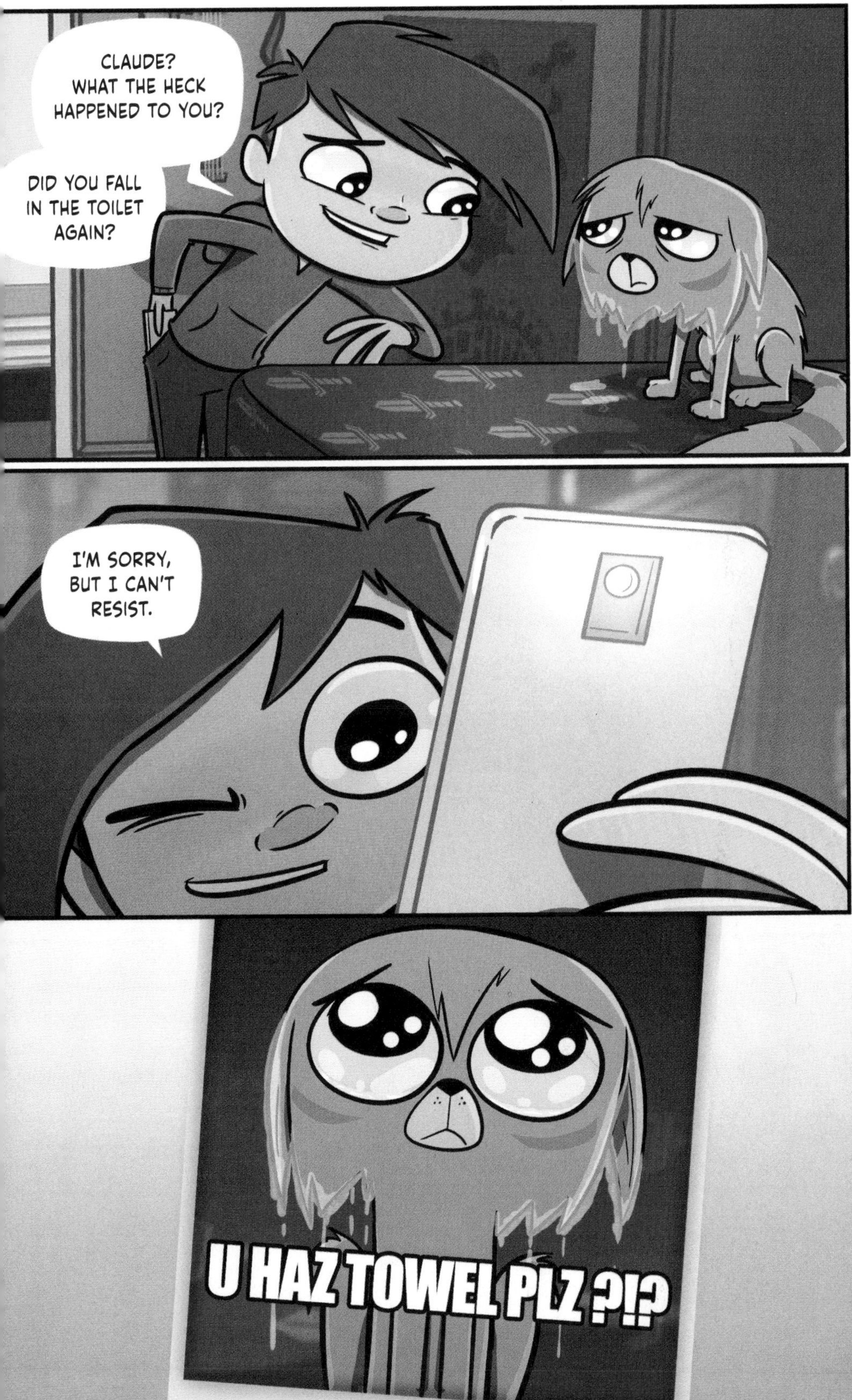
CLAUDE?
WHAT THE HECK
HAPPENED TO YOU?
DID YOU FALL
IN THE TOILET
AGAIN?
I'M SORRY,
BUT I CAN'T
RESIST.
U HAZ TOWEL PLZ ?!?

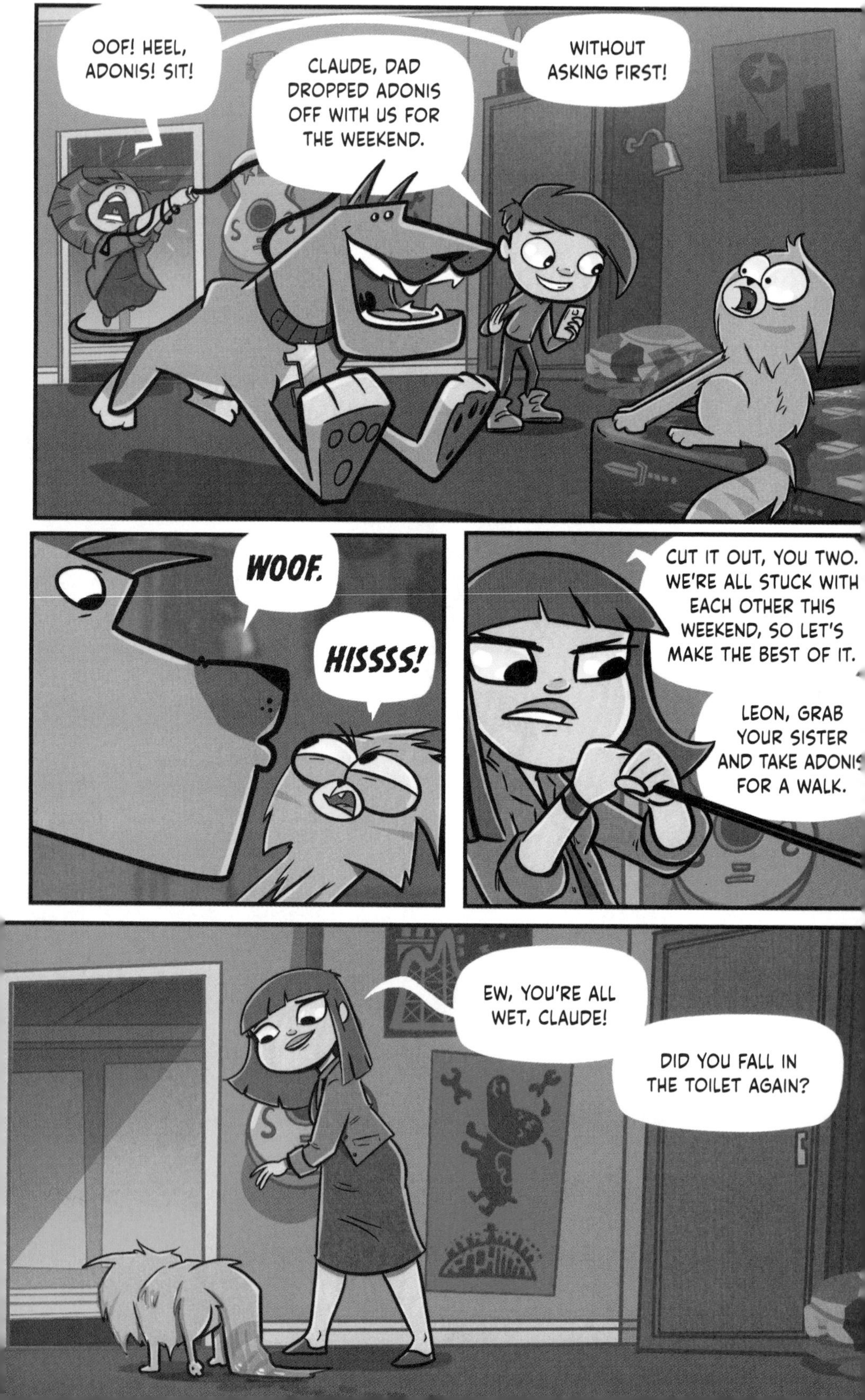
OOF! HEEL, ADONIS! SIT!
CLAUDE, DAD DROPPED ADONIS OFF WITH US FOR THE WEEKEND.
WITHOUT ASKING FIRST!
WOOF.
HISSSS!
CUT IT OUT, YOU TWO. WE'RE ALL STUCK WITH EACH OTHER THIS WEEKEND, SO LET'S MAKE THE BEST OF IT.
LEON, GRAB YOUR SISTER AND TAKE ADONIS FOR A WALK.
EW, YOU'RE ALL WET, CLAUDE!
DID YOU FALL IN THE TOILET AGAIN?

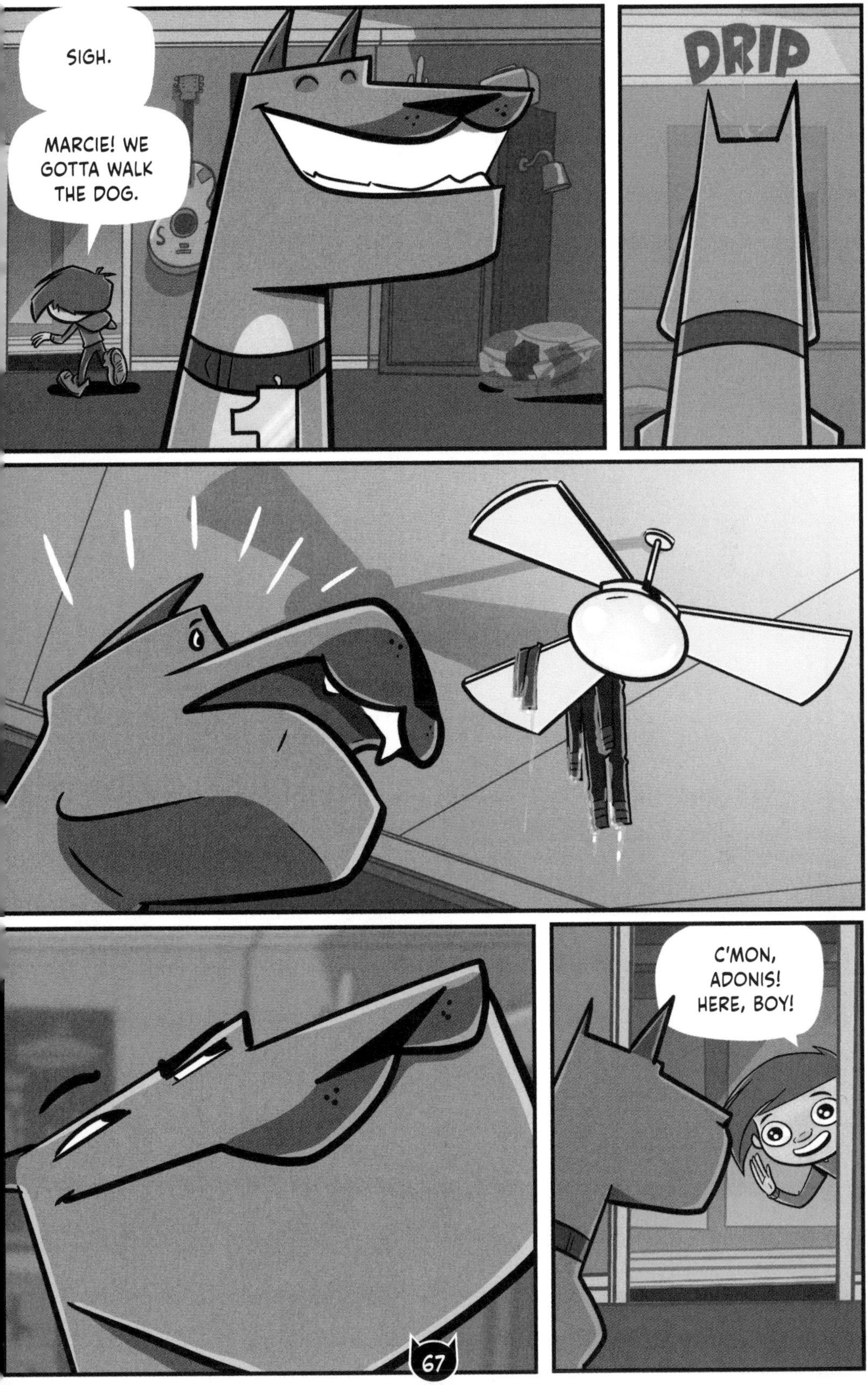
SIGH.
MARCIE! WE GOTTA WALK THE DOG.
DRIP
C'MON, ADONIS! HERE, BOY!

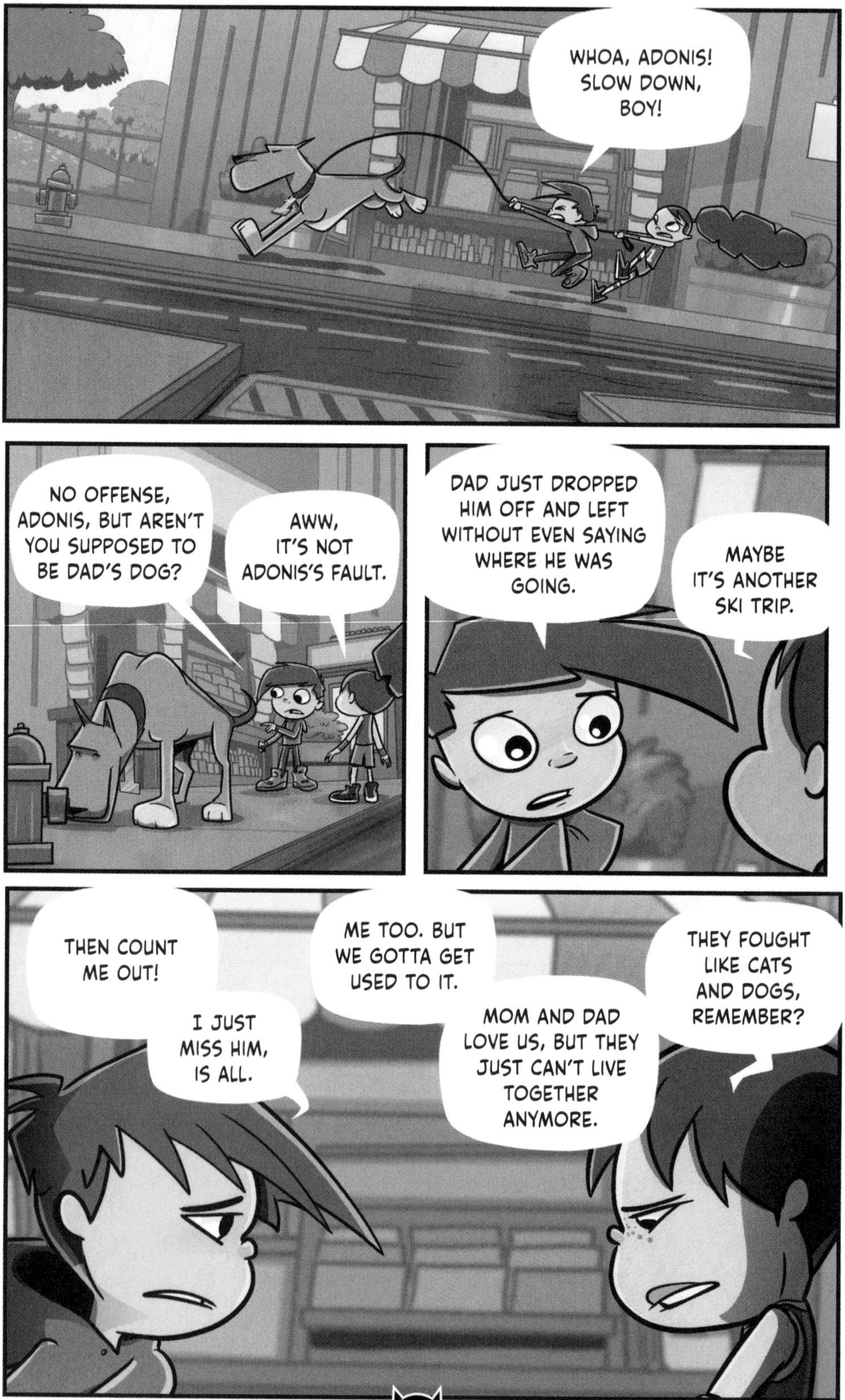
WHOA, ADONIS! SLOW DOWN, BOY!
NO OFFENSE, ADONIS, BUT AREN'T YOU SUPPOSED TO BE DAD'S DOG?
AWW, IT'S NOT ADONIS'S FAULT.
DAD JUST DROPPED HIM OFF AND LEFT WITHOUT EVEN SAYING WHERE HE WAS GOING.
MAYBE IT'S ANOTHER SKI TRIP.
THEN COUNT ME OUT!
I JUST MISS HIM, IS ALL.
ME TOO. BUT WE GOTTA GET USED TO IT.
MOM AND DAD LOVE US, BUT THEY JUST CAN'T LIVE TOGETHER ANYMORE.
THEY FOUGHT LIKE CATS AND DOGS, REMEMBER?

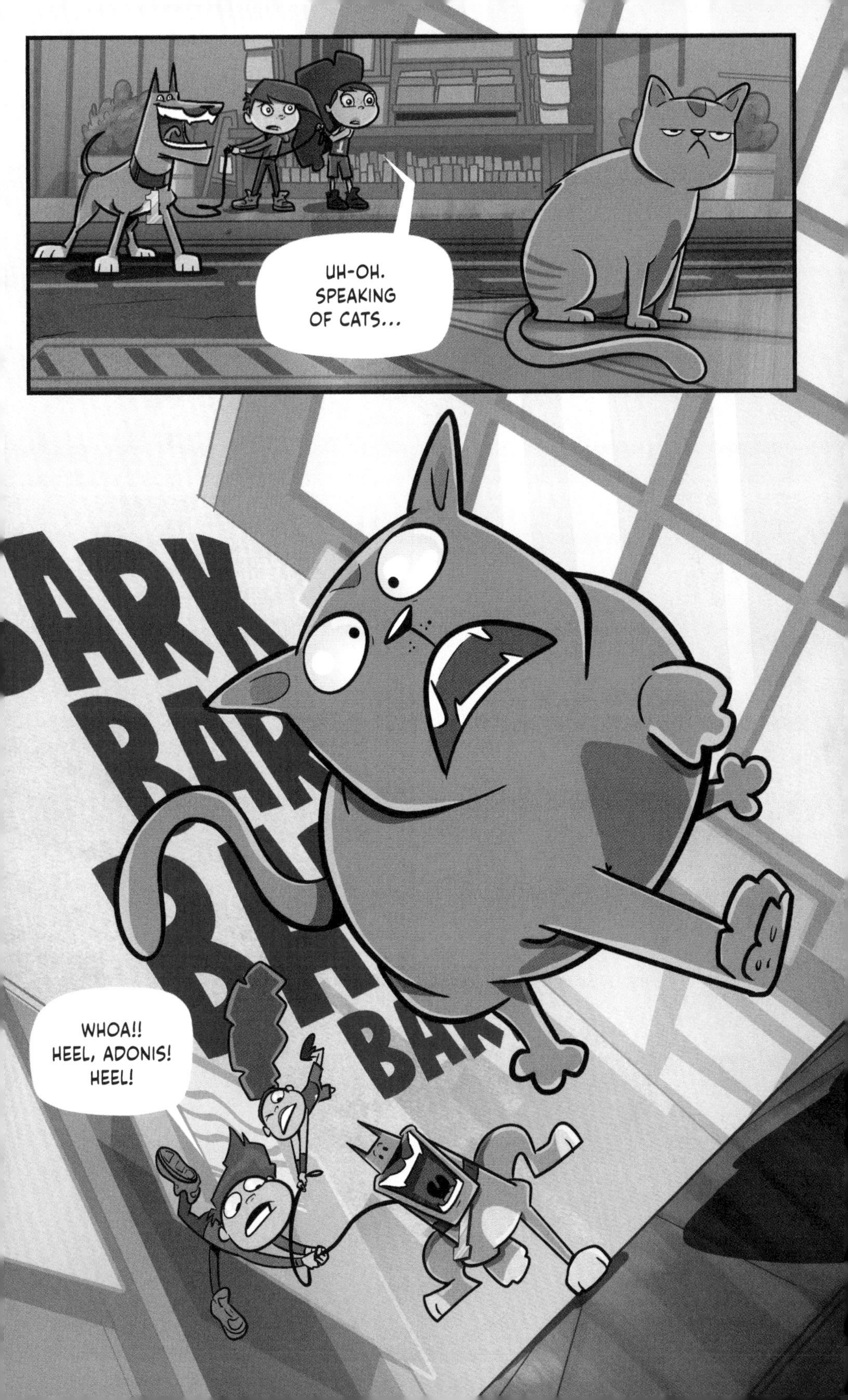
UH-OH. SPEAKING OF CATS...
WHOA!! HEEL, ADONIS! HEEL!

YOU FEELING LEFT OUT TOO, MR. SQUEAKS?

YEAH, SOMETHING'S WEIRD ABOUT THAT DOG. AND NOT JUST BECAUSE MY EX-HUSBAND DROPPED HIM OFF WITHOUT EVEN A PHONE CALL.

ALTHOUGH, THAT'S ANNOYING.

FOR ONE THING, HE'S AS STRONG AS A TRUCK!

AND, I DUNNO, MAYBE IT'S THE WAY HE STARES AT YOU. LIKE HE'S LOOKING RIGHT THROUGH YOU.

I MUST SOUND LIKE A CRAZY PERSON OR SOMETHING.

I MEAN LOOK AT ME, TALKING TO A HAMSTER ABOUT A DOG.

I GUESS WE'RE BOTH OLD NEWS, MR. SQUEAKS.

MAYBE I SHOULD BUY THE KIDS A PONY JUST TO KEEP UP.

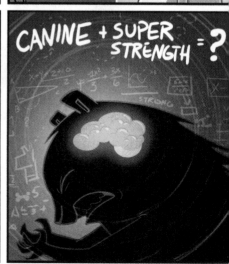

CANINE + SUPER STRENGTH = ?

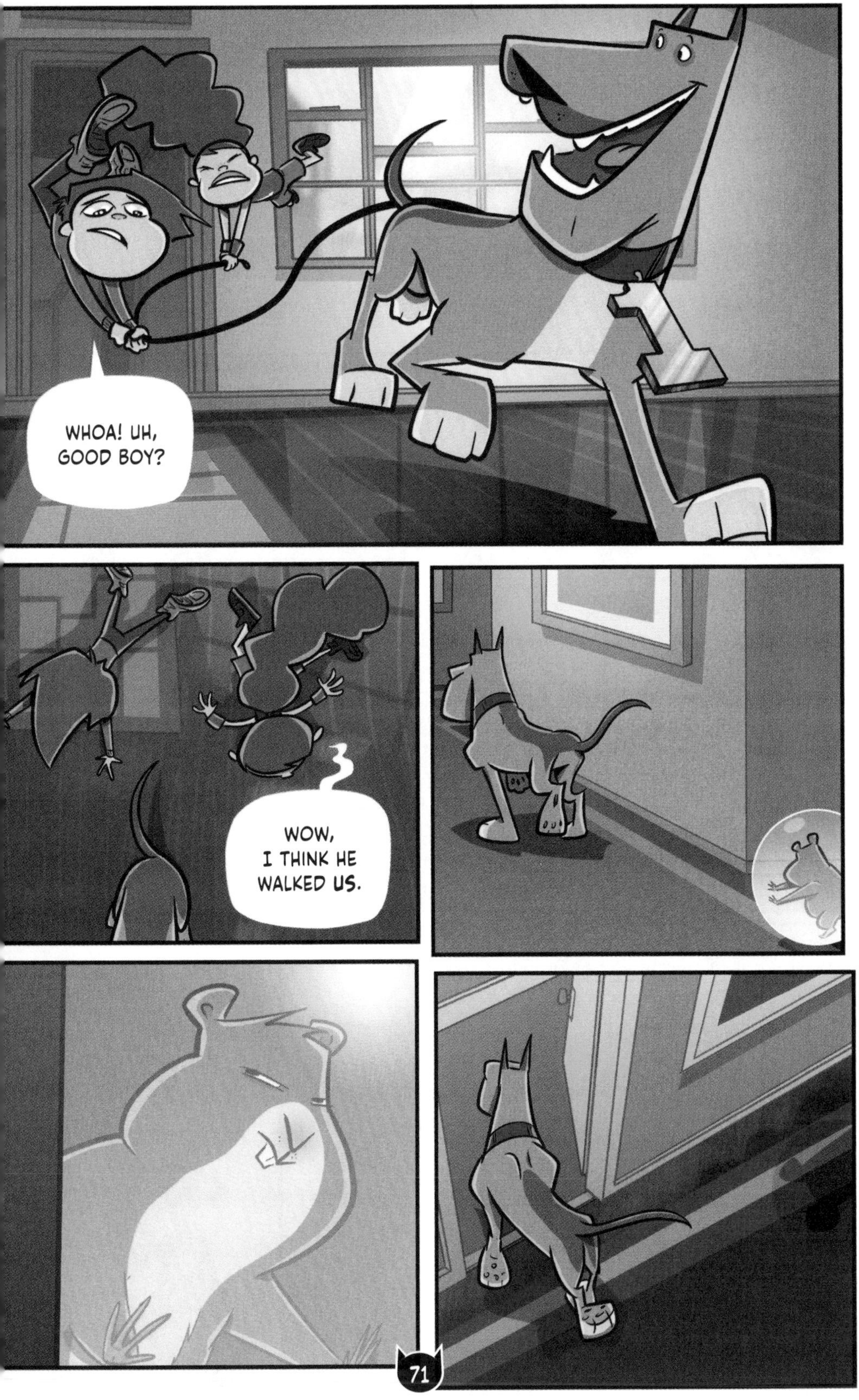
WHOA! UH, GOOD BOY?
WOW, I THINK HE WALKED US.

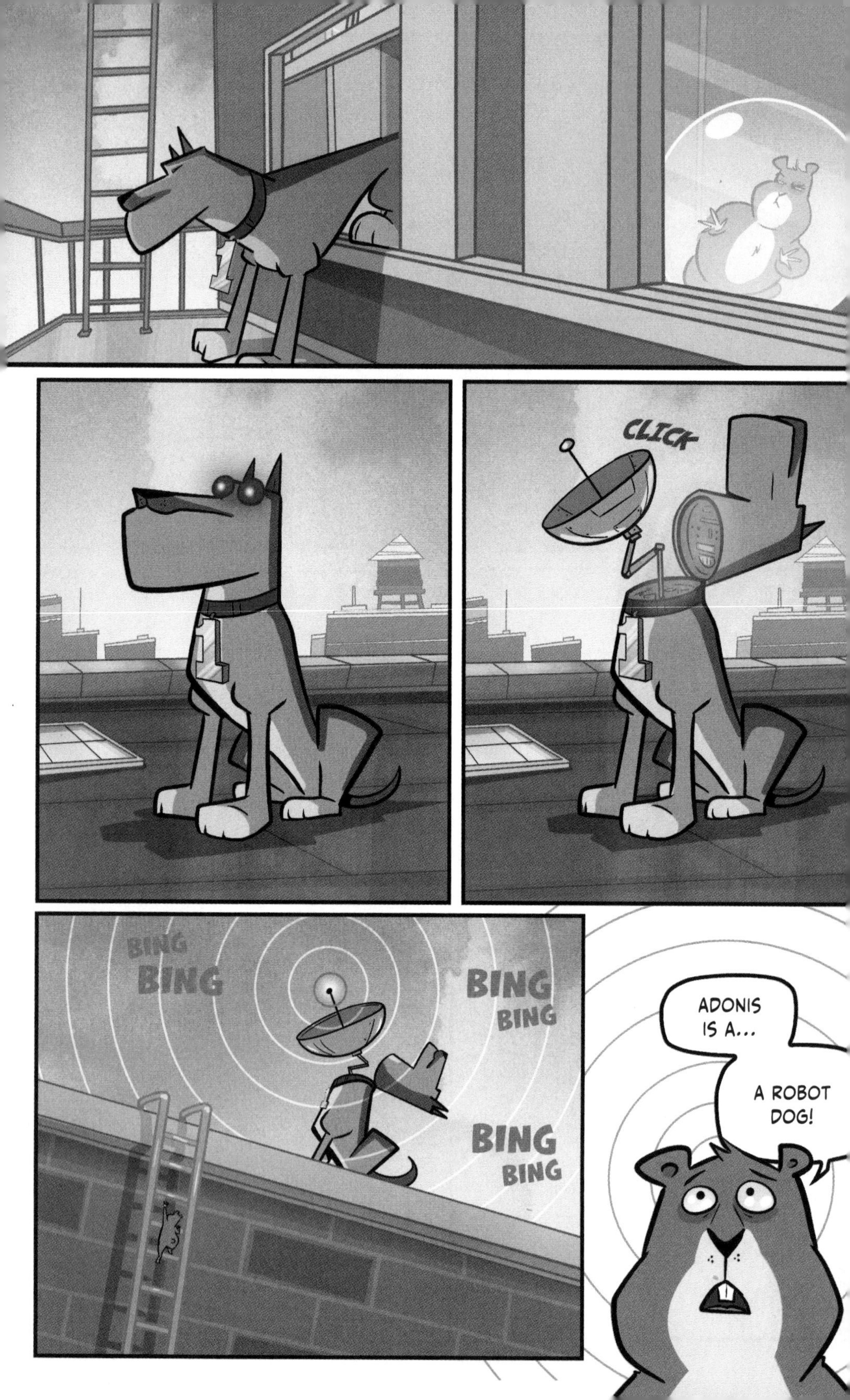
CLICK
BING
BING
BING
BING
BING
BING
ADONIS IS A...
A ROBOT DOG!

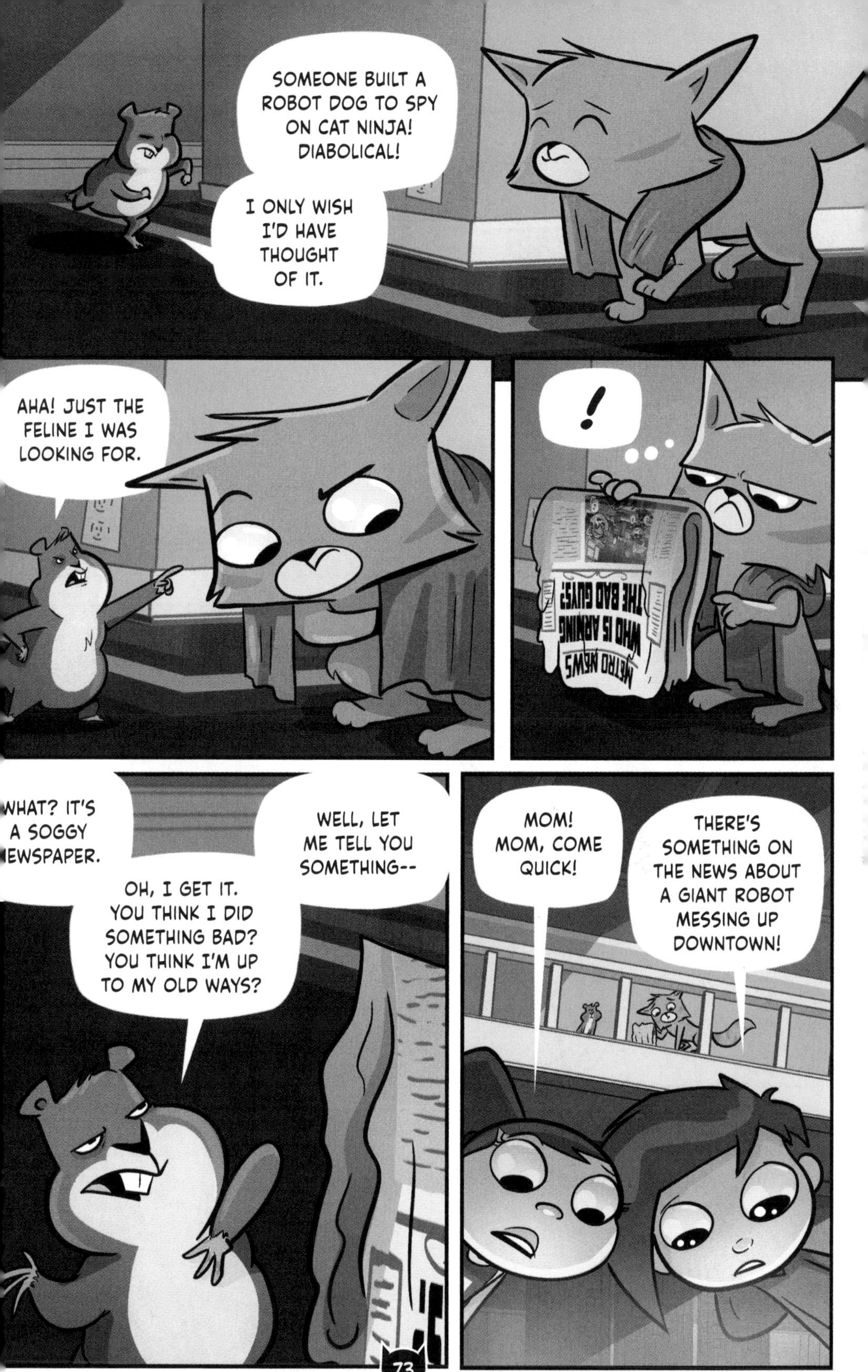
SOMEONE BUILT A ROBOT DOG TO SPY ON CAT NINJA! DIABOLICAL!
I ONLY WISH I'D HAVE THOUGHT OF IT.
AHA! JUST THE FELINE I WAS LOOKING FOR.
!
WHAT? IT'S A SOGGY NEWSPAPER.
OH, I GET IT. YOU THINK I DID SOMETHING BAD? YOU THINK I'M UP TO MY OLD WAYS?
WELL, LET ME TELL YOU SOMETHING--
MOM! MOM, COME QUICK!
THERE'S SOMETHING ON THE NEWS ABOUT A GIANT ROBOT MESSING UP DOWNTOWN!

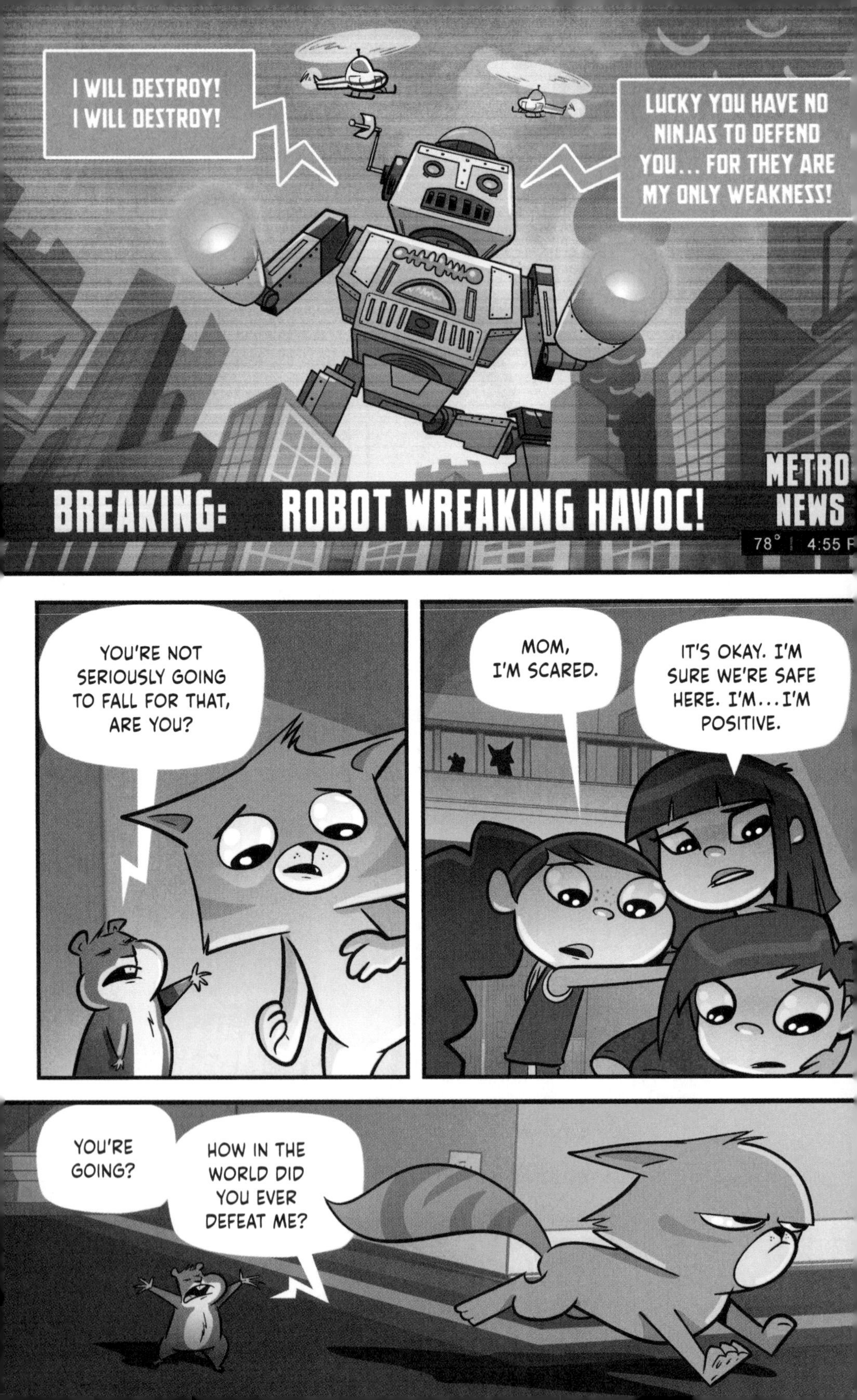
I WILL DESTROY!
I WILL DESTROY!
LUCKY YOU HAVE NO NINJAS TO DEFEND YOU... FOR THEY ARE MY ONLY WEAKNESS!
BREAKING: ROBOT WREAKING HAVOC!
METRO NEWS
78° | 4:55
YOU'RE NOT SERIOUSLY GOING TO FALL FOR THAT, ARE YOU?
MOM, I'M SCARED.
IT'S OKAY. I'M SURE WE'RE SAFE HERE. I'M...I'M POSITIVE.
YOU'RE GOING?
HOW IN THE WORLD DID YOU EVER DEFEAT ME?

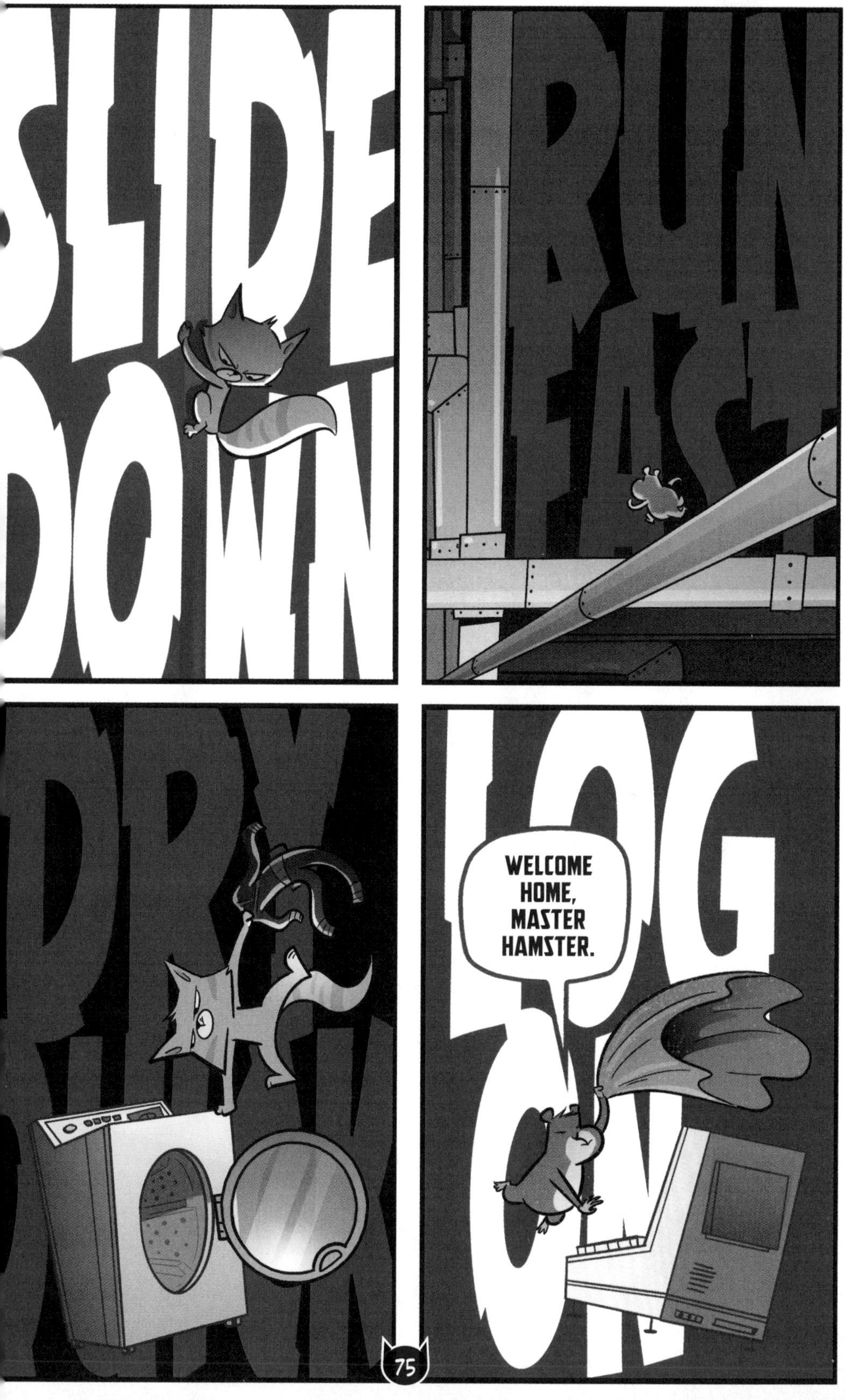
SLIDE DOWN
RUN FAST
LOG ON
WELCOME HOME, MASTER HAMSTER.

TAKE THAT, FIRE HYDRANT!
TAKE THAT, CAR!
THERE ARE NO NINJAS TO SAVE YOU NOW!

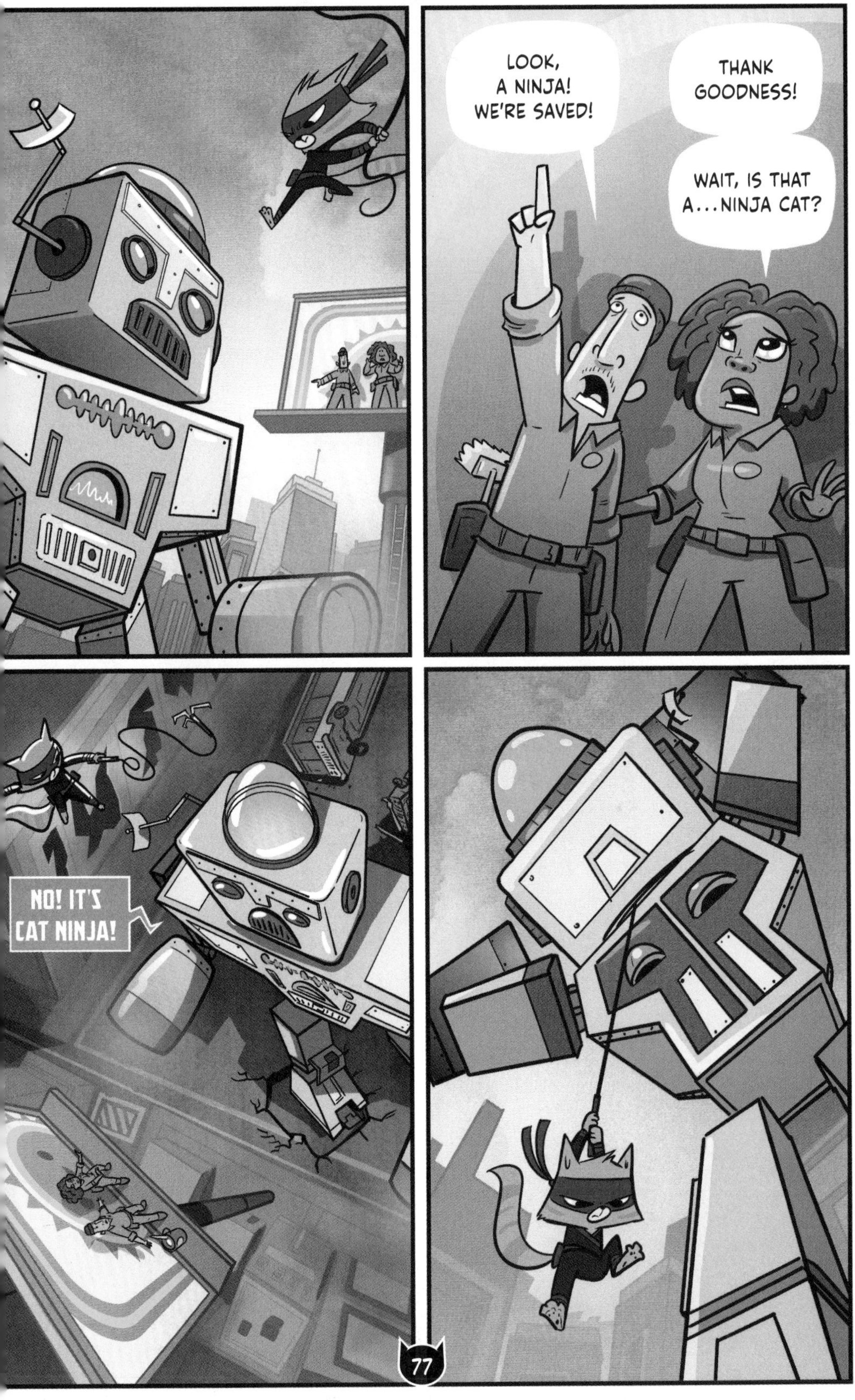
LOOK, A NINJA! WE'RE SAVED!
THANK GOODNESS!
WAIT, IS THAT A...NINJA CAT?
NO! IT'S CAT NINJA!

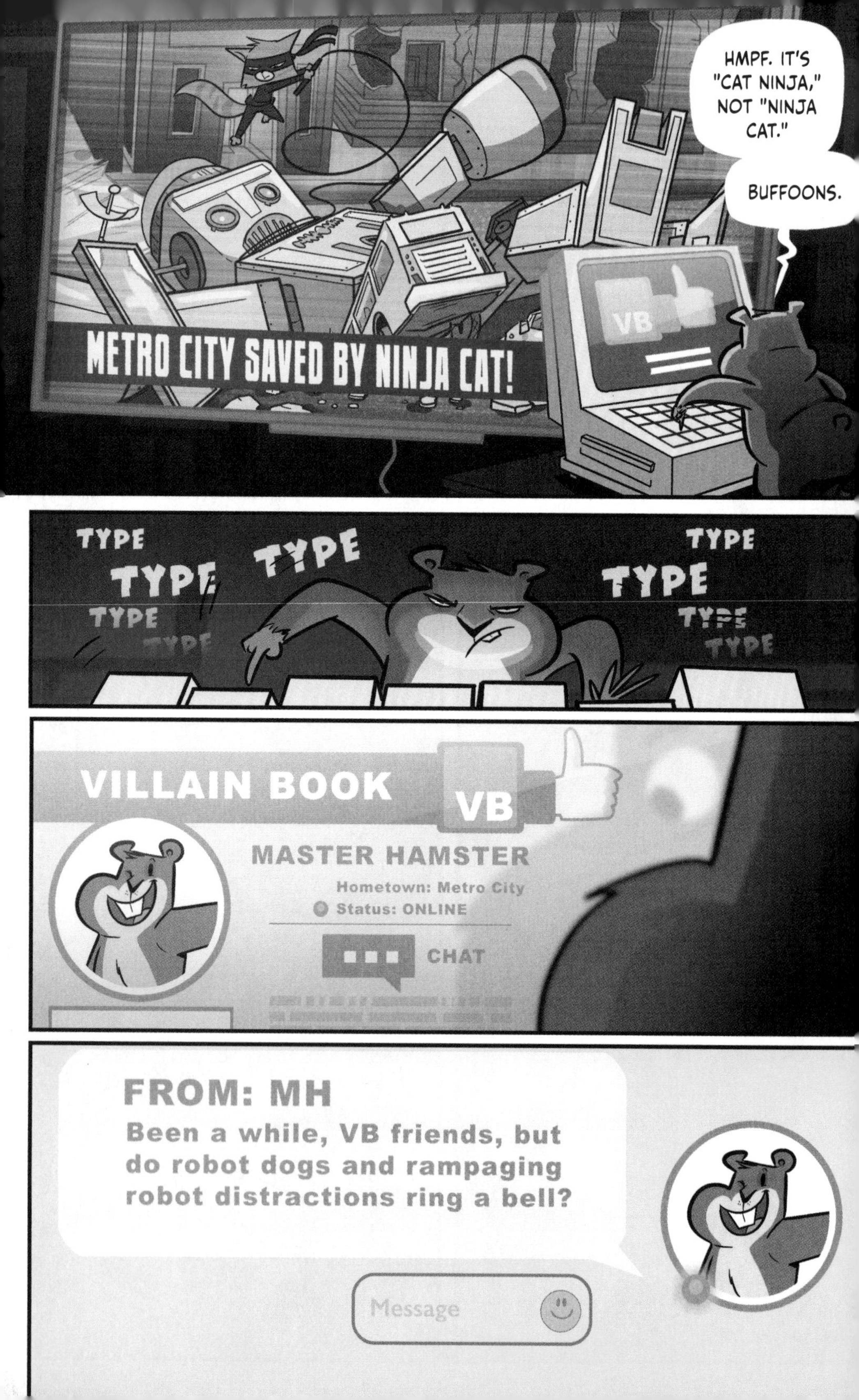
METRO CITY SAVED BY NINJA CAT!
VB
HMPF. IT'S "CAT NINJA," NOT "NINJA CAT."
BUFFOONS.
TYPE
TYPE
TYPE
TYPE
TYPE
TYPE
TYPE
TYPE
TYPE
VILLAIN BOOK
VB
MASTER HAMSTER
Hometown: Metro City
Status: ONLINE
CHAT
FROM: MH
Been a while, VB friends, but do robot dogs and rampaging robot distractions ring a bell?
Message

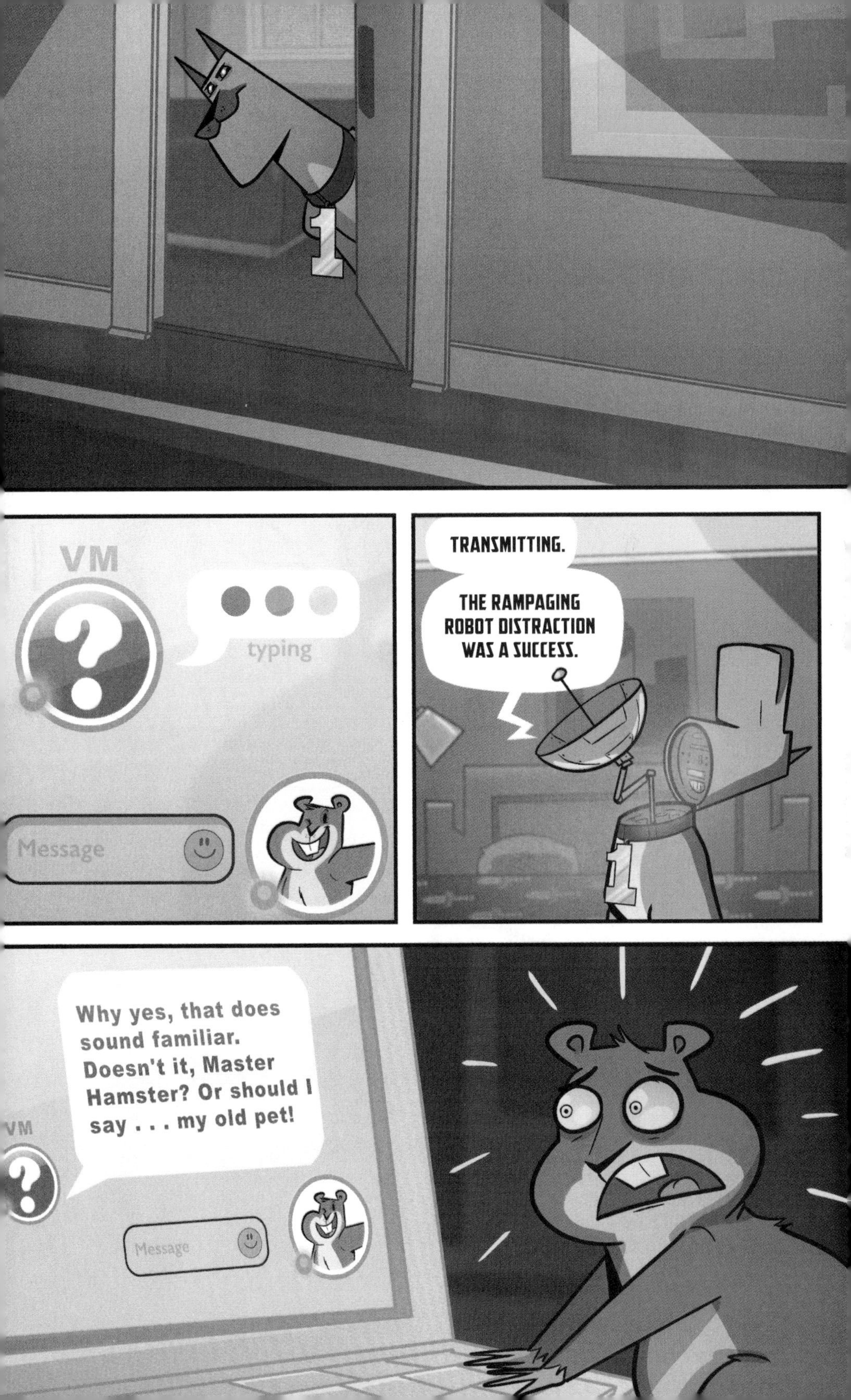

VM
typing
Message
TRANSMITTING.
THE RAMPAGING ROBOT DISTRACTION WAS A SUCCESS.
Why yes, that does sound familiar. Doesn't it, Master Hamster? Or should I say . . . my old pet!
VM
Message

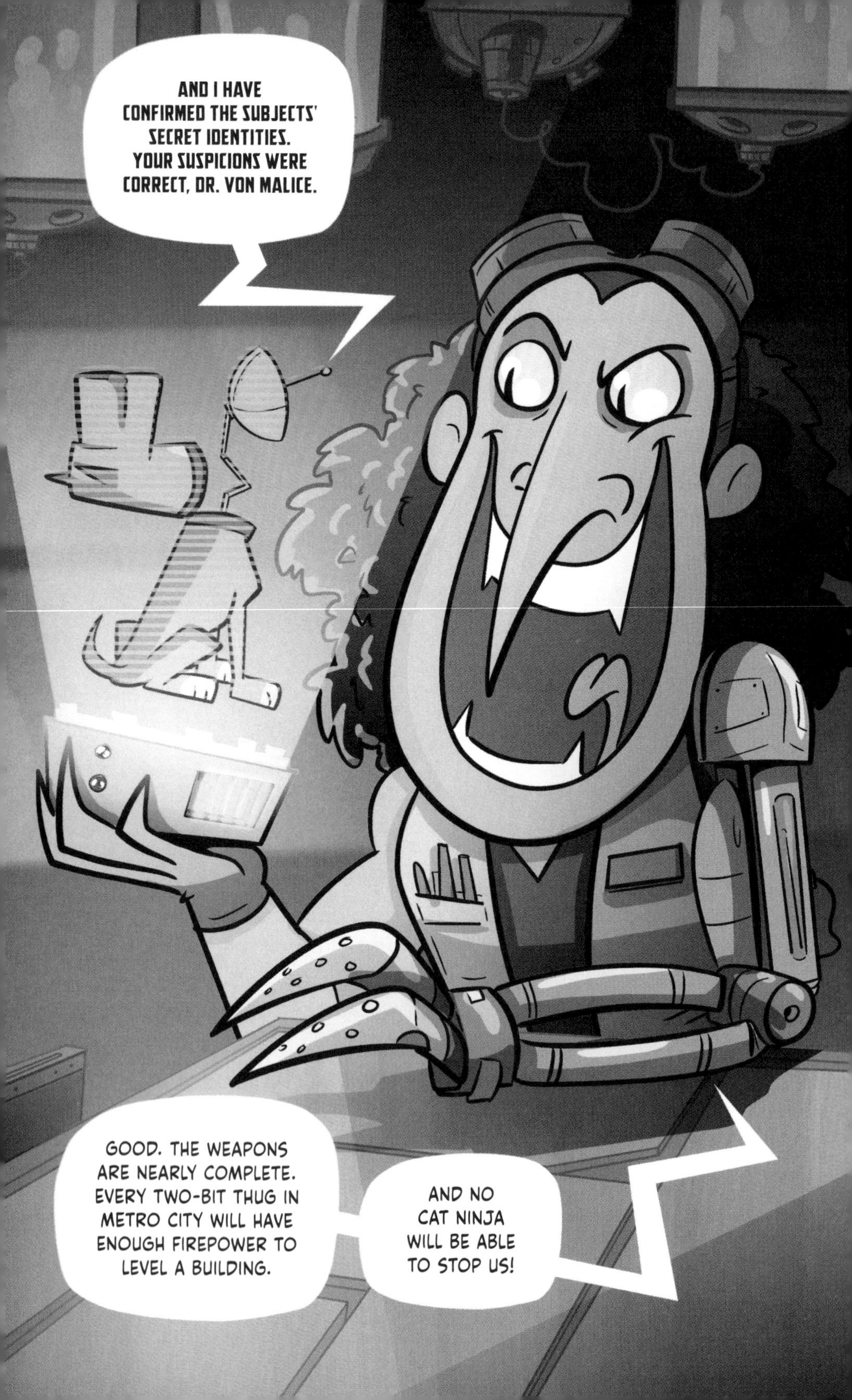
AND I HAVE CONFIRMED THE SUBJECTS' SECRET IDENTITIES. YOUR SUSPICIONS WERE CORRECT, DR. VON MALICE.
GOOD. THE WEAPONS ARE NEARLY COMPLETE. EVERY TWO-BIT THUG IN METRO CITY WILL HAVE ENOUGH FIREPOWER TO LEVEL A BUILDING.
AND NO CAT NINJA WILL BE ABLE TO STOP US!

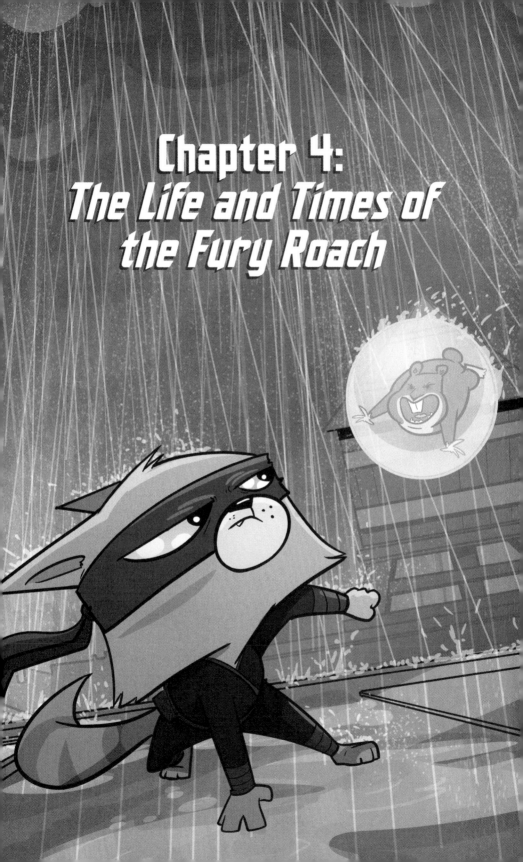

Chapter 4:
The Life and Times of the Fury Roach

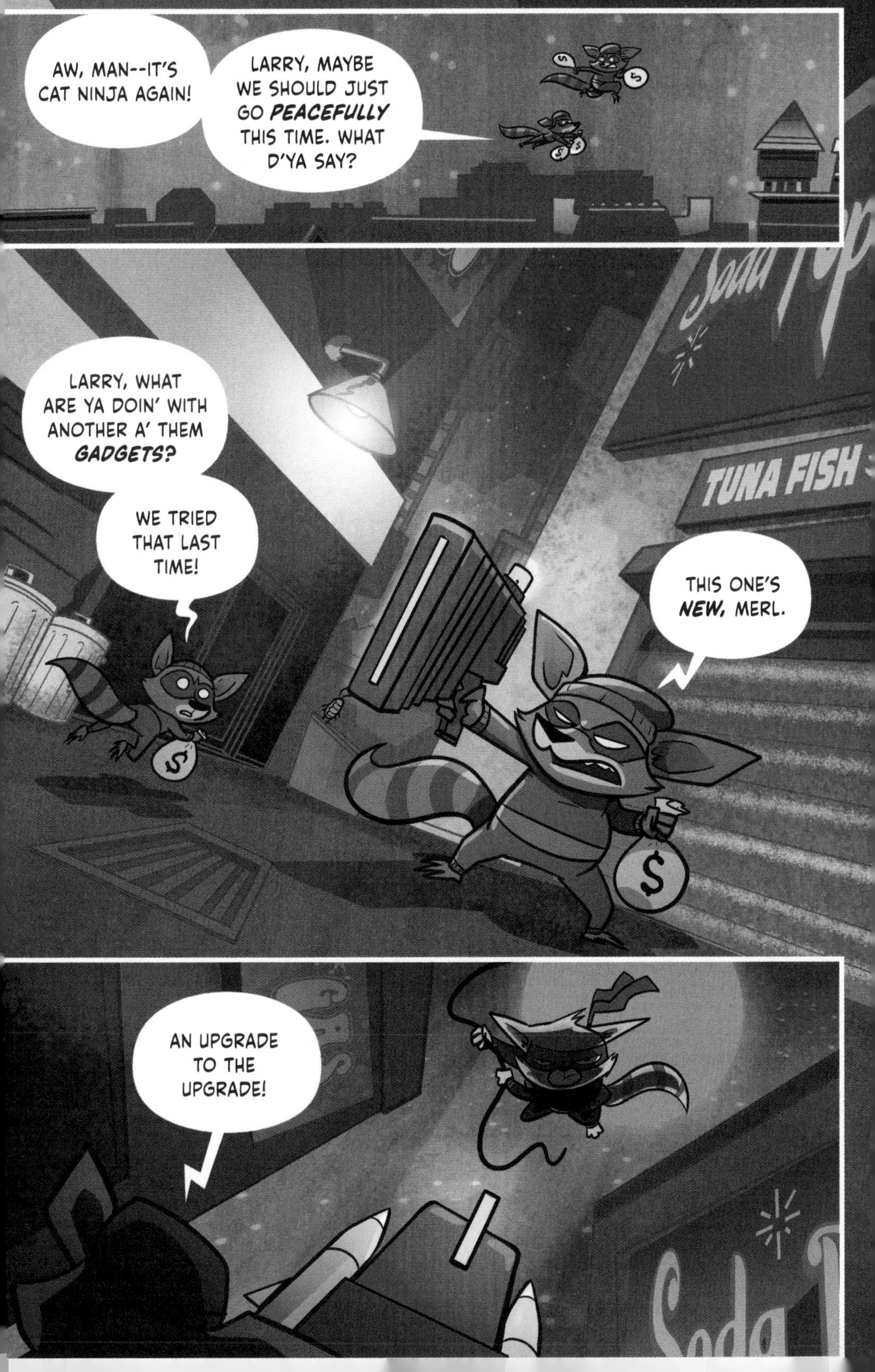
AW, MAN--IT'S CAT NINJA AGAIN!
LARRY, MAYBE WE SHOULD JUST GO PEACEFULLY THIS TIME. WHAT D'YA SAY?
LARRY, WHAT ARE YA DOIN' WITH ANOTHER A' THEM GADGETS?
WE TRIED THAT LAST TIME!
TUNA FISH
THIS ONE'S NEW, MERL.
AN UPGRADE TO THE UPGRADE!

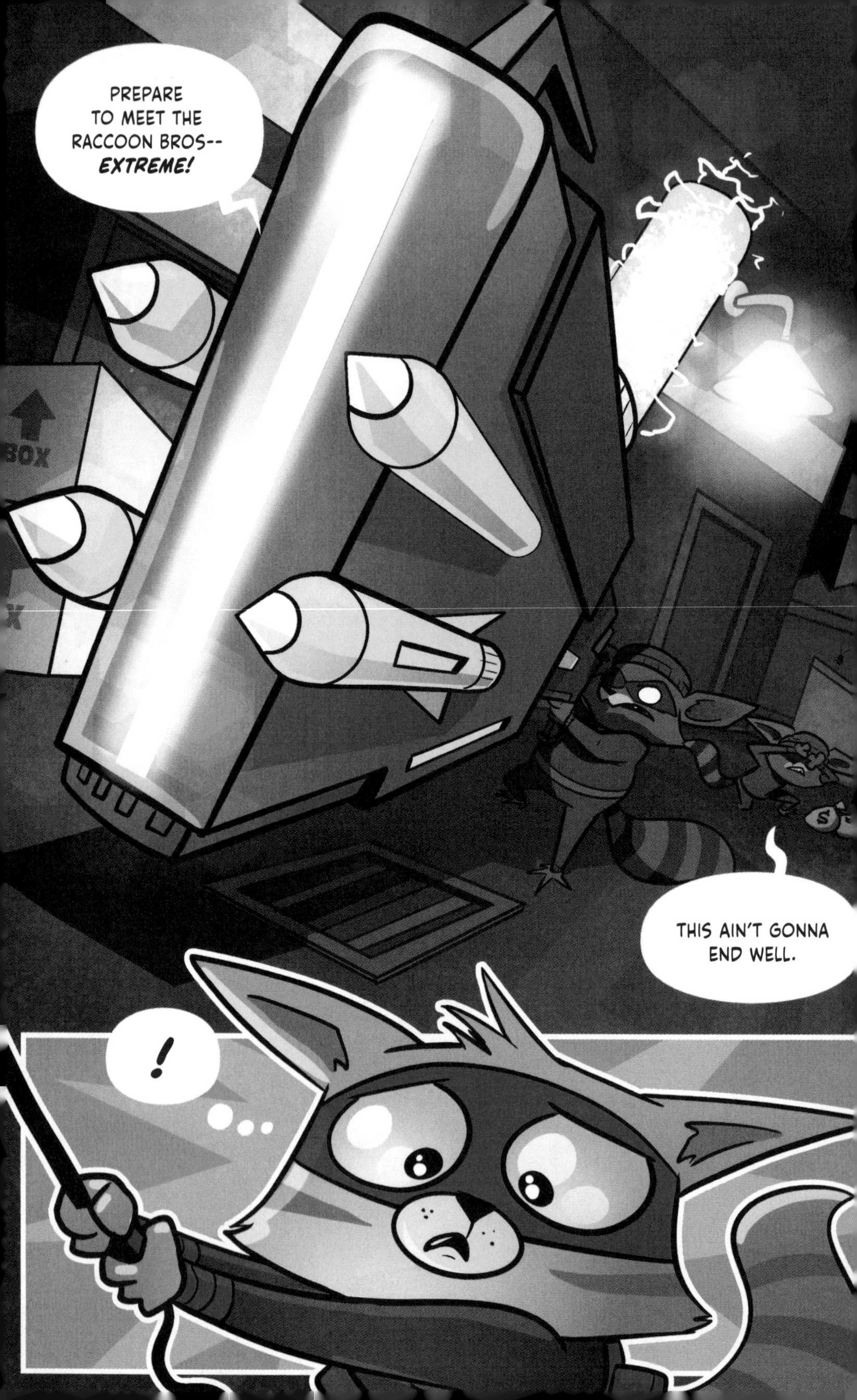
PREPARE TO MEET THE RACCOON BROS-- ***EXTREME!***
THIS AIN'T GONNA END WELL.
!
BOX

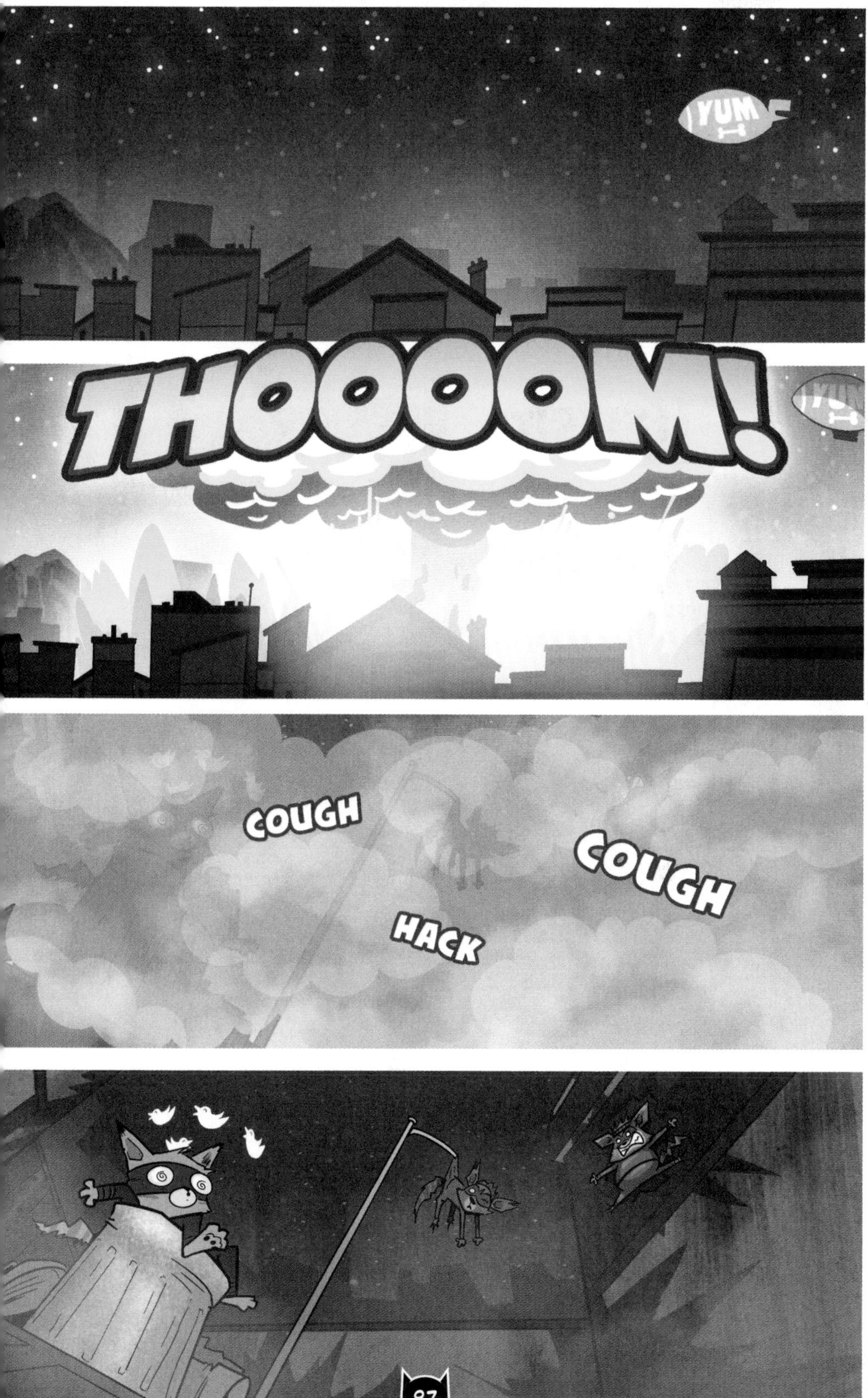
YUM
THOOOOM!
YUM
COUGH
COUGH
HACK

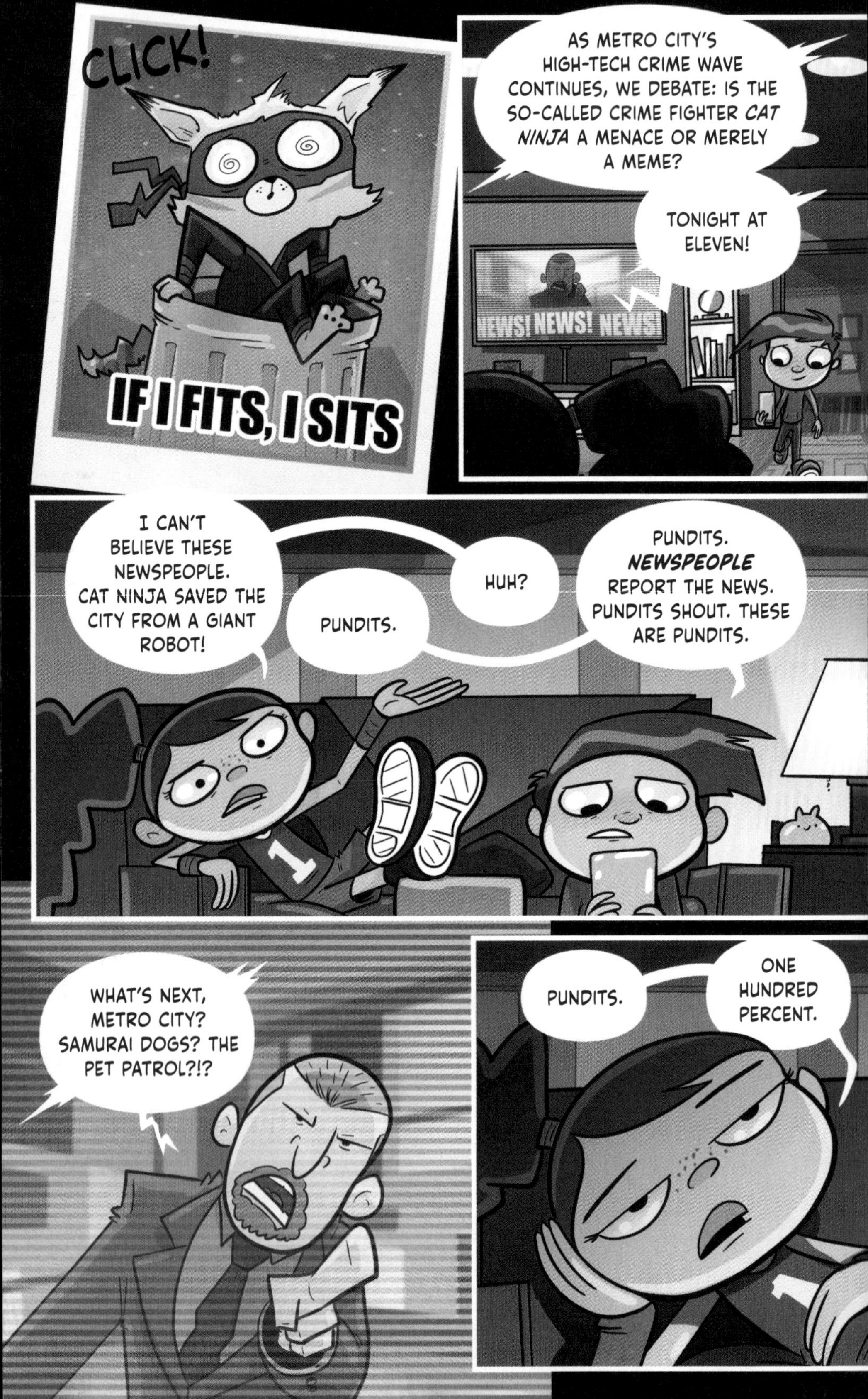
CLICK!
IF I FITS, I SITS
AS METRO CITY'S HIGH-TECH CRIME WAVE CONTINUES, WE DEBATE: IS THE SO-CALLED CRIME FIGHTER *CAT NINJA* A MENACE OR MERELY A MEME?
TONIGHT AT ELEVEN!
NEWS! NEWS! NEWS!
I CAN'T BELIEVE THESE NEWSPEOPLE. CAT NINJA SAVED THE CITY FROM A GIANT ROBOT!
PUNDITS.
HUH?
PUNDITS. ***NEWSPEOPLE*** REPORT THE NEWS. PUNDITS SHOUT. THESE ARE PUNDITS.
WHAT'S NEXT, METRO CITY? SAMURAI DOGS? THE PET PATROL?!?
PUNDITS.
ONE HUNDRED PERCENT.

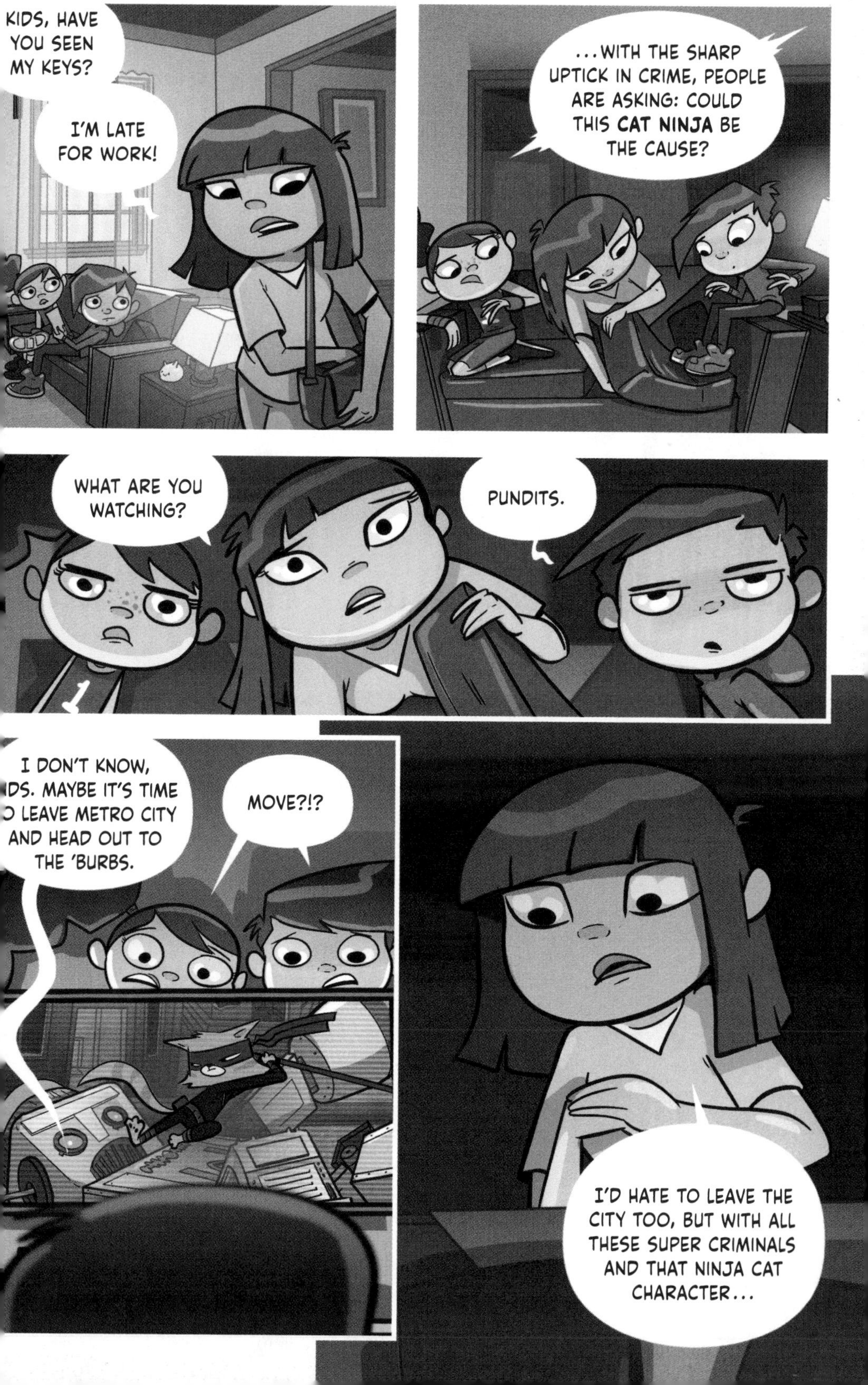

KIDS, HAVE YOU SEEN MY KEYS?
I'M LATE FOR WORK!
...WITH THE SHARP UPTICK IN CRIME, PEOPLE ARE ASKING: COULD THIS **CAT NINJA** BE THE CAUSE?
WHAT ARE YOU WATCHING?
PUNDITS.
I DON'T KNOW, IDS. MAYBE IT'S TIME O LEAVE METRO CITY AND HEAD OUT TO THE 'BURBS.
MOVE?!?
I'D HATE TO LEAVE THE CITY TOO, BUT WITH ALL THESE SUPER CRIMINALS AND THAT NINJA CAT CHARACTER...

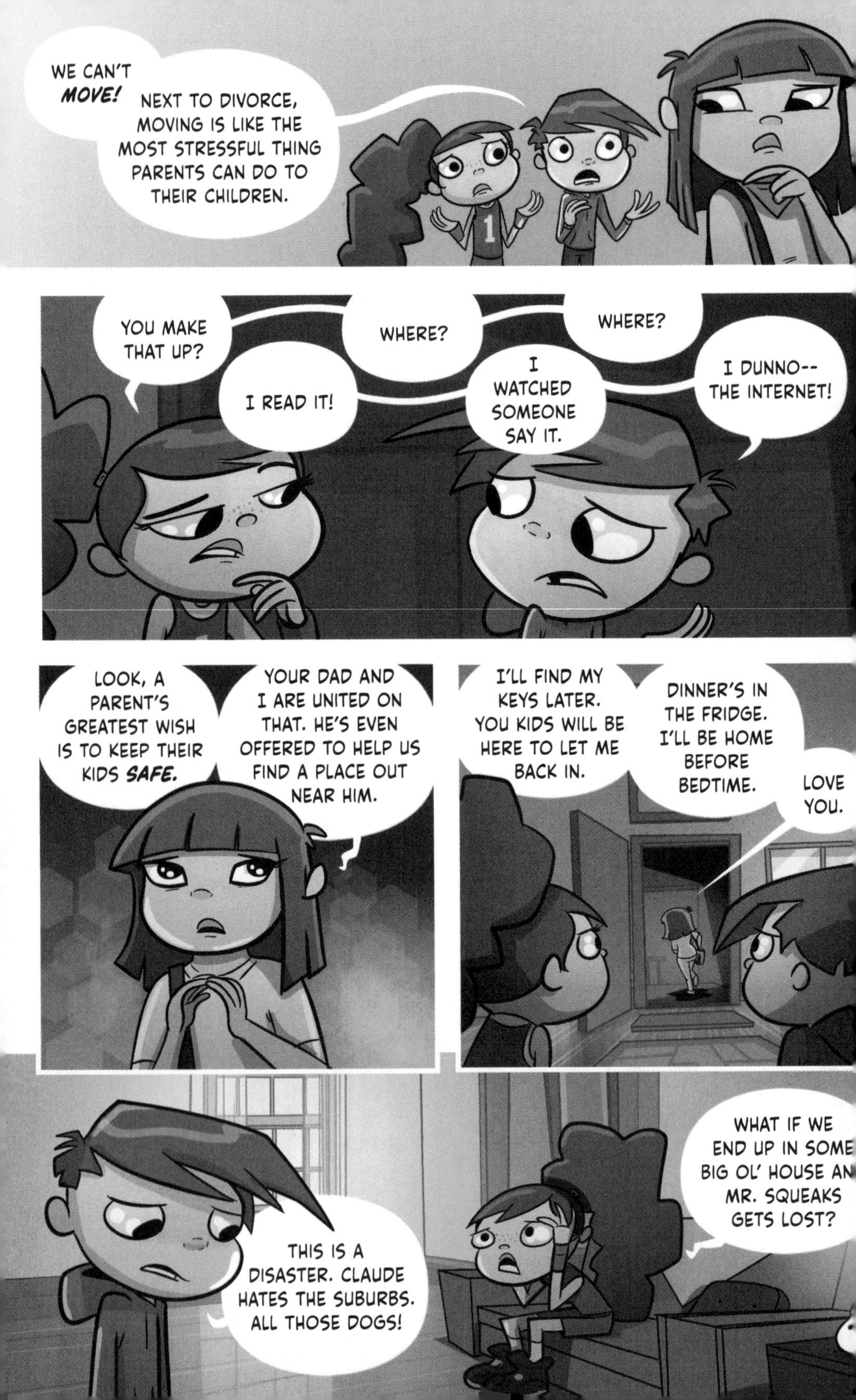
WE CAN'T *MOVE!*
NEXT TO DIVORCE, MOVING IS LIKE THE MOST STRESSFUL THING PARENTS CAN DO TO THEIR CHILDREN.
YOU MAKE THAT UP?
I READ IT!
WHERE?
I WATCHED SOMEONE SAY IT.
WHERE?
I DUNNO-- THE INTERNET!
LOOK, A PARENT'S GREATEST WISH IS TO KEEP THEIR KIDS *SAFE.*
YOUR DAD AND I ARE UNITED ON THAT. HE'S EVEN OFFERED TO HELP US FIND A PLACE OUT NEAR HIM.
I'LL FIND MY KEYS LATER. YOU KIDS WILL BE HERE TO LET ME BACK IN.
DINNER'S IN THE FRIDGE. I'LL BE HOME BEFORE BEDTIME.
LOVE YOU.
THIS IS A DISASTER. CLAUDE HATES THE SUBURBS. ALL THOSE DOGS!
WHAT IF WE END UP IN SOME BIG OL' HOUSE AN MR. SQUEAKS GETS LOST?

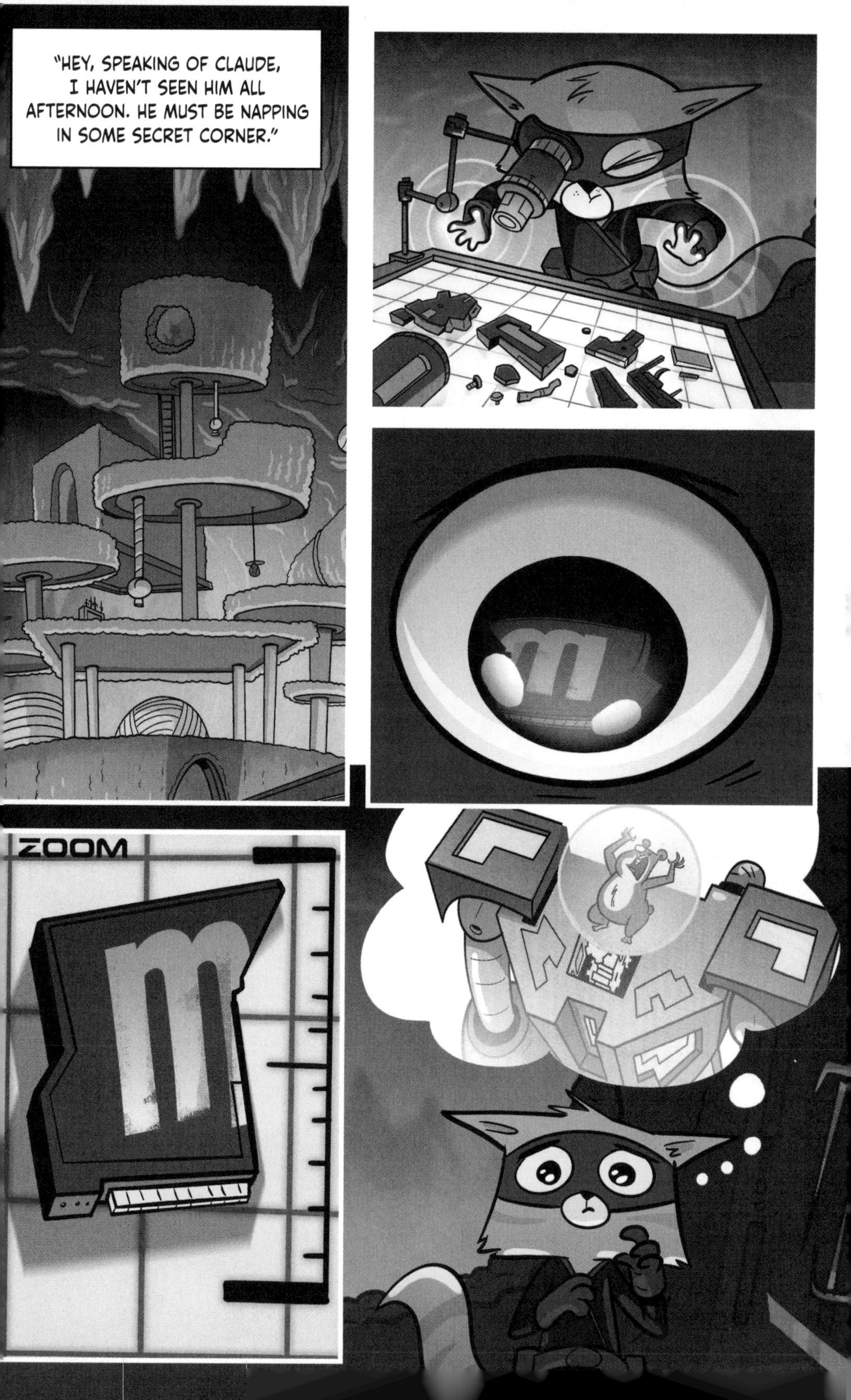
"HEY, SPEAKING OF CLAUDE, I HAVEN'T SEEN HIM ALL AFTERNOON. HE MUST BE NAPPING IN SOME SECRET CORNER."
ZOOM

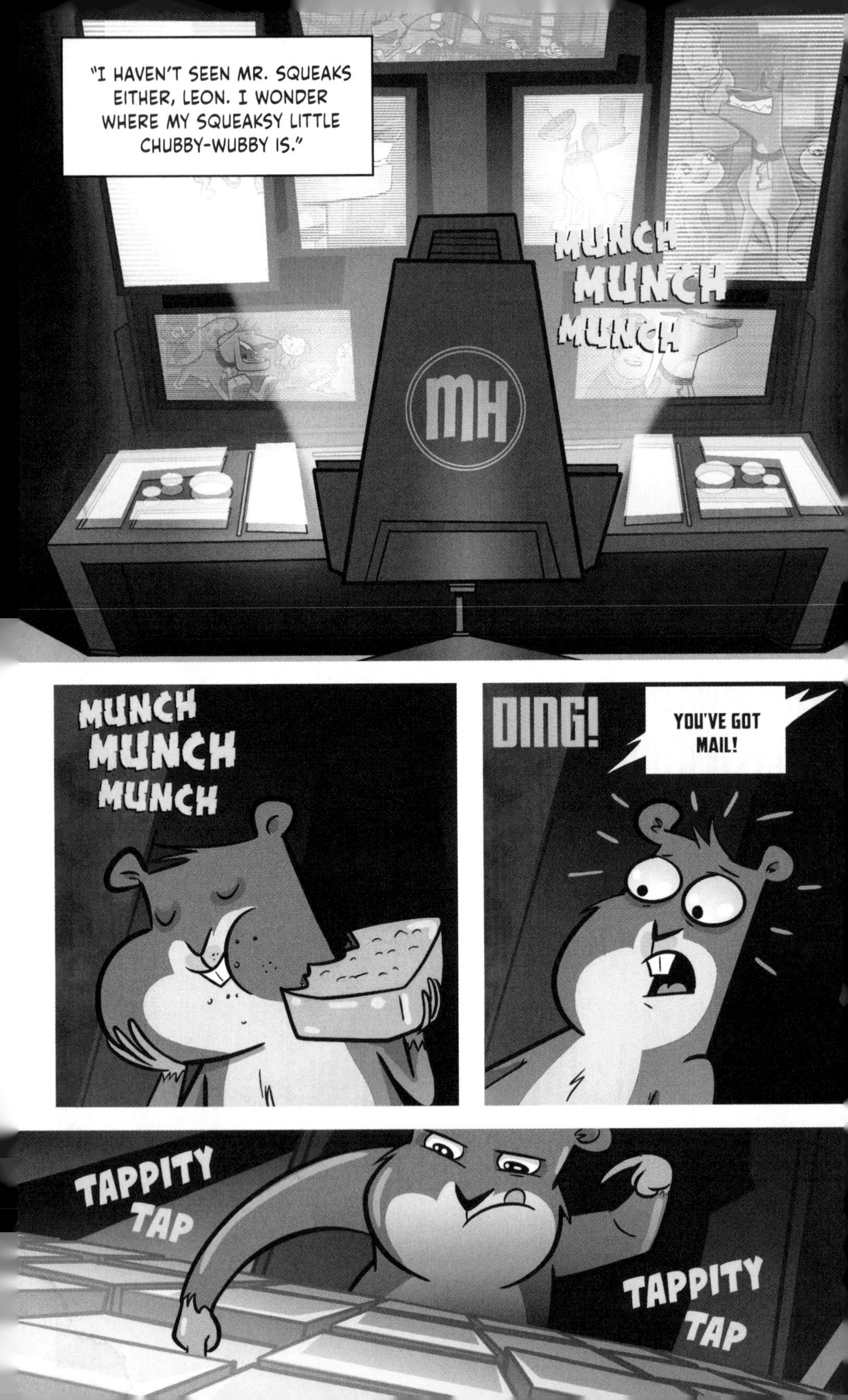
"I HAVEN'T SEEN MR. SQUEAKS EITHER, LEON. I WONDER WHERE MY SQUEAKSY LITTLE CHUBBY-WUBBY IS."
MUNCH
MUNCH
MUNCH
MH
MUNCH
MUNCH
MUNCH
DING!
YOU'VE GOT MAIL!
TAPPITY
TAP
TAPPITY
TAP

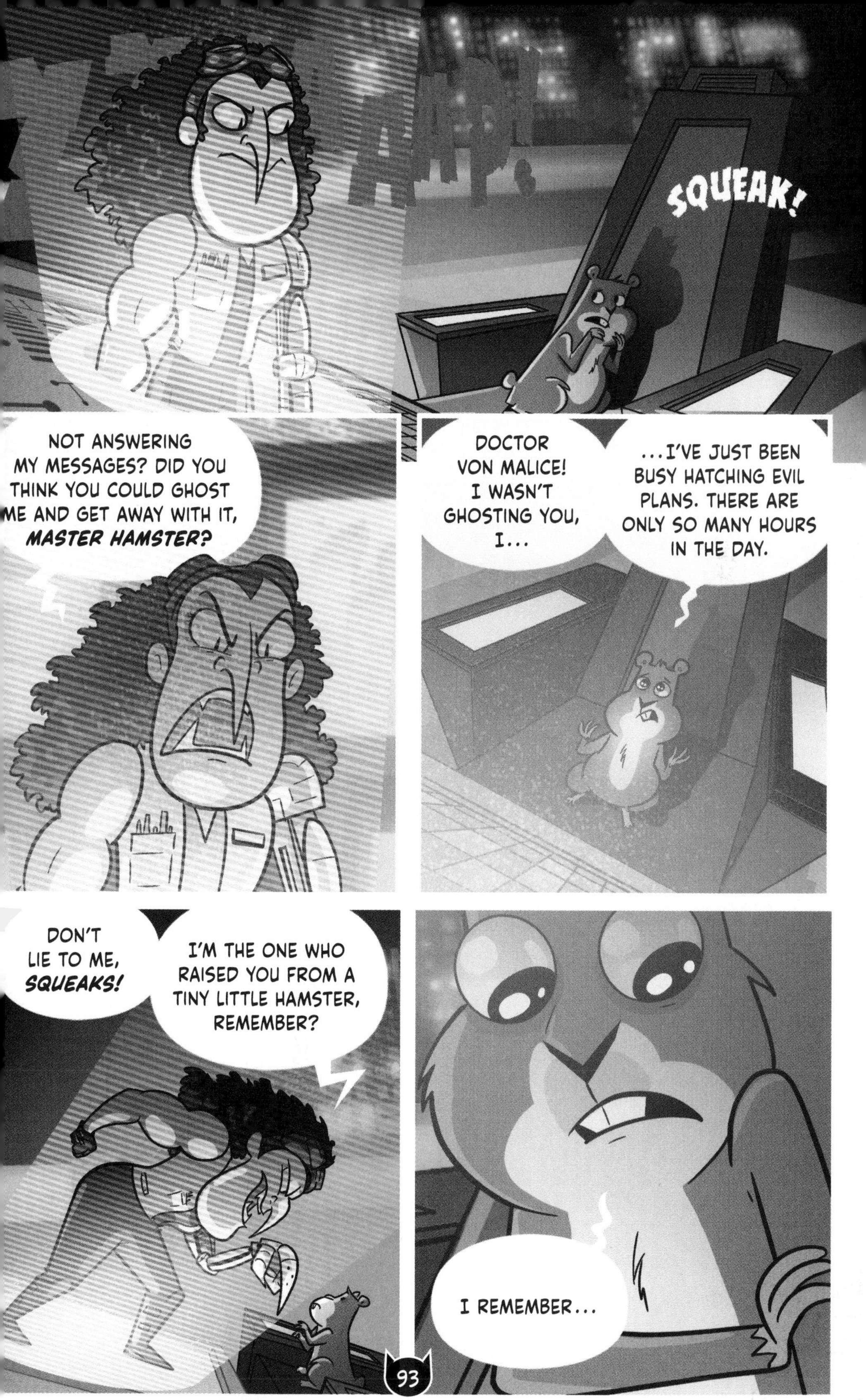
SQUEAK!
NOT ANSWERING MY MESSAGES? DID YOU THINK YOU COULD GHOST ME AND GET AWAY WITH IT, MASTER HAMSTER?
DOCTOR VON MALICE! I WASN'T GHOSTING YOU, I...
...I'VE JUST BEEN BUSY HATCHING EVIL PLANS. THERE ARE ONLY SO MANY HOURS IN THE DAY.
DON'T LIE TO ME, SQUEAKS!
I'M THE ONE WHO RAISED YOU FROM A TINY LITTLE HAMSTER, REMEMBER?
I REMEMBER...

YEARS AGO...

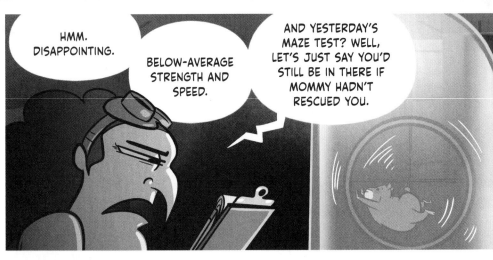

HMM. DISAPPOINTING.

BELOW-AVERAGE STRENGTH AND SPEED.

AND YESTERDAY'S MAZE TEST? WELL, LET'S JUST SAY YOU'D STILL BE IN THERE IF MOMMY HADN'T RESCUED YOU.

HARDLY MUTANT-RODENT ASSASSIN MATERIAL, ARE YOU?

SQUEAK!

STILL, MAYBE I'LL KEEP YOU AROUND FOR A WHILE. YOU NEVER KNOW WHEN YOU MIGHT NEED A BELOW-AVERAGE SPECIMEN.

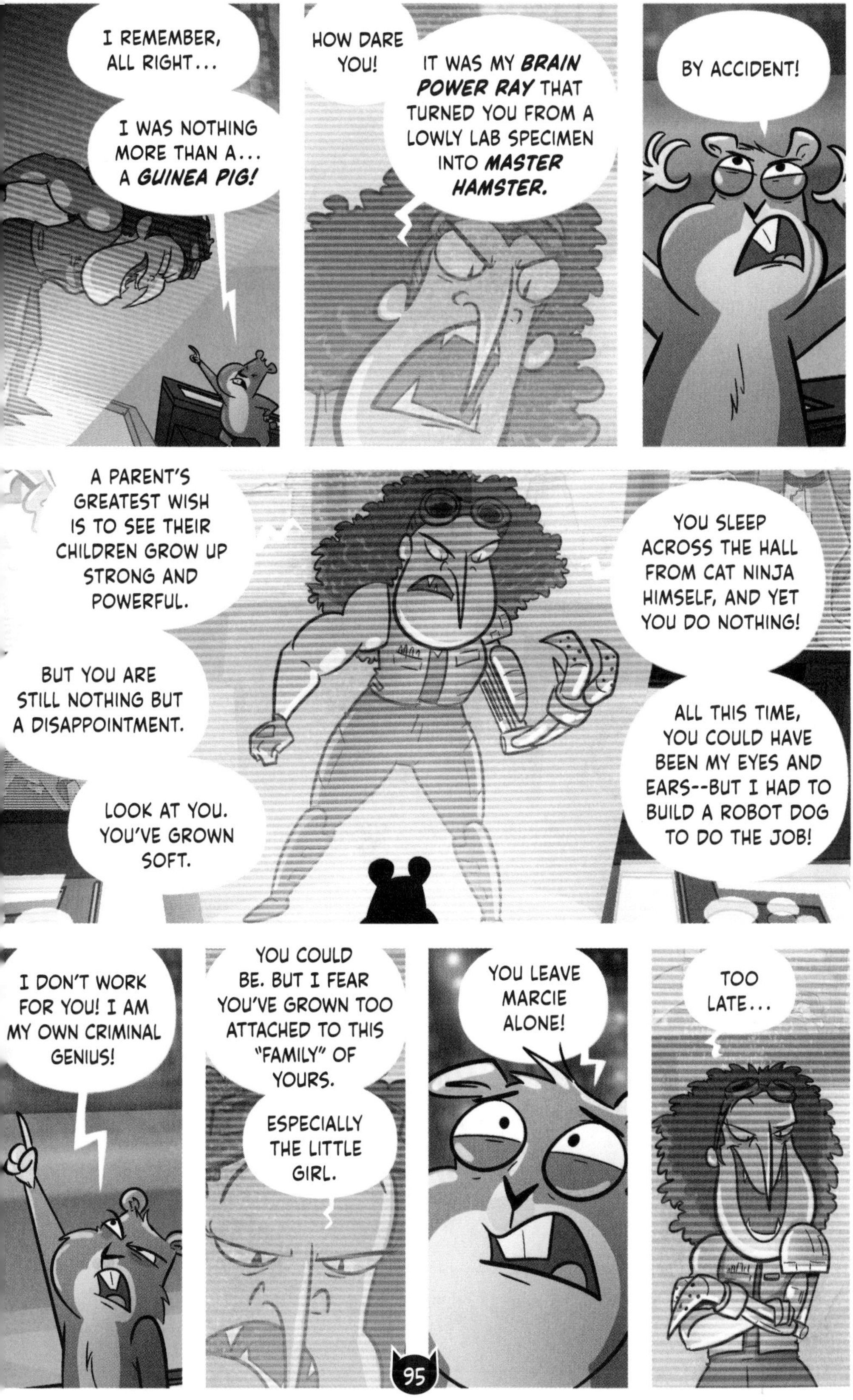
I REMEMBER, ALL RIGHT...
I WAS NOTHING MORE THAN A... A *GUINEA PIG!*
HOW DARE YOU!
IT WAS MY *BRAIN POWER RAY* THAT TURNED YOU FROM A LOWLY LAB SPECIMEN INTO *MASTER HAMSTER.*
BY ACCIDENT!
A PARENT'S GREATEST WISH IS TO SEE THEIR CHILDREN GROW UP STRONG AND POWERFUL.
BUT YOU ARE STILL NOTHING BUT A DISAPPOINTMENT.
LOOK AT YOU. YOU'VE GROWN SOFT.
YOU SLEEP ACROSS THE HALL FROM CAT NINJA HIMSELF, AND YET YOU DO NOTHING!
ALL THIS TIME, YOU COULD HAVE BEEN MY EYES AND EARS--BUT I HAD TO BUILD A ROBOT DOG TO DO THE JOB!
I DON'T WORK FOR YOU! I AM MY OWN CRIMINAL GENIUS!
YOU COULD BE. BUT I FEAR YOU'VE GROWN TOO ATTACHED TO THIS "FAMILY" OF YOURS.
ESPECIALLY THE LITTLE GIRL.
YOU LEAVE MARCIE ALONE!
TOO LATE...

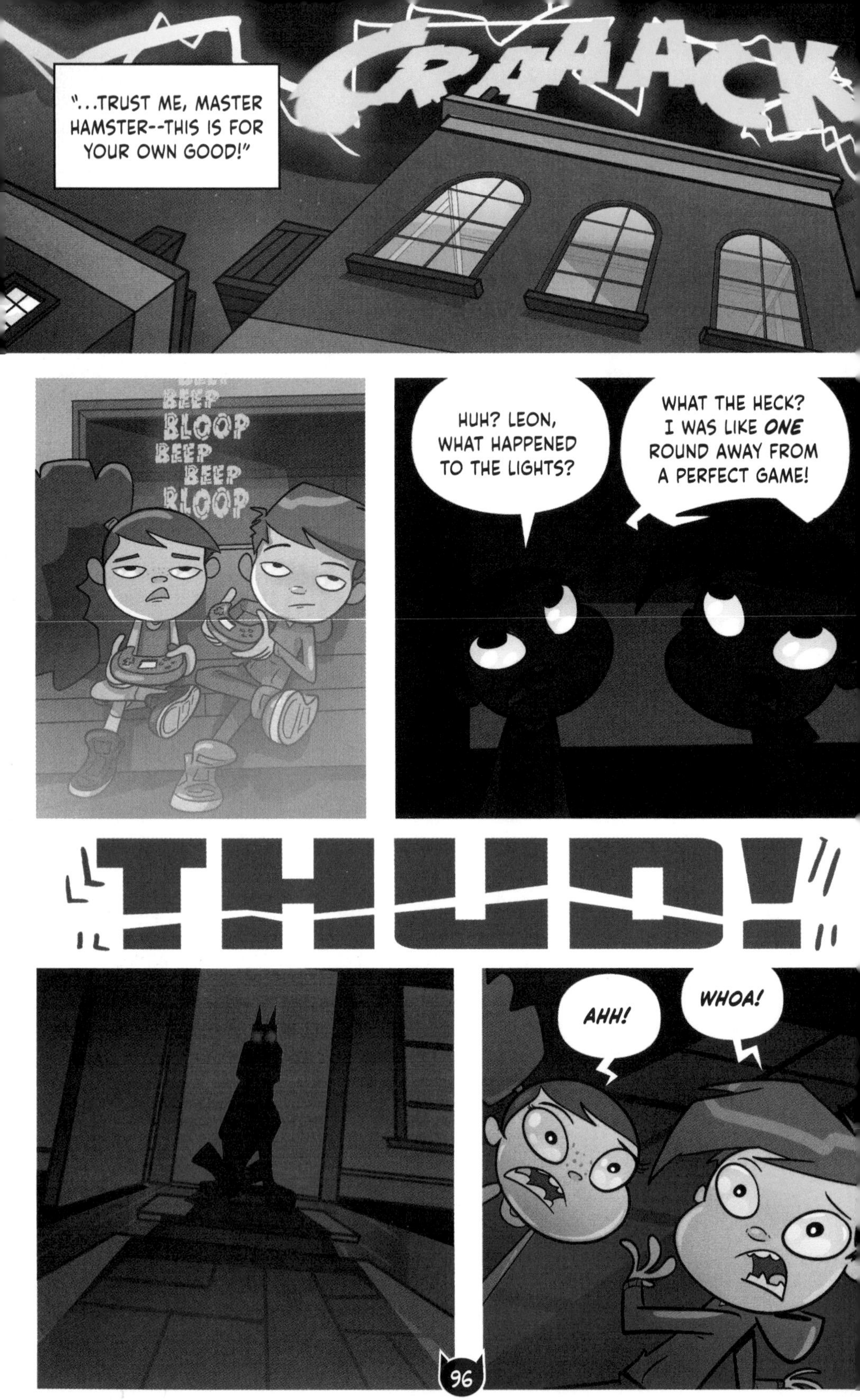
"...TRUST ME, MASTER HAMSTER--THIS IS FOR YOUR OWN GOOD!"
CRAAACK
BEEP
BLOOP
BEEP
BEEP
BLOOP
HUH? LEON, WHAT HAPPENED TO THE LIGHTS?
WHAT THE HECK? I WAS LIKE *ONE* ROUND AWAY FROM A PERFECT GAME!
THUD!
AHH!
WHOA!

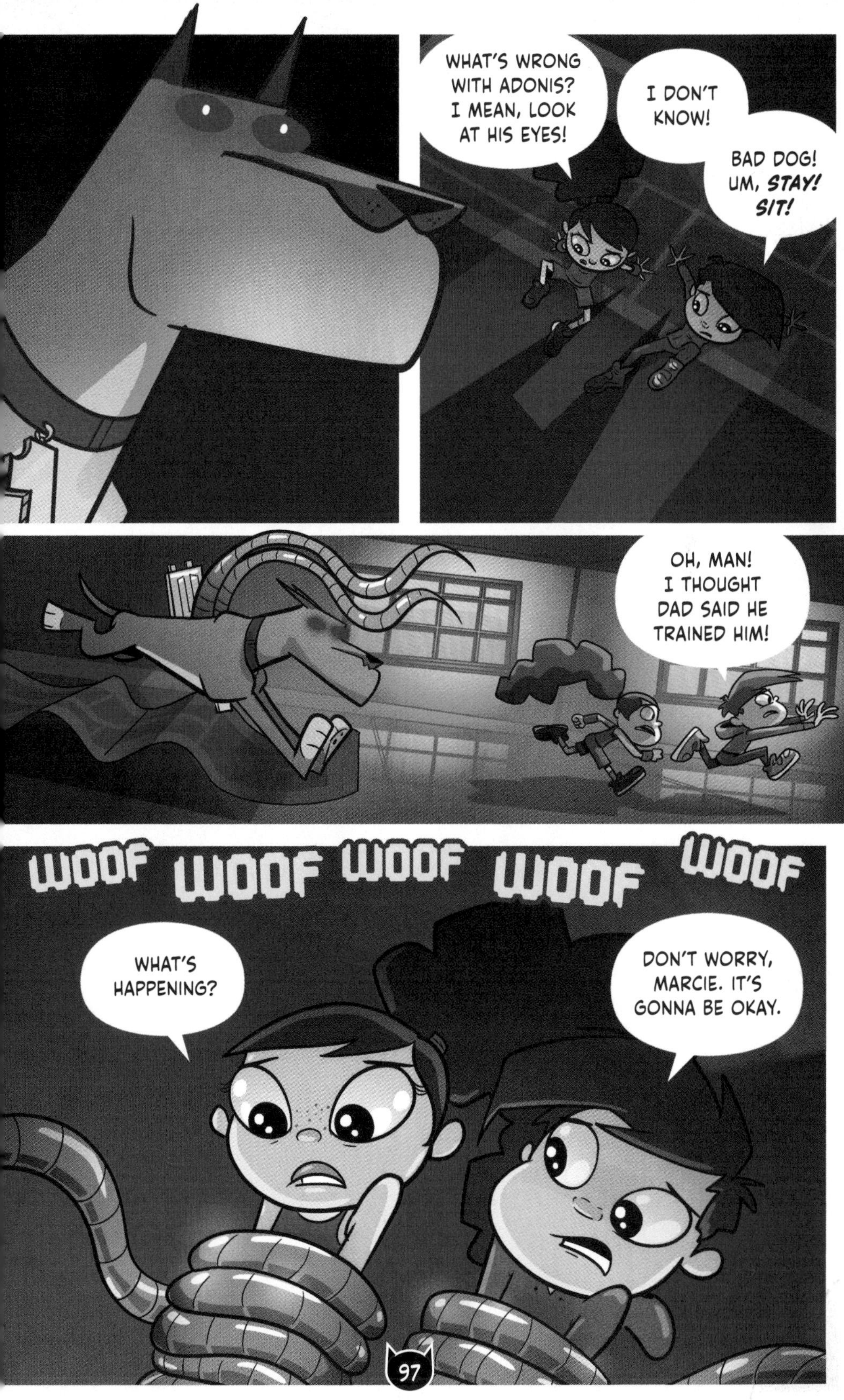
WHAT'S WRONG WITH ADONIS? I MEAN, LOOK AT HIS EYES!
I DON'T KNOW!
BAD DOG! UM, STAY! SIT!
OH, MAN! I THOUGHT DAD SAID HE TRAINED HIM!
WOOF WOOF WOOF WOOF WOOF
WHAT'S HAPPENING?
DON'T WORRY, MARCIE. IT'S GONNA BE OKAY.

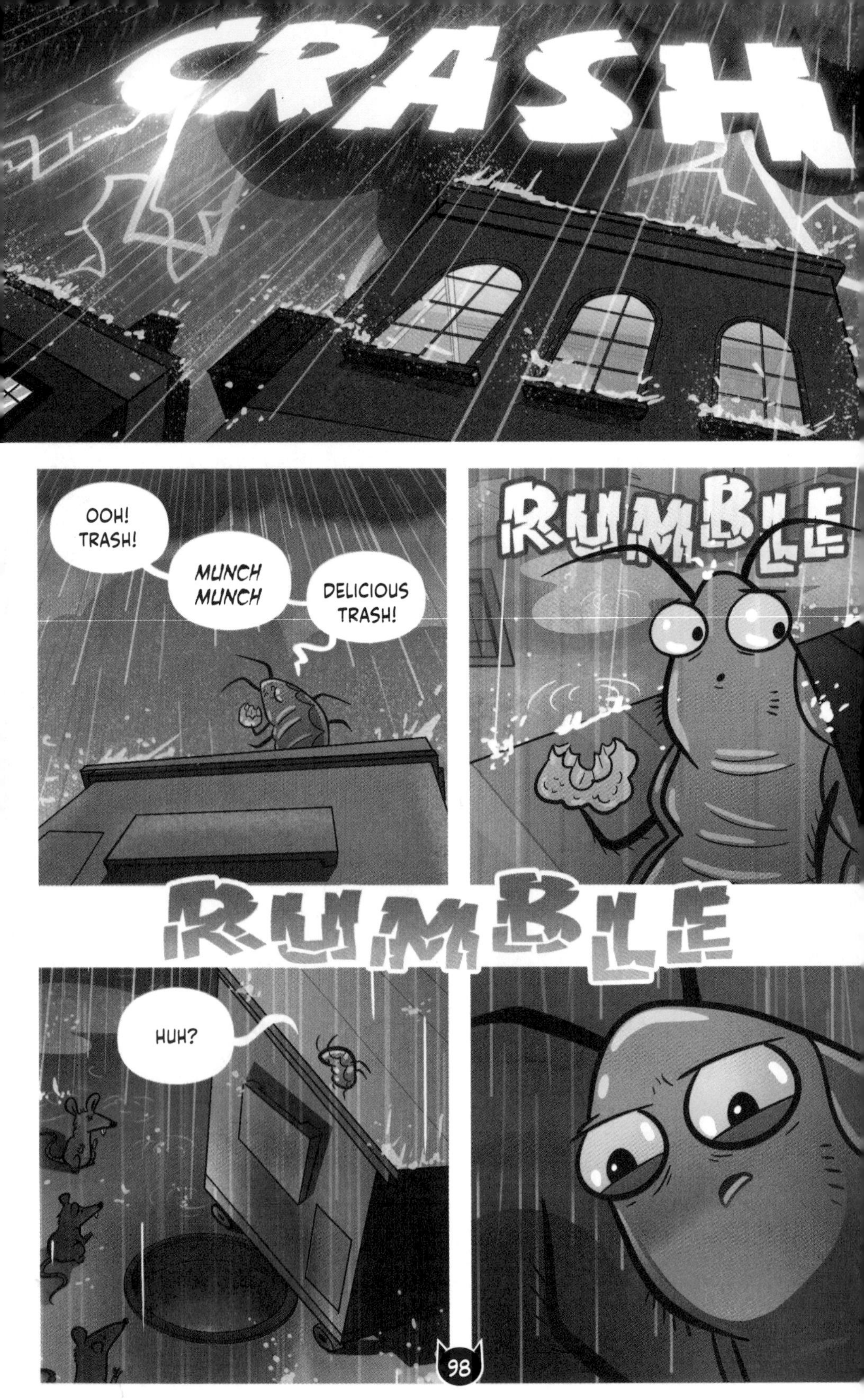
CRASH
OOH! TRASH!
MUNCH MUNCH
DELICIOUS TRASH!
RUMBLE
RUMBLE
HUH?

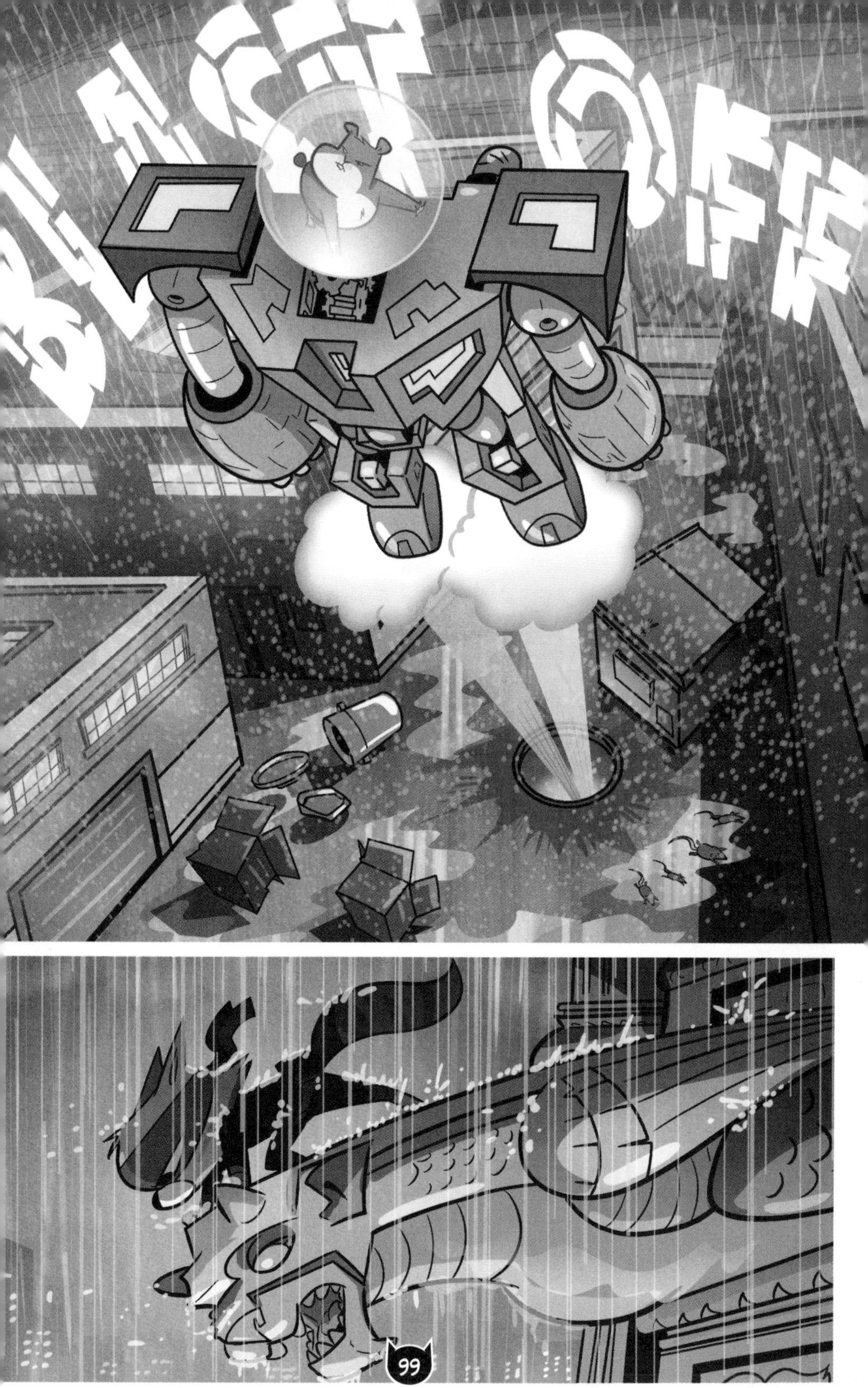

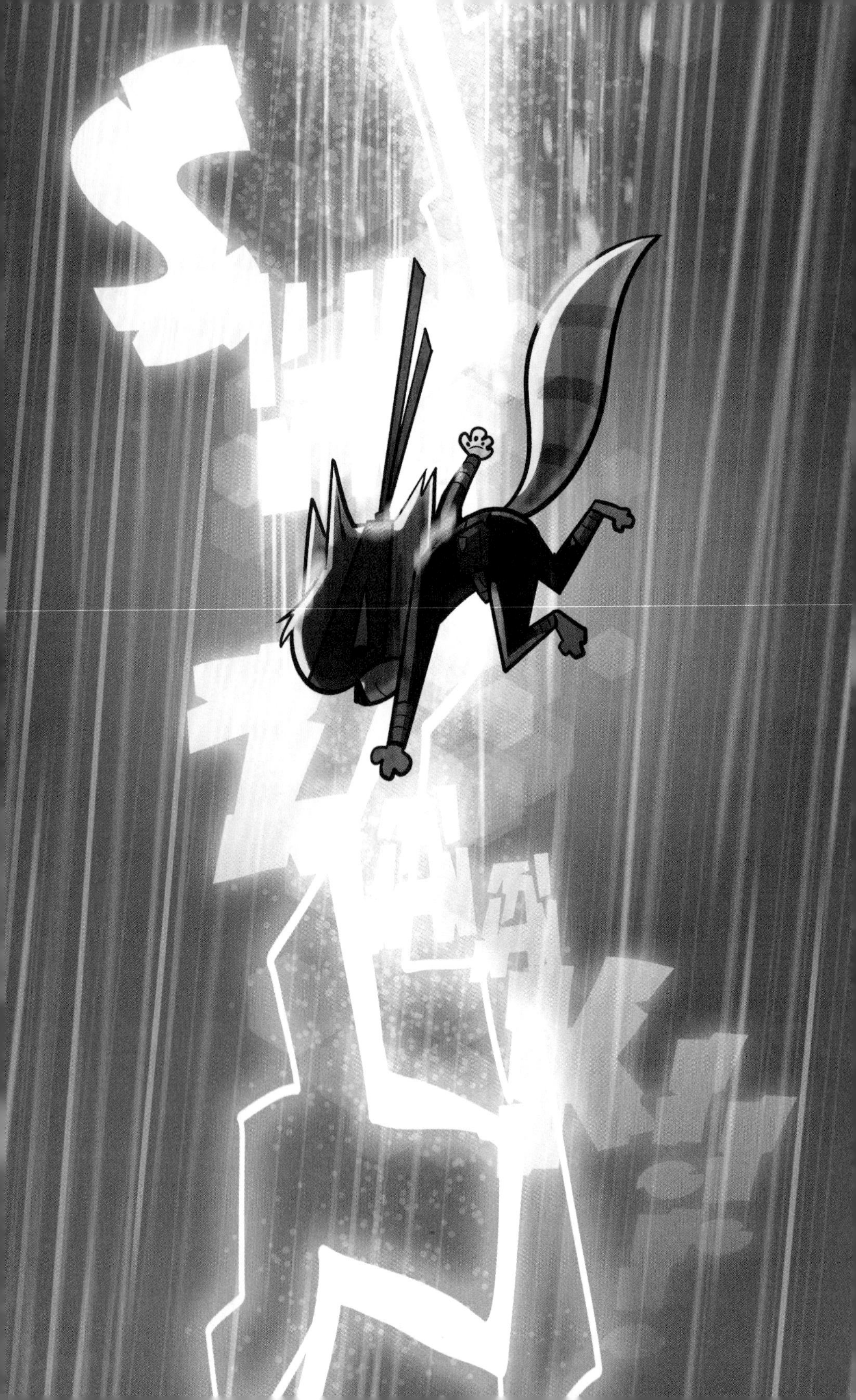

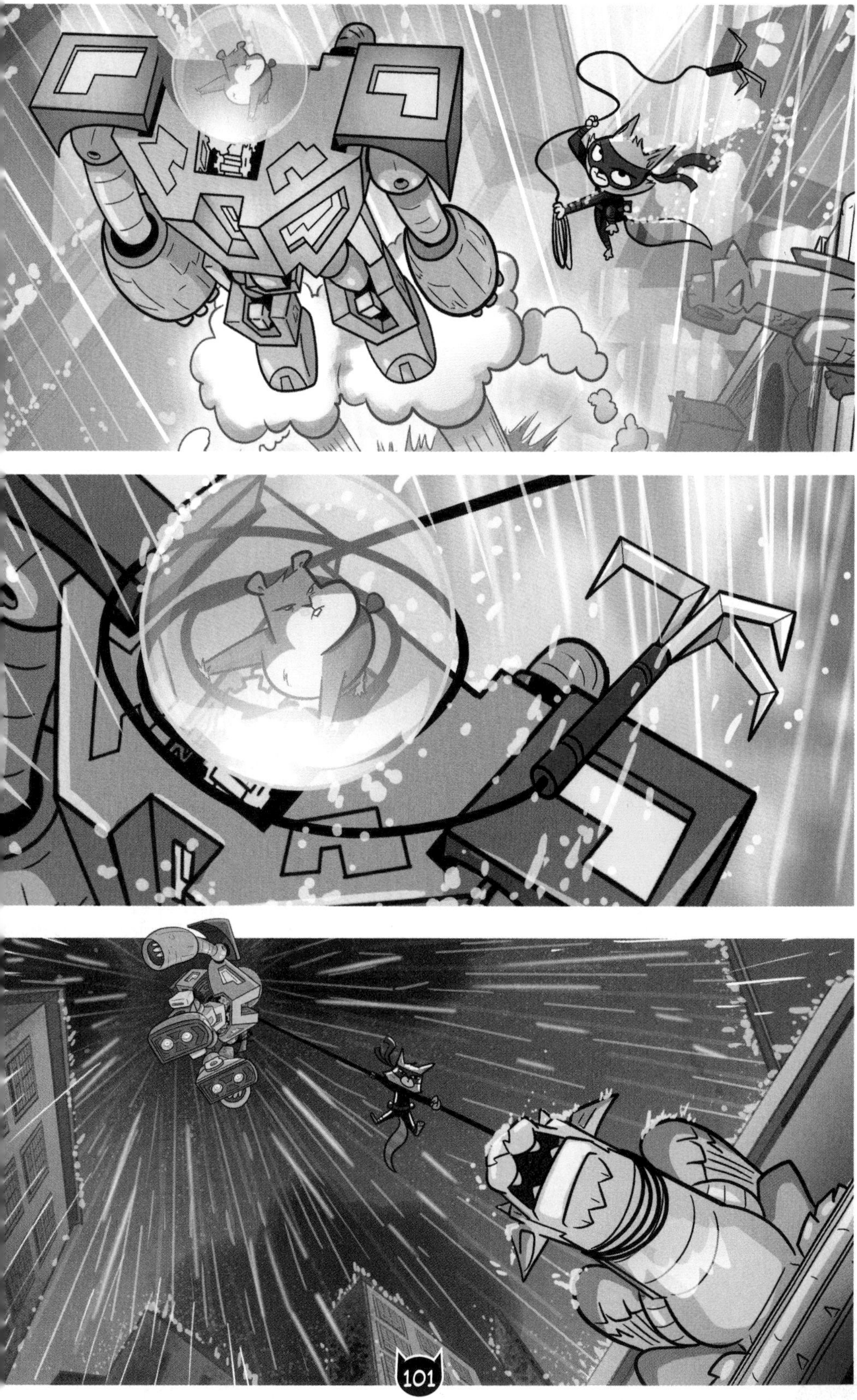

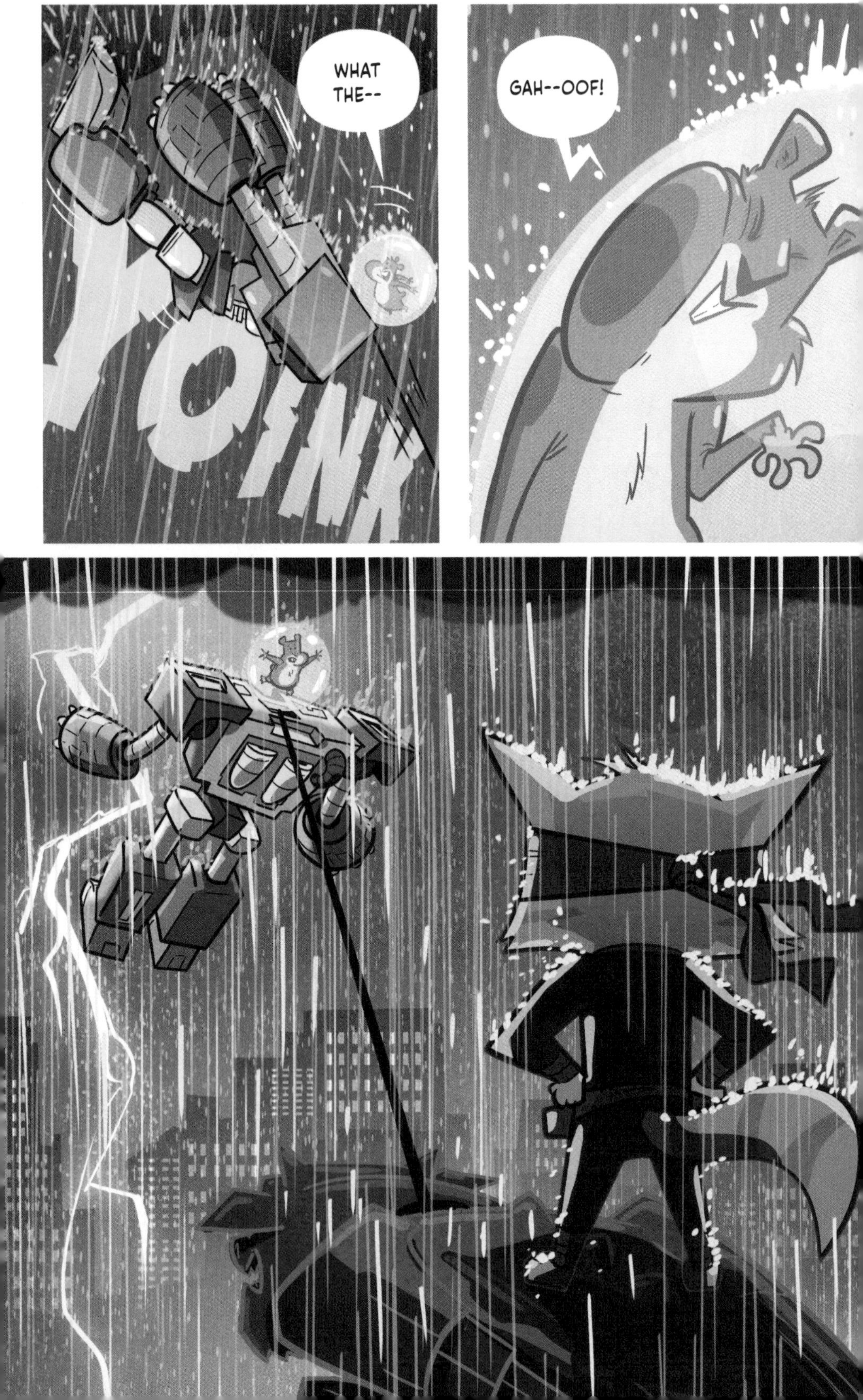
YOINK
WHAT THE--
GAH--OOF!

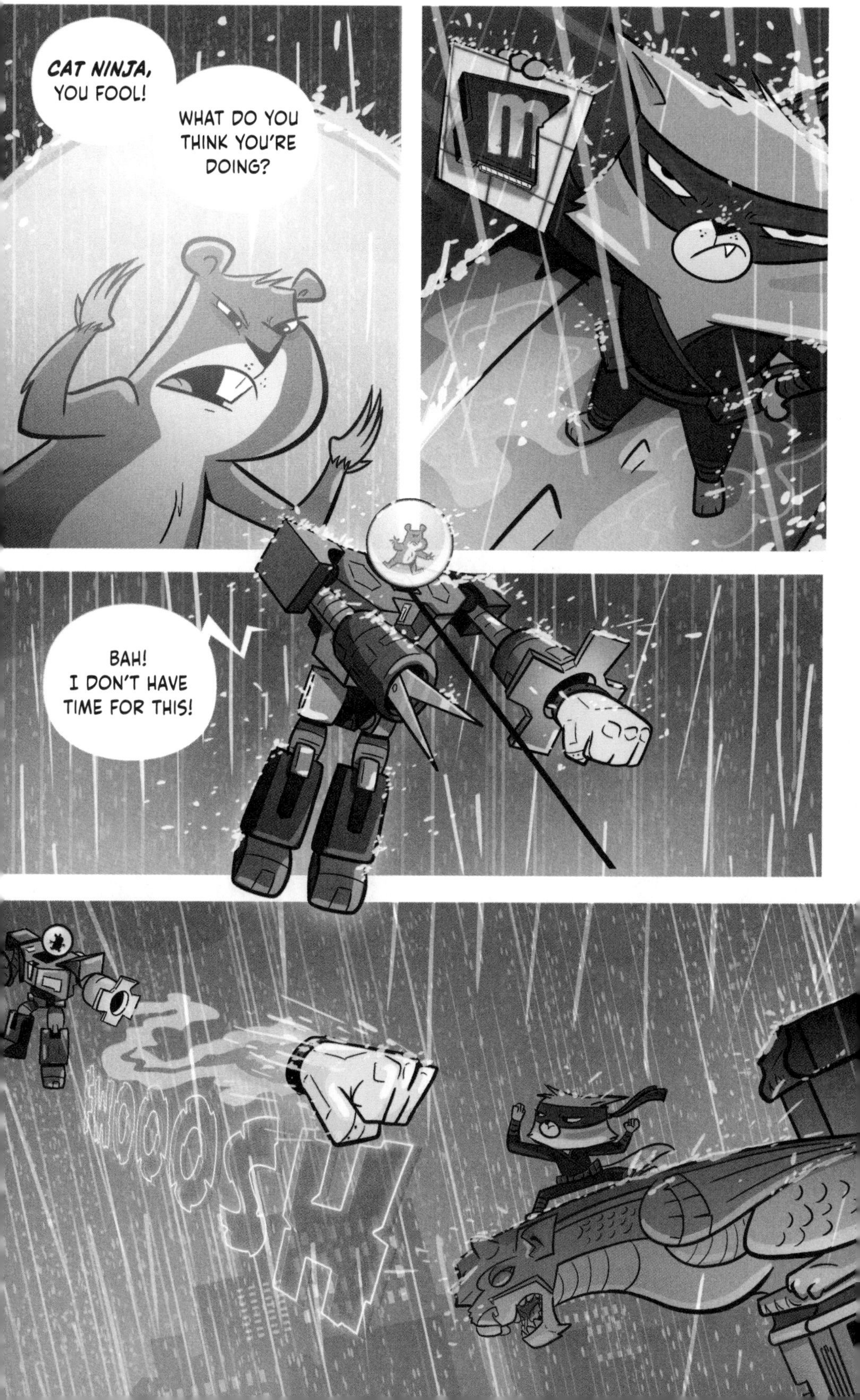
CAT NINJA, YOU FOOL!
WHAT DO YOU THINK YOU'RE DOING?
BAH! I DON'T HAVE TIME FOR THIS!
FWOOOOSH

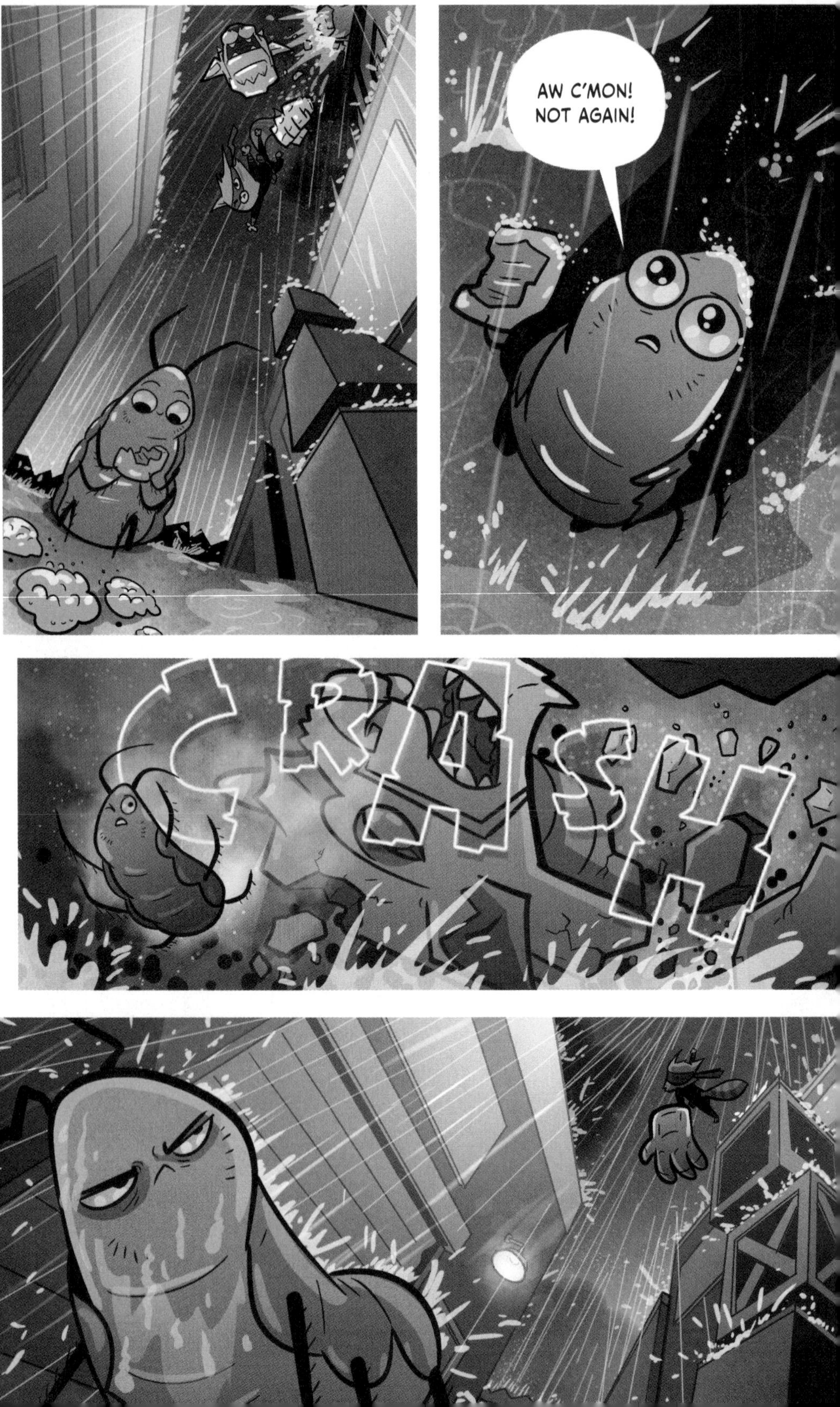
AW C'MON! NOT AGAIN!
CRASH

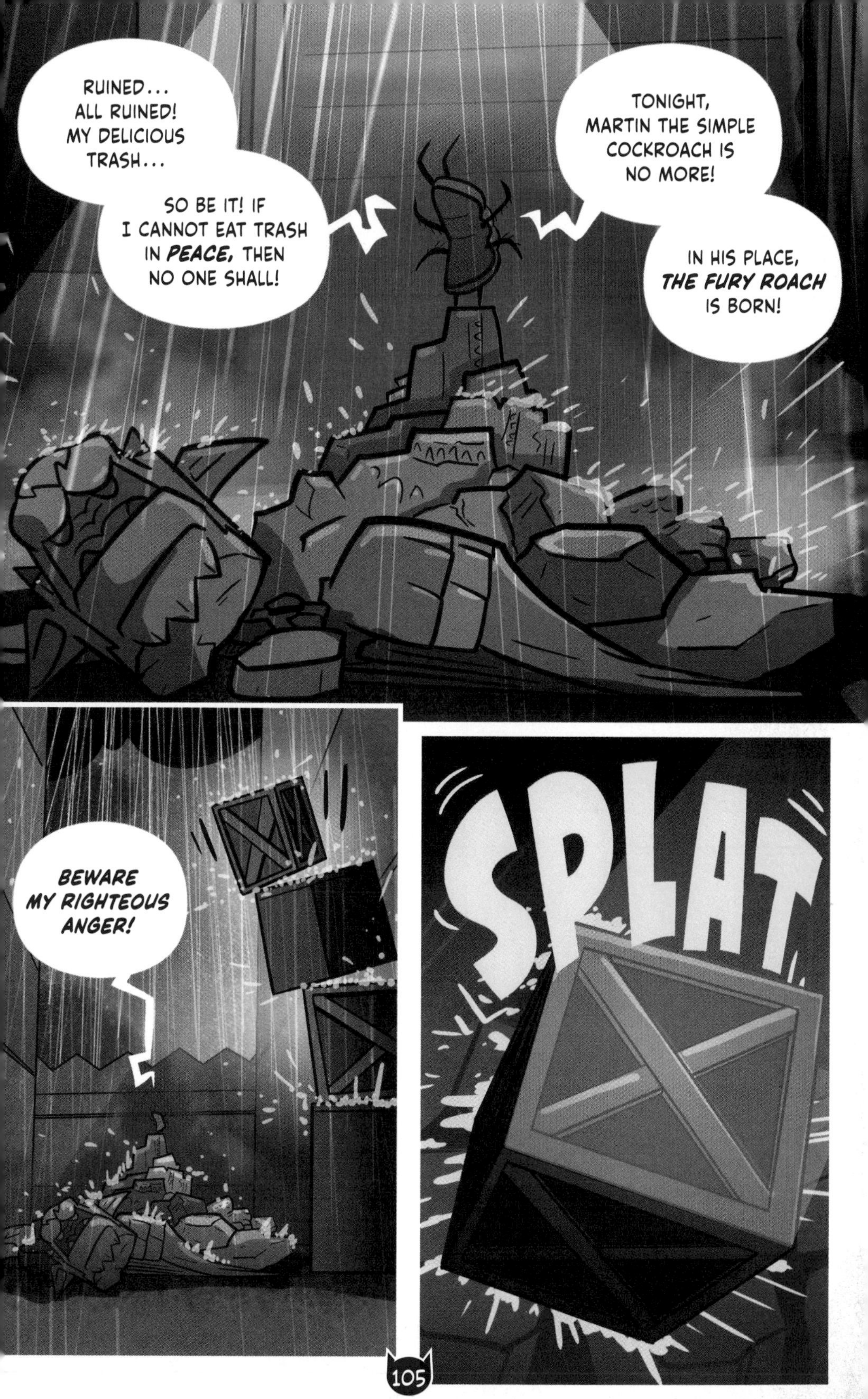
RUINED... ALL RUINED! MY DELICIOUS TRASH...
SO BE IT! IF I CANNOT EAT TRASH IN *PEACE,* THEN NO ONE SHALL!
TONIGHT, MARTIN THE SIMPLE COCKROACH IS NO MORE!
IN HIS PLACE, *THE FURY ROACH* IS BORN!
BEWARE MY RIGHTEOUS ANGER!
SPLAT

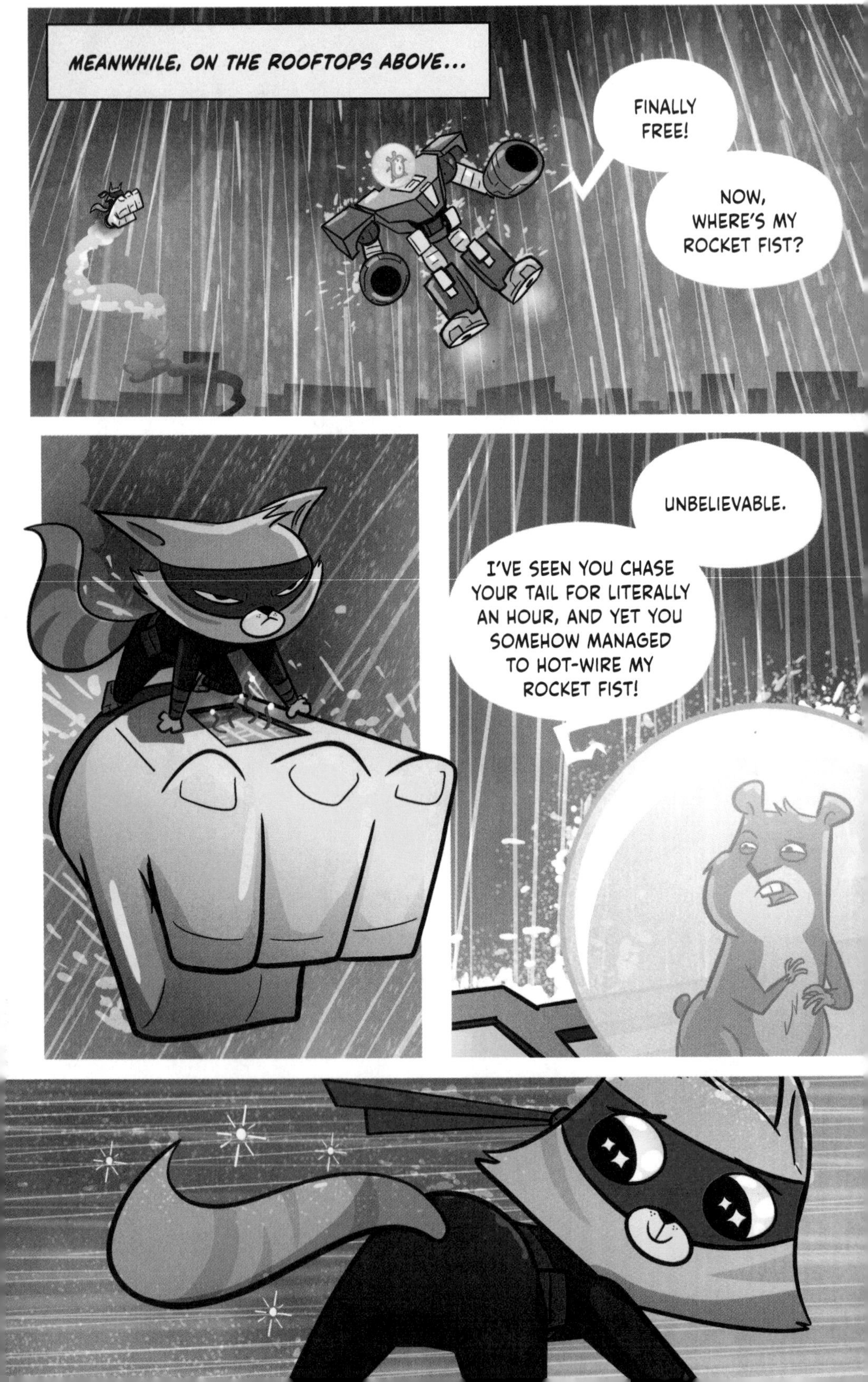

MEANWHILE, ON THE ROOFTOPS ABOVE...
FINALLY FREE!
NOW, WHERE'S MY ROCKET FIST?
UNBELIEVABLE.
I'VE SEEN YOU CHASE YOUR TAIL FOR LITERALLY AN HOUR, AND YET YOU SOMEHOW MANAGED TO HOT-WIRE MY ROCKET FIST!

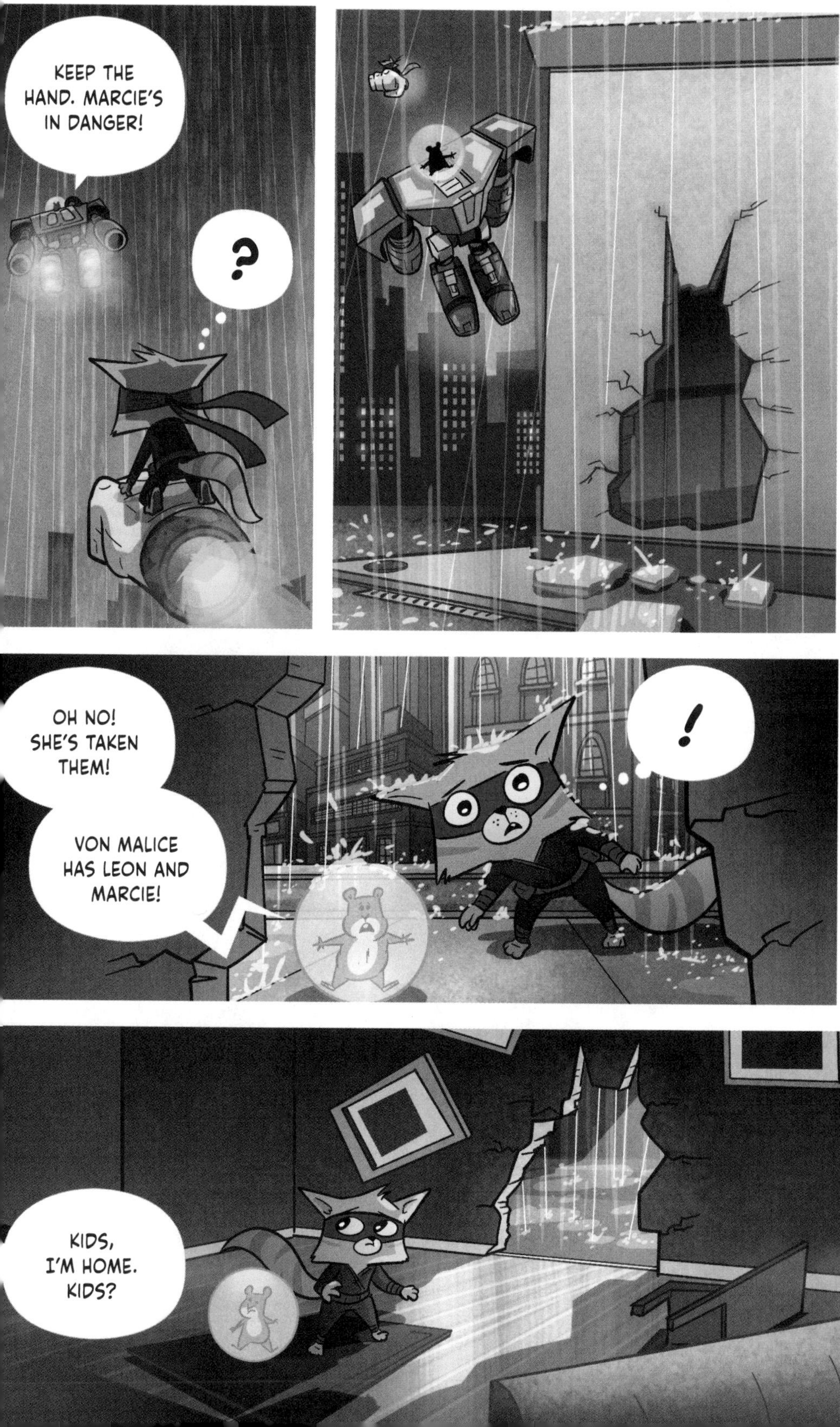
KEEP THE HAND. MARCIE'S IN DANGER!
?
OH NO! SHE'S TAKEN THEM!
!
VON MALICE HAS LEON AND MARCIE!
KIDS, I'M HOME. KIDS?

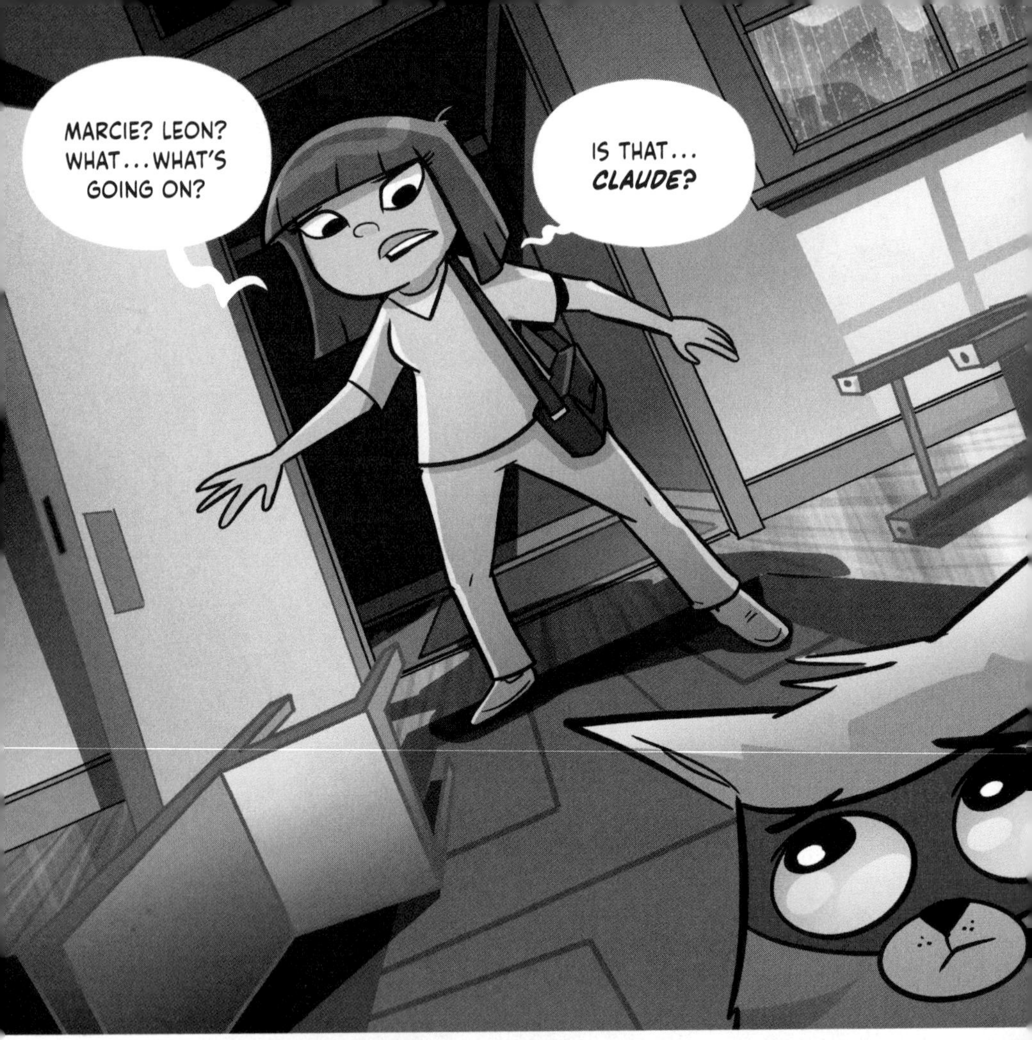
MARCIE? LEON? WHAT...WHAT'S GOING ON?
IS THAT... *CLAUDE?*

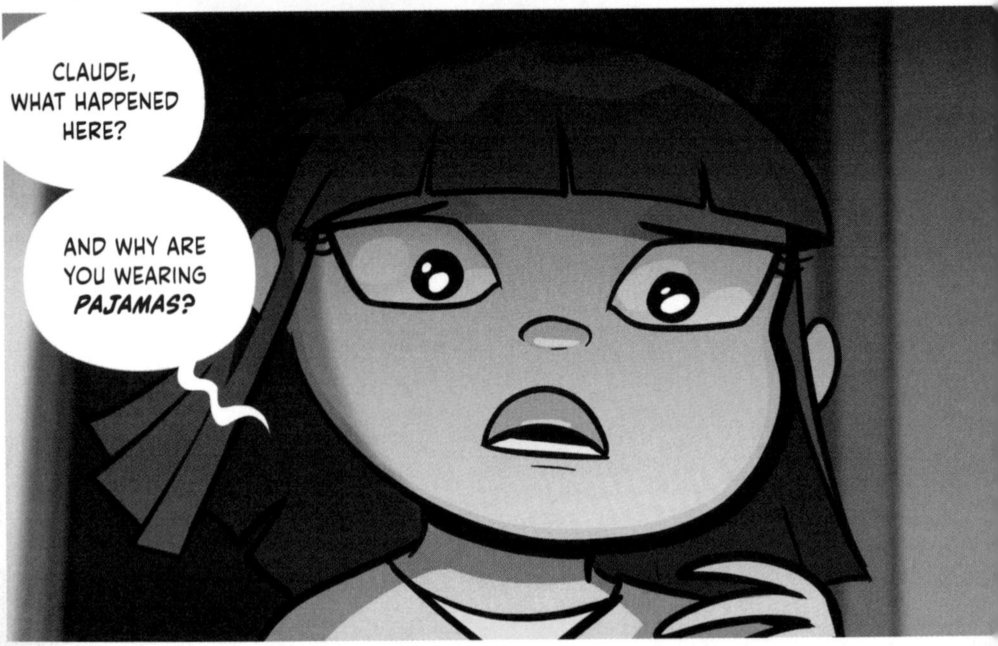
CLAUDE, WHAT HAPPENED HERE?
AND WHY ARE YOU WEARING *PAJAMAS?*

Chapter 5: *Family Squabbles*

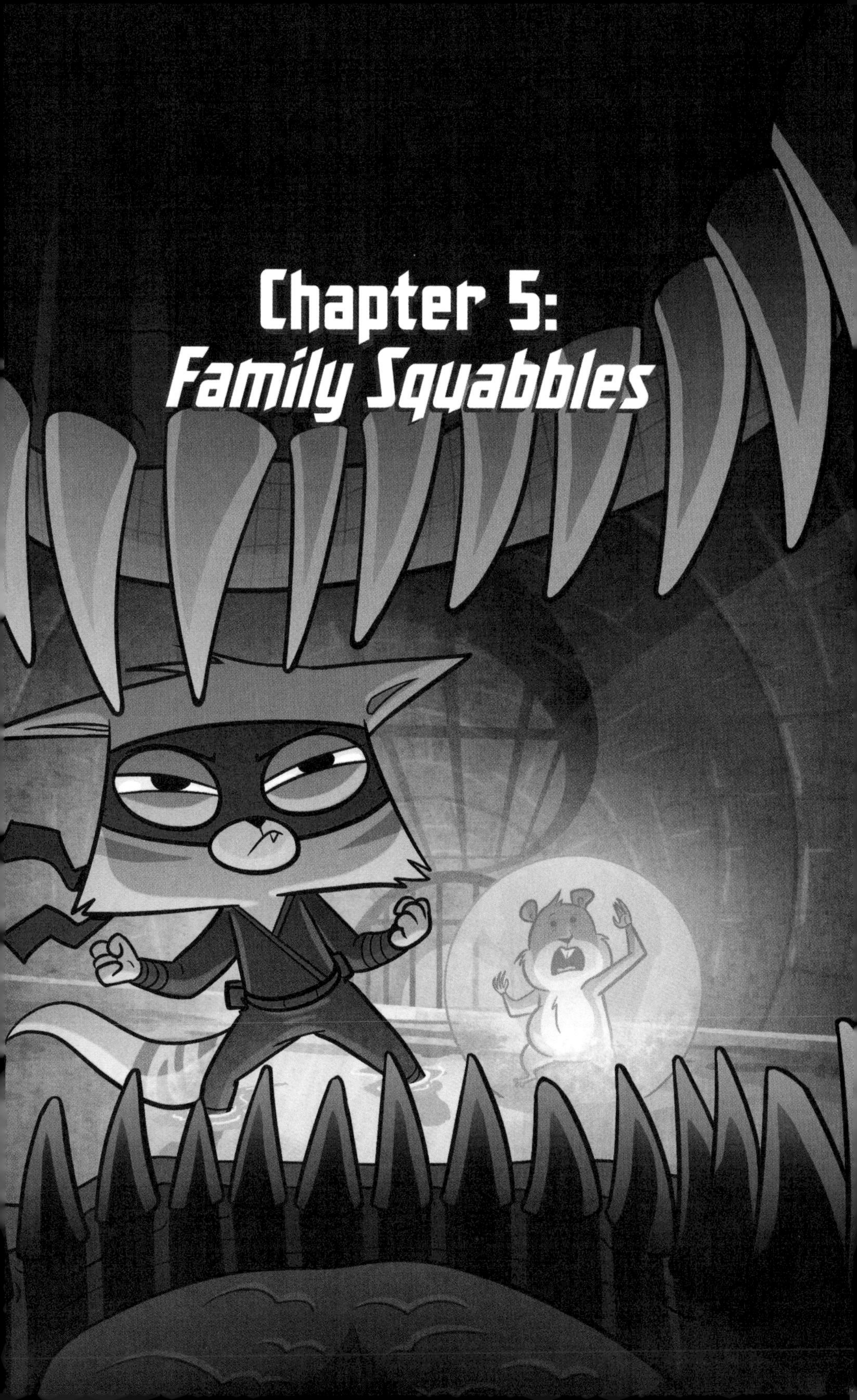

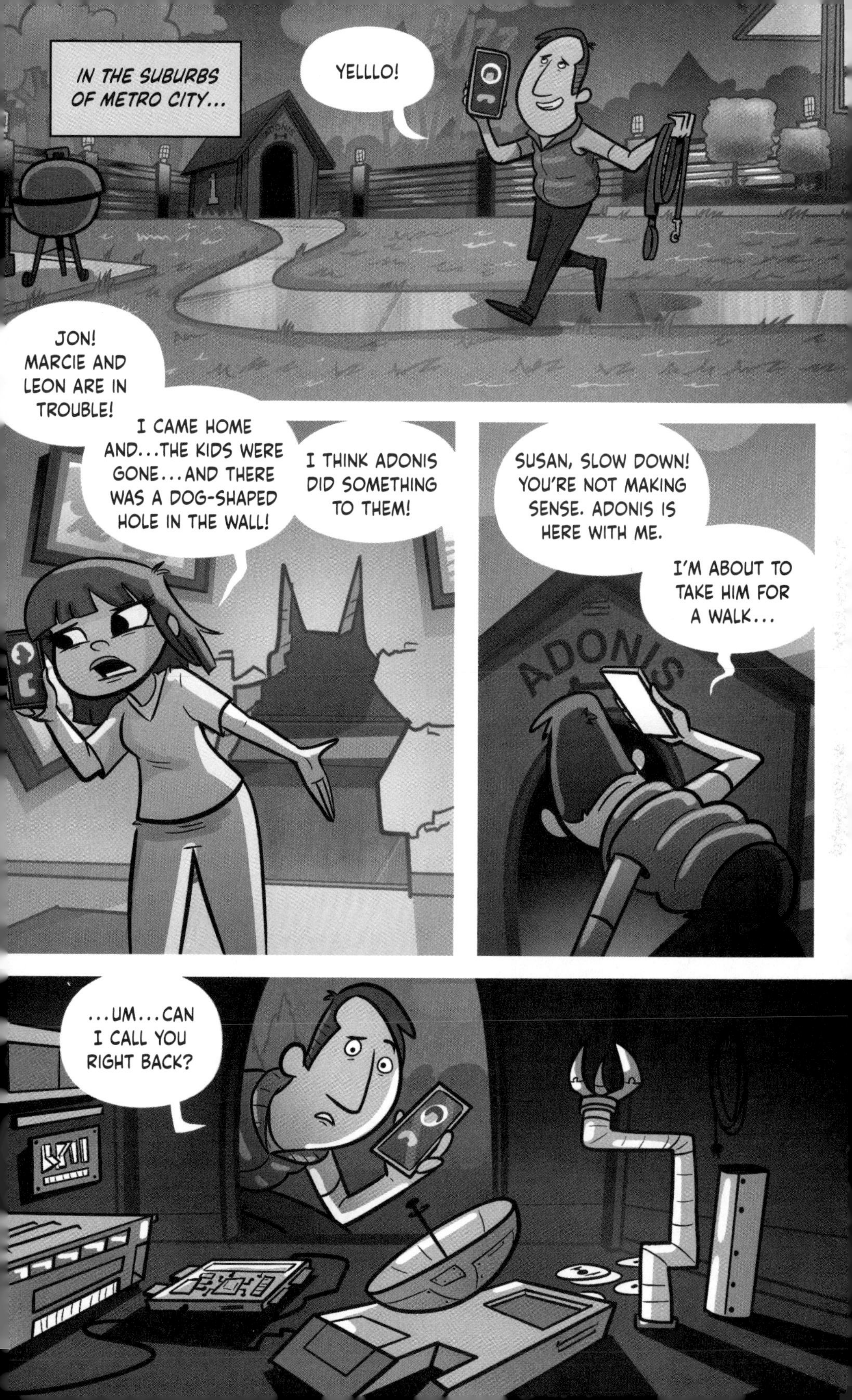
IN THE SUBURBS OF METRO CITY...
BZZZ
YELLLO!
ADONIS
JON! MARCIE AND LEON ARE IN TROUBLE!
I CAME HOME AND...THE KIDS WERE GONE...AND THERE WAS A DOG-SHAPED HOLE IN THE WALL!
I THINK ADONIS DID SOMETHING TO THEM!
SUSAN, SLOW DOWN! YOU'RE NOT MAKING SENSE. ADONIS IS HERE WITH ME.
I'M ABOUT TO TAKE HIM FOR A WALK...
ADONIS
...UM...CAN I CALL YOU RIGHT BACK?

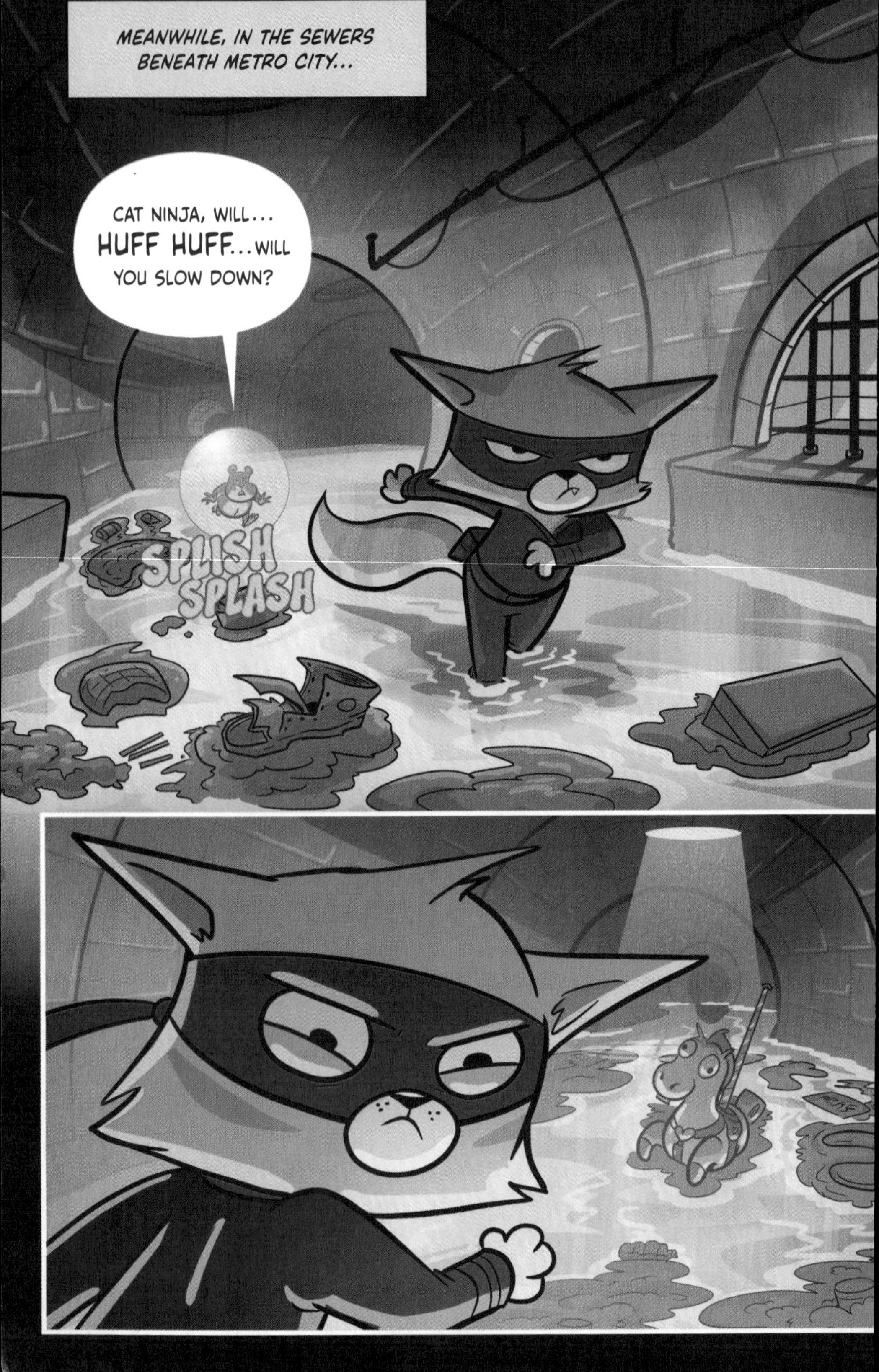
MEANWHILE, IN THE SEWERS BENEATH METRO CITY...
CAT NINJA, WILL... HUFF HUFF... WILL YOU SLOW DOWN?
SPLISH SPLASH

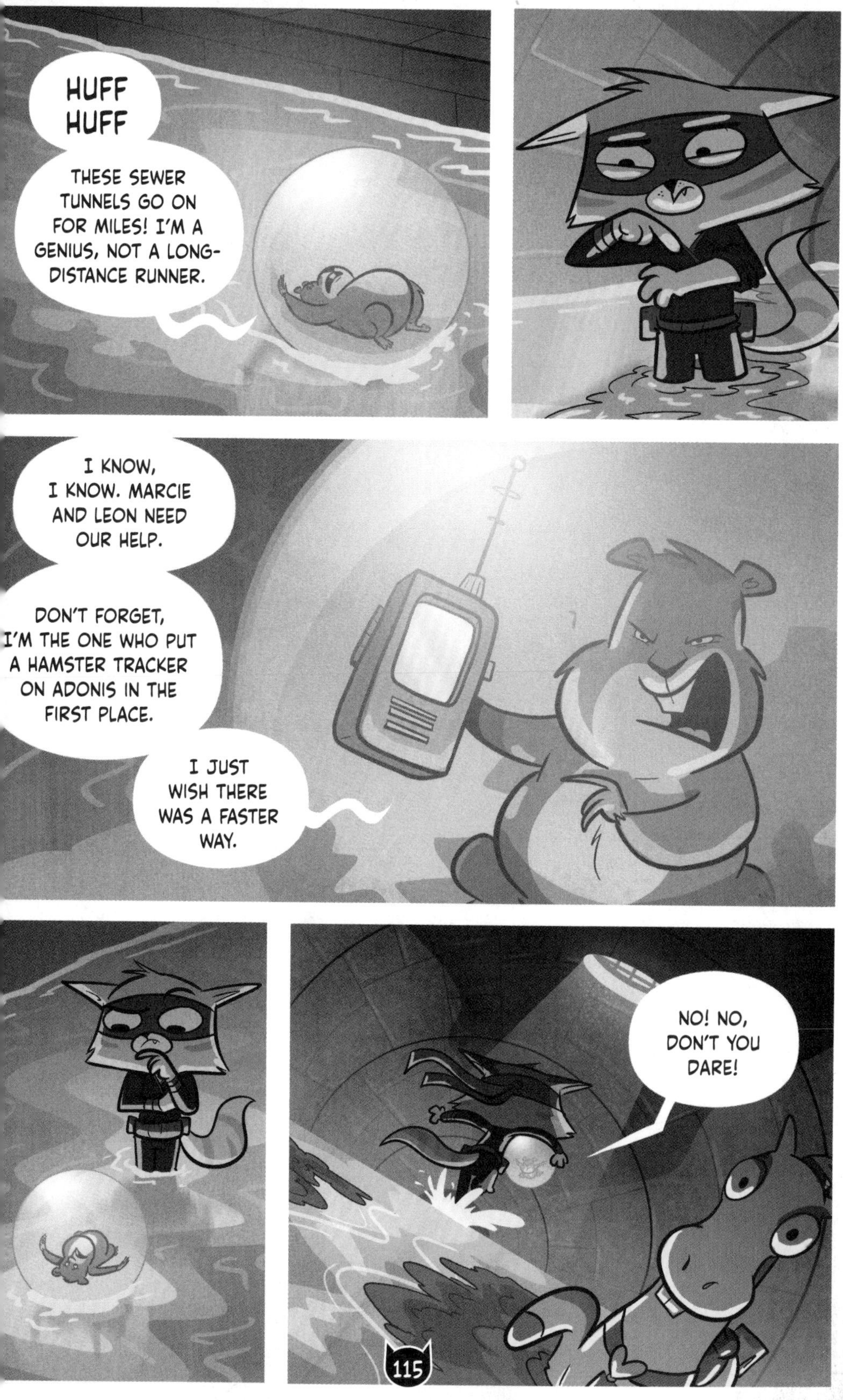
HUFF
HUFF
THESE SEWER TUNNELS GO ON FOR MILES! I'M A GENIUS, NOT A LONG-DISTANCE RUNNER.
I KNOW, I KNOW. MARCIE AND LEON NEED OUR HELP.
DON'T FORGET, I'M THE ONE WHO PUT A HAMSTER TRACKER ON ADONIS IN THE FIRST PLACE.
I JUST WISH THERE WAS A FASTER WAY.
NO! NO, DON'T YOU DARE!

PUT ME DOWN THIS INSTANT!

I AM A *CRIMINAL MASTERMIND* AND WILL *NOT* BE CARRIED!

YOU REALLY ARE THE WORST.

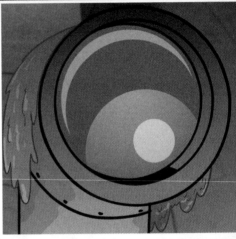

CAT NINJA. RIGHT ON SCHEDULE.

AND WHAT'S THIS? A NEW *SIDEKICK*?

MASTER HAMSTER HAS FALLEN TO A NEW LOW.

SEWER CROC

POISON GAS

SPIKEY TRAP

LET'S SEE IF WE CAN'T SOFTEN THEM UP A BIT BEFORE THE MAIN EVENT.

116

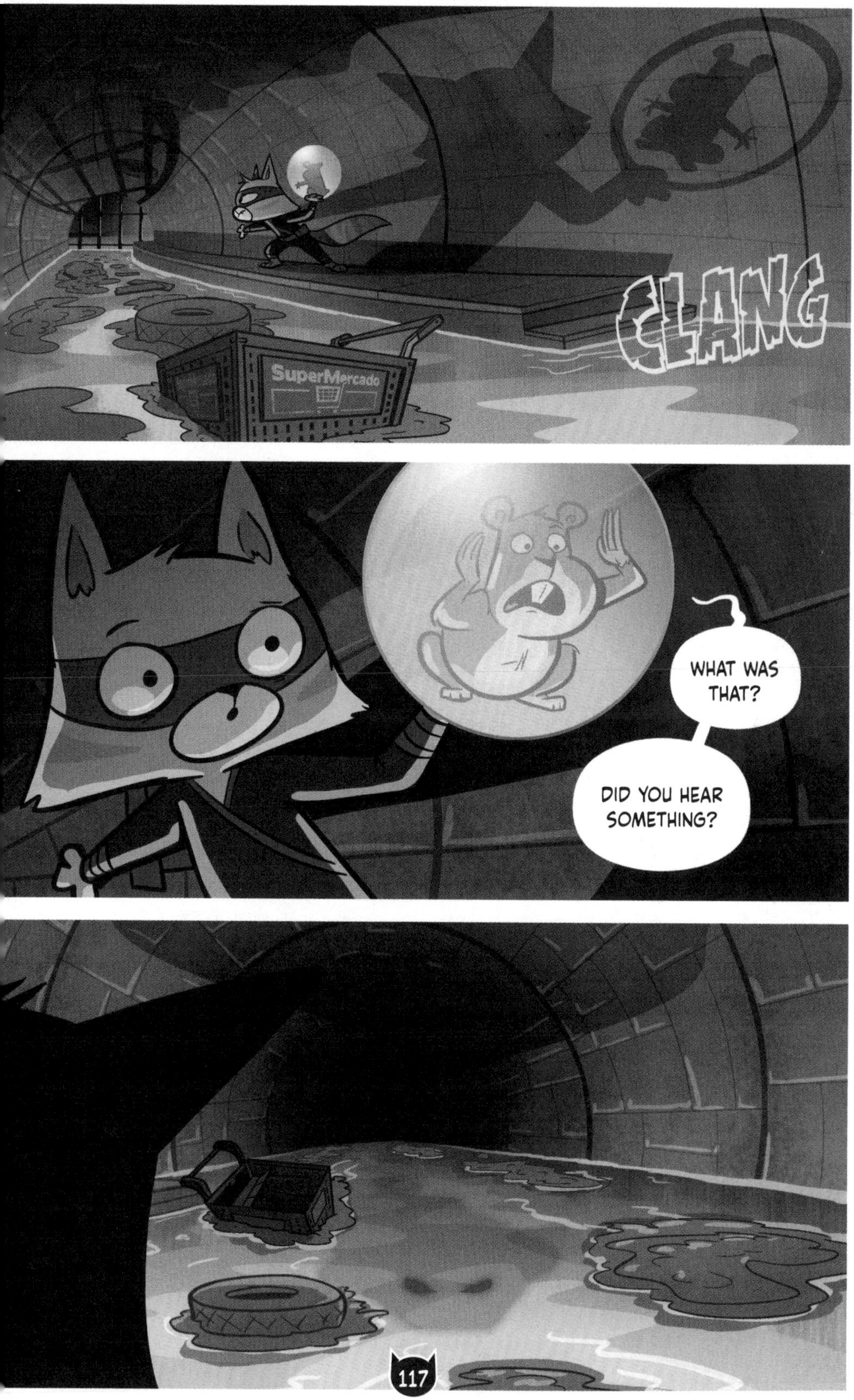
CLANG
SuperMercado
WHAT WAS THAT?
DID YOU HEAR SOMETHING?

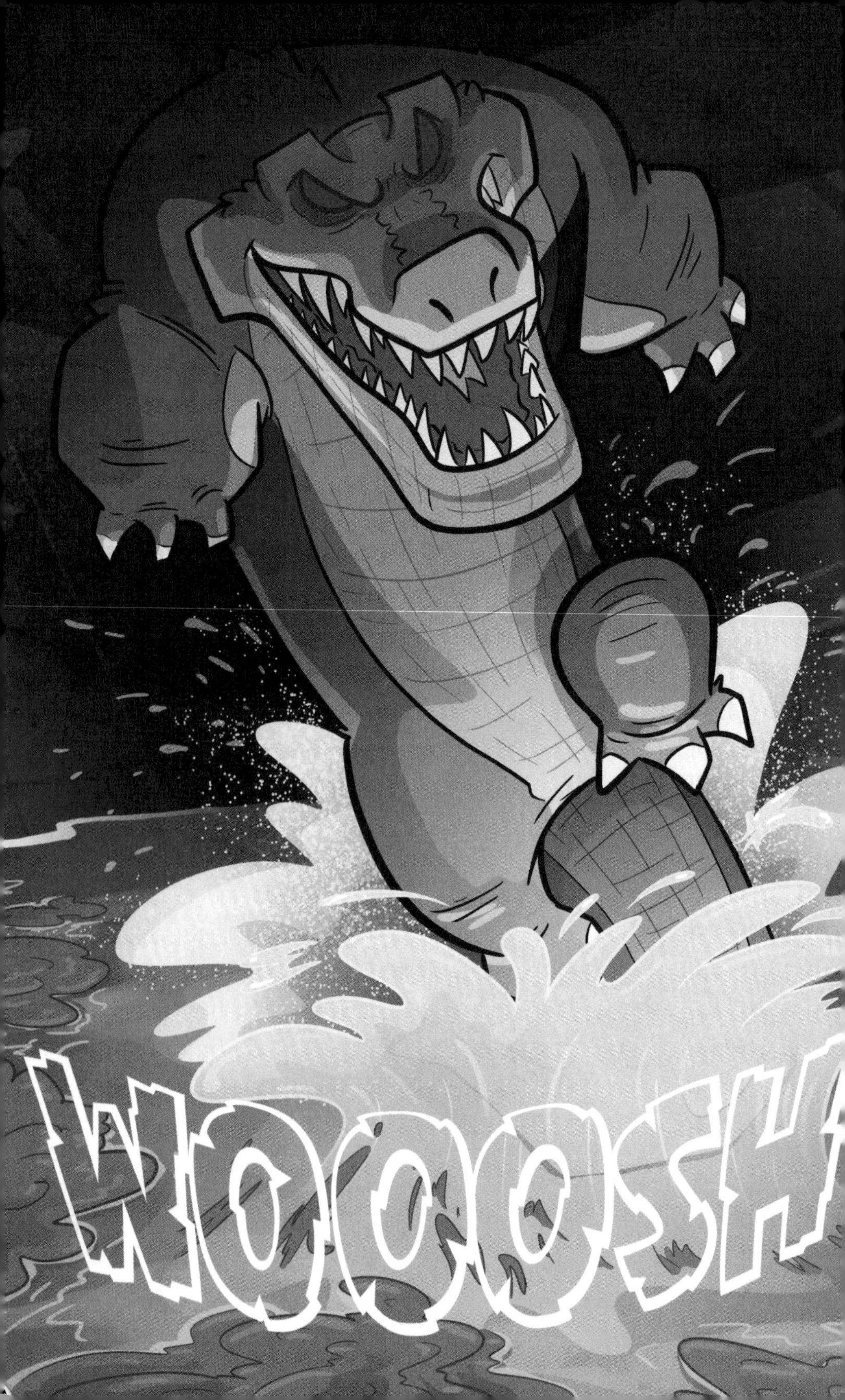
WOOOSH

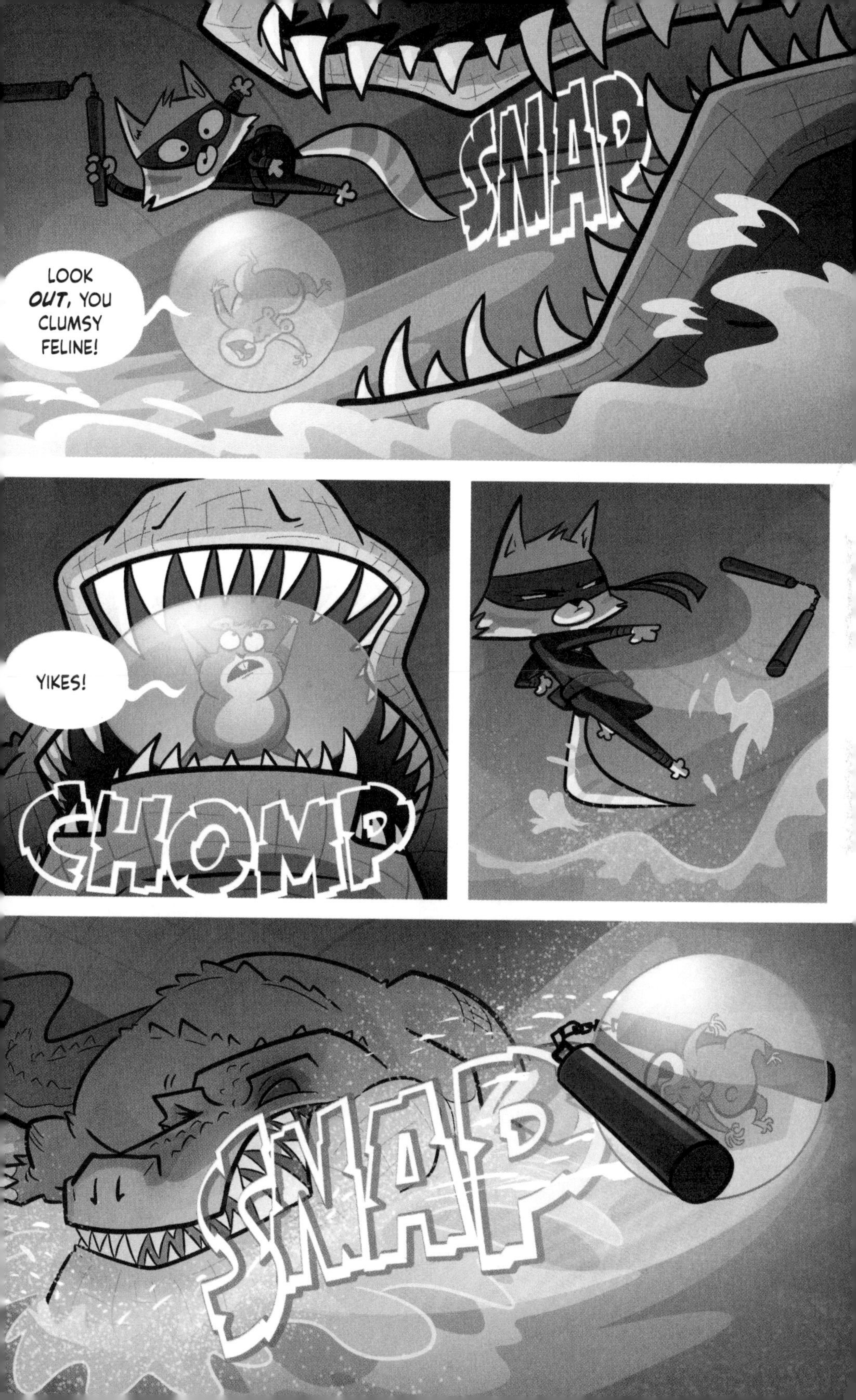
SNAP
LOOK OUT, YOU CLUMSY FELINE!
YIKES!
CHOMP
SNAP

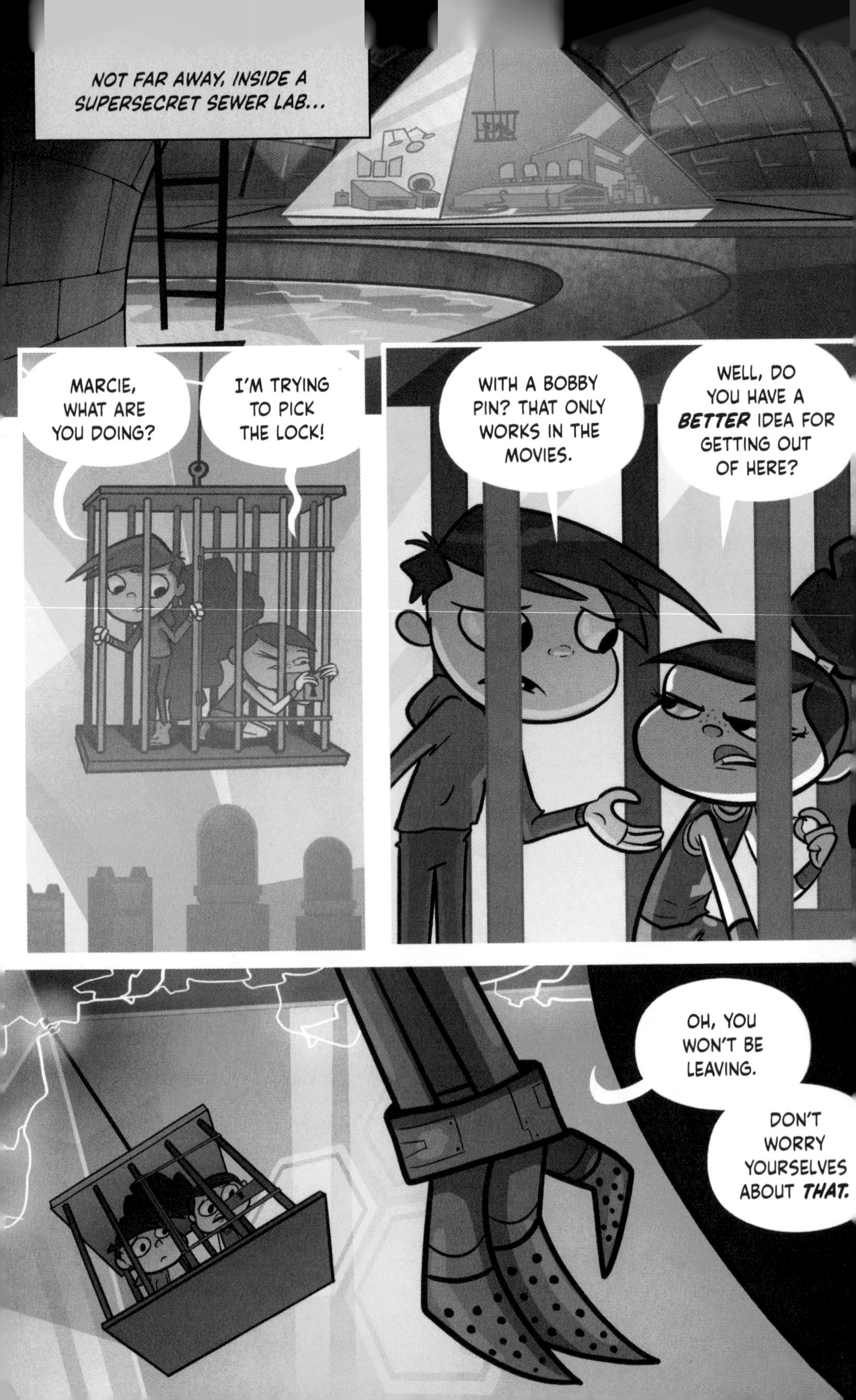
NOT FAR AWAY, INSIDE A SUPERSECRET SEWER LAB...
MARCIE, WHAT ARE YOU DOING?
I'M TRYING TO PICK THE LOCK!
WITH A BOBBY PIN? THAT ONLY WORKS IN THE MOVIES.
WELL, DO YOU HAVE A BETTER IDEA FOR GETTING OUT OF HERE?
OH, YOU WON'T BE LEAVING.
DON'T WORRY YOURSELVES ABOUT THAT.

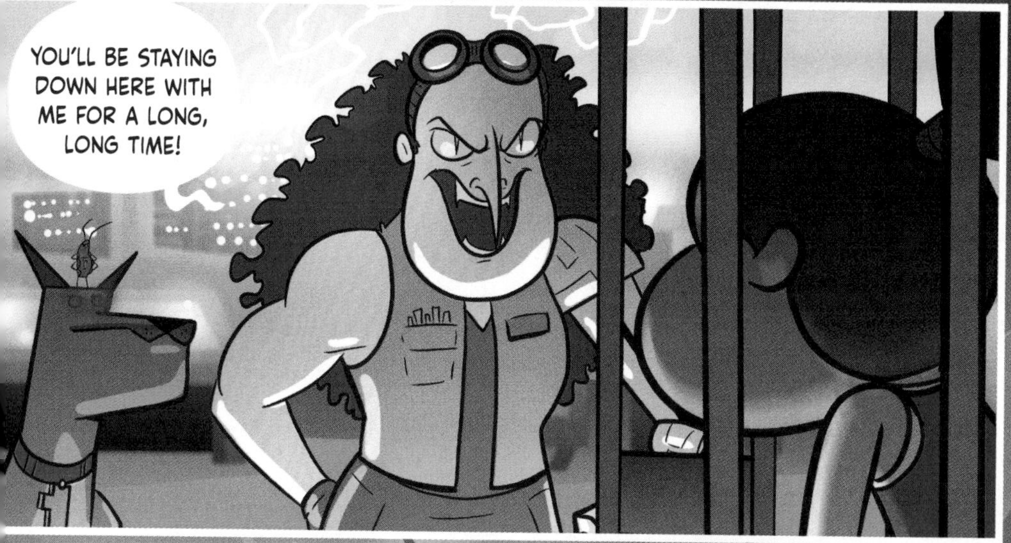
YOU'LL BE STAYING DOWN HERE WITH ME FOR A LONG, LONG TIME!

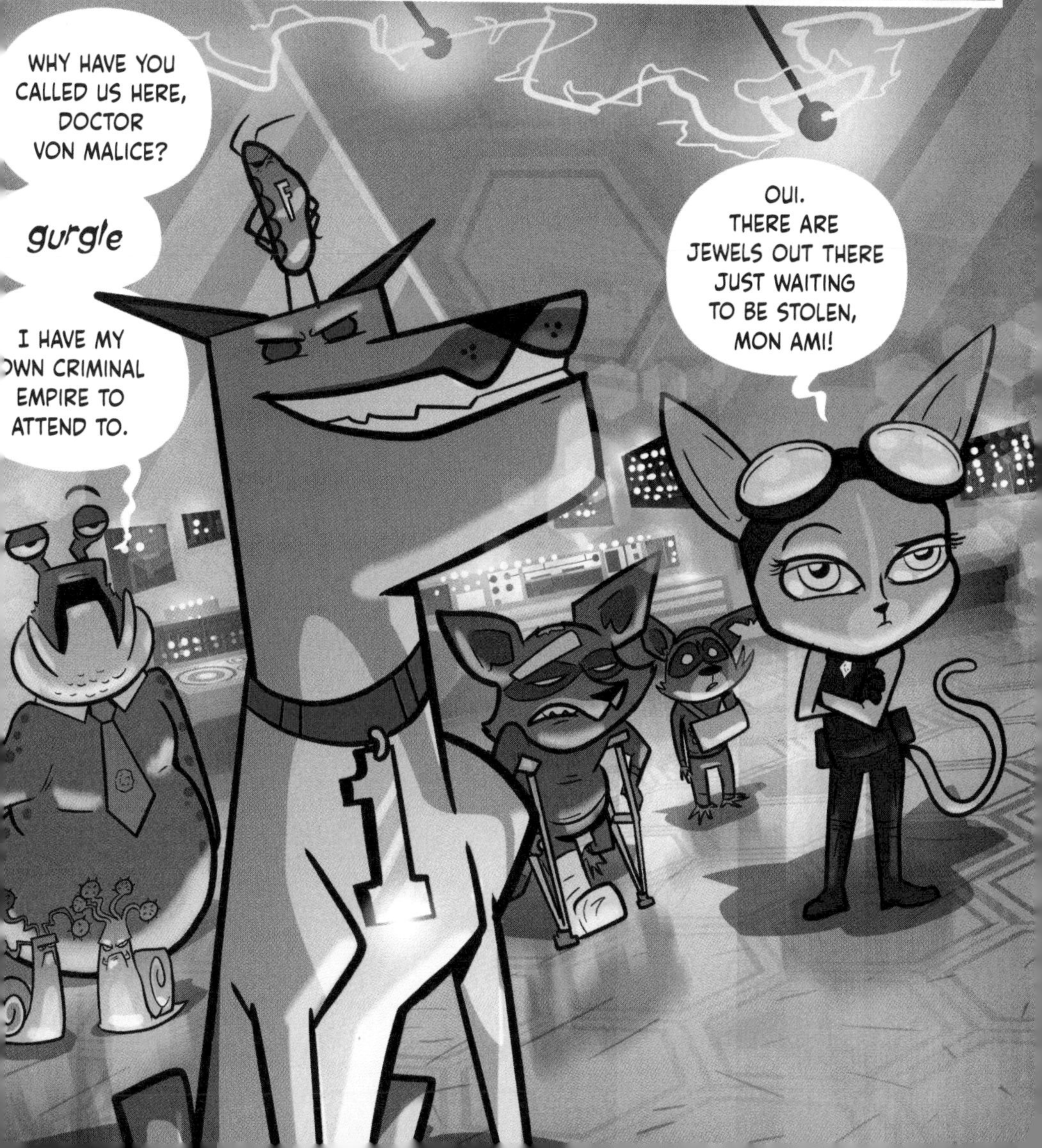
WHY HAVE YOU CALLED US HERE, DOCTOR VON MALICE?
gurgle
I HAVE MY OWN CRIMINAL EMPIRE TO ATTEND TO.
OUI. THERE ARE JEWELS OUT THERE JUST WAITING TO BE STOLEN, MON AMI!

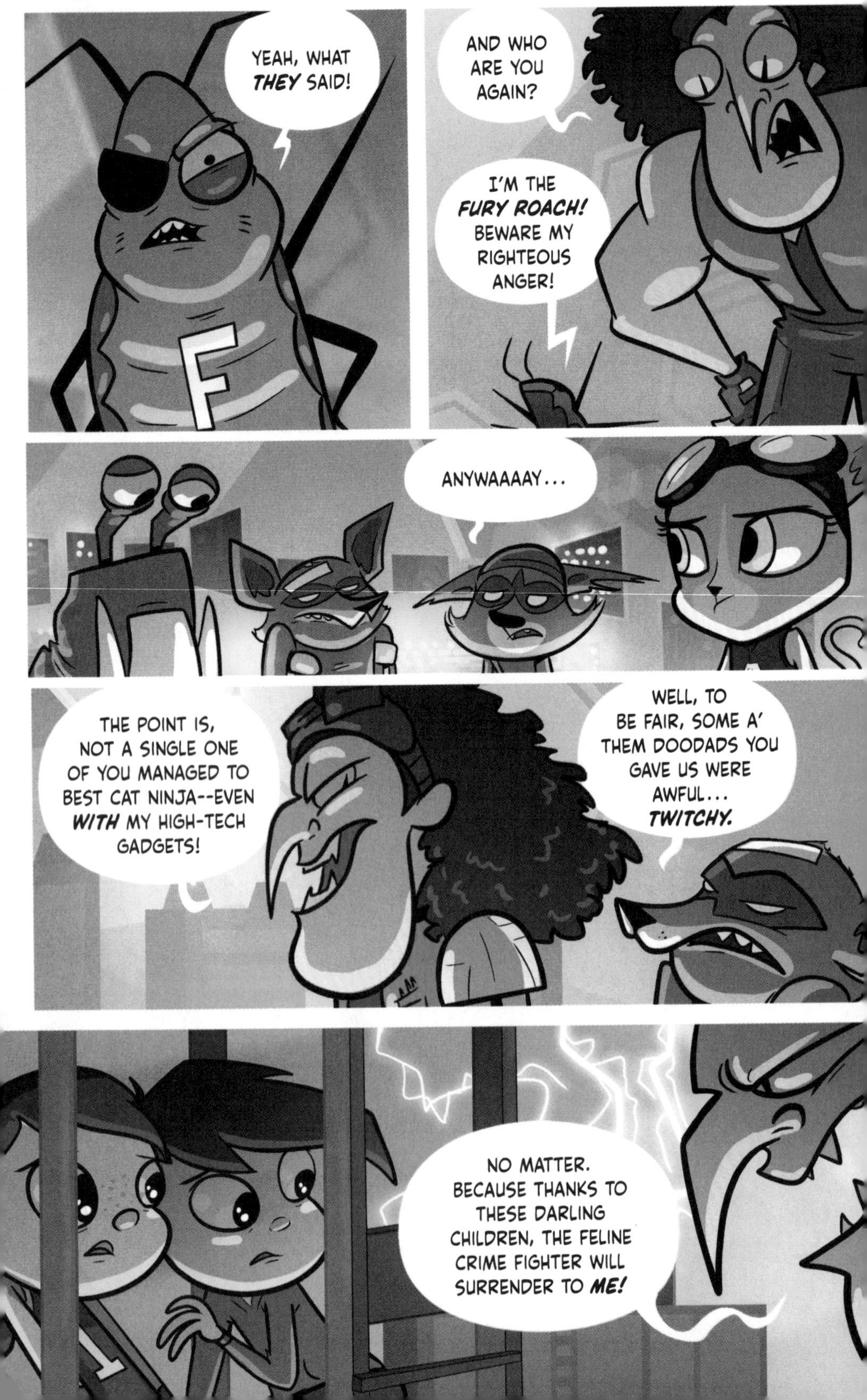
YEAH, WHAT *THEY* SAID!
AND WHO ARE YOU AGAIN?
I'M THE *FURY ROACH!* BEWARE MY RIGHTEOUS ANGER!
ANYWAAAAY...
THE POINT IS, NOT A SINGLE ONE OF YOU MANAGED TO BEST CAT NINJA--EVEN *WITH* MY HIGH-TECH GADGETS!
WELL, TO BE FAIR, SOME A' THEM DOODADS YOU GAVE US WERE AWFUL... *TWITCHY.*
NO MATTER. BECAUSE THANKS TO THESE DARLING CHILDREN, THE FELINE CRIME FIGHTER WILL SURRENDER TO *ME!*

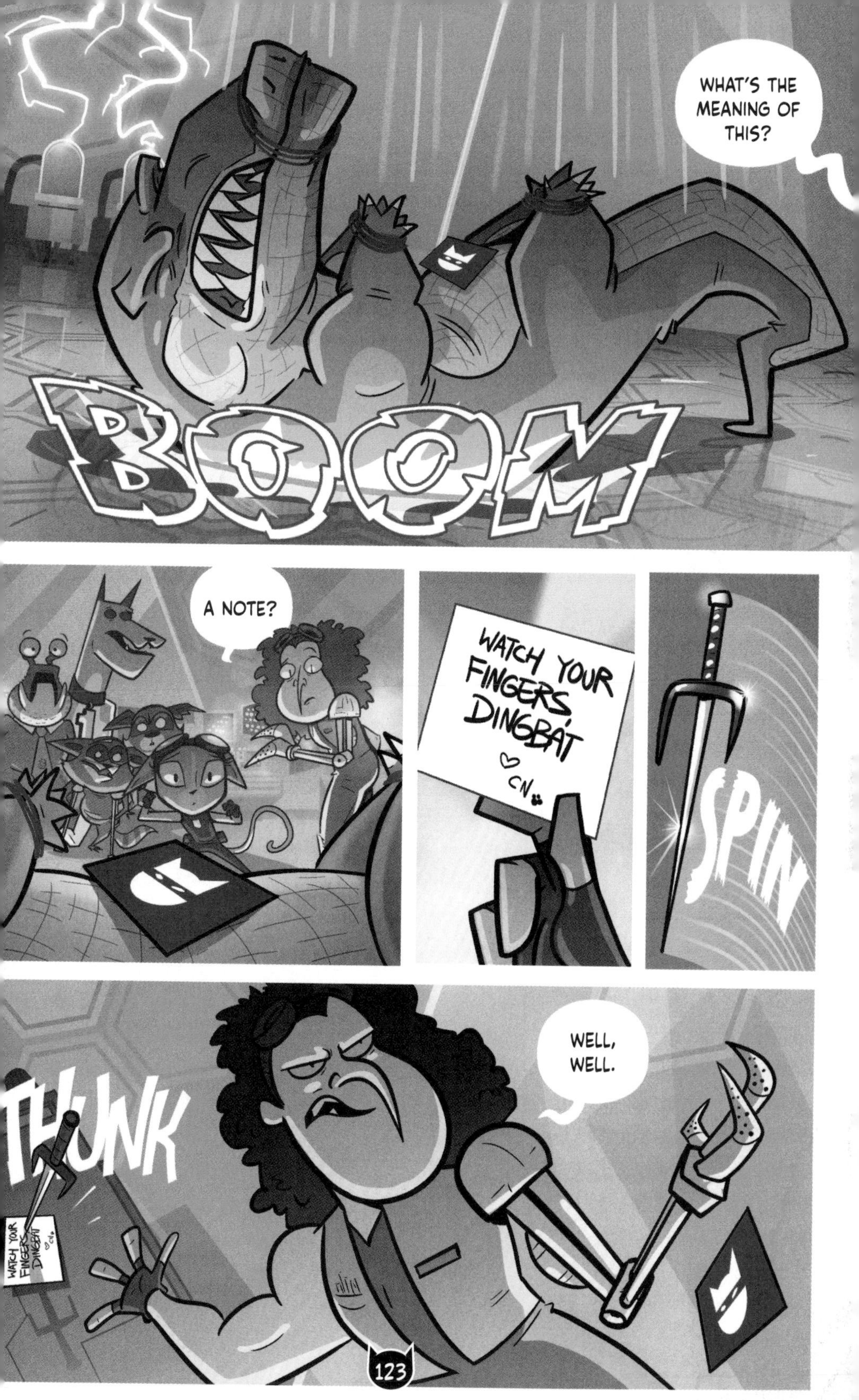
WHAT'S THE MEANING OF THIS?
BOOM
A NOTE?
WATCH YOUR FINGERS, DINGBAT
CN
SPIN
THUNK
WATCH YOUR FINGERS, DINGBAT
WELL, WELL.

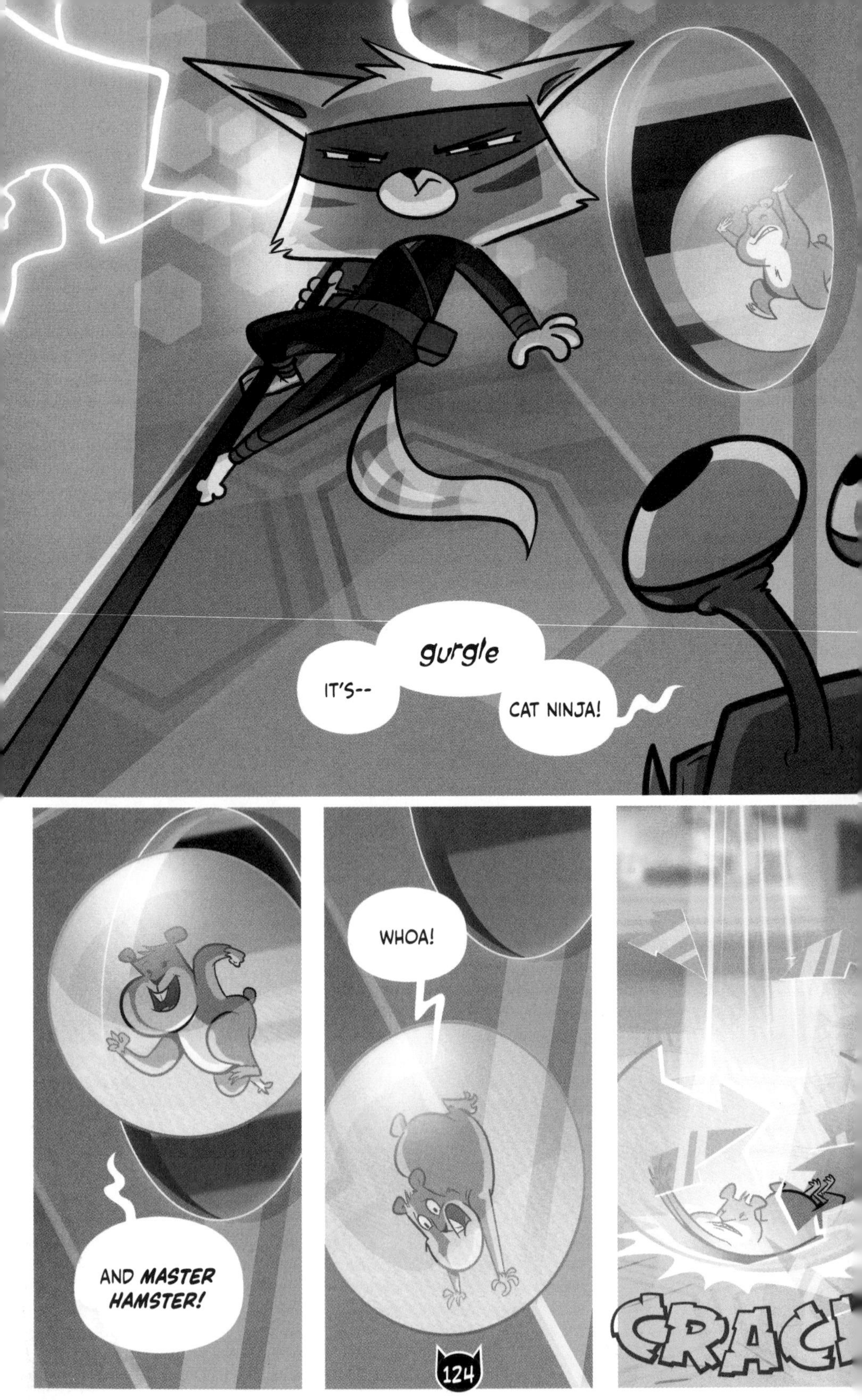
IT'S--
gurgle
CAT NINJA!
AND MASTER HAMSTER!
WHOA!
CRAC

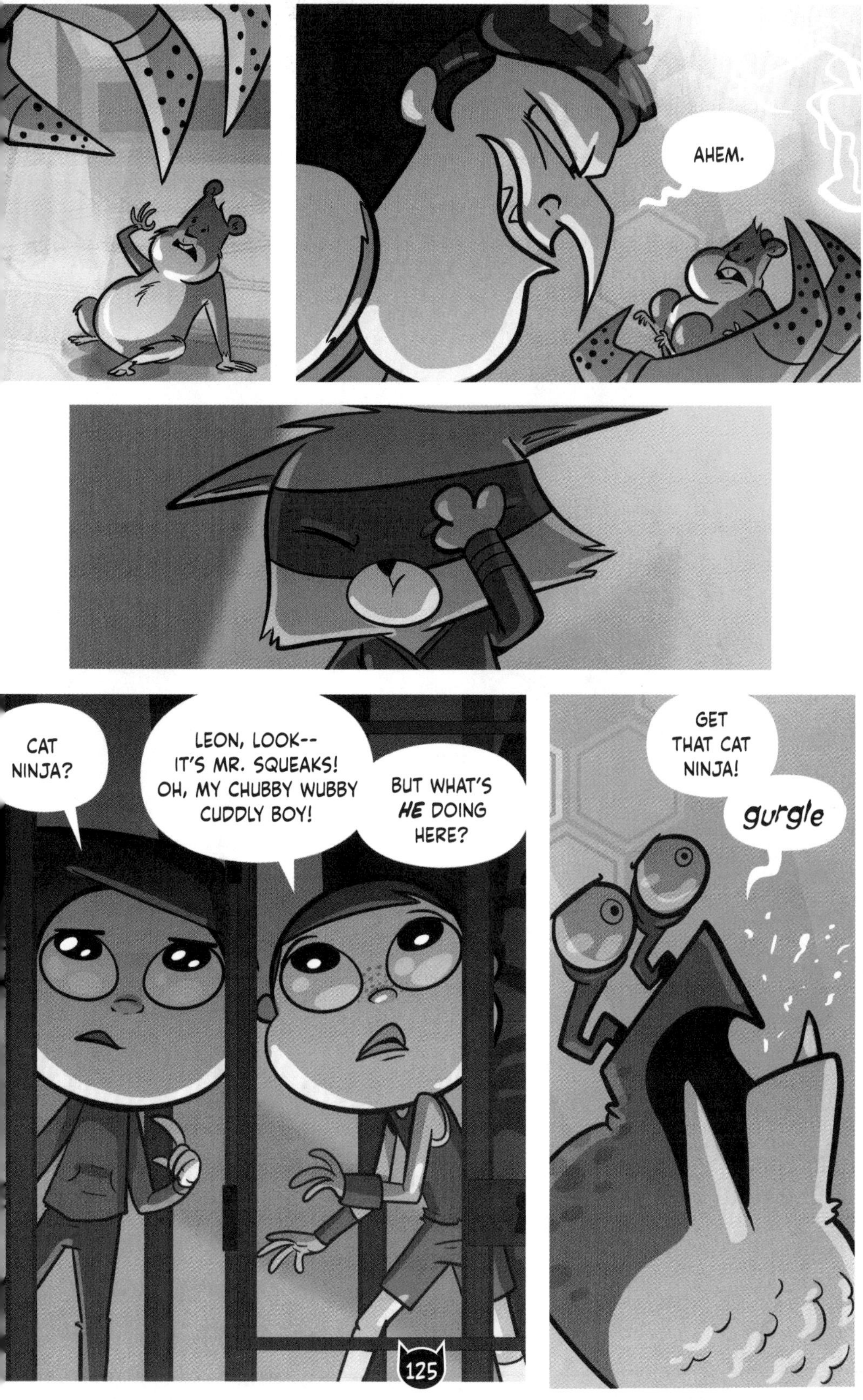
AHEM.
CAT NINJA?
LEON, LOOK-- IT'S MR. SQUEAKS! OH, MY CHUBBY WUBBY CUDDLY BOY!
BUT WHAT'S *HE* DOING HERE?
GET THAT CAT NINJA!
gurgle

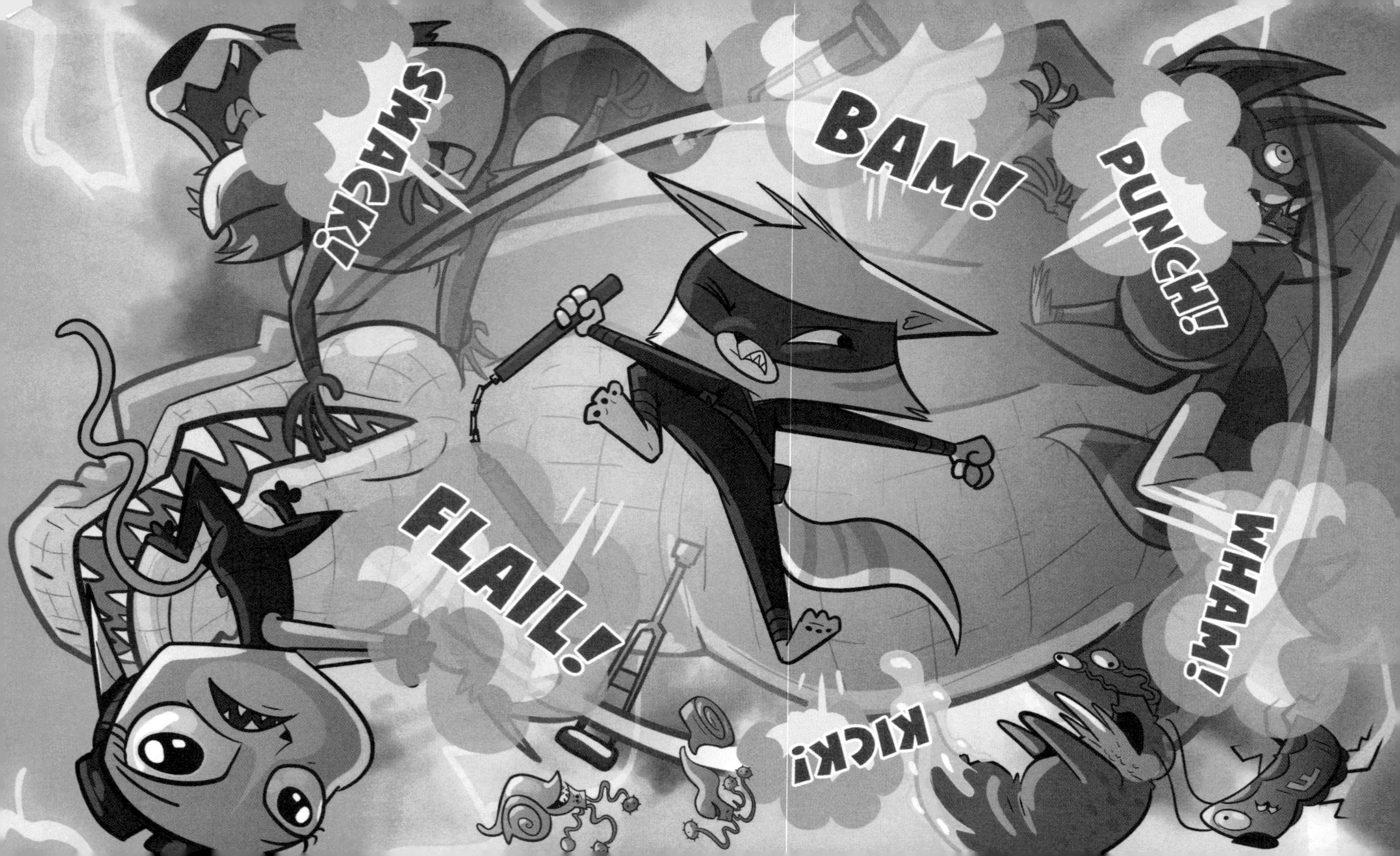
SMACK!
BAM!
PUNCH!
FLAIL!
WHAM!
KICK!

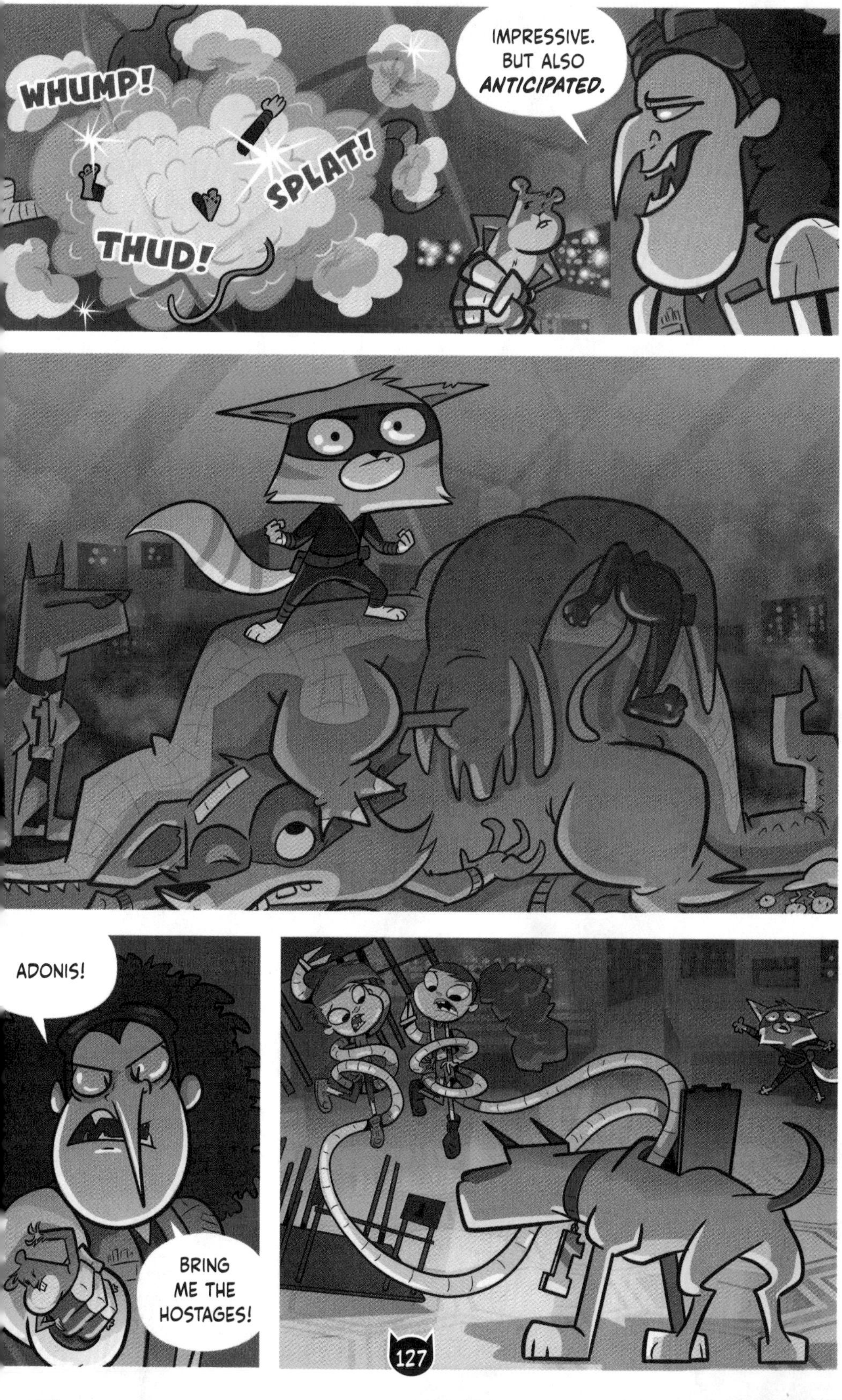
WHUMP!
SPLAT!
THUD!
IMPRESSIVE. BUT ALSO ANTICIPATED.
ADONIS!
BRING ME THE HOSTAGES!

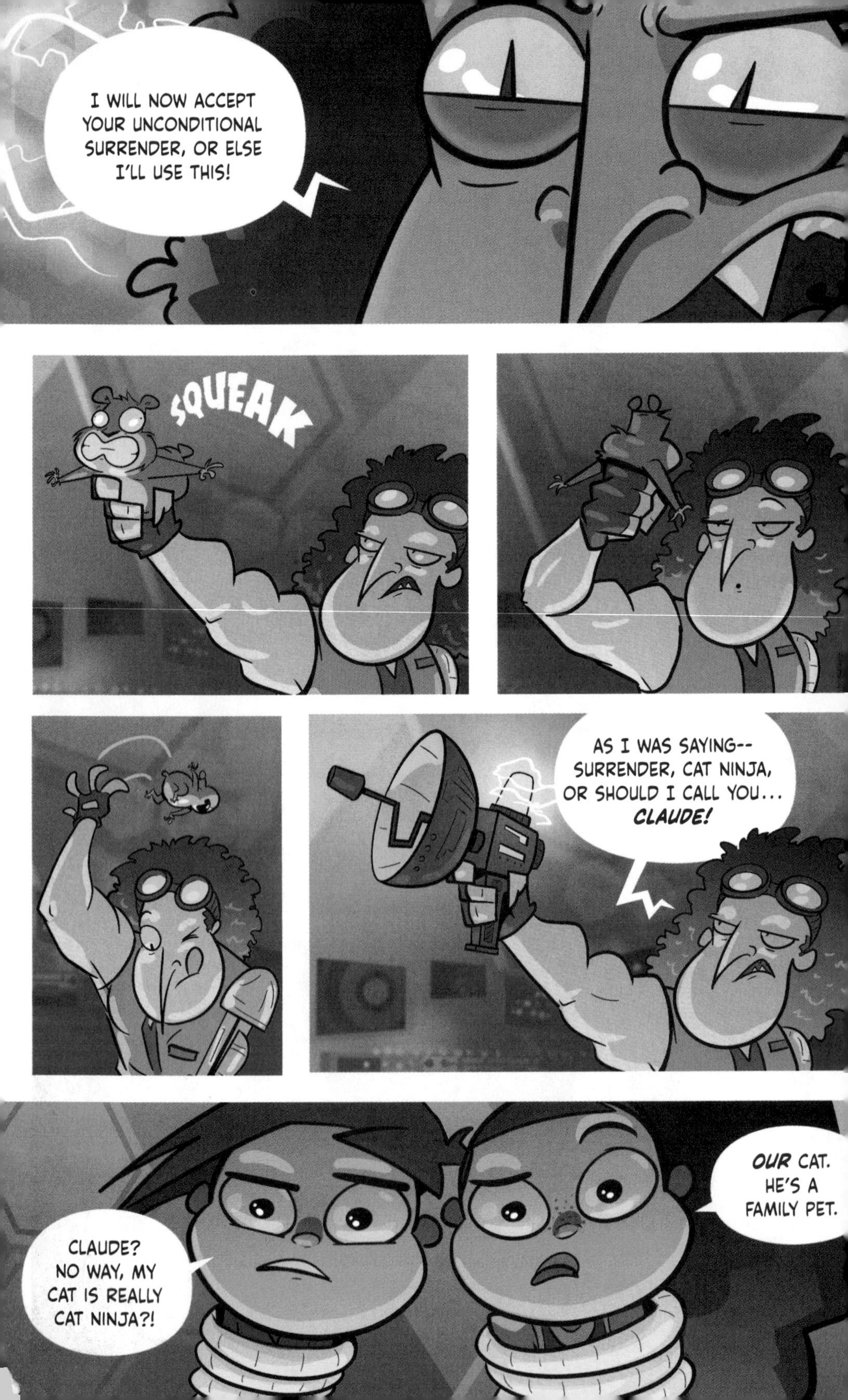
I WILL NOW ACCEPT YOUR UNCONDITIONAL SURRENDER, OR ELSE I'LL USE THIS!
SQUEAK
AS I WAS SAYING-- SURRENDER, CAT NINJA, OR SHOULD I CALL YOU... *CLAUDE!*
OUR CAT. HE'S A FAMILY PET.
CLAUDE? NO WAY, MY CAT IS REALLY CAT NINJA?!

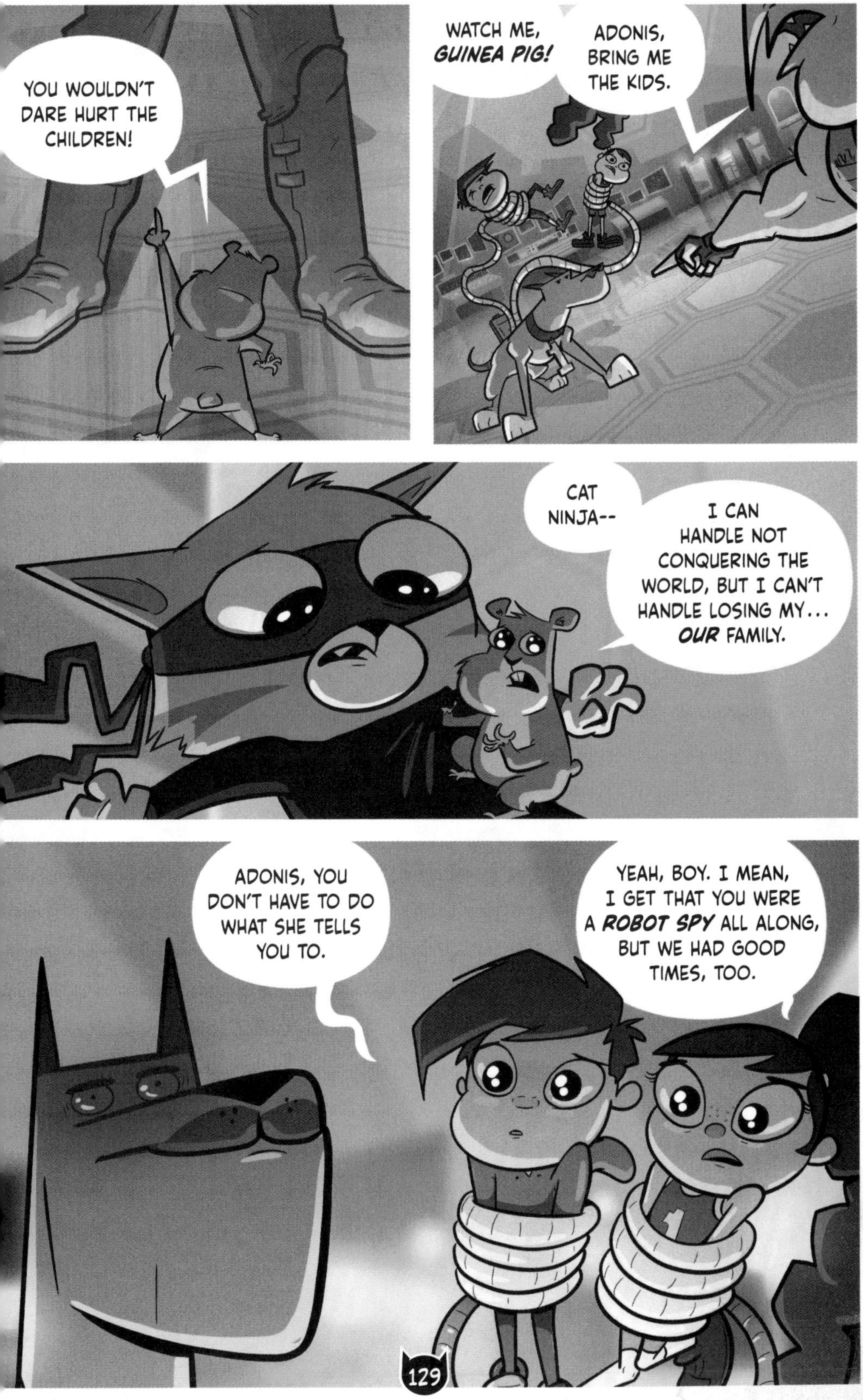
YOU WOULDN'T DARE HURT THE CHILDREN!
WATCH ME, *GUINEA PIG!*
ADONIS, BRING ME THE KIDS.
CAT NINJA--
I CAN HANDLE NOT CONQUERING THE WORLD, BUT I CAN'T HANDLE LOSING MY... *OUR* FAMILY.
ADONIS, YOU DON'T HAVE TO DO WHAT SHE TELLS YOU TO.
YEAH, BOY. I MEAN, I GET THAT YOU WERE A *ROBOT SPY* ALL ALONG, BUT WE HAD GOOD TIMES, TOO.

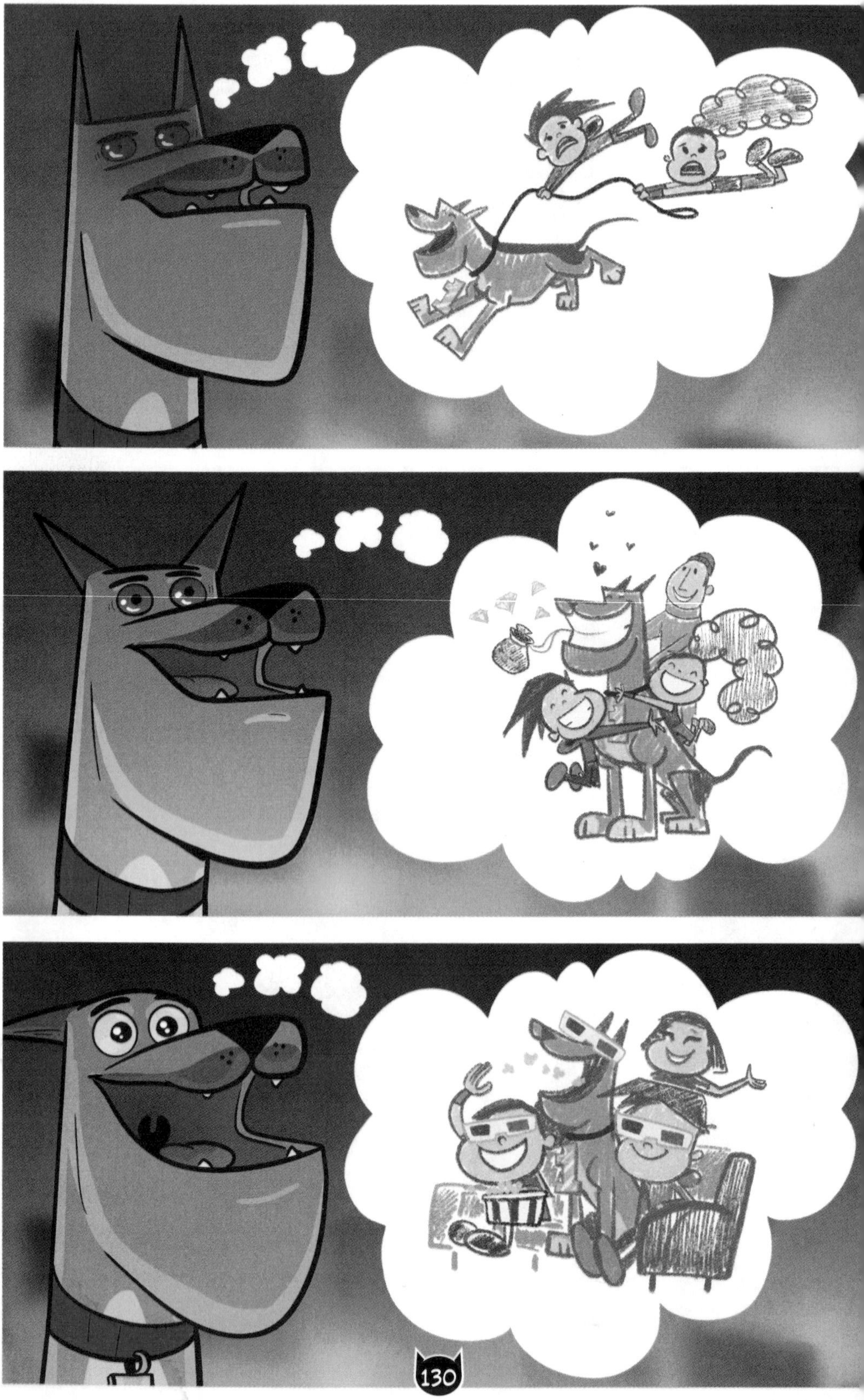

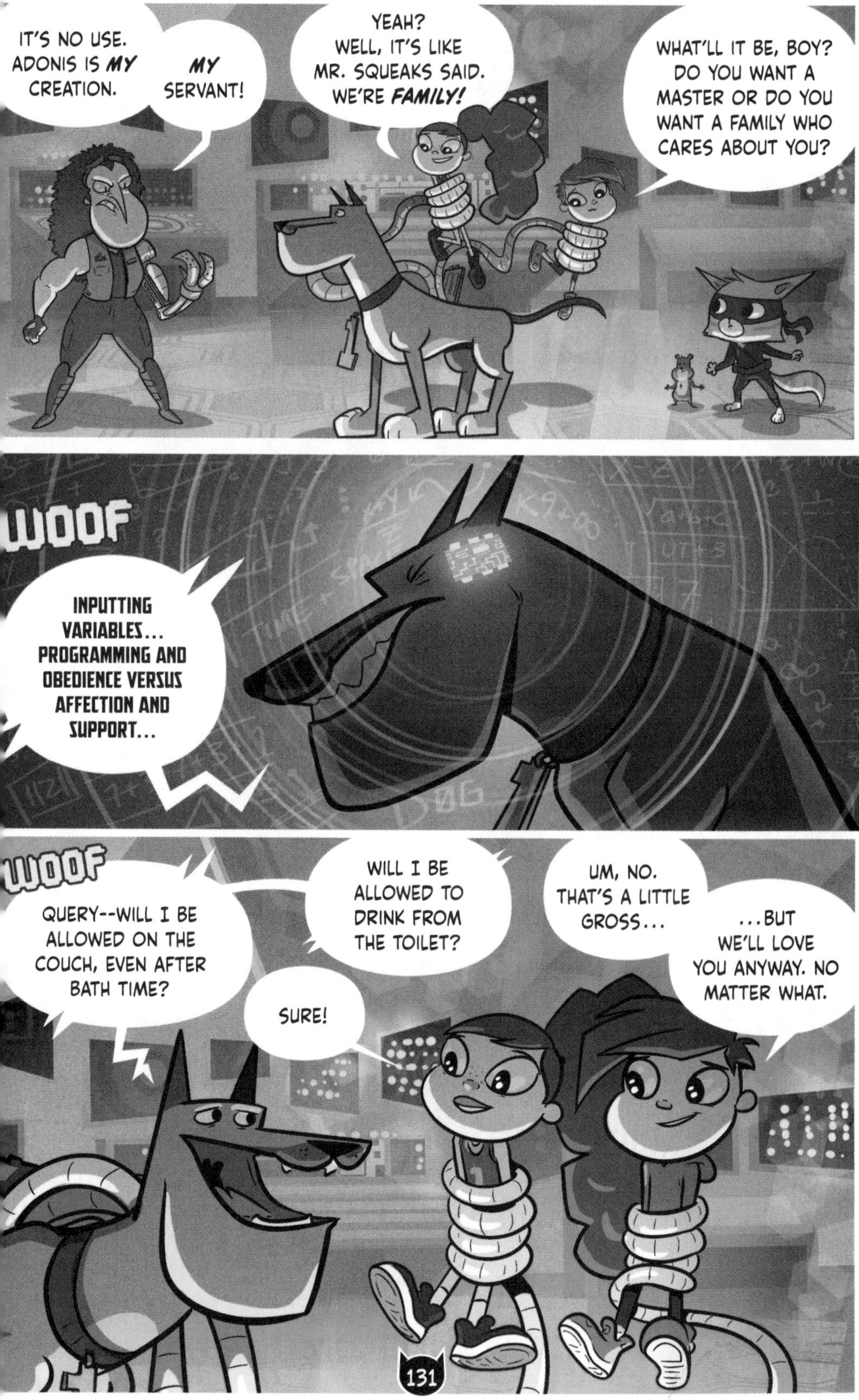
IT'S NO USE. ADONIS IS MY CREATION.
MY SERVANT!
YEAH? WELL, IT'S LIKE MR. SQUEAKS SAID. WE'RE FAMILY!
WHAT'LL IT BE, BOY? DO YOU WANT A MASTER OR DO YOU WANT A FAMILY WHO CARES ABOUT YOU?
WOOF
INPUTTING VARIABLES... PROGRAMMING AND OBEDIENCE VERSUS AFFECTION AND SUPPORT...
WOOF
QUERY--WILL I BE ALLOWED ON THE COUCH, EVEN AFTER BATH TIME?
SURE!
WILL I BE ALLOWED TO DRINK FROM THE TOILET?
UM, NO. THAT'S A LITTLE GROSS...
...BUT WE'LL LOVE YOU ANYWAY. NO MATTER WHAT.

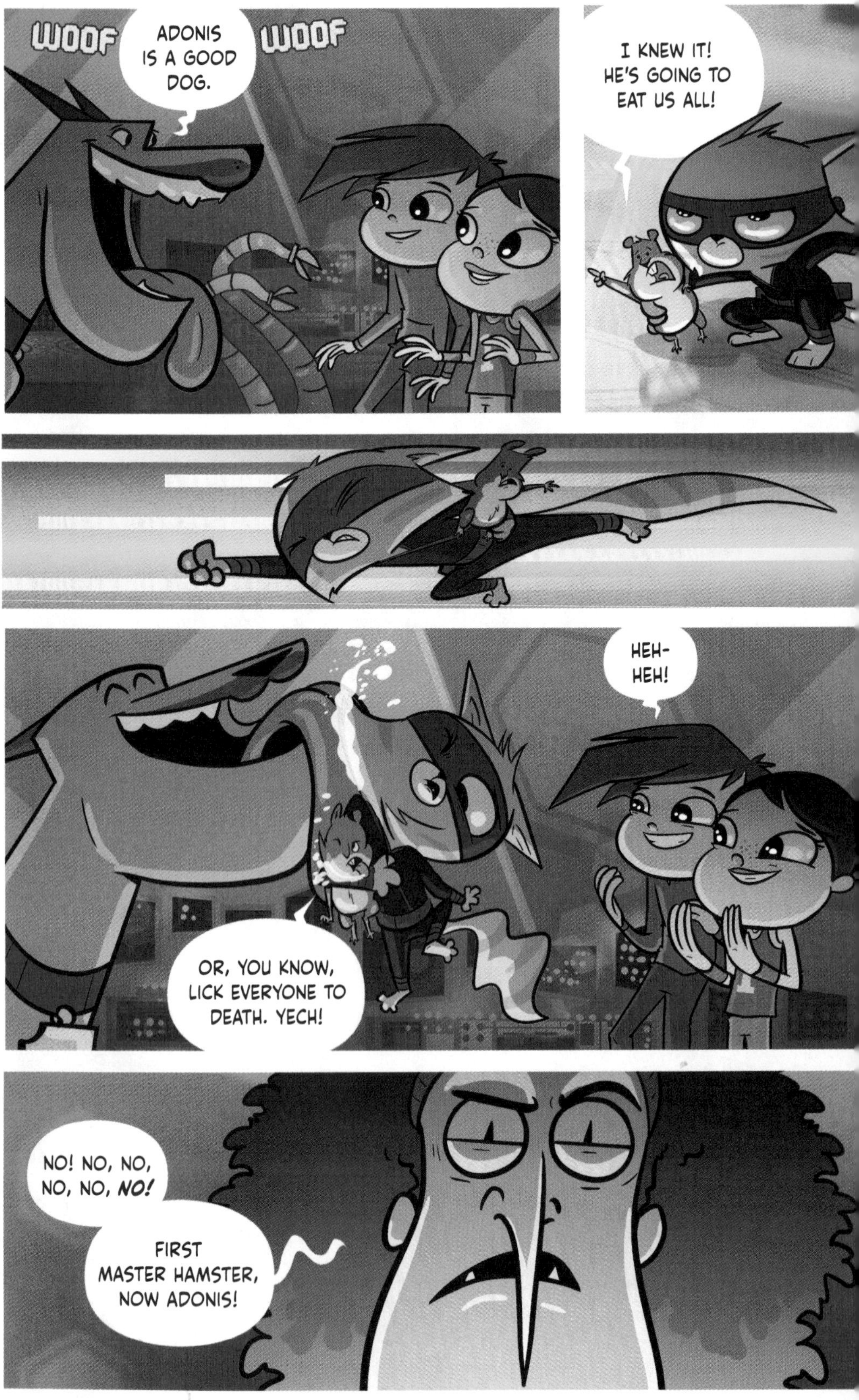
WOOF
ADONIS IS A GOOD DOG.
WOOF
I KNEW IT! HE'S GOING TO EAT US ALL!
HEH-HEH!
OR, YOU KNOW, LICK EVERYONE TO DEATH. YECH!
NO! NO, NO, NO, NO, *NO!*
FIRST MASTER HAMSTER, NOW ADONIS!

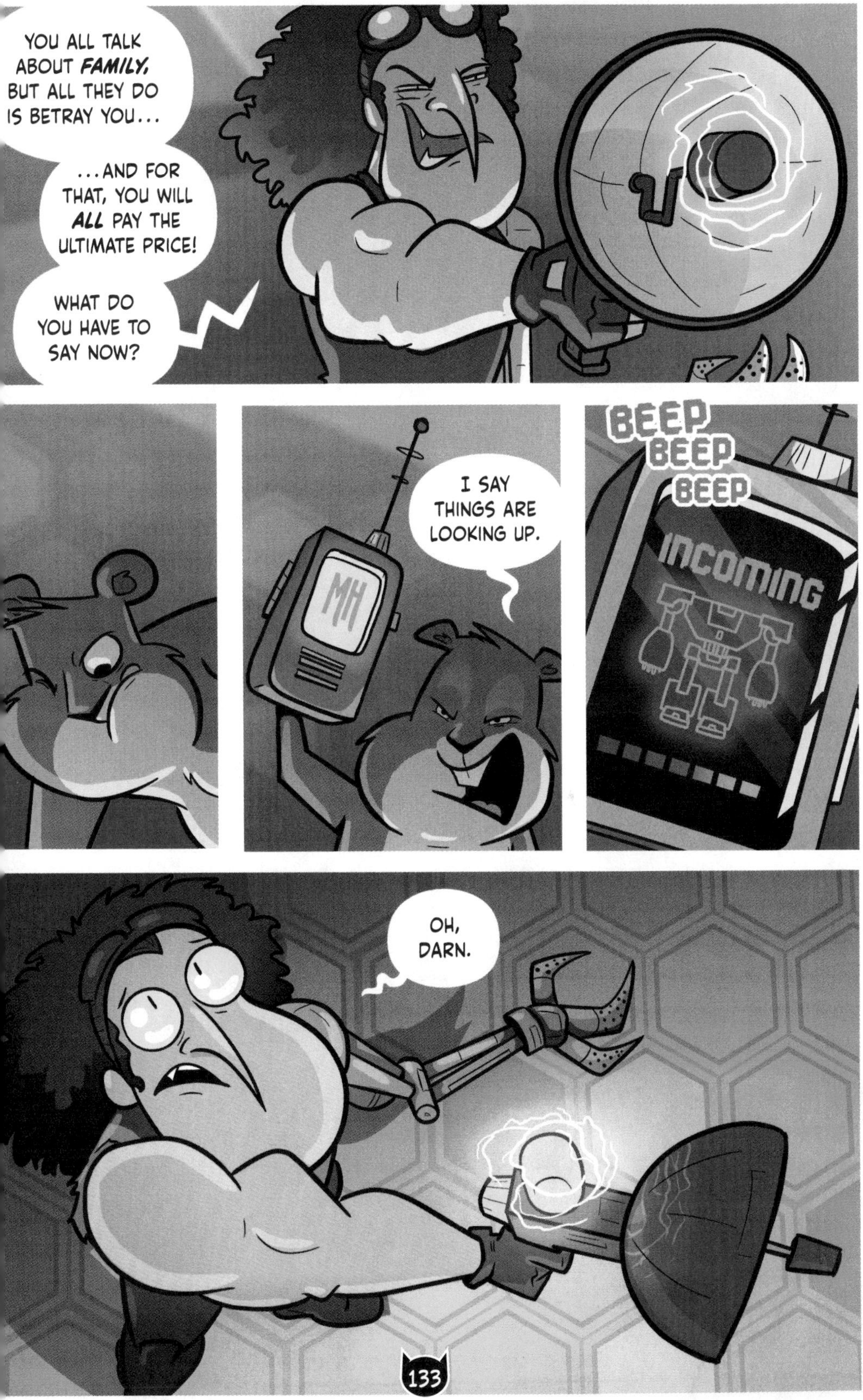
YOU ALL TALK ABOUT FAMILY, BUT ALL THEY DO IS BETRAY YOU...
...AND FOR THAT, YOU WILL ALL PAY THE ULTIMATE PRICE!
WHAT DO YOU HAVE TO SAY NOW?
I SAY THINGS ARE LOOKING UP.
MH
BEEP BEEP BEEP
INCOMING
OH, DARN.

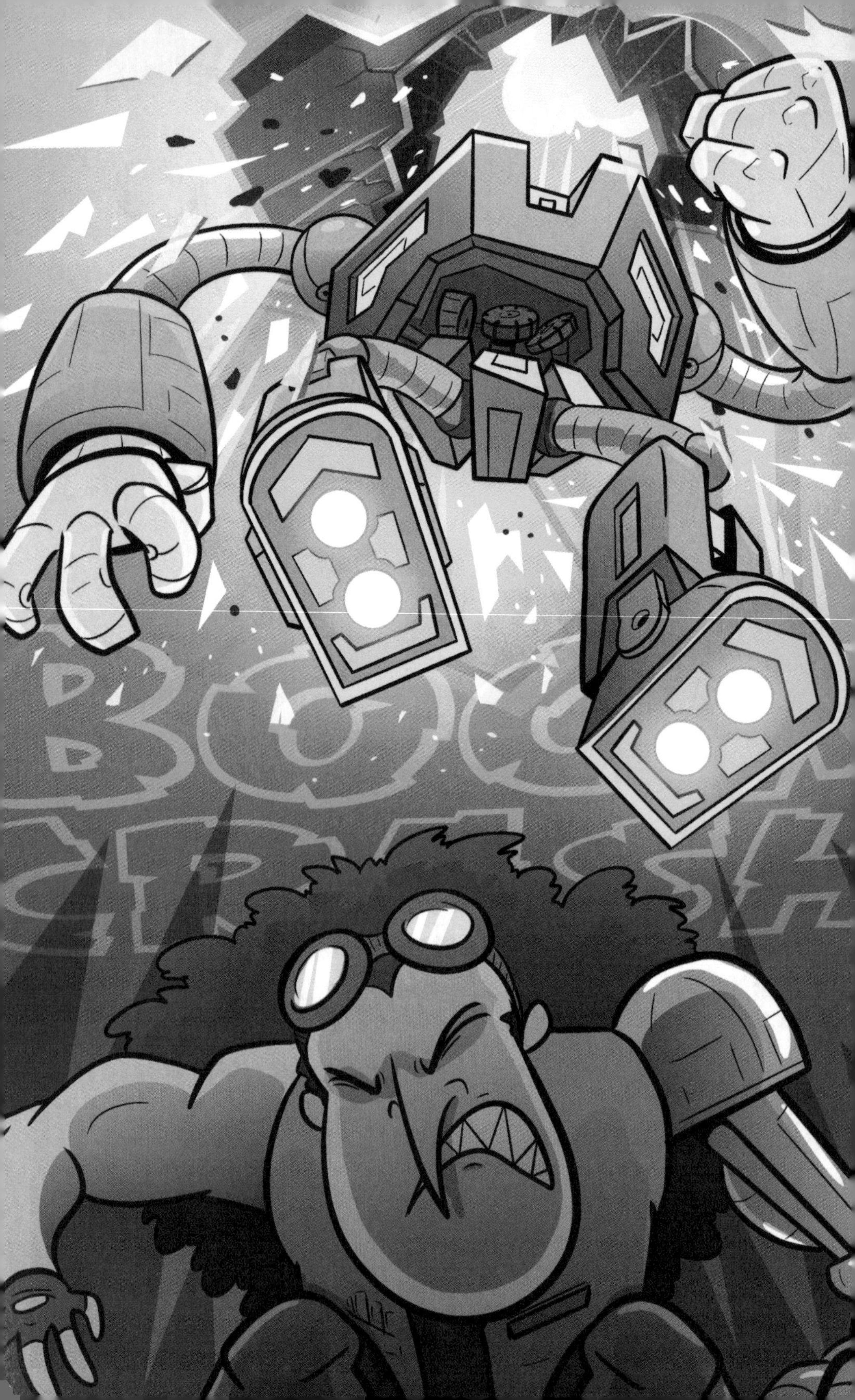

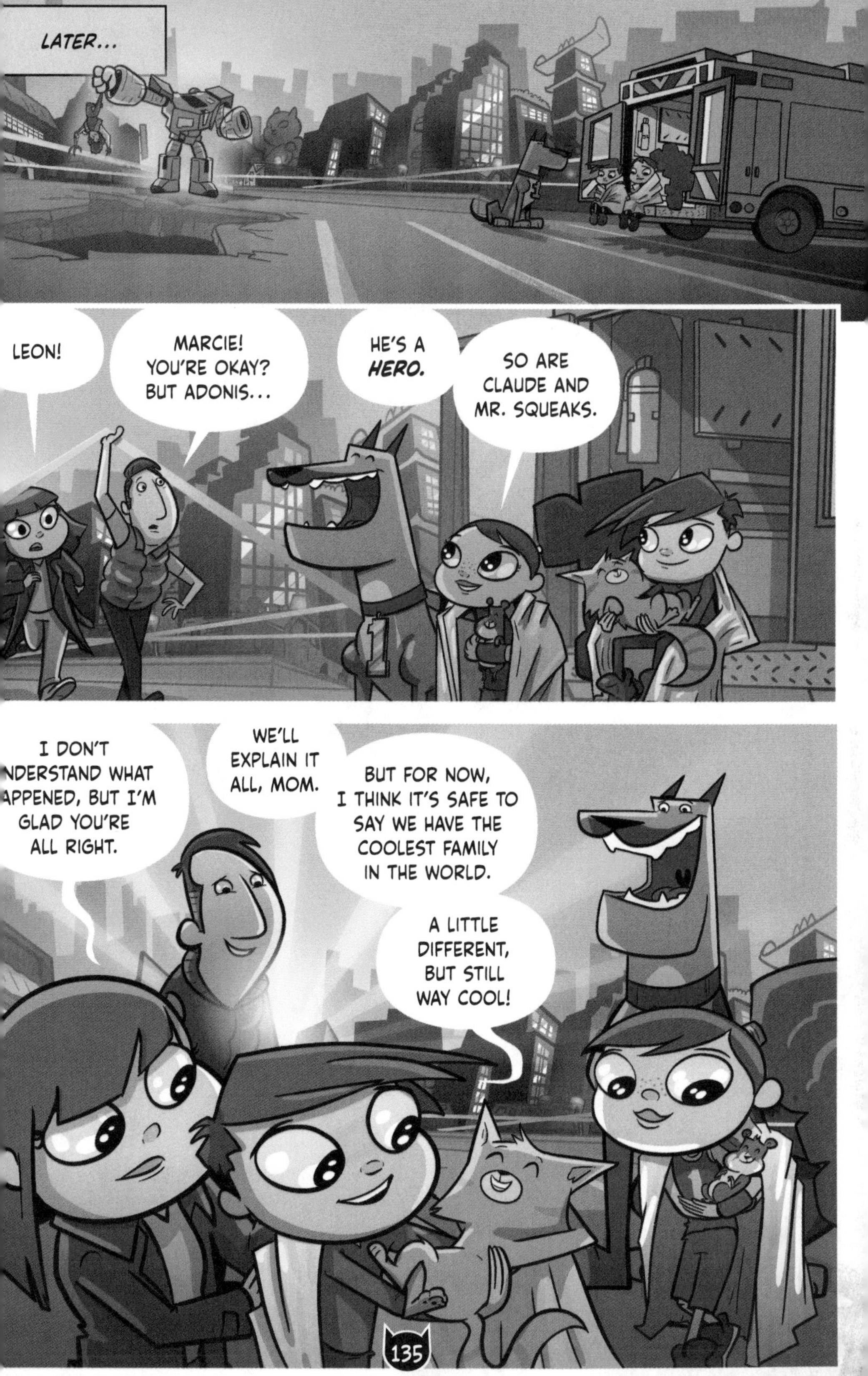
LATER...
LEON!
MARCIE! YOU'RE OKAY? BUT ADONIS...
HE'S A *HERO.*
SO ARE CLAUDE AND MR. SQUEAKS.
I DON'T NDERSTAND WHAT APPENED, BUT I'M GLAD YOU'RE ALL RIGHT.
WE'LL EXPLAIN IT ALL, MOM.
BUT FOR NOW, I THINK IT'S SAFE TO SAY WE HAVE THE COOLEST FAMILY IN THE WORLD.
A LITTLE DIFFERENT, BUT STILL WAY COOL!

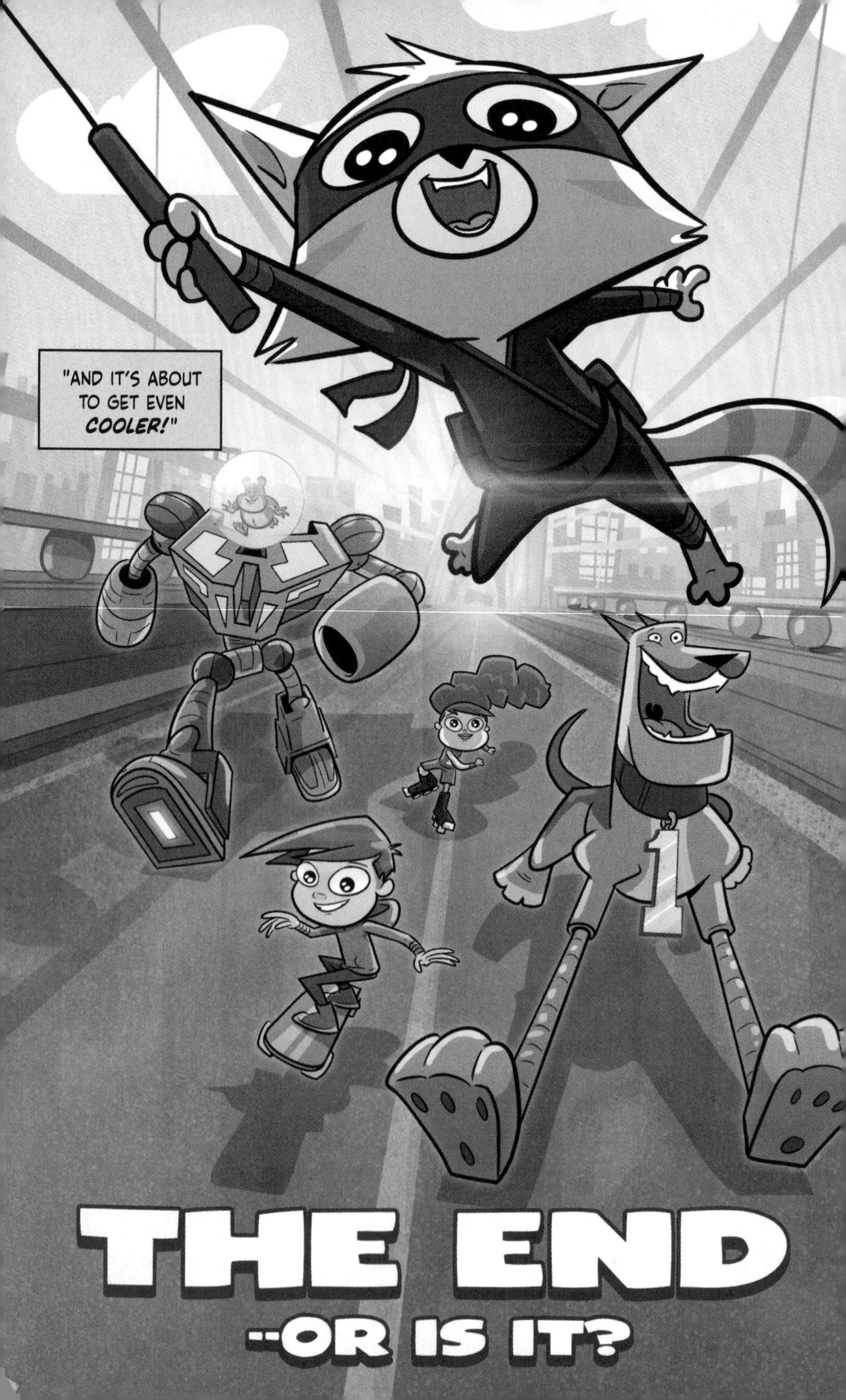
"AND IT'S ABOUT TO GET EVEN COOLER!"
1
THE END
--OR IS IT?

About the Author

MATTHEW CODY is the author of several popular books, including the award-winning *Supers of Noble's Green* trilogy: *Powerless, Super,* and *Villainous.* He is also the author of *Will in Scarlet* and *The Dead Gentleman,* as well as the graphic novel *Zatanna and the House of Secrets* from DC Comics. He lives in Manhattan with his wife and son.

About the Illustrator

YEHUDI MERCADO was born in Mexico City and raised in Houston, Texas. He is a former Disney art director turned successful graphic novelist. His graphic novels as writer-illustrator include *Buffalo Speedway, Pantalones, TX, Rocket Salvage,* and *Sci-Fu: Kick it Off.* He is currently showrunning a narrative podcast based on his graphic novel *Hero Hotel.*

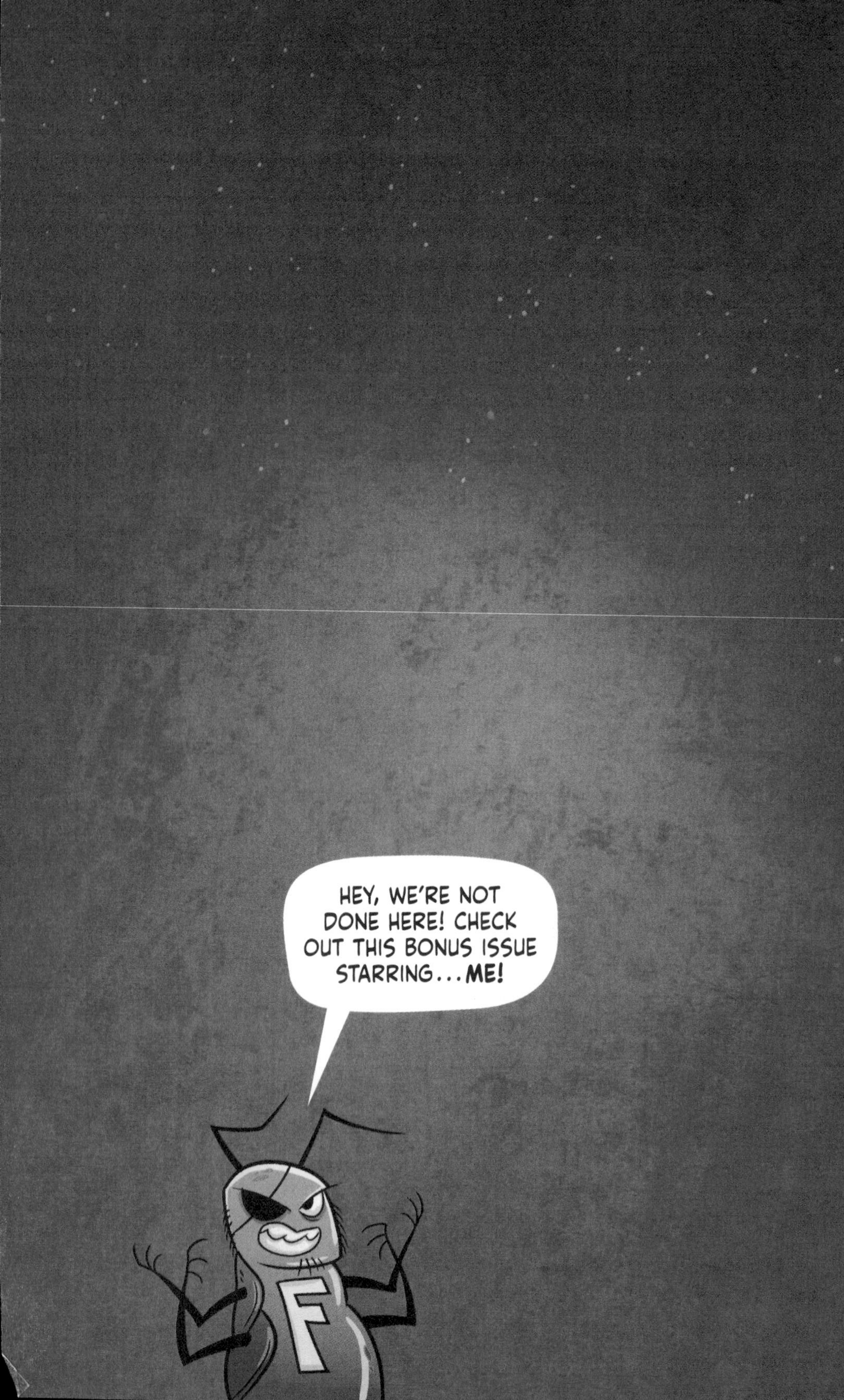
HEY, WE'RE NOT DONE HERE! CHECK OUT THIS BONUS ISSUE STARRING...ME!

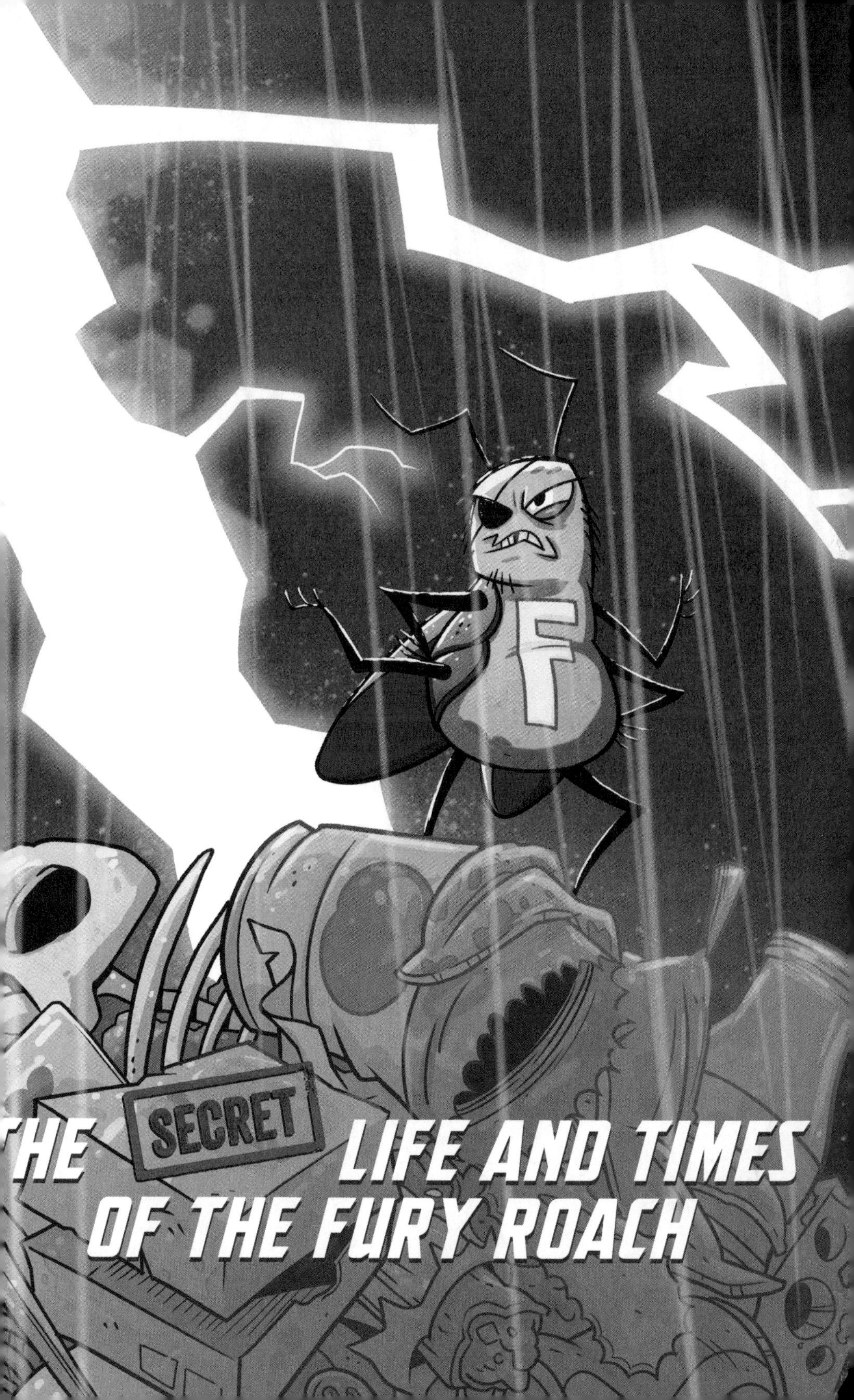
THE SECRET LIFE AND TIMES
OF THE FURY ROACH

Written by
Colleen AF Venable
Art by
Chad Thomas
Colors by
Warren Wucinich

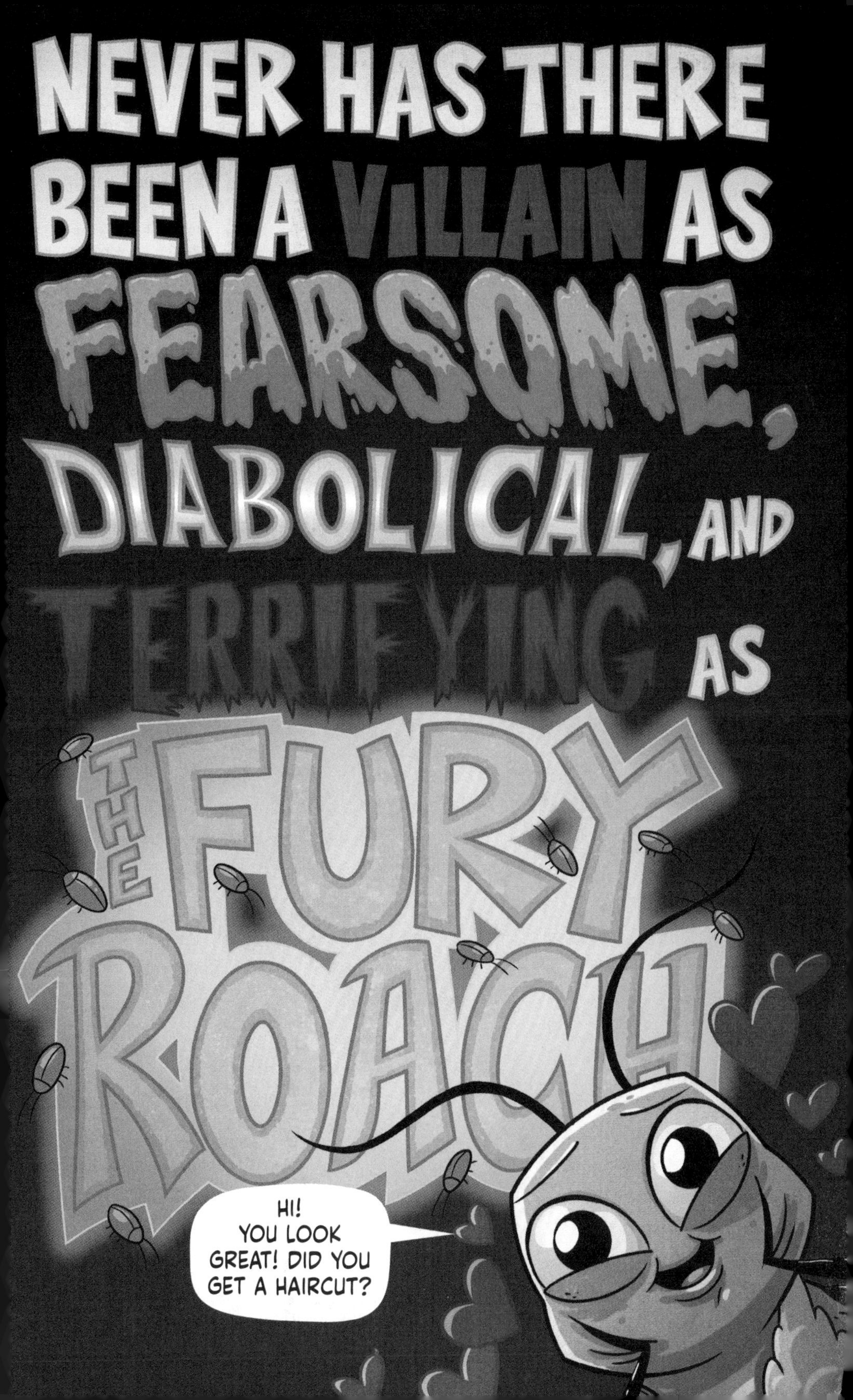
NEVER HAS THERE BEEN A VILLAIN AS FEARSOME, DIABOLICAL, AND TERRIFYING AS
THE FURY ROACH
HI! YOU LOOK GREAT! DID YOU GET A HAIRCUT?

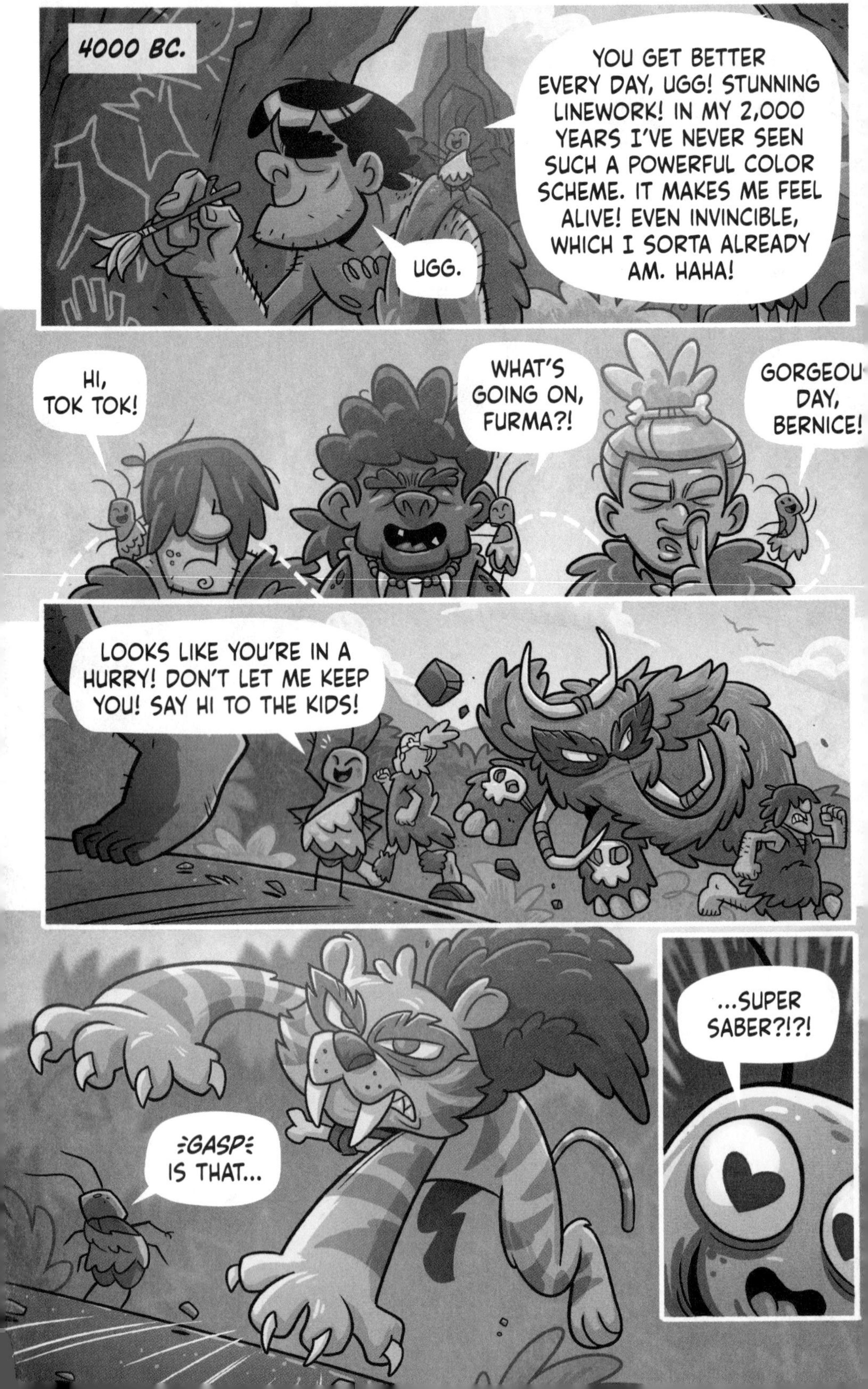
4000 BC.
YOU GET BETTER EVERY DAY, UGG! STUNNING LINEWORK! IN MY 2,000 YEARS I'VE NEVER SEEN SUCH A POWERFUL COLOR SCHEME. IT MAKES ME FEEL ALIVE! EVEN INVINCIBLE, WHICH I SORTA ALREADY AM. HAHA!
UGG.
HI, TOK TOK!
WHAT'S GOING ON, FURMA?!
GORGEOU DAY, BERNICE!
LOOKS LIKE YOU'RE IN A HURRY! DON'T LET ME KEEP YOU! SAY HI TO THE KIDS!
GASP IS THAT...
...SUPER SABER?!?!

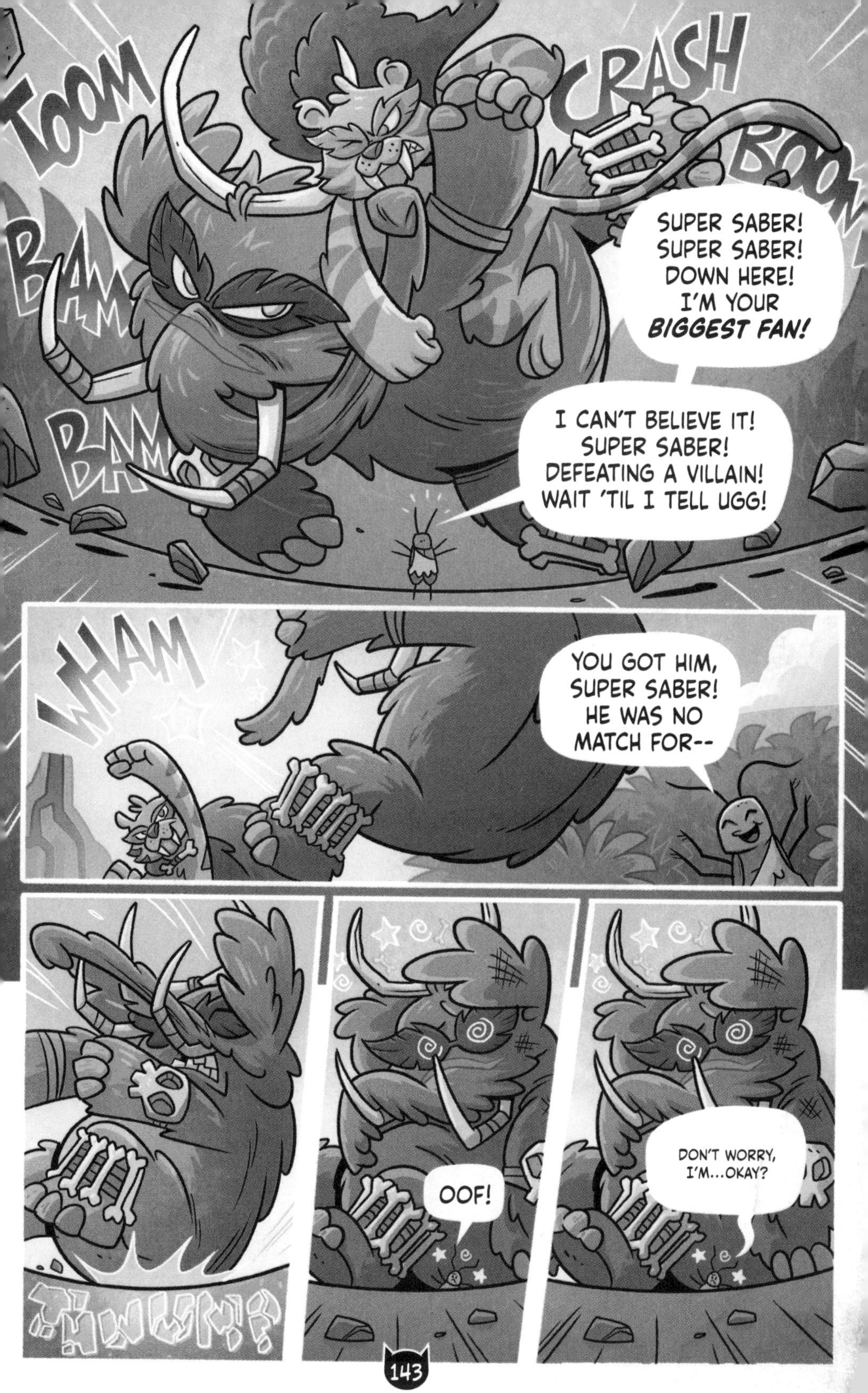
TOOM
CRASH
BOOM
BAM
BAM
SUPER SABER! SUPER SABER! DOWN HERE! I'M YOUR *BIGGEST FAN!*
I CAN'T BELIEVE IT! SUPER SABER! DEFEATING A VILLAIN! WAIT 'TIL I TELL UGG!
WHAM
YOU GOT HIM, SUPER SABER! HE WAS NO MATCH FOR--
OOF!
DON'T WORRY, I'M...OKAY?

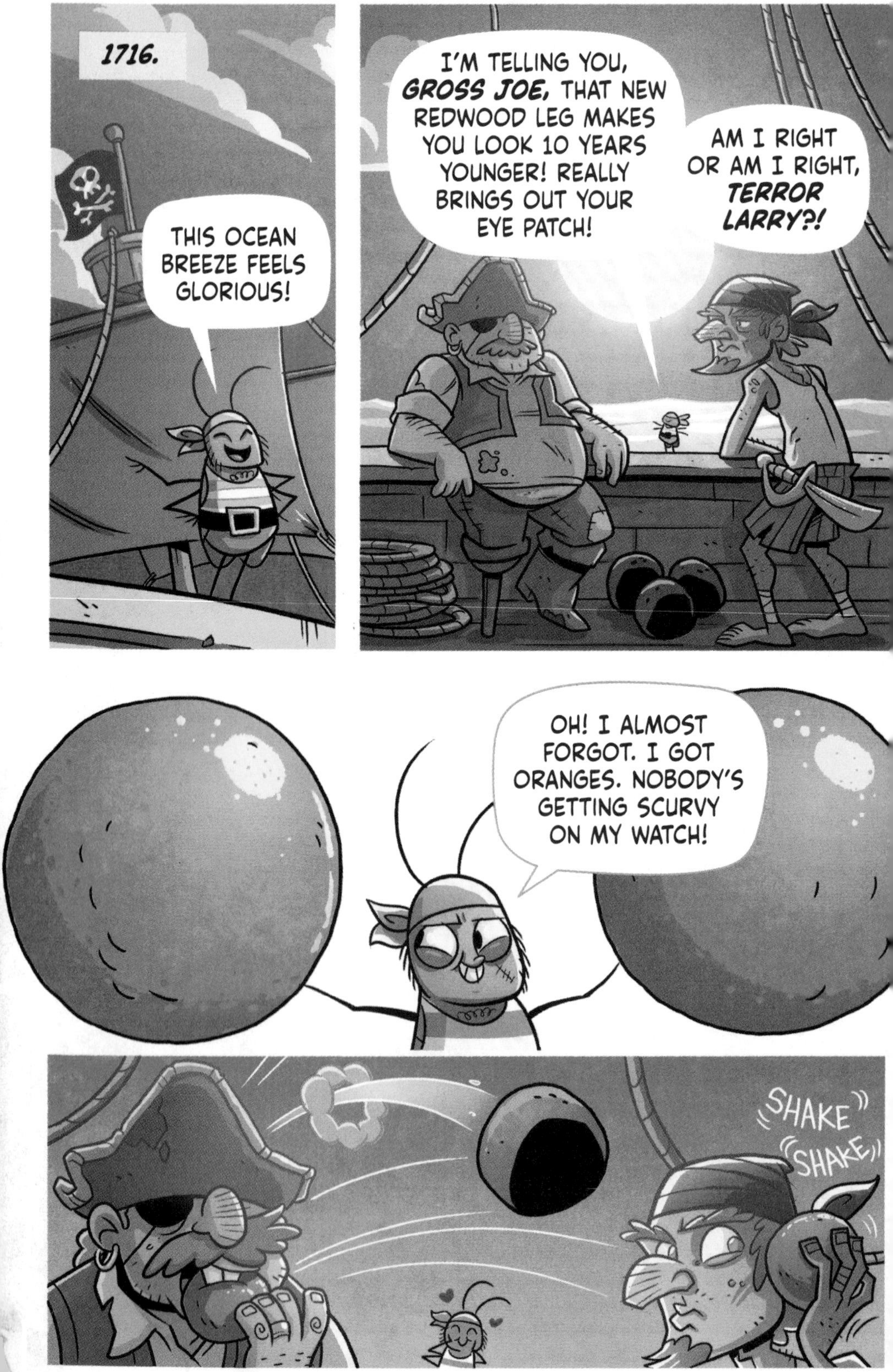
1716.
THIS OCEAN BREEZE FEELS GLORIOUS!
I'M TELLING YOU, **GROSS JOE,** THAT NEW REDWOOD LEG MAKES YOU LOOK 10 YEARS YOUNGER! REALLY BRINGS OUT YOUR EYE PATCH!
AM I RIGHT OR AM I RIGHT, **TERROR LARRY?!**
OH! I ALMOST FORGOT. I GOT ORANGES. NOBODY'S GETTING SCURVY ON MY WATCH!
SHAKE
SHAKE

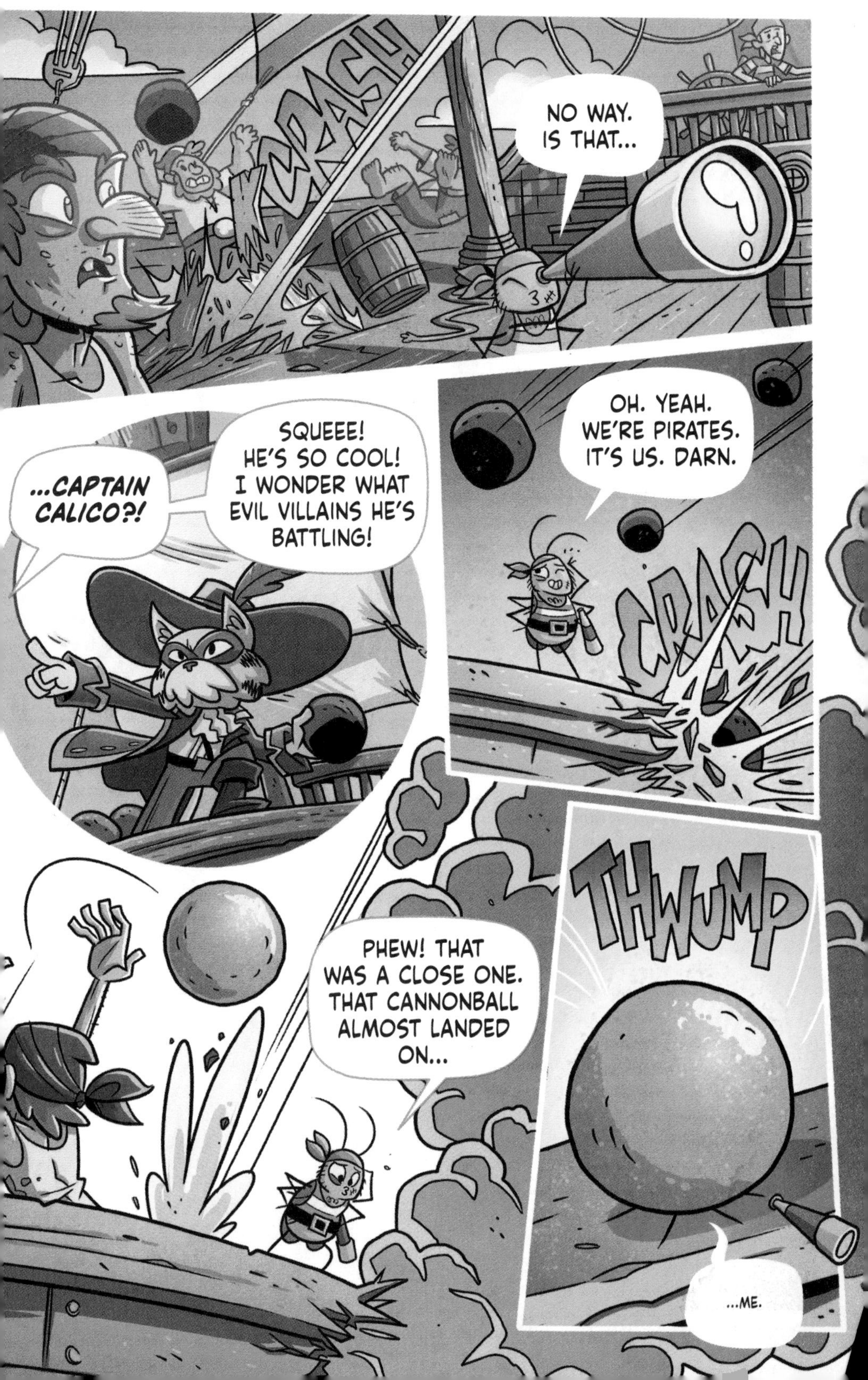
CRASH!
NO WAY. IS THAT...
...CAPTAIN CALICO?!
SQUEEE! HE'S SO COOL! I WONDER WHAT EVIL VILLAINS HE'S BATTLING!
OH. YEAH. WE'RE PIRATES. IT'S US. DARN.
CRASH
PHEW! THAT WAS A CLOSE ONE. THAT CANNONBALL ALMOST LANDED ON...
THWUMP
...ME.

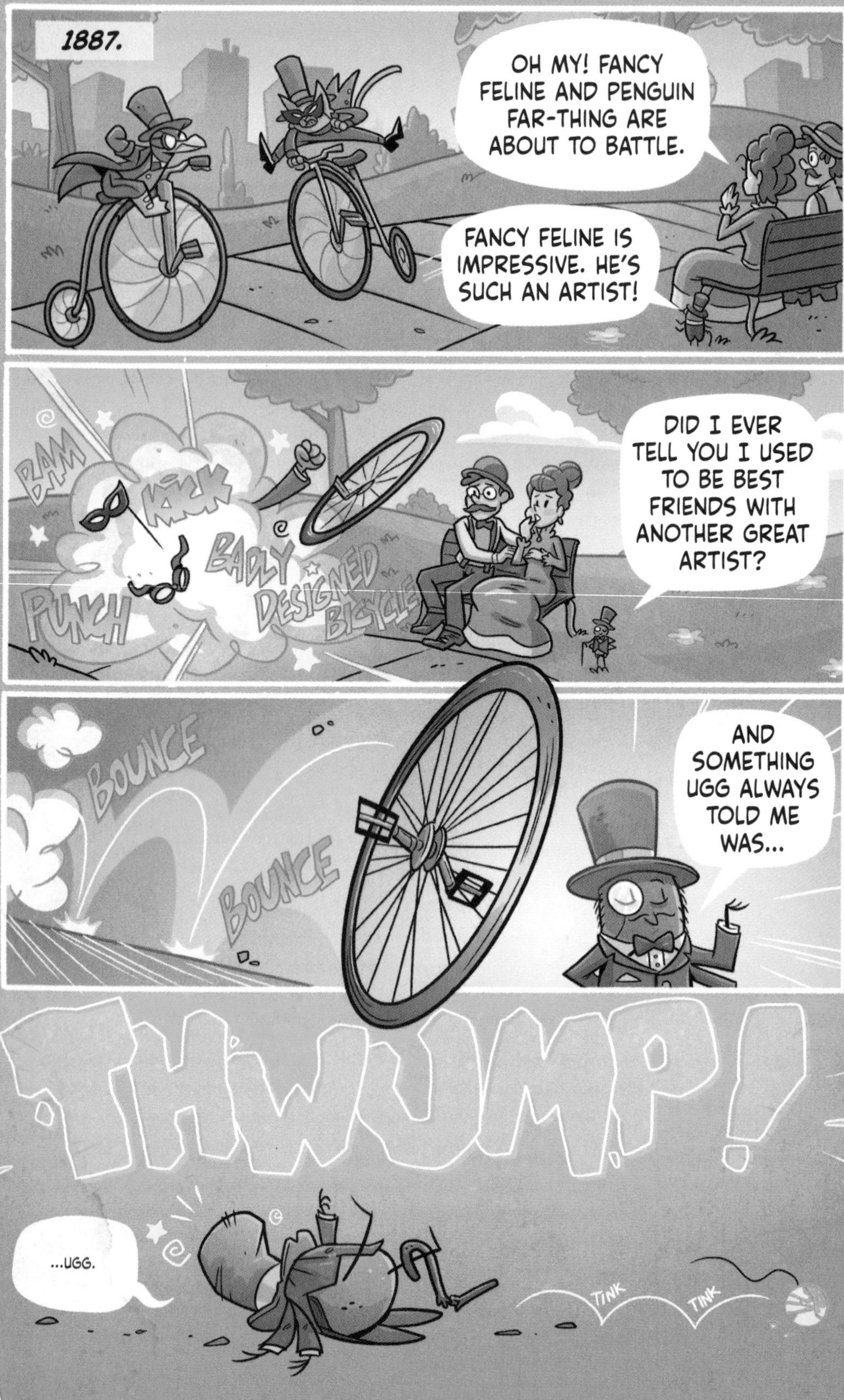
1887.
OH MY! FANCY FELINE AND PENGUIN FAR-THING ARE ABOUT TO BATTLE.
FANCY FELINE IS IMPRESSIVE. HE'S SUCH AN ARTIST!
BAM
KICK
BADLY DESIGNED BICYCLE
PUNCH
DID I EVER TELL YOU I USED TO BE BEST FRIENDS WITH ANOTHER GREAT ARTIST?
BOUNCE
BOUNCE
AND SOMETHING UGG ALWAYS TOLD ME WAS...
THWUMP!
...UGG.
TINK
TINK

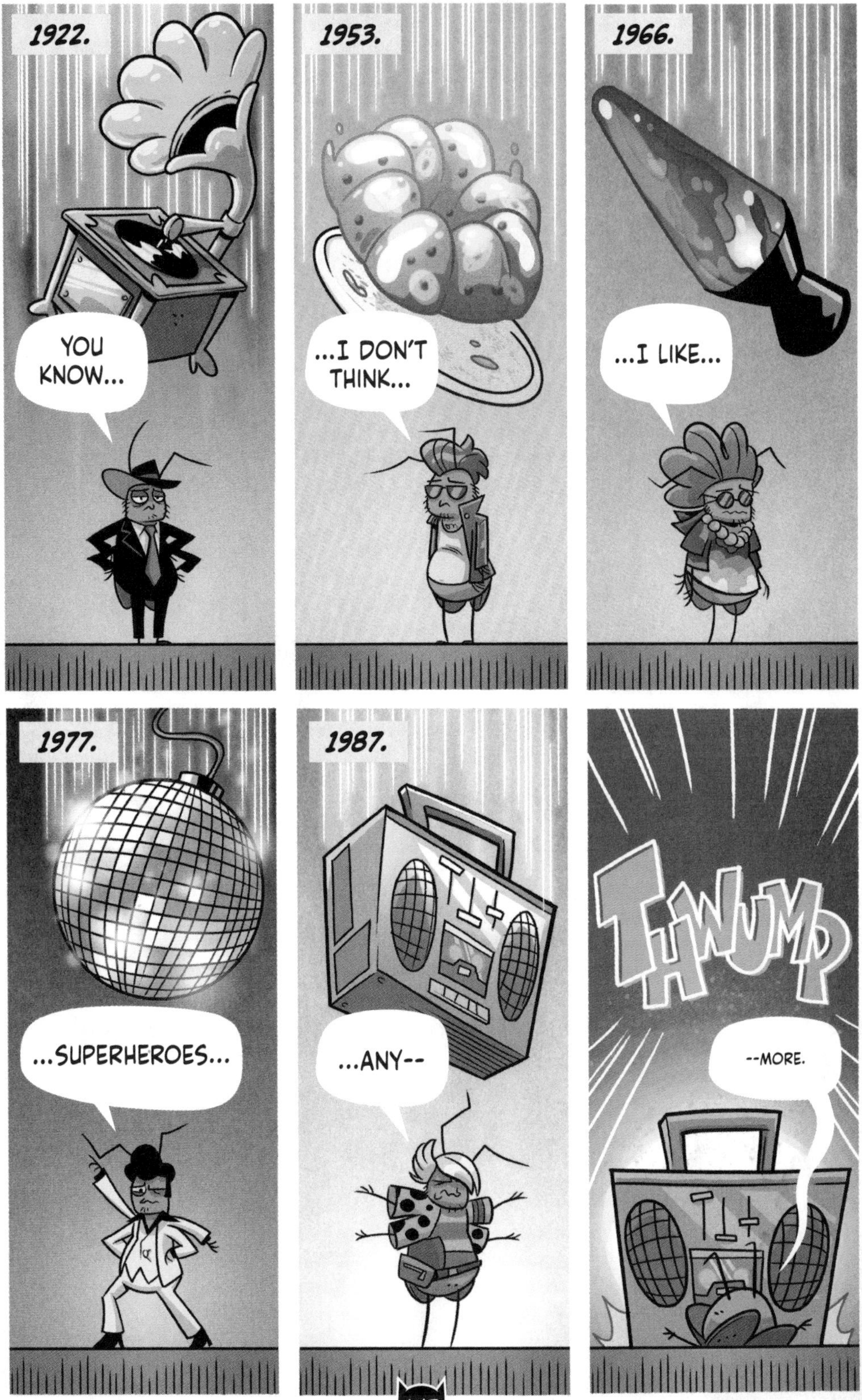
1922.
YOU KNOW...
1953.
...I DON'T THINK...
1966.
...I LIKE...
1977.
...SUPERHEROES...
1987.
...ANY--
THWUMP
--MORE.

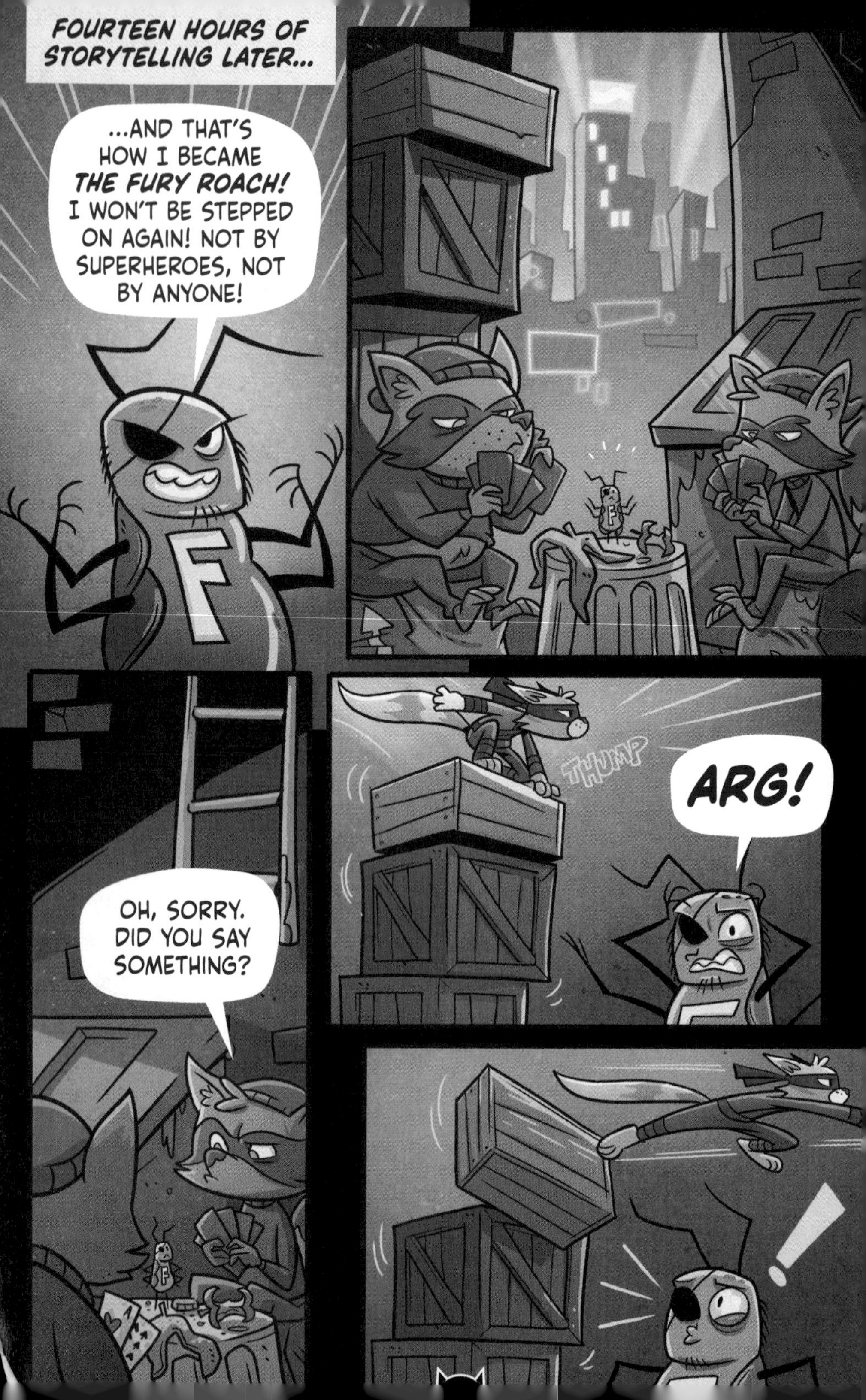
FOURTEEN HOURS OF STORYTELLING LATER...
...AND THAT'S HOW I BECAME *THE FURY ROACH!* I WON'T BE STEPPED ON AGAIN! NOT BY SUPERHEROES, NOT BY ANYONE!
OH, SORRY. DID YOU SAY SOMETHING?
THUMP
ARG!
!

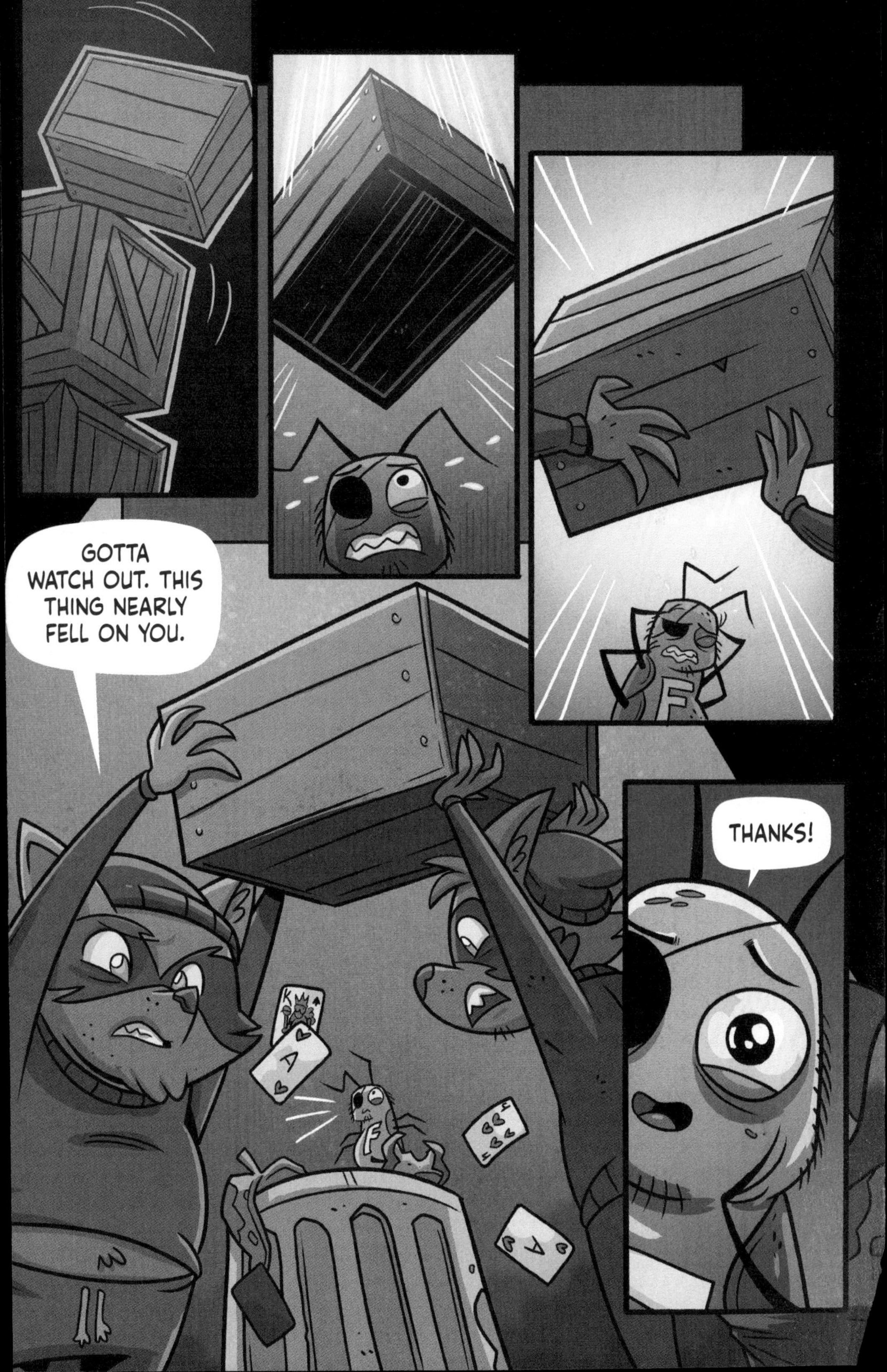
GOTTA WATCH OUT. THIS THING NEARLY FELL ON YOU.
THANKS!

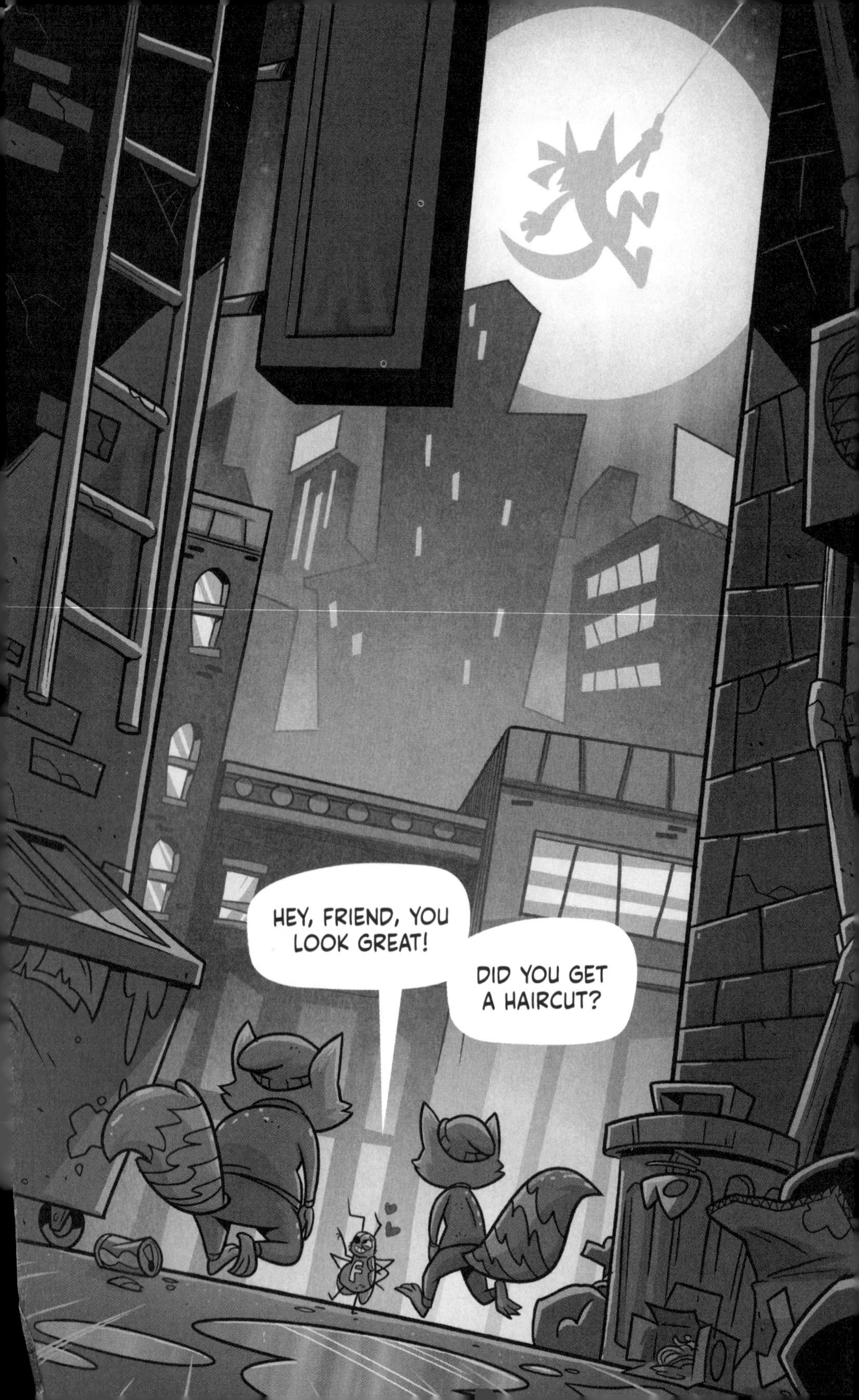
HEY, FRIEND, YOU LOOK GREAT!
DID YOU GET A HAIRCUT?

Is Your Pet a Superhero or a Supervillain?

Answer the following questions and then tally up your responses to find out. (If you don't have a pet, use your favorite houseplant instead!)

1. When I want to snuggle with my pet, they:
   A. Stash their nunchucks and curl up next to me for a cuddle session.
   B. Stare at me blankly, then ask for more yum-yums.
   C. Sometimes want a head rub and sometimes just walk away.

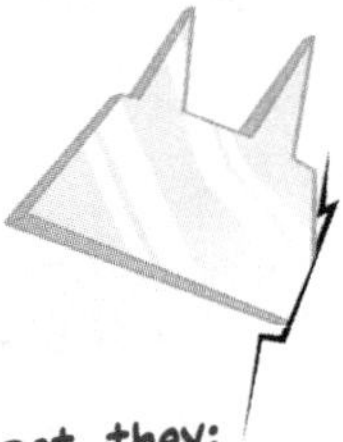

2. My pet's favorite toy is:
   A. A throwing star.
   B. A brand-new freeze ray.
   C. A ball.

3. When my pet sees another pet, they:
   A. Always seem happy to make a friend--or ally.
   B. Hiss, bark, or glare like they have a secret feud.
   C. Don't even notice them.

4. My pet is strong:
   A. At surprising moments--like when I get captured by an evil scientist's minion.
   B. All the time. It's almost like they have robot strength!
   C. I'm not really sure. I've never tried arm wrestling my pet.

5. My pet's special hiding spot contains:
   A. Ninja gear.
   B. Weird electronic gadgets.
   C. Chewed-up shoes.

6. When I offer my pet special treats, they:
   A. Take just enough to keep up their energy for justice.
   B. Grab as many as they can fit into their mouth. Need more yum-yums!
   C. Nibble a few? Eat the whole bag? It depends on the day.

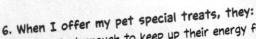
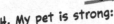

7. When a giant robot messes up the city, my pet:
   A. Puts on a mask and mysteriously disappears.
   B. Snorts because they know they could've done better.
   C. Snores on the couch.

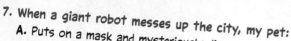

8. When I talk to my pet about a problem, they:
   A. Always listen to my troubles and give me extra love.
   B. Stare right through me. Sometimes their eyes even...glow?
   C. Keep on snoring.

9. When I wake up in the morning, my pet:
   A. Seems tired, but content, like they spent the night foiling crimes.
   B. Seems grumpy, like they spent the night watching their crimes get foiled.
   C. Is still snoring. Seriously, how much can one animal sleep?

10. My pet came from:
   A. A rescue group run by a wise old ninja master.
   B. A championship breeder (who may or may not be an evil scientist).
   C. Who knows? They just showed up at my house one day!

If your answers were...

Mostly A's:

You've got yourself a superhero pet! You spend all day snuggling with your pet, but when the sun goes down, and you're fast asleep in your bed, your stealthy pet springs into action and defends your neighborhood from dastardly foes! Well done, superpet!

Mostly B's:

Your cuddly ball of fur is actually a supervillain! When your head hits the pillow, your innocent-looking pet is probably setting an evil plan in motion to take over the entire neighborhood! Whatever you do, don't get on your supervillain pet's bad side.

Mostly C's:

It may be too soon to tell whether you're dealing with a superhero or a supervillain. Look for clues that might lead you more in the superhero direction of saving neighbors or the supervillain direction of plotting mass chaos in the local park.

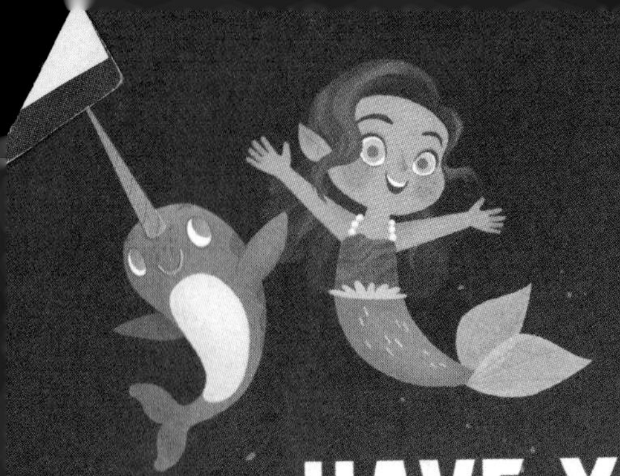

HAVE YOU HEARD ABOUT epic! YET?

We're the largest digital library for kids, used by millions in homes and schools around the world. We love stories so much that we're now creating our own!

With the help of some of the best writers and illustrators in the world, we create the wildest adventures we can think of. Like a mermaid with a narwhal who solve mysteries. Or a pet made out of slime.

We hope you have as much fun reading our books as we had making them!

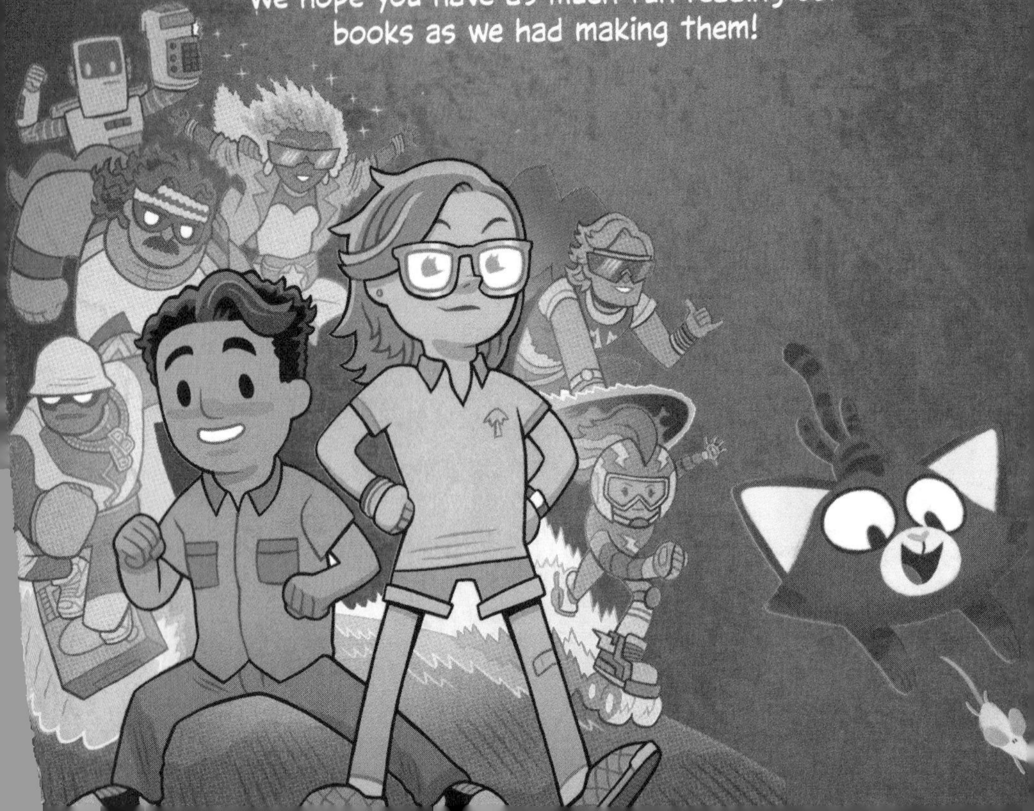

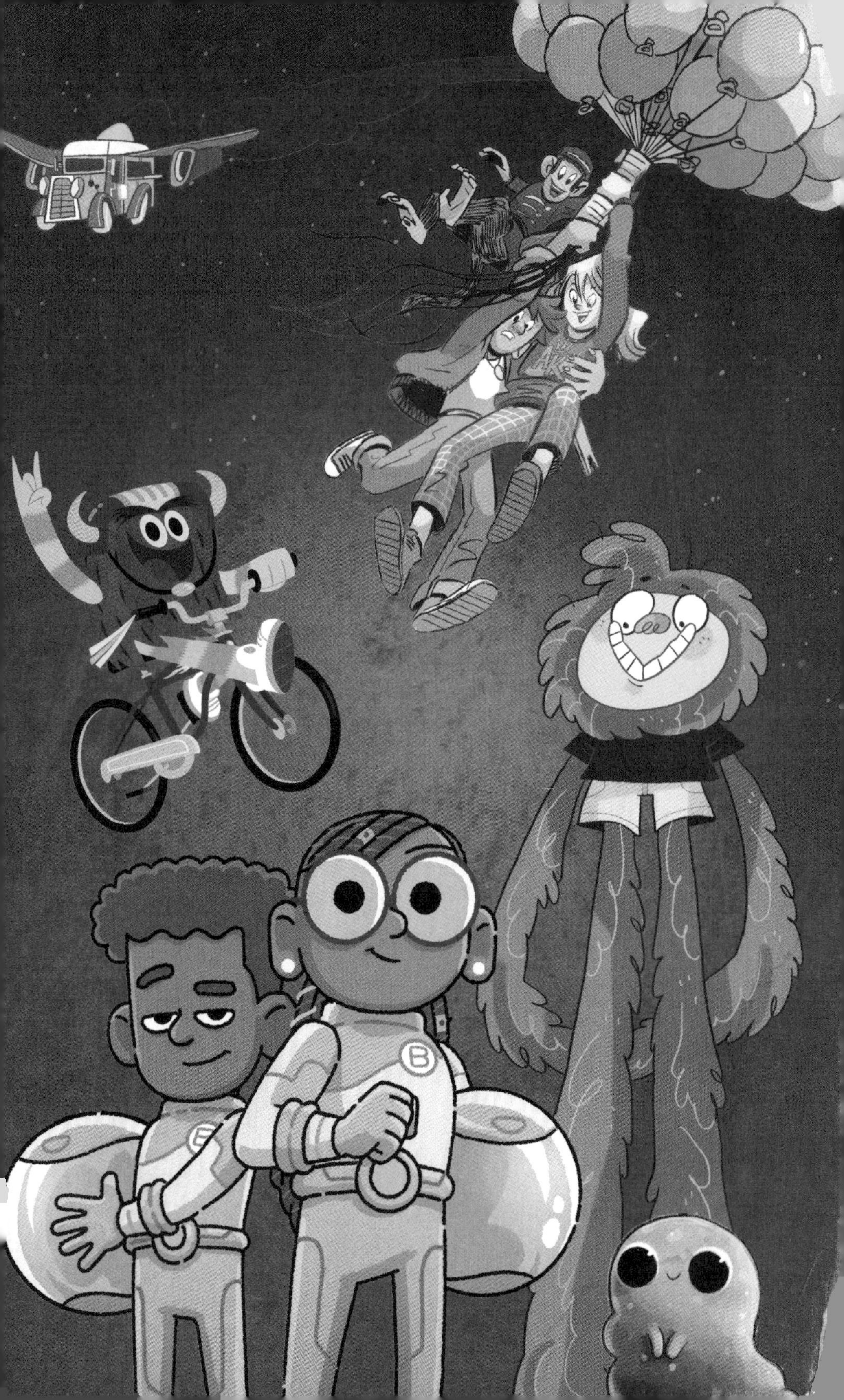

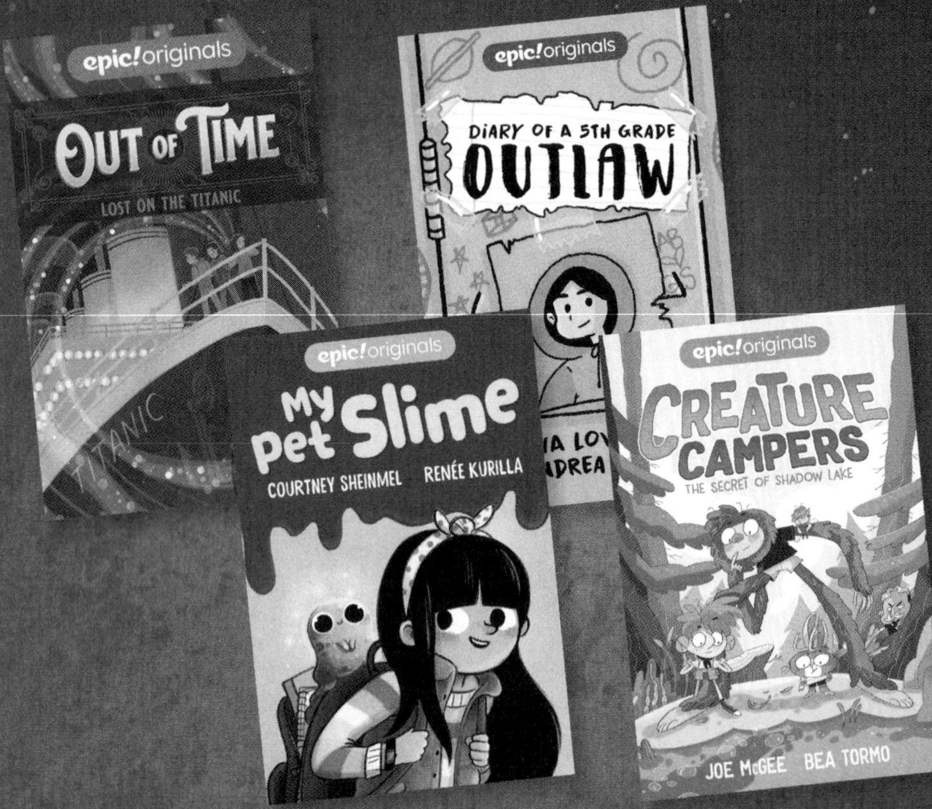
epic! originals
OUT OF TIME
LOST ON THE TITANIC
epic! originals
DIARY OF A 5TH GRADE
OUTLAW
epic! originals
My pet Slime
COURTNEY SHEINMEL
RENÉE KURILLA
epic! originals
CREATURE CAMPERS
THE SECRET OF SHADOW LAKE
JOE McGEE
BEA TORMO